The Long Way Home

The Long Way Home

by

Roslyn Bane

Desert Palm Press

The Long Way Home

By Roslyn Bane

©2017 Roslyn Bane

ISBN-(book) 9781942976516
ISBN-(epub) 9781942976523
ISBN (pdf) 9781942976530

Desert Palm Press
1961 Main Street, Suite 220
Watsonville, California 95076
www.desertpalmpress.com

Editor: Mary Hettel
Cover Design: Michelle Brodeur (eebooWORX)

Printed in the United States of America
First Edition July 2017

Acknowledgments

This book would not have been possible without assistance from others. Thanks for your support and ideas. Thank you to my beta readers; Brenda, Judy C., Danielle Z., and Anya. Your feedback was invaluable.

Special thanks to: Sarah W. at Ability Prosthetics, Linda at Drayer Physical Therapy, Adam H. at Wellspan Physical Therapy, Heather H. and 'Doc' Morales at Wellspan Orthopedics. Your knowledge is incredible and you serve your patients well. It was a pleasure to work with you.

To the instructors at the Golden Crown Literary Society (GCLS) Writing Academy, my classmates, and mentor Catherine, thanks for an incredible year of guidance and fellowship.

Thank you to Jan who took infinite care and skill, to help refine this story. Thanks for taking on what Sister Mary Joseph gave up on.

Thanks to Mary, my editor at Desert Palm Press, who helped polish it, and Michelle Brodeur for the cover. Thanks Lee for taking a chance with this book.

Thank you to the folks at Wounded Warrior Project who help our wounded veterans and their families on their journey of healing and to the many wounded veterans who shared their stories with me, this book could not have been written without your input. Thank you for your service.

Finally, to my family; thank you for your support. Bonum possit venire de rerum mutatione.

.

Dedication

To Female Veterans who have served their country with honor and integrity

Chapter One

"KEEP YOUR LOOKOUT SHARP, there's been fighting on that second ridge all morning." Major Samantha "Sam" Davies interrupted the easy conversation of her flight crew to redirect their attention to the mountains outside their helicopter.

"Roger that, Major. Heads up, guys. Watch your sectors. Let's get this bird back in time for some hot chow today."

As the crew chief called out instructions to the young Marines manning the guns, Sam provided coordinates to her copilot. Alternating her scan from the instrument panel to the terrain outside, she watched for unfriendlies and other hazards to her team. They had just finished a resupply mission to a forward operating base and were heading back to camp. The weather was typical for Afghanistan, hot and dry. There had been no rain for weeks, and the wind blew up clouds of dust that could quickly cause brownout conditions. Sam licked her cracked lips, her eyes constantly in motion, watching as the copilot, a young first lieutenant, handled the big helo. *Did he realize it was easy for the enemy to hide behind the craggy rocks, and in deep ravines? That they popped up like woodchucks but weren't nearly as friendly. Here, in this god-forsaken land, death bloomed. Death thrived. And Death was always hungry.* Her gaze swept across the instrument cluster and noticed the altitude. "Bring us up, Lieutenant. Remember your scan pattern, outside and inside. With all this brownout here and with so few trees, you'll start to lose some of your depth perception."

"Yes, Major."

Over the intercom, the crew chief shouted, "Got something. Two o'clock." A loud bang on the airframe behind her head and the high-pitched squeal of metal tearing overpowered the noise of the rotors. Her stomach lurched, and sweat dripped down her back. Adrenalin kicked in and her vision sharpened, and reflexes tuned to precision, she started calling out instructions.

Sam shouted "Left," even as she took the controls and pushed the helo left. "Chief, what have we got?"

"They're on the ridge," the chief shouted as she continued to bank the big helicopter to the left, moving them away from the gunfire.

The helo echoed with the distinct bwap, bwap, bwap, bwap as her crew unleashed bursts of gunfire. The smell of gunpowder tinged the air. Her crew shouted to each other.

"I saw a flash."

"Three o'clock."

"I got one at four o'clock."

"Shit! They've got something big! It's going high, down, Major, down!"

Sam lowered the collective to bring the helo lower, and the chopper dropped two hundred feet and continued to bank left.

"Muzzle flash, oh shit! It's coming right for us." The shriek of metal tearing, the instant beeping and buzzing of multiple alarms, filled her ears. Warning lights flashed on the instrument panel, and circuit breakers popped in the cockpit. "We're hit! We're hit!" the crew chief yelled.

The helicopter started a slow spin, and Sam shouted over the intercom, "We lost the tail rotor. Hang on. We're going to land it. It's going to be fast." She lowered the collective all the way down and pushed on the right rudder pedal to adjust for the loss of torque.

The first lieutenant was on the radio. "Mayday! Mayday! This is sierra foxtrot two four seven we're going down, grid five four seven two Echo. Mayday! Mayday this is sierra foxtrot two four seven."

The crew chief yelled over the shouts of the crewmen to hook their restraints. The console was an array of flashing lights, alerting Sam to catastrophic failure. Buzzers and beeps, the engine winding down and the wind all combined to form layers of sound. *Get away from the ridge, find a clearing. It's gonna be tight, watch the boulders.* She spotted a potential landing zone.

"We're dropping fast. This is going to be rough. Brace for impact!" The helo spun faster and faster. Sam pulled the cyclic backward to raise the nose, adding more right rudder. Her stomach lifted with the negative g-forces as the helo dropped. She focused on the landing zone as the chopper spiraled down faster and faster. Her vision narrowed as she fought against the blurring. She checked the altimeter, and pulled the collective up hard to slow the speed of descent and pulled the cyclic aft. The nose came up, as the wheels impacted the ground, even as the spin continued. Screams filled the air as the main rotor blades struck several large boulders on the side of the mountain, splintering on impact. The chopper rolled to the left flipping several times. The deafening sound of metal twisting and glass popping filled the air and darkness descended.

***

Sharp daggers of pain penetrated her legs, and her head throbbed. Sam became aware of a faint beeping and her name being called from behind and below her. Dry, hot wind blew against her face, and the smell of jet fuel was thick on the air. She struggled to open her eyes and shook her head to clear it. Knifelike pain sliced through her ribs and she gasped. She wiped a gloved hand over her eyes and bewildered, looked at the blood on her glove. Her vision blurred and she wiped again. Sam heard her name again, and she tried to speak. She tasted blood and grit in her mouth. Turning her head to the left, she realized the helicopter was leaning to its left side.

"Major, wake up. Come on we've got to get out of here." It was Martinez, her gunner. "Let's go."

She looked at him, and then beyond to where the lieutenant sat motionless, crumpled against the airframe his head at an unusual angle, blood trickling from his mouth and from under his helmet. His eyes were open, dark and unfocused. *Oh God, he's dead*. Martinez' face was covered with dirt and sweat, his nose was angled to the side, and a jagged cut ran the length of his jaw.

As Sam reached for her harness, pain ripped through her side, and she hissed in agony. Staring at her legs, she watched as blood slowly spread across her flight suit. She pulled her legs back and groaned as pain ripped through her right leg. "Fuck." Her stomach clenched tight, *Oh shit, it's stuck. Get it out, get it out.* She leaned forward to push on the console and pain exploded again.

"Wait, let me see." Martinez crawled over to her. "It's stuck. I'm gonna push, you're going to have to pull it out. Ready? Go."

Sam braced her left foot on the deck and pushed down. Bones shifted, their ends grinding past each other making a sound like dry wood splintering and cracking. White hot bolts of pain shot deep within her and waves of nausea roiled through her gut. An animal-like howl escaped from deep within her, and her focus dimmed. *Oh fuck*. Sweat poured down her face, and she squeezed her eyes tight against the pain. With her pulse pounding in her ears she pulled again, using her hands to yank at her thigh.

"Stop, Major." Martinez reached his hand down into the small gap, and she shuddered as his hand gripped her leg. She flinched as his fingers sank into her flesh. He jerked and pulled his hand back. It was covered in blood. "I'll get a tourney on, Major." He reached up to his left shoulder and pulled off the combat application tourniquet from his shoulder strap. "Hold on."

Heart racing, she gritted her teeth as he positioned the tourniquet mid-calf and started to tighten the windlass. She groaned as the band squeezed tighter around her leg. Leaning her head back, Sam clenched her teeth and held her breath against the pain until the lifeless body of the lieutenant burst free in a huge gasp. "That's good. Stop! Uh, it's tight." She grabbed his hand, restricting his movement.

He reached down to her leg again, ran his fingers along it, before pulling back his hand. "It's not bleeding now. Major, you don't look too good."

She panted against the intense pain. "Corpsman?" she grunted.

Martinez shook his head. "I'll get his stuff. He's got morphine. I'll be back."

Sam gripped the cyclic between her knees and stared blankly at the instrument panel, and the cracked and buckled gauges. Licking her lips, she panted out small breaths to minimize her chest movement. Her vision narrowed, and nausea returned. She focused on the sound of Martinez as he cursed and threw gear to the side. It thudded heavily onto the floor, echoing in the metal frame. *Gotta get help.* Radio. A prick in her thigh caused her to look down, and she saw Martinez pull back with the auto injector in his hand.

"It's the morphine, Major. It'll help."

Sam clutched at his arm. "Who's here?"

"Mitchell's gone, Roberts too. The LT. Jakes is outside with a gun." Sam closed her eyes tightly as heaviness settled into her chest. She shook her head slightly and swallowed against the sudden thickness in her throat. *Damn. Three of my men. And I'm sitting here stuck.* She ground her teeth and pulled her leg again, her vision fading with the effort.

"Major, I gotta get outside and get the radio going."

Sam let go of his arm and wiped the sweat from her face. Stomach clenching, she stared at the lifeless body of the lieutenant. A few moments later she recognized Martinez' voice as he called over the radio. Her brain was fuzzy, and her pain subsided, as thick gray fog replaced the desert brown. Silence descended.

***

Sam awakened slowly to the sound of gunfire. *Where is it? How many?* She couldn't make sense of it. Everything was heavy and slow moving. After several more minutes of sporadic gunfire, it grew quiet. Her hair stood on end as boots scraped along the floor behind her. Someone crawled through the chopper toward her, their breath harsh in the silence. *Who is it? Who's left? Don't let them take you. Not like this. Hell no.* Her breathing slowed, her muscles tightened, a drop of sweat fell into her eyes and was blinked away. Barely breathing she slowly and quietly drew her sidearm from the holster on her chest. *Can't miss from here. Soon as they come around the corner.*

"Major, it's me, Martinez."

She lowered the handgun onto her lap, and let out a huff of air. Martinez looked at her, "Good, you're awake. And you've got your weapon. We got 'em, Major. I don't know how long it will be till more come. You stay quiet in here. Stay still. Don't let them know you're alive. Save your ammo."

"Radio?" She shook her head to clear the fuzziness, but the pounding in her head intensified.

"Radio's busted. Jakes is trying to fix his comms."

"Outside...keep watch." She gasped as breathing became more difficult.

"Roger that."

As he retreated, she pushed with her left foot against the metal again, her attempts intensifying her pain. Her hands trembled as her right leg still wouldn't budge.

***

A few minutes, or was it hours later, she heard someone approach. "Major, listen to me," Martinez said. "We got five unfriendlies coming up the ridge. We gotta let them get in close so we can get them. Stay quiet in here. I'll be behind. Jakes is in front." He pressed her weapon into her hand. "Don't shoot unless someone comes inside. Do you understand?"

She nodded, or she thought she did, and heard Martinez move away. The wind through the shattered windscreen blew grit across her face, and sweat and blood ran down her neck and back. The heat in the chopper intensified as the sun continued to bake down. Every breath hurt, but she stayed quiet. The sound of gunfire erupted around her and pinged against the helicopter. Heart racing she remained still. Her eyes were heavy, so she closed them and listened closely. *Someone's out there, watching. Waiting. Looking.* Uneasiness washed over her, and she opened her eyes. Her stomach tightened in surprise as a shadow crossed to the left in front of the chopper. The figure ignored her and crept along moving slowly forward. She shifted her eyes and saw that Jakes was looking the opposite way. *Jakes, turn around. Turn around. Hell no, not one more.* Raising her weapon, she aimed at the shadowy figure, fired and missed. The man spun to face her, their eyes locked, and they both raised their weapons. A sharp crack sounded, and the man dropped suddenly as Jakes turned and fired. After several seconds it was quiet.

Sam turned her head to the side as Jakes crawled up next to her, his huge muscular body barely fitting into the narrow space. "Thanks, Major." He looked down at her leg. "Let me try to move this." He pushed with his arms against the console. Unable to shift it he flipped onto his back, lay across the bent floor, and pushed with his legs. The metal moved only a fraction of an inch. Sam bit down on her lip trying to remain quiet as the pain intensified with his push. *Do it. Push harder. Come on.* She groaned softly, and the coppery taste of blood filled her mouth.

When he could push no longer, he got up. "Shit. Fuck, Major! It's been two hours. I'm giving you another hit. Martinez is keeping watch. I'm going to try to call out again. I don't know if we're getting through." He reached into his kit, pulled out a morphine injector and released it into her thigh.

***

Lieutenant Commander Kristine Matthews pulled off her gown and gloves, rolled them together and dropped them into the medical waste bin in the operating room. Her mask quickly followed, and then she rubbed her hands across her lower back, hoping to ease the ache. After seconds of futile effort, she bent forward and touched her toes, sighing as the stretch eased some of the kinks out of her back. She straightened up and twisted side to side, smiling at the nurse who was placing the surgical instruments into the racks. "Thanks for your help. It went well today. The team was on top of things."

"We're a well-oiled machine, Commander."

"That we are. Is there anyone left?"

"That's it for you. David...ah, Dr. Williams is here, and Dr. Lewis is on call. You're off unless the shit hits the fan."

Kris yawned and stretched her arms overhead. "I'm beat."

"I bet. I heard some good news. The Afghan kids we shipped out yesterday are doing okay."

She shook her head, trying to clear the images of the children who had arrived in a decrepit bus with burns and multiple fractures after their school was intentionally firebombed for teaching girls. "That's good to know. They were so young. I don't understand how anyone can do that to children. There's just no way to make sense of it." Kris took a deep breath and released it slowly while raising her hands overhead and stretching. "I never will understand."

"It's been a long week, Doc, get some sleep."

"I'm going to try." Kris stepped outside for a breath of air. A layer of reddish brown dust hung on the horizon. She wiped at the sweat on her brow and hoped that the AC in her quarters was working. Maybe if it was cool, she could get a few hours sleep, if she could get the images of the older school girls who had been beaten and raped out of her mind. She swallowed hard against the rage that bubbled up like a geyser inside her.

Kris turned at the sound of a woman wailing. The woman struggled with a guard and pulled free. She clung tightly to a package and ran toward Kris. Horrified, Kris watched a guard raise his rifle and aim at the woman. "Stop! Don't shoot!" Kris screamed as she ran toward the familiar woman waving her arms frantically. "Don't shoot." She grabbed at the woman. "Waseema, what's wrong?"

Waseema thrust the bundle into her arms, and Kris' heart stuttered as tears flowed down Waseema's face. Her breath caught in her throat as she pulled the wrappings back and whimpered as she looked at the familiar toddler's lifeless body, already rigid and cold. *Oh, dear God. No. No. Not Yagana.* The dark hair was matted with blood and dirt. Seconds passed until Kris could breathe again. "Waseema, come inside with me." She took her by the hand and led her inside to the coolness of the hospital. "I'm sorry. It's too late. There is nothing I can do." She wiped sticky blood from the toddler's face with the blanket and closed the lifeless dark brown eyes. After several agonizing minutes Kris handed the child to a nurse. She spoke calmly to Waseema trying to console her until an interpreter arrived. "Let them take her, so she can be cleansed.

You'll be taken to her soon." She stayed thirty more minutes, whispering softly and holding the hands of her friend until she calmed and was led away.

Kris walked away, her stomach tight and her mind numb. She wiped a tear from her cheek and hoped she could make it to her bunk before she broke down. She walked through the crowded hallway as nurses and corpsmen moved about the small hospital making their rounds, checking on the injured marines, and resupplying, getting ready for the next emergency. Numb, she went into a changing area and put on her camouflage uniform and boots. Loud voices caught her attention, and she hurried down the hallway. As she neared a small workstation, she realized that Dr. David Williams, the lead surgeon, and a senior chief, were listening to a Marine Colonel as he spoke, his gruff voice booming down the halls. "They've been taking fire. The pilot's leg is trapped, a tourniquet's on. Their corpsman is dead. A sergeant's been doing what he can, but there's been sporadic fighting. They've been able to defend. There's no sign of activity in the area now. We need them out of there quick."

"I'll go," Kris interrupted. "We're not busy now." Kris started running down the hall. "Get me a corpsman, I'll grab a jump bag." She pulled several medications from drug supply and loaded them quickly. She didn't stop when she heard a voice behind her.

"Are you sure?" David said.

Kris stole a quick look into his steel grey eyes. "Yes. We can't send a corpsman in alone. The pilot needs more advanced care."

Her stomach tightened as she reached for a power saw and blades. As she grabbed for battery packs, a hand closed over hers. She turned and saw David's brow furrow and the deep lines at the corners of his eyes. "Be safe." Kris swallowed hard, her mouth suddenly dry, and nodded. She loaded the batteries in the bag and tightened the straps. Before she could speak, she heard a familiar voice behind her.

"Doc, I'm your medic. Let's do this."

Kris almost smiled as she realized one of their most experienced corpsmen was coming too. "Let's go, Morales." With the jump bags slung over their shoulders, they ran out the door to a chopper just touching down. A moment after they lifted off, a dangerous looking marine handed them body armor and told them to put it on. The chopper raced forward into the desert.

Chapter Two

"HURRY, COMMANDER, SHE'S IN here. You've got five minutes! Ten at best. We've been taking fire for a few hours. We get a few bastards at a time taking shots. Sometimes they actually try to move in."

Jumping from their chopper, Kris and Morales ran to the downed helicopter. *Someone survived this?* It was leaning precariously to the left, pinned against the boulders. Mangled metal and aircraft parts lay across the field. The main rotor was completely destroyed, its blades shattered. The tail was bent in half.

Kris' feet rolled and slid across rock as she ran. The sound of brass chattering as she kicked up spent rounds was almost musical. She tossed her bag into the helicopter and climbed up. Creeping over the crumpled seats and bags, she gripped the mangled wall for balance. Her eyes adjusted to the dim light as she picked her way forward. Twisted metal blocked easy access to the front cabin, and she dropped her gear and crawled into the cockpit.

The windscreen was gone, and the smell of fuel, oil, dirt and sweat mingled together. Through it all came the overpowering stench of blood and bowel. The air was thick with it. It took Kris a mere second to realize the copilot was dead. His body had released his fluids sometime after death. She reached forward and closed his eyes, and turned her attention to the remaining pilot. Blood and dirt caked the major's face. Kris' breath hitched as she realized she was looking at the delicate features of a woman whose eyes were nearly swollen shut. A ribbon of dried blood from under her helmet tracked past split and swollen lips and dIsappeared under the collar of her flight suit.

"Major? Can you hear me?" Kris shouted to be heard over the noise of the waiting helicopter. She reached for the pilot's neck and found a pulse, slow, weak, but steady. Relief surged through her, but faded when she noticed the pilot's leg disappear into the middle of a tangle of twisted metal. Blood covered the legs of her flight suit.

"She's had two doses of morphine. It's been over three hours. Our corpsman's dead. I got the tourney on right away. I didn't know what else to do. We tried to get her out, but couldn't shift the metal. Her leg is stuck. I tried to push and, at first, she was trying to pull it free. Not anymore."

Kris continued her assessment as the sergeant spoke. "It's okay. You did well." Kris moved closer to her patient. "Major? Answer me, Major. Sergeant, what's her name?"

Martinez shouted over the noise of the helicopter on watch overhead. "Major Davies."

"Major Davies, look at me!" The pilot's left eye opened suddenly and Kris jolted. The deep green of her eye was obscured by brilliant red, filling the white of her eye completely. The red glared in stark contrast to her pale dirty face. "Tell me what you feel."

She panted. "Pain. Head hurts, leg...bad, stuck."

"I am going to take a look. I am getting you out of here." Kris moved her hands down across the pilot's arms, the top of her chest. *Ribs broken, arms good.*

"No. Stuck. Shoot me."

It took Kris a moment to comprehend the garbled words. She shook her head vigorously "What? No!"

"Taliban. Come back. Leave. Shoot me."

Kris looked at her in disbelief and finally saw the pistol in her lap. "No! No way." She carefully removed the gun from the major's lap.

"Sergeant! Take this gun. Give me my bag."

She ran her hands down the pilot's leg feeling the stickiness of drying blood. Unable to find any fresh bleeding she relaxed marginally. Reaching further down, she encountered metal and snaked her hand through a gap in the wreckage, ignoring the scrapes of metal across her hands. Narrowing her eyes, she concentrated, and her hand closed on tattered, soft gobs of flesh and jagged pieces of bone as the contour of the leg changed abruptly. *Shattered, muscles torn, bones exposed, contaminated, no fresh bleeding.* She withdrew her hand, now stained with sticky blood and pulled scissors from her gear bag. She cut through the bloody pants removing them down to where the tourniquet held tight. She cut the fabric below the tourniquet and tugged it free. Lying across the console, she tried to reach around the metal to free the leg. "It won't move." She heard someone come up from behind her.

"Doc, what do you need?"

"Give me another tourniquet and betadine."

Morales handed her a tourniquet and Kris attached it two inches above the other. She grabbed the antiseptic and doused the leg with it.

Gunfire sounded behind her and she jerked her head up.

Morales shoved her head down. "Stay down! Commander, you gotta hurry."

"Start an IV, saline." Morales squeezed into the opening between the seats, pulled one of the major's arms down to her side, quickly inserted the IV, and started the fluid running. Kris pulled on new gloves and readied her equipment.

"Get the Versed. Push it." Morales grabbed the medicine and administered it quickly; the major sighed out a long breath as her head fell forward.

"Scalpel."

He handed her the scalpel. "Jesus, you're not really going to—"

"Give her some morphine, hold her down." She looked at the major, considered what she was about to do and worried how much the woman would feel. "Major, this is going to hurt," she warned even though the major appeared unresponsive.

Her jaw set, Kris took a deep breath and moved with precision. She sliced quickly across the leg, moving the blade from right to left. She cut deep getting down to the bone and narrowly avoided getting kneed in the jaw as the major jumped and screamed.

"Hold her steady," Kris ordered.

The major slumped forward, held up by her seat restraint. Kris reached her hand up. "Clamp." There was a quick thwack of the instrument as Morales placed it in her hand. She wiggled the clamp under the bone, prying it beneath the muscle. "LAP." The sponge was instantly pressed into her hands. Gunfire sounded again, and she flinched but kept her head down. Her pulse pounded in her ears, and then everything became strangely quiet. She grabbed the lap sponge with the clamp and tried to wiggle it back and forth under the bone. "Damn, I need a few more inches. I can't get enough force. Take this." She tugged the quick release of her body armor and lay across the console. Closer now, she grabbed the sponge and pulled it rapidly back and forth until she could grab both ends. She pulled on the ends and lifted the bone toward her. "Give me the saw."

"What?"

"The saw! It looks like—"

"I got it." He thrust the heavy piece into her hands.

Dear God, let her not feel this. With steady hands, she turned the saw on and using her left hand, aligned it the best she could in the cramped space and pressed it to the bone. The scream lasted only a second, but she knew she would remember it for the rest of her life. Kris pulled harder with the sponge, using it as a retractor to lift the bone further as the cut through the tibia deepened. Chips of bone and marrow flew up. There was a jerk as the saw cleared the tibia and she turned it quickly on the fibula. She finished the cut through the bone, flicked the switch off, and thrust the saw back toward Morales. Without asking he handed her the scalpel again and she quickly used it to cut through the remaining muscle and skin. Kris took a deep breath, her shoulders dropping momentarily. She glanced up at the major, her mouth open as she hung unconscious in her harness. *Breathing shallow. Needs oxygen, fluids. Antibiotics. Get her sedated.*

Gunfire bounced off the sides of the helicopter. Someone hollered into the wreckage, "We gotta go!"

"Get her out." Kris pushed her hands up against the pilot's shoulders as Morales unhooked the harness, and the Major collapsed onto her, still mercifully unconscious. She supported the pilot's chest, and felt ribs shift, while Morales and the sergeant wrestled the major out of her seat. They pulled her back into the belly of the chopper and onto a stretcher. Climbing over the console, Kris scrambled back to them. She grabbed two Kelly clamps, clamping two vessels oozing blood.

"Doc, now!"

"I need a few seconds." She grabbed some sponges and applied a pressure dressing. "Go, go, go!"

They moved as fast as they could toward the back of the downed chopper. She grabbed the jump bag and one side of the stretcher. The four of them ran toward the Evac helicopter as it was touching down a hundred yards away. Gunfire sounded all around them. *Where are they? Where's it coming from…where's air cover?* Dirt flew up at their feet. Suddenly fire erupted in her chest, and her hands stung with the bite of rocks cutting into them.

Morales screamed, "Fuck, doc's hit, doc's hit."

Before Kris could roll over, strong arms lifted her, and she realized she was hanging upside down over Morales' shoulder. Pain pounded through her with each step Morales took. Moments later she felt more arms grabbing her, as she was wrestled inside the chopper. She had a momentary feeling of weightlessness and realized they were airborne.

"Doc, talk to me."

"Oh my God! How…how bad is it?" She panted, already breathless. "Where is it?" Her hands grabbed at her chest, she felt blood on her hands. She licked at her lips and gulped for air, as white-hot pain flashed through her body. She tried to sit up, but he held her down.

"Move your hands, let me see. Lie still."

Everything ceased to exist except for Morales and her pain. Her mind scrambled trying to keep up with what he was doing. He worked quickly, cutting through her shirts and exposing her chest. She heard him mutter "Fuck" as he looked at the wound.

"Can't...breathe...up."

"Stay down." She watched as Morales reached into his bag, ripped open a package and pulled out an occlusive dressing. His firm hands pressed down onto her chest where she knew the air was rushing out. He grabbed gauze and applied a pressure dressing to her shoulder. "You'll be all right, doc, I've got you. You'll feel less pressure in your chest now."

Kris nodded and whispered, "Help her."

"She can wait."

The sergeant had come over "She doesn't look good. Geeezus Christ."

"Shut up! Be quiet," Morales hollered. "Ignore him, doc." He grabbed a stethoscope, and she watched as he closed his eyes, his head cocked to the side. "Breathe, doc, breathe." He put the stethoscope down and looked at her wound, "You're still bleeding a little. I'm going to clamp it. Doc, look at me. Stay focused on me." It was quiet for several seconds as he studied the wound. He muttered, "There has to be another bleeder. I gotta find it."

Kris hissed as his fingers probed into her, she reached for his hand. "Hurts." Something sprayed across her face. *Oh, Fuck.*

"There it is. It's a little one, near your shoulder." He sprinkled quick clot on the wound and covered it with gauze. "You're doing good, doc. Stay with me."

Kris looked over at the major. She tugged on Morales' sleeve. "Fluid." She pointed a finger at the major, shuddering between gasps. "Give her fluid." Hearing gagging, she turned her head and watched as the Sergeant vomited in the back of the helicopter.

Kris heard the gunner groan, "Holy mother of God, her tit is gone."

"I got it, doc. Stay still. I got you both." His voice was reassuring and calming. She felt a prick of pain in her arm, and she knew he had started an IV. Her vision grayed. "Up, can't breathe, up." Jakes propped her up slightly as Morales moved over to the major. Kris watched as he hung another bag of fluid above the major and checked her dressing.

"No blood?" she muttered.

"No. Keep your eyes open. Doc, look at me." He placed an oxygen mask on her, and the cool air flowed across her face. "Keep breathing, doc. Come on. Breathe with me. Watch me."

From far away she heard someone call out "How much longer?"

"Three minutes to wheels down. They need an update."

Kris saw his mouth move but heard nothing. She bit down against the pain and closed her eyes. Jostling awakened her and she grabbed the hand that pulled back the bandage. Through blurred vision she recognized David. He looked at her, and she saw the alarm in his eyes.

"Kris, you'll be all right. I'll take care of you."

She shook her head. "Pilot."

"We've got it." She opened her mouth to speak. He looked down. "Quiet, I know what to do."

Then it was dark.

***

Sam became aware of sound, a steady beep in time with her heartbeat, a squeaking wheel as it moved by, the sound of footsteps on the floor. *Where am I? My head hurts. Hell, everything aches. I need water.* She remained quiet. Everything was dark, subdued, like she was looking through a thick fog. She tried to remember. *What had happened?* She tried to speak but nothing came out. Someone lifted her arm, warm fingers pressed along her wrist. She tried to turn but pain flashed bright into her head. The quick prick along the inside of her elbow was virtually painless. More footsteps and muffled voices. Finally, she heard a voice close by. "How is she doing?"

"Vitals are stable. She's had another unit of blood. Fluids are running now."

"Awake yet?"

"Not yet."

I am awake. I am here. Don't you see? I'm right here. Look at me.

"Well, let's take a look."

Someone pried open her eyelid, shined a light in it, and allowed the lid to flick closed. The other lid was subjected to the same sequence. Someone was pushing on her legs. Yanking them around. *Damn, were they hitting them with hammers?* She tried to pull away. Unfamiliar voices sounded confident but urgent, and she tried in vain to follow their conversation.

"The bandages are off."

"Okay, let's see what we have. Hmm. Okay. Let's take her in. Get this cleaned up. Get another dose of antibiotics on board. When's the next flight?"

"In six hours."

"Good, let's get her out. Where's Kris?"

"She's in the OR already."

The voices became softer as footsteps moved away. *What the hell is going on? Someone is still here.* "Hey, Major. You might be able to hear me. I'm going to give you antibiotics and some more pain medicine. You're heading home." The female voice was calm, and Sam sighed. Warmth spread through her arm and the fog thickened until all was silent.

***

Sam awakened with a jerk, and had the feeling that a long time had passed. *Where was she? Damn this fog. Her throat hurt.* She tried to call for help, but nothing happened. Although she tried again, no sound came out. Something held her down as she tried to sit up. *Voices were clearer now, loud, fast, yet not chaotic. English. Many people were moving around. I'm being carried. Footsteps on metal.* Straps were placed down over her and pulled snug. Something soft and warm covered her. *A blanket?*

"Chief, this is Major Samantha Davies, thirty-one-year-old female, no allergies. Blood type A positive. Right below knee amputation, concussion, fractured ribs, right, four through eight, no pneumothorax. Pain medication on board. Light sedation. Foley is in."

Cool air flowed through the mask snugged to her face. More movement surged around her, snaps and clicks, multiple voices, and many conversations. There was the sound of a large door moving, and darkness enveloped her. She recognized the distinctive high-pitched squeal of an aircraft engine starting. There was a deep rumbling around her and then movement. *I'm going somewhere.*

Chapter Three

LANDSTUHL, GERMANY

SAM WOKE GRADUALLY, A deep ache in her legs. She tried to open her eyes, but they felt gritty. Finally, one eye popped open, and she saw a shadowy figure in dark blue clothing moving nearby. The air held a peculiar odor, and she tried to recall the smell. It took several seconds, and a feeling of unease rippled through her as she recognized the smell of a hospital. The subtle odor of disinfectant lingered. Sam glanced at the brightly lit monitors, their screens filled with numbers which constantly changed. A door stood ajar, and she recognized the sounds of English and German being spoken nearby. The figure moved closer. She was a woman with blonde hair tied up in a bun and wore a single silver bar signifying her rank as a first lieutenant.

The woman's eyes widened in surprise. "Hi, Major, it's good to see you awake. I'm one of your nurses, Lieutenant James. You can call me Emily if you like."

"Where am I?" Sam's words came out raspy, her throat was dry.

"You're at Landstuhl, Major."

Germany. "How long have I been here?" Sam fidgeted under the blanket, trying to get comfortable. Her ribs hurt and it was painful to draw a deep breath. She had a headache that was getting worse by the minute and trying to outrace the crushing molten lava pain in her legs. She kicked trying to get more comfortable. The pain eased up in her left, but her right foot continued to throb and was becoming excruciating. She wiggled her legs, felt the sheet rub across her feet, irritating them more.

"Almost two days, ma'am. You will be heading back to the States tomorrow."

Two days? "Back to the States? Why?"

A warm hand picked up hers and pressed into her wrist. A soothing voice, spoke softly to her, "You were injured, ma'am. You're on your way home. Can you see me all right?"

"Little blurry. What happened?" Before the nurse could answer, the door opened, and a lanky, dark-skinned man dressed in scrubs arrived. His bald head reflected the light, distracting her momentarily. "Good morning, Major. It's nice to see you're awake."

"Morning, sir." She croaked out, her voice gravelly.

He pulled a chair over to the bed and sat down. "I wanted to talk to you about your injuries. Can I bring the bed up some?"

Sam nodded and groaned quietly as the bed moved her into a semi-reclined position.

"How's your pain level?"

She bit down hard, struggling to swallow against the dryness in her mouth. "It's bad."

"Major, let me tell you the rules here." His eyes that were so dark brown they nearly concealed his pupils. Subtle wrinkles marked the corners of his eyes. "When you're in pain you say something so you get the right amount of medicine. You will recover faster if your pain is controlled. You won't be completely pain-free, but our goal is to keep the level manageable."

"Yes, sir."

"Where do you hurt?"

"Head, neck, ribs. Legs hurt. Bad. Hurt like hell." She bit her lip and grimaced against the pain that continued to expand like a balloon filling with air.

"Major, do you remember what happened?"

"Helo crashed. Leg is busted." She stared at the wall trying to remember. "I was trapped." She stared at him for several seconds, her heart started to thud, and she squeezed her eyes tight against sudden tears. "Some of my crew didn't make it."

"That's right. You lost some of your crew. Do you remember anything else?"

Sam sat quietly for a few moments trying to recall the events. "There was an attack. Jakes, Martinez. Two, maybe three times." Her heart started to race, and the beep of a monitor momentarily distracted her. Sweat rose on her neck and back. She rubbed her palms on the blanket and looked down at her legs. She closed her eyes, picturing the helicopter.

"That's right, there were some skirmishes, and you were trapped. How did you get out?"

Sam stared at the wall and shook her head. "I don't know."

He placed his hand over hers and lowered his voice. "Your

helicopter crashed and you were seriously injured. Your right leg was trapped and injured."

Her stomach tightened. "I broke it. It hurt too much to move it."

He picked up her hand and gave it a squeeze. "There was severe bleeding, extensive tissue damage. I'm sorry, but you lost your leg."

Sam jolted in bed, trying to sit up as her body went on alert. Her heart pounded, and blood rushed to her head. The light brightened in the room as her pulse throbbed in her ears. Her skin was damp with sweat. "No!" She tried to sit up, but collapsed with the effort. She looked at the blanket covering her legs. "Broken that's all." She was light-headed, and the room started to spin.

He squeezed her hand firmly. "No, Major. It was badly damaged and trapped. You've had three surgeries. The first was at the field hospital, and you've had two more here. We've been cleaning out the wounds, taking out the damaged tissue. You're heading home tomorrow. You'll be going to Bethesda. It's possible you'll need more surgery there."

"No. You're wrong. I can feel them! My feet are there. Right there." She pointed at her legs and kicked. But the blanket only moved a little. She deliberately wiggled her left foot, watching the blanket move. She repeated the action with the right foot but nothing happened. Pain exploded in her right foot, but the blanket didn't move. Nausea roiled up, as her gut clenched. She shook her head in denial. "It hurts. I can feel it."

"Major, I am going to lower the blanket so you can see. What you're experiencing is phantom pain. The nerves are firing, and your brain is trying to figure out what is going on. It's normal for you to experience this."

She shook her head. "No, it's there."

The doctor spoke calmly, "Major, you have a below knee amputation. You've lost your leg at about mid-shin."

Her headache exploded as she violently shook her head. "No."

"Your leg is bandaged. Do you want to see?"

Staring at the wall, she tried to push up, and gasped as pain exploded in her chest.

"Careful. You have four broken ribs."

"Up." Her voice was too high. "Up, let me up."

"You want the bed up more? Let me help you. Are you ready?"

Sam looked at him and realized he was serious. With her heart pounding in her chest so hard it hurt, she took a deep breath that caused the pain in her chest to flare. She let it out slowly, stared into his dark brown eyes for several seconds and nodded. She looked down. *Holy fuck. No, no, no.* Her thigh was swollen, and heavily wrapped with bandages that spiraled down over her knee, before stopping abruptly. There was nothing left. Her leg ended at the shin. Her right foot throbbed, pulsing with pain, like some crazy, sick magic trick even though her foot and lower half of her shin were gone.

She looked up in a panic, opened her mouth to say something and started to dry heave. Her upper body shook as contractions racked her body. Sweat beaded on her skin and trickled down her face in front of her ears. *Oh fuck. What am I going to do? What? How? Oh, my God. I can't walk. Or drive.* The doctor's voice carried through the chaos of her thoughts but didn't register. After several minutes, she became aware of him still speaking calmly, "We're going to keep you here another day. Tomorrow you head for Bethesda. You're going home, Major."

She lay motionless, staring at the wall as the doctor and nurse got her situated under the covers. "I'm going to give you something else for the pain. Get some rest. I'll be back later, and we can talk some more. Your family has been notified, and they have been getting updates daily. Perhaps later, after we meet again, you would like to call your family. I'm sure they would love to hear your voice."

Sam watched as the nurse mixed the medicine into her IV line. Almost instantly darkness closed in.

***

Kris awakened slowly, her eyes heavy, the room was blurry. The smells and sounds of a hospital were similar but somehow different. The room was modern and brightly lit. It wasn't an open bay like the field hospital. She watched a monitor as it recorded the vital signs. *Heart rate and breathing were a little slow. Blood pressure slightly elevated. Temperature good.* Distractedly she looked for the patient, but she saw no bed or patient. *This isn't right. Think, think.* Kris shook her head from side to side and grimaced. Her vision wasn't clear. Lifting her arm to rub her eyes, pain flew into her chest, and she hissed against the discomfort. *Oh God! I am the patient! Where am I? What happened?*

Voices around her, "Doctor Matthews, Kris, you're waking up. You're in Landstuhl. Can you hear me?"

One voice among several was familiar. *Who? Landstuhl?* Struggling to focus she squeezed her eyes shut several times. There was pain. Pain everywhere, gnawing, creeping around the edges of awareness. "Kris, do you hear me? Look at me."

She looked toward the voice, struggled to focus, and recognized her old roommate from medical school and her first lover. "Vicki?" Her voice was weak and scratchy. Her mouth and throat were dry. "Where?"

"You're in Germany, Kris. At Landstuhl. You've been here for four days."

"Ger…? Why?" Kris shook her head slightly. *Afghanistan. Field hospital.* "How?"

"Kris, you were hurt. You took a hit to your shoulder and chest. Do you understand me?"

"Chest…hurts," she gasped. She tried to reach for her chest, but her arm didn't move.

"Kris, listen to me. You had a chest injury. Your lung collapsed. There's a wet seal in. You have a wound vac on too."

She bit at her lip and stared at Vicki silently. *Wet seal? Wound vac? Germany?*

"Kris, do you understand?"

She shook her head and whispered, "No."

"You have a wet seal in. You are going to need the chest tube and suction for a few more days. Do you understand what I am saying?"

Kris lay still, wincing against the pain, after a few seconds she nodded as she envisioned the two tubes leading into her chest and pulling out blood and fluids. "Why?"

"You were hit." The bed was moved into a sitting position, and the nurse helped Kris sit up. Kris gasped with the pain. "Easy, let us support you." The cool stethoscope pressed against her side and back and she did her best to breathe despite the pain in her chest. Deep and stabbing, it tugged painfully all the way to her shoulder.

"Your lungs sound good. How is your pain level? Do you need something for pain?"

Kris nodded and tried to swallow. "Yes. Thirsty."

Vicki adjusted the medication running through the IV. "Here is a little more. Try to relax." She turned slightly and spoke to the nurse. "Lieutenant, can you bring some water in?" She motioned for the nurse to go and waited until the door closed. "Your parents were notified. And Shelly. They haven't been updated since yesterday. Do you want me to call them and update them personally or do you want the official call through the command?"

"You. They trust you." Kris reached for her chest. "What happened?"

"Tell me what you remember."

"I left the hospital, going to my quarters. Woke up here." Kris saw concern pass over her friend's face. "What hap…"

She quieted as the nurse returned with a water pitcher, and watched as the nurse poured water into a pink plastic tumbler and soaked sponge swabs in the water. The nurse placed one in her mouth so she could suck the water out. Cool, fresh water spread over her dry tongue and mouth. It vanished before hitting the back of her throat, and she reached for more. "Take it easy. Nice and slow. Let's see how you do." She accepted the swab sticks, sucking greedily for the few drops of water.

"What happened?" But even as Vicki started to talk Kris' eyes grew heavy, and she drifted back to sleep.

Chapter Four

SAM LOOKED AROUND THE unfamiliar surroundings. The room was sparsely decorated, with a two-drawer cabinet, a chair, a stool, and on the far wall hung a television. The second hand on a face clock ticked audibly. Several monitors and an IV pole were nearby, standing guard. A soft, steady beep, kept time with the rhythm of her heart. There was a surprising amount of open floor space. A door stood open which led to a bathroom. *Hospital. I was going home.* Lifting her arm, she followed the tubing down from the largest bag of fluid, until it joined with an orange topped needle and disappeared into her hand.

The bed rails were pulled up, keeping her from rolling out of bed. She read the buttons and raised the head of the bed, pain grabbing at her ribs. Stopping the bed movement, she pulled the blanket down and peaked inside her gown. Deep purple and blue ran along her ribcage and around her side as far as she could see. "Damn, I'm glad that doesn't hurt as bad as it looks. They didn't send me home for that. Did they?" She let her gown drop back into place, "Something's not right."

She sat quietly trying to remember something, anything. *Think Sam. What are you forgetting? Why does my foot keep itching?* She reached down to scratch her leg and remembered. *My God. My leg, part of my leg is gone.* Her chest tightened and sweat formed on her forehead. Her muscles tensed until air burst from her lungs. Shaking uncontrollably, she jerked up to a sitting position, ignoring the grinding in her side, and tried to lower the rails. An alarm sounded, something tugged at her chest, and pulled at her skin.

The door burst open, and Sam looked up in surprise. "Stop. Major, get back in bed. Come on, lean back. Let me get you settled." Warm hands gently pressed her back until she was lying down.

"I want to sit. Let me up." She panted.

"Shh. It's okay. You'll be all right. Relax, slow down your breathing. Look at me, Major. Breathe in slow, through your nose. Hold it. Out through your mouth and nose. A little slower. Come on, with me."

Her muscles slowly relaxed and the beeping grew slower. Sam

swallowed hard before croaking out, "Where am I?"

"Bethesda, ma'am." The nurse looked at the EKG monitor, pressed a button silencing the alarm. "Let me look, Major, I think you pulled off one of your leads." Sam sat still as the nurse opened her gown. "You did. Two of them are loose, let me put new pads on."

She ignored the tugging on her skin as the adhesive was peeled off the rest of the way, and two cold pads were placed along her ribs. "What day is it?"

"It's Wednesday, a little after eight in the morning. You arrived late last night. How are you feeling?'

"Confused. My ribs hurt, and you're a little blurry. My leg is gone. It's not a dream. Why can't I remember?"

"I'm sorry, Major. It's not a dream. You're in good hands here. Your confusion is due in part to your concussion. You have a lot going on right now, so feeling confused is normal. I'll let the doctors know that you're awake. Would you like some water? You've been given the okay for that."

"Yes. Thank you."

The nurse finished reconnecting the leads prior to writing a few notes on her chart. "Your vitals look good. I'll go speak with your medical team and get some water for you. Are you hungry?"

"No."

"Someone will be back in with the water soon. Here's your call bell, and the TV remote. The phone is here if you want to call your family." She pulled the phone over, and placed it on a stand, moving it next to the bed. "Ring the bell if you need anything."

***

LANDSTUHL, GERMANY

"Kris, how are you feeling?"

"Vicki? What are you doing here?"

"I arrived a few months back. You don't remember talking to me yesterday?"

"I thought maybe I dreamed it. Yesterday is pretty blurry."

"You are in Landstuhl. Do you understand what happened to you? How you were hurt?"

"Landstuhl? How long have I been here?"

"This is day five."

"Five? What happened? Why am I here?"

"Do you remember anything?"

Kris was silent for several moments and then spoke hesitantly. "I remember finishing up in the operating room." She closed her eyes thinking back. "We did a turnover, I grabbed my gear and went back to my quarters to get some sleep."

"Hmm. Okay. What about your injuries? Do you understand what happened?"

Kris shook her head. "I don't." She was quiet for several seconds, as she stared intently at the wall, "You said I was hit, and my arm was hurt. And that my lung collapsed. I don't understand how that could happen. Everything is a little confusing."

"That would be the pain medications. How is your pain level today?"

"If I don't move it's a seven. Vicki, what's going on?"

"You were hit by shrapnel in your left shoulder and chest. You have severe chest trauma. You had a collapsed lung. The shoulder damage was surprisingly mostly superficial. You had some penetration there, but overall the nerves and muscles did well. No bone injury either."

"You're not telling me something."

Vicki reached over and took her right hand. Kris looked down at their joined hands. "You have a wound vac on now, trying to help pull the skin edges closer, and the chest seal, drawing out fluid from the chest wound and your lung."

"A wound vac?" Kris reached up and felt the plastic bandage across her chest, touched the tubing, and followed it with her hand until it disappeared over the edge of the bed. Tracing the tubing back up, she ran her hands over the plastic again and laid her hand flat on it. "Oh, my God" She jerked in bed trying to sit up but was easily pushed back down by Vicki. "My breast, it's gone! It's gone?"

"Shh. Kris, calm down. You had a blast injury. One piece of metal made it all the way into your lung and collapsed it. That was removed and your lung re-inflated quickly. But the rest, you had fifteen shards, removed from the chest muscles and your breast tissue. You've had four surgeries here, and one at the field hospital. It's been almost a week since you were hurt. They were able to repair the major blood vessels under your arm, that's why you're in the sling. To let that rest and heal. You almost bled out. Kris, your corpsman, saved your life. He kept you going until the medevac returned."

"What? Why was I in a medevac? I work at the hospital. Were we attacked? Was there another suicide bomber?"

"No. You had to go out to the field. Do you remember that?"

"No."

"Hmm. Let me go make a few calls. I want to get a neurologist down here. I spoke with your parents last night. I told them that you had been awake and that you were confused but doing better. I couldn't get a hold of Shelly, but I left a message on your home phone."

"Okay. Thank you. Can I make a call? I want to talk to them."

"Absolutely." Vicki pulled the phone closer, "Take your time. But don't wear yourself out."

Kris waited until she walked out before laying her head back on the pillow. *What the hell happened?*

Chapter Five

BETHESDA, MARYLAND

"HOW ARE YOU DOING this morning, Major? I'm Lieutenant Shorb. I'm a physical therapist and will be working with you the next few weeks. Today we want to get an idea of what you can do right now. Your broken ribs are going to make this a little harder so if you need to catch your breath let me know, and we'll stop for a little while. Looks like before your injury you were in excellent shape, but with your injuries, surgeries, and inactivity you'll have deconditioned some."

She bit her lip, and watched him closely. "Okay. What do I have to do?"

"Let's see if we can get you sitting up on your own, and getting in and out of bed from a chair. If you do well, maybe we can get you standing. This helps us find out how much assistance you are going to need getting in and out of bed, into a chair, into the bathroom, and getting dressed. The sooner we can get you moving the sooner we can get the catheter out and leave it out. Initially, we're going to do the exercises in here, and as soon as you're ready, you'll start taking sessions in the PT clinic, twice a day. Before we start, how are you feeling today?"

"I'm a little sore."

"A little? Sorry, Major, I don't buy that. Most folks here right now are in a fair amount of pain. This will go a lot better if you're honest. So, on a scale of one to ten, with ten being the worst, where would you set your pain at?"

"A five, maybe six."

"Do you want something else for pain?"

"Not right now."

Once Shorb explained the different things Sam would need to do to get to a seated position, he helped her transition from lying flat to a full, upright seated position. She did it several times, occasionally grimacing from the pain in her ribs. "Damn that hurts."

"Like I said, your ribs are going to make this harder, but we have to get you up and moving. Do it again."

Sam lay back, collapsing the last few inches. Her breath rushed out as her ribs shifted. A wave of nausea hit her, and she covered her mouth quickly with her hands.

"Major? Are you okay?"

"Yes. Coming back down didn't feel too good."

"Try to control your descent. Don't just fall. One more time and then you'll try something else."

Sam took several deep breaths, and pulled herself up into position. The air whooshed out of her with the effort, and she bit down to keep from groaning.

"Did that feel any better?"

Sam wiped at the sweat on her brow. "Not really. I feel like I'm uneven and twisted."

"You want to be balanced. Make sure you're sitting with your weight evenly distributed."

"LT, I think I know how to sit."

"Major, I have no doubt that you do. But since you've never had a missing limb, I want to make sure you're not sitting in such a way that you start to get pressure sores on your stump or on your backside. "

"How do I know if that's happening?"

"Shift around until you feel comfortable. Lift as you reposition, don't slide. Pillows will be helpful." The therapist wedged a pillow against her buttocks to keep her from sliding down and placed another pillow under the stump. "Do you feel balanced now?"

"I do."

"Good. I'm going to lower the side rail, and you're going to turn and sit on the edge. Push with your arms." Sam wiped her sweaty palms against the sheets and followed his instructions. Soon she was sitting with her legs dangling over the side of the bed. "It's been over a week since you last stood up, so it's not unusual to get dizzy. I'm going to wrap this belt around your pelvis, and lower the bed a little closer to the floor. Don't try to stand up yet."

"Okay. What is the belt for?"

He wrapped his arms around Sam, positioned and fastened the thick, wide strap. "This is an assist strap. I am going to use it to help you get in that chair. This minimizes the risk for everyone."

"Okay, what's next?"

"I'm going to show you how to get in the wheelchair." He

demonstrated the technique several times, giving her several pointers she had to be aware of so she wouldn't end up on the floor.

"When you're ready, go ahead."

Sam placed her foot on the floor and pushed with her arms to a half standing position. She started to pivot toward the wheelchair, and the room faded to gray. Her knee felt like a sponge, and she swayed. A tight pull across her waist got her attention, and she was pushed back against the bed.

"Sit down. "

"I got light-headed. Why?"

"Because you have been lying down for almost ten days. It will get better. Take a few seconds, and we'll do more."

She took several deep breaths, grimacing against the grinding of her ribs. "Let's do it."

After several more attempts, she was performing the maneuver relatively quickly. Ignoring the sweat that ran down her face, she sat down on the bed.

"Only a few more minutes until the morning session will be over. I want to see if we can get you standing all the way up."

He unfolded a walker and set it up in front of her. She scowled and grumbled, "That's for old people."

"It's for injured people. We can't get you on crutches until we know you can stay balanced using a walker. The harder you work, Major, the sooner you'll get up and move on your own. Ready to do this?"

"Yes."

He positioned the walker for her, and showed her how to stand and balance with the device. After a few tries, she could perform the maneuver without difficulty. "Okay, Major, that's it for the morning."

"Already?"

"It's been an hour. You'll have another session this afternoon, possibly with another therapist. You'll do these exercises here. After that you're going down to the therapy room. I think you're strong enough to start doing more. Do you want to sit in the wheelchair or get back in bed?"

"The chair. By the window."

"Okay. Ring the call bell if you need something. Do not try to get in bed by yourself. Not yet."

"I understand."

He watched as she got into the wheelchair and rolled herself over to the window. He moved the water pitcher and tumbler closer to her. "Remember to drink, Major."

Sam nodded her head and watched as he walked out of the room. The door closed and she sucked in a breath and tugged at her hair. *Dear God can I really do this? What am I going to do? I have no strength. What if I can't fly? I can't stay in. I can't go back. Not again.*

Her eyes filled as she fought back the despair. Two steady breaths quieted the hammering in her chest. She concentrated on controlling her breathing and gradually her muscles relaxed, and her head fell forward.

"*Hi, Sam. Welcome to your new home. I know you're a little scared right now. You've had sleepovers here with Lauren. Now instead of leaving in the morning, you get to stay.*"

"*Thank you for letting me stay here until my dad comes back.*"

"*Of course, honey. Mr. Jim and Justin will help bring in the rest of your things. Lauren is upstairs waiting for you. You two will sleep in the same room. Whenever you're tired of being in her messy room, you can help us decorate your own room.*"

"*Okay. But I think my dad will be back soon. He'll be wondering why we aren't at home.*"

Sam jerked awake, and tugged at her hair. She muttered, "Why did I dream about that?" Uncomfortable from sitting so long she shifted in the chair and flinched from the discomfort of the catheter. "That's it. This comes out." She wheeled over to the bed and pressed the call bell. The nurse arrived quickly. "I want this catheter out. Now."

"Yes, ma'am. Lieutenant Shorb said you did well today. Let's get you in bed, and I'll get it out. You'll need help getting to the restroom later though."

"I don't care. Go ahead and get it out."

Chapter Six

LANDSTUHL, GERMANY

"DR. MATTHEWS?" A TALL, dark-haired man came into her room. "Hi. I'm Dr. Rohrden, one of the surgeons here. How are you feeling?"

"Weak. Pain is a seven." Kris spoke slowly avoiding the deep breaths that increased her pain. She pointed to the monitor that was keeping track of her vital signs. "My oxygen saturation is good. It drops a little periodically. I have to remember to take deeper breaths."

"Any leg pain?"

"No." She knew he was asking her questions, assessing her risk for a blood clot. "I feel good. What is your plan for taking off the wound vac? I could move better if I didn't have to be tethered to it."

"That's what I wanted to talk to you about. It is not ideal to send you across the Atlantic with it on. Certainly, we've done that before but not usually on the chest. You have minimal drainage from the chest wound now. We would like to do a skin graft to close the wound here."

Kris shook her head. "Here?"

"Yes. We would take the graft skin from your thigh. The procedure itself doesn't take long. I'm sure you're familiar with the technique."

"I am. I've done them back home."

"You would be here a few more days. As soon as it looks like the graft is healing, we'll get you home. Your oxygen levels are consistently dropping through the night."

"I wasn't aware of that," she murmured as she looked over at the monitor.

"With the reduced air pressure when flying, keeping you here a few more days while everything heals will help you tolerate the flight better."

"I see. When would this be done?"

"We hope to do it tomorrow."

"All right let's do it. How much of a gap in the wound is there now?"

"The largest gap is three inches by about two inches. There are several areas where you have had great results with the wound vac. However, there are still a few spots where there is a half inch gap, a little like you had been hit by buckshot, Commander. I think for the long run its best to remove the damaged skin and get a healthy flap on. I don't want to leave those tissues exposed much longer and increase the risk of infection."

"Tomorrow," Kris whispered.

"How is your shoulder?"

"It doesn't bother me at all. I think the pain from the chest is completely overshadowing the arm discomfort."

"Good. I see you're eating solid food again. Enjoy your dinner tonight. You know the routine, nothing to eat or drink after midnight."

"I do. Thank you."

"I'll see you tomorrow."

Chapter Seven

BETHESDA, MARYLAND

SAM SAT ON THE edge of a low padded table, her foot bouncing on the floor. Around her was a flurry of activity with therapists and corpsmen helping other patients, several were missing legs, one was missing both. A cheer went up as a young Marine climbed up a flight of six steps, his arms raised in triumph.

"How are you feeling?" Lieutenant Shorb asked.

"I'm okay. I was tired after this morning's therapy session though. I fell asleep in the chair afterward."

"It's normal for you to be tired. Your body is working hard to recover. This morning was to get an idea about what you could do and to teach you how to move around safely. We'll keep working on those activities, but now we're going to start to get your leg, your residual limb, ready, for when you get your prosthesis."

Sam furrowed her brow and bit down on her lower lip. "When is that usually?"

"There is no set timeframe, Major. Everyone is different, and there are many factors. How much of the limb was lost? Are there other injuries? Was the patient in shape prior to the injury or were they overweight? Two things are definite for every limb loss. One, swelling must be reduced so you can get a good fit with the prosthesis. Two, the loss of flexibility will greatly limit what you can accomplish, and it will affect the type of prosthesis you will receive. Also, a prosthesis for someone who wants to run is different than one for someone who is going to be less active."

"Our goal is to keep the muscles in both your legs stretched out. So, we're going to spend a lot of time with flexibility exercises. You'll do strengthening, and we will start desensitization training also. That will help with some of the strange sensations you're experiencing now. Since you have on shorts and a T-shirt, are you ready to get started?"

Sam thumped her hands down on the table. "Let's do it."

"Okay, lie down with your legs out straight."

Sam lay down on the padded table, her head resting on a thin pillow.

"Do you see how your left leg is fully straight but your right knee is bent? Straighten that."

Sam tried but couldn't. "I can't, it's stuck."

"That's what we're going to work on. A lot. Let's go through the exercises. Some you'll do on your own, others you will need help with, especially the first few times. Remember, if you're not sure how to do something, ask someone first. We don't want you getting hurt."

She nodded. "Okay, let's do it."

Thirty minutes later drenched in sweat, Sam lay back on the table. "How is it possible to be this tired? I haven't moved from here."

"Because you had an intense stretching session. Your hamstrings are incredibly tight."

"Hamstrings? I was beginning to think they were harp strings."

They both laughed for a few seconds.

"One last exercise. Roll over onto your stomach and let your leg relax. Let gravity help force your knee straight. The better flexibility you have in your residual limb, the better you will do with the prosthesis. If you get a muscle contracture, it may mean having to permanently use a walker or crutch along with the prosthesis."

Sam frowned. "I don't like that term. Residual limb. It reminds me of something nasty, discarded."

"I see. Well, that's what it's usually called. What term would you prefer we use?"

"I don't know…how about…the unleg?"

"The unleg?"

"Yes, or the stump. But I think unleg is better." She flashed a quick smile at him.

"Unleg it is."

"I'm going to go make a few notes in your chart. I'll be back in ten minutes. Call out if you need help, Major. As you can see there are plenty of people around."

Sam lay on the bed, as the sweat slowly dried. *How can I be so exhausted from just a few exercises? My leg is hot. Ask if that is normal.* She watched as a therapist demonstrated a one-handed shoe tie to a young female missing an arm. *She looks like she's a teenager. Poor kid.*

"All right, Major."

Sam jumped, surprised and embarrassed that she had fallen asleep.

"Oh sorry, didn't take you long to fall asleep. Let me help you roll over."

The therapist watched Sam roll over and push herself up to a sitting position. His hand brushed against hers as he handed her a towel. "You feel a little warm, Sam. Do you feel okay?"

"I'm tired. And my leg is hot."

"Let me check your wound." He started to remove the bandage from the stump. "Have you seen this yet?"

"No. I don't like to look at it. They've been doing the wound care."

"You aren't the only one. Let us know if you want to see it."

Sam watched the therapist's face as the wound was uncovered. She decided she wouldn't want to play poker with the man because his face gave absolutely nothing away. "Is it okay?"

"It's a little warm."

"Well, I have been exercising, and it's all wrapped up. Shouldn't it be warm?"

"Perhaps. I'll let the doctor know what I see." He touched the end gently. "Does this hurt?"

Her leg jerked back, and she shrieked loud enough that others in the clinic turned to look.

"That's a little more sensitive than I expected. Let's get this covered up, and a corpsman will take you back."

Sam moved into the wheelchair easily, and wheeled herself down the hall. She made it most of the way, but her heart began to pound against her sore ribs. As she struggled to keep the chair moving the corpsman started to push the wheelchair, not commenting when Sam became too tired to continue. He watched as Sam transferred herself back to the bed without assistance.

"Major, show me how to position the pillows to avoid pressure sores."

Sam did as he asked. A slow moan escaped as her leg started to pulse.

"Are you in pain?"

"Yes."

"I'll send the nurse in. Get some rest. You're scheduled with the LT again tomorrow at oh eight hundred."

Sam nodded. After several seconds, she looked at the TV hanging on the wall. *She wasn't in the habit of watching TV. Perhaps she could ask for a book or newspaper.*

The nurse came in quickly. "Tired from your therapy today, Major?

The therapists are pleased with how well you've done. I just want to check your wound, before we get you cleaned up." As she unwrapped the ace bandages and cotton gauze from the stump, Sam watched her carefully. There was a quick flash of concern before a poker face appeared. "I'm going to leave this uncovered for a few minutes. I want the doctor to look at this. Let me get your vitals and then I'll be back with some water."

"Is there something wrong?"

"It's a little redder than I like. I'll have the doctor paged."

Sam sat staring at the wall, alternated with counting the dots in the ceiling tiles. Anything to avoid looking at the stump, at the unleg, at the residual limb. *Whatever the hell it was.* Finally, the doctor arrived. She wondered what had taken so long, but after she looked at the clock on the wall, it had only been five minutes.

"Hi, Major. I understand there is some concern about your leg. Let me take a look." She watched as a frown appeared and his brow furrowed. "Is this sore?" He rubbed it.

Sam flinched pulling her leg away sharply. "Yes." She ground her teeth together and pressed her head back into the pillow. "What's going on?"

"Major, I need you to rollover."

The nurse lowered the head of the bed until Sam was flat and she rolled over. A hand touched her butt and slowly moved lower pressing firmly on her leg. "Tell me where you start to have any pain."

His hand crossed her knee joint and slid down her calf. She hissed, "Right there."

"Has she been running a fever?"

"No, sir. Her vitals have all been normal."

"Antibiotics?"

"Only oral antibiotics now. Four times a day. Her pain level has been consistently five or six, with no increase in pain medication."

Sam remained quiet as the conversation went on around her. Finally, she cut in. "Will you tell me what's going on?"

"Yes. Rollover. Let's get this bandaged."

Sam rolled over. "I want to see it. What's wrong?"

"It appears you have an infection. It may be just the skin, but we should have the orthopedist evaluate you. I am going to order some x-rays and see what the bone looks like."

"I want to see. Let me see." She sat up and looked down. Her heart hammered as she looked at her uncovered leg for the first time. The stump was bulbous and swollen. It looked soft and was light red. More flushed than the rest of her leg. She reached her hands down and touched it. As her fingers touched the line of sutures, she realized it was tender.

"It's bright red along the back of your leg and at the tip. There is some sloughing of the skin too. I want to get a light bandage over this." He turned to the nurse. "Let's get orthopedics in. Let them know x-rays are ordered. Get an IV and antibiotics going again."

Two hours later Sam sat quietly in the dim light of her room staring at the ceiling, her dinner untouched, pushed away on the tray. Nausea swept through her. *Were they going to take more of her leg? How much?* She was sitting on the edge of the bed her good leg swinging back and forth when two of her doctors walked in. From the look on their faces, she knew it wasn't good news. "You're going to take more off, aren't you?"

"Yes. The bone looks like it is infected. Any open fracture is considered a high-risk wound. Your leg bone was exposed for several hours. We don't want to delay any longer."

"How much more will you take?"

"We won't know until we get in there. If we act fast, there is an excellent chance that you will keep your knee. That makes using the prosthesis so much easier. There is no substitute for a healthy human knee."

"When will it be?"

He gestured to her food tray. "Did you eat?"

"Not since noon. I'm not hungry."

"You're getting your fluids through the IV now so don't eat or drink anything. We'll take you in after midnight. I don't want to wait until morning."

"We'll take good care of you, Major. We'll get you through this."

Chapter Eight

LANDSTUHL, GERMANY

KRIS SAT IN BED and did her best to take deep breaths. The respiratory therapist was encouraging her to continue breathing forcefully.

"Only a few more, Commander, and we'll be done. After that you can rest for a few minutes before they get you up and moving."

Kris finished with the breathing exercises and took the mask off her face. She dried the mist from her mouth and chin and handed the mask back to the corpsman. "There you go. Are you coming back later?"

"Someone will be by this afternoon for your next treatment. Remember to do the deep breathing exercises on your own every hour for ten minutes."

"I understand."

"I'm sure you do, doc. Be sure you do them."

"I'll be good."

After he left the room, she lowered her gown and looked at the large bandage covering most of her chest. She could see nothing else. The ache in her chest was diminished as the pain medication was at a good level. Her arm wasn't painful at all. She wished she could come out of the sling for some movement, but the repaired blood vessels needed minimal movement while they healed. She pulled her gown back up, snapped it, and pulled it up to her waist to look at the bandage on her thigh. Her leg below the bandage covering the graft site was a little swollen, which was to be expected. She leaned back and closed her eyes. *In twenty-four hours, I'm going home.*

***

BETHESDA, MARYLAND

Sam became aware of movement around her. She opened her eyes and realized she was in recovery. Everything was blurry. She tried to rub at her eyes, but a nurse stopped her. "Don't rub your eyes, Major."

"Blurry."

"I'll get it for you. Keep them closed, and I'll wipe off the ointment."

Something soft dabbed across her closed eyelids and when she reopened them everything was clear. Sam sighed. "That's better. What time is it?"

"It's oh five hundred, Major. You going somewhere?"

"How much?"

"The doctor will be along shortly to talk to you. Your surgery went well."

"Now. Tell me now." Sam had grabbed the nurse's hand and wouldn't let go. She wasn't squeezing, she didn't have the strength, but her voice was commanding despite its low volume.

"Major, I can't."

"Knee?"

"Knee? Oh, do you still have your knee? Yes. Yes, you do."

Sam let go of her, and sighed, laying her head back on the pillow. "Thank you."

***

BETHESDA, MARYLAND

Kris awakened slowly, gradually recognizing the noises around her. She caught the faintest whiff of perfume. She turned her head toward the scent. "Shelly?"

"Hi, babe." A strong warm hand held hers tightly and lips pressed lightly to hers.

"How long have you been here?"

"I got here late last night. Too late to visit. They said by late morning things would be settled enough to see you. How are you feeling?"

"Tired. Sore. I'm so happy to see you." She lifted Shelly's hand to her lips and kissed it. "I've missed you."

"I missed you too. I was so scared. They didn't share a lot of details. I think your parents got more information. Being able to speak the doctor talk, they knew what questions to ask. They kept me informed." She leaned forward, kissed Kris on the head. "They're here. They stopped downstairs for some coffee and probably to give us a few minutes alone. Thank God, you're home. I can sleep easier at night knowing you're back here safe and sound, where you belong."

Kris reached for the water pitcher and gasped, clutching at her chest. "I'll get that for you." Shelly filled the pink plastic water cup and held the cup and straw while Kris drank. "You look uncomfortable. Are they giving you enough pain medication? You shouldn't be hurting."

"I have enough. I don't need anymore, it makes me too tired."

"You do look tired. What happened, Kris? They didn't really explain it."

Before Kris could answer there was a soft knock at the door, and it pushed open slightly. Her mouth curled up as her parents entered. "Mom, Dad."

"Oh, Krissy." Her mom hurried over, tears immediately sliding down her face. "It's so good to have you back. How do you feel?"

Kris reached her arm up to try to hug her mother, grimacing as the pain ripped through her chest. She kissed her cheek, and gave a weak hug to her father. "I'll be okay. I need time, that's all."

"You gave us quite the scare." Kris heard the emotion in her dad's voice.

"I'm sorry." Kris stopped speaking as the nurse came in the room, and checked Kris' vital signs, IV, and bandages. As soon as the nurse left the room, everyone started to talk at once.

Kris held up her hand, silencing everyone. "Please. Let me explain." She flinched as a flash of pain stabbed into her chest. She took several shallow breaths. "I don't remember everything. In fact, I don't remember how I was hurt at all. They've told me I went outside the wire, uh, outside the camp. I went out to help. And I was hit."

"You went outside the camp?" Shelly jumped up. "Why would you do that?"

"Someone needed help."

"For God's sake, Kris. You could—"

Kris' mother cut her off. "So you're not sure how you were hurt?"

"No. There's a...um, some amnesia around the events."

"But..." Shelly looked at Kris' parents "Is that all right?"

Kris' mom spoke first. "It's concerning. Of course, so much has happened, a little confusion is reasonable." She gave Kris' hand a gentle squeeze. "I'm sure with time things will become a little clearer."

Her father spoke softly, "How do you feel?"

Kris looked at her parents. "I feel okay. Better now that I am back in the States."

Kris' dad spoke, "I feel better now that you're back home too."

There was a rap on the door, and it opened right away. "Good morning. Whoa! Big crowd. Sorry for the interruption but I wanted to see how the patient was doing this morning." He smiled at Kris. "I'm Dr. Martin, one of the civilian physicians here. Who are your visitors, Commander?"

"These are my parents, William and Irene Matthews. Both of my parents are physicians. My dad is a family practice physician, and my mom is a general surgeon. This is my partner, Shelly Delabrois." Kris saw the doctor's smile waver for a split second, but he recovered and smiled politely.

He looked at everyone. "Could I have a few moments to speak with the patient alone?"

"Yes," William said, and ushered them all from the room.

"Commander Matthews, can I call you Kristine?"

"Kris."

"I've read over your recent medical records. Everything appears in order. We'll remove the graft bandages later today for another look. They were checked on your arrival last night, but I want to examine you myself. We can wait until your family leaves though, and Orthopedics will be by later to look at your arm. Is your pain controlled well?"

"I'm fine unless I sneeze or cough."

Dr. Martin pulled a chair up and sat next to the bed. "You will continue on respiratory therapy here until you are consistently holding high blood oxygen levels. While you were sleeping, on the flight back, your saturation level dropped pretty low."

"It did?"

"Yes. The oxygen brought your level back up quickly, and you slept without any other incidents. Would you like me to speak to your parents and um...your partner about your injuries?"

"Talk to my parents. I'll tell my partner."

Chapter Nine

"HEY BABE. THE DOC said you wanted to talk to me alone. I don't think he likes me. Or maybe that we're a couple. Are you okay with that?"

"I don't care. Not now. Shelly, we need to talk."

"Do you need something?"

"Just for you to sit down and listen." Kris yawned. "Sorry, the pain medicine makes me sleepy. I need to tell you this now. When I was hurt, I was hit up near my shoulder—"

"Yes, I can see that. That's why you have a sling."

She shook her head. "There's more. I was hit in the chest. It's…it's bad, Shelly."

"The chest? What do you mean?" Her eyes drifted down to Kris' chest, covered with the blankets, "What kind of injury?"

"I…most of my breast, the left one. It's gone."

"Gone? What do you mean?"

"It's gone. It was damaged, by shrapnel. It hit my shoulder and chest."

"But you have body armor."

"I don't know what happened. I don't remember it all. Shelly, it's gone. My left breast is gone. They had to graft skin to cover the wound."

"What do you mean? You have nothing there? Not even skin?"

Kris saw Shelly getting pale, heard her voice growing sharper. "There's skin now. They took a graft from my leg to cover it."

"I don't understand. Let me see."

"I can't. It's bandaged."

"Let me see the bandage." Shelly came to the bed and gently pulled the blankets down. She unsnapped the shoulder portion of the gown and lowered it, revealing Kris' heavy bandages. "There's one on your leg too?"

"That's where they took the graft from."

"Oh, my God. You could have been killed." She sat down, pale, her hands trembling.

"Shelly, it's okay. I'm home. Calm down and come sit with me, here on the bed."

Shelly came to the bed and Kris did the best she could to comfort her. To reassure her that she was indeed okay and she whispered, "I'm sorry. I didn't know a better way to tell you."

***

A few minutes later Kris' parents came into the room, they paused momentarily as they saw Shelly sitting on the bed with Kris, and tears running down their daughter's face. Kris looked up at her parents. "Did you speak with the surgeon?"

"We did." Irene and William moved into the room, pulling chairs up next to the bed, and Shelly moved down to the foot of the bed, wiping her face with tissues. William grasped Kris' hand. "He said that you are doing well and that your lung had minimal damage. Your chest injuries are doing well, all things considered. You were lucky."

"I know."

Shelly interrupted, "Lucky? How is this lucky?"

"What I mean is that she could have lost a lung or had a heart injury. She could have lost her life."

"Oh yes. I understand. But I wouldn't call this lucky."

Kris yawned and shook her head trying to stay awake. Irene noticed. "Kris, honey, don't fight it. Go to sleep, I will be here when you wake up."

"Okay. Sorry," she mumbled as she slipped into sleep.

***

The counselor sat down by the window next to Sam. "Sam we've received several calls from your family asking for updates on your condition. While that is certainly common when people are first injured it is less common later. Is there a reason why you are not keeping your parents and siblings up to date?"

"They're my foster parents."

"I see. How long were you with them?"

Sam was quiet for several long seconds while she thought about what she had said. She started to bounce her leg. "Since I was eight. That really wasn't fair, what I said. I mean they are my foster parents, but I was with them longer than my father was ever with me or my siblings." Sam noticed the look on the counselor's face. "My father left

44

us. My siblings and I were together for a short period after that, but eventually, we were separated. I don't know where any of them are."

"A woman has called and said she was your sister, Lauren."

"Oh, that's my fost...yes, I would say she is my sister, not by blood. But it's better. She, they, wanted me in their life. I...I don't want them to see me like this."

"That's common, Sam. You are feeling weak, and scared. A good many warriors don't want their loved ones to see them when they're first injured."

"I don't want them to think they have to keep taking care of me. They've done enough. I have to be able to do this by myself."

"You don't have to do this by yourself. In fact, trying to do it alone will make it infinitely harder. We're here to help you. All the staff is here to help you recover, but you'll still do the actual work. How well you recover has a lot to do with the effort you put in, but also the support that you receive. Use your resources here. The staff, the counselors, all the others in here who are injured can and will help. The activities that are available are helpful too. You lost more than a part of your leg. Ask for help."

"I will."

"Now what do you want to do about your parents? They're worried and want to see you."

"They can come. Can you call? I'm not sure that I can talk with them right now."

"We'll take care of that for you. They should be able to stay in family quarters at Fisher House."

"Great, thank you."

Chapter Ten

KRIS AWAKENED AND LOOKED about the room. Her mother sat in a chair looking tired as she thumbed through a magazine. Kris noticed for the first time the lightening of her hair at the temples, as the light brown gave way to wisps of gray. The crow's feet along her eyes had deepened, and her cheeks were thinner. Irene took a deep breath and glanced over at Kris, eyes widening when she realized she was being watched.

"I didn't realize you were awake." Irene stood up, walked over to her. "How do you feel?"

"I'm okay." Kris' voice cracked, and she reached for the water cup, wincing as pain seared into her chest.

"Let me get that."

Kris sipped from the cup, and nearly sighed as the cool water soothed the soreness in her throat. After several seconds she nodded, and her mother pulled the cup away. "Thanks, Mom. Why didn't you go back to…where are you staying?"

"We're here at Fisher House. It's only a few minutes away. I wanted to be here when you woke up. So, we could talk privately until your father comes back."

"You spoke with the surgeon?"

"Yes, both the plastic surgeon and the orthopedic surgeon. The skin flaps look healthy. They had done muscle flaps during one of the earlier surgeries."

"I remember him saying that. He said I could eventually have reconstructlon, but that's a long way off. About a year." Kris heard her mother's sigh. "What's wrong?"

"It seems as if you're only worried about your breast. I know to you that is the more obvious injury, but you can live without your breast, Kris. Your arm was damaged too, and you have yet to ask about it. What they found and what they did to repair it."

"They told me previously there was minimal damage to the bicep and deltoid. But that it would heal well. The bones and cuff were not damaged. I was lucky, I realize that. It doesn't hurt at all, or not in comparison to my chest. Or what's left of it."

Irene pulled the chair closer to the bed. "Does it worry you? I'm sure you have some concerns."

"Mom, I've done mastectomies. It was an injury, not cancer. I know what the women who have their breast removed worry about."

"I know you do. However, this is the first time you've felt it as a patient. Stop trying to be so analytical. Let yourself feel something. Don't be so stoic."

"What do you want me to do? I can't fix it." She tried to lower her voice, but she felt a lump rising in her throat. She rubbed her temple and swallowed hard. "I trust these guys like they trust me."

"I'm not questioning their skills. I want you to tell me how you feel. Not as a physician but as my daughter. I imagine you're scared, at least a little." Kris stared at her mother in silence. "Okay Kris, I misunderstood. I thought you might have some concerns and that you would want to talk about it. Losing a breast is a very personal thing. I am here if you want to talk about it. How did...never mind. Would you like some more water? Are you hungry? They should probably be bringing your lunch soon."

"How did what, Mom?" She stared at her mother and waited as the seconds ticked by.

Irene sighed. "I was wondering how Shelly took the news."

Kris' cheeks started to burn. "It caught her off guard. But we'll be fine. She'll be back later and I'll explain it to her in more detail."

"What about your shoulder? What did the surgeon say about that?"

"Nothing. Mom, do you talk to your patients about their treatment outside your specialty? No. We have to wait for the orthopedic doc. But it doesn't hurt. In fact, it's like I can't even feel it."

Kris saw her mother's eyebrows arch. "You can't feel it, or it doesn't hurt?"

"It doesn't hurt. See my hand works..." Her voice drifted off. She attempted to move her fingers, and they stayed motionless. *What? Oh, My God.* She reached over and grabbed her left hand with her right. She felt nothing with her left. She tried to form a fist with her left hand. Her heart raced, and the room became overly bright. Her breath burst in and out. "Mom! I can't feel it. It's not moving. I can't...Oh no!" Buzzing filled her ears. She started shaking, and sweat slid down her face and neck. "How did I not see this?"

Irene was instantly at her side. She scratched along the back of her left hand leaving abraded skin. "Do you feel that?"

"No."

Irene reached over and pressed the call bell.

***

At Kris' insistence, her parents remained in the room while the orthopedic surgeon performed his evaluation. He tested her sensation and muscle function in her left arm and scribbled some notes down. "Your arm is definitely not responding normally. I am ordering x-rays to make sure some metal wasn't somehow left in there. If that's normal, we'll get an MRI to see if we can see anything with the nerves. While you were in Germany, you had movement in your hand. The sling was to minimize your arm motion while the blood vessels and grafts healed. The good news is we know the entire arm is getting excellent blood flow."

Kris said, "And if that is normal, then what?"

"We'll take you back in and look around. I'll have to avoid cutting through the healing graft, so the approach will be unusual. I'm going to request the tests now. I'll be back after the results are available and we can talk more. I will tell you that this is unusual. Whatever it is, we'll find it."

Roslyn Bane

Chapter Eleven

GOD, THAT'S ANNOYING. THE rhythmic click and squeak of the crutches were irritating. *Can't they make quiet crutches? Everyone turns around and watches.*

The corpsman interrupted her thoughts. "Where you going, Major?"

"To that window at the end of the hall."

"Great. You're pushing yourself. You almost got there yesterday. There's a nice view of the garden from there. I'll let you take a rest and come back to get you."

"Good. I want to see something other than these walls." Sam paused to wipe sweat from her brow, and wiped her hand on her shirt. After a few more steps she sat down on the couch and placed the crutches on the floor. She settled in and stared out the window. Fluffy white clouds whisked along in the bright blue sky. Forsythia bushes and daffodils, heavy with their yellow crowns, moved soundlessly in the breeze. She watched as someone moved a wheelchair out next to a bench and held it while their companion shifted from chair to bench. Together they sat holding hands, and after some time she saw them lean their heads against each other. *They have each other.*

A heavy sigh had Sam looking over her shoulder. A woman with brown hair, which almost reached her shoulders, was coming down the hall using a cane and breathing heavily. Around her waist was an assist belt, and a corpsman walked beside her encouraging her to continue. They reached the window, and she stopped and leaned against it. Sweat ran down the woman's pale face. She was ashen, with dark shadows under her eyes. Her exposed hand was bruised and swollen. Sam almost cringed imagining the pain that came with having a hand that looked like that.

"Do you want to sit down, Commander? I'll get another chair."

"Okay, but only for a minute."

"Sit here." Sam reached for her crutches and started to get up.

"Don't get up. There's enough room for both of us." Kris sat down, wincing as she scooted back further. "Thanks."

"Let me take that belt." The therapist unfastened the belt. "I'll leave you here. I'll be back in a few minutes."

Sam watched as the therapist walked down the hall, and the woman next to her whispered, "Christ this sucks. Whoever thought it would be so hard to breathe."

"I feel the same way. Even sitting up hurts," Sam said quietly.

"It does." The woman looked at Sam for several seconds. A puzzled expression appeared on her face before she extended her hand. "I'm Kris."

Sam's stomach clenched uncomfortably, and she hesitated briefly prior to shaking Kris' hand. The skin was soft and damp, her grip firm. "Sam. Nice to meet you. How long have you been here?"

"One week. How about you?"

"Two weeks." Sam looked outside. "Looks like a nice day out."

"Sure does. Although I heard it was chilly."

"I am hoping to go outside to that little garden." Sam pointed out the window. "I think they're afraid I might make a break for it though."

Kris smiled. "I can create a diversion if you like, but you need to swing back around and get me."

Before Sam could respond the corpsman returned. "Ma'am, you have to get moving. You have an appointment down in the orthopedic clinic."

Sam retrieved the crutches and pushed herself up, grimacing from the discomfort. She turned back to Kris. "Good luck."

As Sam moved down the hall she stopped and looked back at Kris. *I've seen her somewhere. Where?*

***

Sam returned from physical therapy as the orthopedic physician arrived. "How are you doing this morning, Major?"

"Good. Therapy is going well. They've added more hip extension exercises. They were worried about me getting a contracture."

"Yes, I've read your therapy notes. We'll keep an eye on it. How is your skin?"

"I think it's healing well. It's not hot or red as it was a few days ago."

"Good. You've been checking daily with the mirror?"

"Yes."

"Let me look." He carefully unwound the bandages on her leg. "As soon as the stitches come out we can get you in a stump shrinker to help with the swelling. It will also help to shape the leg, preparing for the prosthesis." He quieted as he examined the stitches that ran along the stump. "This looks great."

Sam exhaled forcefully, unaware that she had been holding her breath. "A shrinker?"

"Think of it as tight sleeve you will wear on your unleg. It helps to squeeze the swelling out and shape your leg. As the limb shrinks, they'll be able to start making the socket for your prosthesis."

"When will the stitches come out?"

"Two or three weeks. You're doing well, Major. Keep up the good work and remember every day to do the checks, and whenever something doesn't feel right with your leg. Make it a habit. You need to do it daily."

As he left the room, Sam gave a silent fist pump. Using her crutches, she headed over to the shower, undressed, placed a waterproof bag over her leg and stepped inside. She propped the crutches against the wall, lowered the shower seat, sat down, and turned on the water. It hit her full blast in the chest. "Shit! Damn, that's cold." She curled her arms across her chest until it warmed. *You'll remember that one, won't you? Aim it away before you turn it on.*

***

Kris, Shelly, and her parents sat and waited, filling the time with small talk about local events, and what had been going on while Kris was overseas. When the orthopedic physician returned they all asked simultaneously, "Well?"

"We can't find any problems on the MRI. I've added you to the surgical schedule tomorrow. We'll take a look and see if we can find what's causing the problem. Nothing to eat or drink after midnight. Someone will be back to restart your IV. The respiratory therapist will be by again tonight, and I am going to ask for another session tomorrow prior to your going into the OR."

Her parents stayed a few minutes longer and then departed. Shelly closed the door and sat on the bed with Kris. "Are you nervous?"

"Concerned. I hope they find whatever is keeping it from moving."

"I'm sure they will. It's getting late. Do you want me to go?"

"Can you stay for a few more minutes?"

"Absolutely." Shelly leaned over and kissed Kris softly on the lips. "Do you want to watch TV?"

"Okay. Will you lie up here with me?"

"I don't think that's allowed."

Kris scooted over and patted the bed next to her. "Sure it is. Trust me. I'm a doctor." Shelly crawled in next to her and Kris sighed. "I missed you. You smell good. You feel good. How long can you stay up here before you head back home?"

"I've been working remotely and sending in reports. I have a few more days until I have to go back."

"That's good. I've missed you."

Shelly kissed Kris on the forehead as Kris settled in to lay her head on Shelly's shoulder. She sighed, and a few minutes later was drifting into sleep.

"I'm going to go. Get some rest, hon. I'll be back tomorrow." She kissed Kris quickly and walked toward the door.

Kris pulled the sheet up and noticed Shelly pulling her phone out. As the door closed, she heard, *"Hi. Where are you? I'm leaving now. Okay, see you soon."*

***

"Ooof! Huh?" Sam rolled on the floor gasping for air while her hip protested from impacting the floor. Flipping to her back, she grabbed her chin to slow the blood flow down her face. Soaked in sweat and trembling she slid across the floor on her back, as warm blood continued to spread. As she reached a chair, the door burst open and the room flooded with light.

"Major, what the he…. Here, let me look at you. What were you doing?" The nurse and a corpsman knelt beside her.

"I don't know what happened." She stayed still while the nurse checked her quickly and pressed gauze to her bleeding chin.

"Other than your chin everything looks okay. Are you hurting anywhere? How's your leg?"

"The missing part hurts. I want to get up."

"Let us help you."

"I want to do it alone."

"That's admirable, Major, but you're not ready yet. Getting up from the floor is different. Let us help you."

The corpsman and nurse placed their arms under her arms and

helped lift her. She wobbled momentarily on her foot, and started hopping toward the bed.

"Major, how did you get out of bed? The side is still up."

"I don't know. I was dreaming."

The nurse looked at her chin. "I'm going to have to get someone up here. You're going to need stitches in your chin, and we need to check under your bandages and make sure your wound didn't break open."

Chapter Twelve

THE ORTHOPEDIST SAT IN the room with Kris and her parents. "We looked with the scope and also opened the arm using a posterior lateral approach. We checked everything. There is no break in the nerve or scar tissue build up. The blood vessels are healing well, and the muscle tissue looks healthy."

Kris trembled, and her voice quivered. "What could be keeping it from moving?"

"Well, it's possible that the nerve was hit sufficiently hard enough that it's been bruised and has not yet recovered. We're going to get you started in therapy and get a brace fitted for your arm. We can't have you developing contractures. In a few days if there is no improvement we'll order some nerve conduction tests. I want to give your arm some time to recover from this latest surgery. Any questions?"

"I understand," she said weakly. *What am I going to do? I can't operate one-handed. I can't do anything. I'm a surgeon for God sake. I need to have both arms functioning. I can't start over.* Struggling to control her breathing she puffed air in and out, over a count of five. She watched vacantly as the surgeon left.

"Kris, calm down. Breathe." William's deep baritone voice got her attention. "Slow it down. That's better. You'll get through this. Give it some time. It's still early."

Kris nodded and whispered, "I'm scared."

***

"Doctor Matthews?"

"Yes."

"Hi. I'm Paul, one of the therapists that will be working with you. I've read through your records about your injuries. I understand your left arm is not moving. I'm going to start moving it for you. Our goal is to keep all those joints and muscles moving. We'll be meeting twice a day. You'll be here, in therapy, a few hours today. You'll also get the brace doc told you about. The respiratory therapist will see you later this afternoon. You'll keep using the cane until you build up enough stamina to walk for longer periods without assistance."

"Okay. Let's get started."

For the next thirty minutes, the therapist moved Kris' arm through a wide range of movements to keep the shoulder, elbow, wrist, and hand flexible. Each finger was moved through its range of motion. Kris willed her fingers to move to no avail. Unable to get lost in her thoughts due to his banter, she looked around. *Wow, there are people around here that are much worse off than me.* She took a few steps with the use of a cane. While the brace was being constructed, another therapist worked with Kris teaching her how to perform a one-handed shoe tie.

Two hours later the therapist helped Kris into a wheelchair. "I think we've worked you hard enough for now." He pushed her back to her room and helped her transfer into the bed. She was asleep before he was out the door.

***

"Good morning, Major. How are you today?"

Sam eyed the psychologist, a Lieutenant Commander. "As well as can be expected."

"That's good to know. How is your chin?"

Sam covered it momentarily. "A little sore. I fell." Sam sighed. "I haven't been sleeping well. I keep dreaming of the crash, but it's not always the same. The other night I was running to help someone and jumped over a wall. That's how I fell and busted my chin."

"Anything else you're worried about?"

Sam clenched her fists and inhaled deeply through her nose. "How about if I will ever walk again? When will I get out of here? Will I be able to stay in the corps? What will I do if I'm not retained? Is this pain ever going to stop? Am I getting addicted to these pain meds?"

"Those are all important questions. Have you spoken to your care team about them? Let's make a list, and you can discuss them with your docs later. You can talk to me about whatever you want, Sam. That's what these sessions are for."

Chapter Thirteen

SOMEONE IS SCREAMING. KRIS sat up abruptly, and her hair stood on end as she climbed out of bed. Kris moved toward the door. Whoever was screaming had stopped, but they needed to be checked. Ignoring the pain in her chest, she pulled the heavy door open and squeezed through the opening. With a hand on the hallway railing, she moved steadily to the nurse's station. The nurses at the workstation looked up in surprise. One of them smiled and approached her.

"Hi Commander, what can I do for you at this time of the evening?"

"I...I heard a scream, I came out to see..."

"I didn't hear anything. Perhaps you had a dream?"

"No. It wasn't a dream. Someone screamed. Horribly."

The nurse took her gently by the arm and led her back into her room. "I'll tell you what, ma'am, I'll go check on the patients if you get back in bed. I'll be back shortly and let you know what we find."

"Okay. Hurry, they sounded like they were in horrible pain." She let the nurse assist her back into bed and watched nervously as her brace was checked.

"I am going to raise the rails so you can't fall."

"They were up. I lowered it earlier so I could use the restroom. I guess I didn't put it back up. Sorry about that."

"Now, Doctor, are you trying to get us nurses in trouble? You must let us do our jobs the way you would expect us to do them for one of your patients. "

"I'm worried about the screaming. Please go check on your other patients." Kris sat back in the bed and waited. She listened for any disturbance but heard none. Ten minutes later the nurse returned and reassured Kris that all was fine. As Kris drifted back to sleep, her thoughts wandered. *The woman today, by the window. Sam. Why did she make me uneasy? Looks like she'd fallen recently. Her chin was sutured and bruised. Her eyes were green, lots of red where it should be white. That's it. It looks strange. Although I should be able to handle that.*

***

Kris lay in bed listening to the surgeon as the dressing from her chest was removed. "As you know, it is essential for the graft to get a good blood supply. I'm going to take the bandages off now. Lay still until they're off and then you can look, if you want to. Sooner or later you have to see it."

"All right." Kris lay still and stared at the wall while the doctor worked the bandage loose. She caressed her ear to dull the deafening throb of her pulse. The surgeon removed the bandage and lifted it to block Kris' view. "This is healing well. There is no sign of infection. The graft looks good, healthy pink skin. Good temperature. Are you ready to look?"

Kris nodded her head and took a deep breath prior to looking down at her chest. "Ah, ha, whh…oh, oh shit."

"Kris, give it time. It's early."

"I…I, need a moment." She looked away, avoiding eye contact with the surgeon and the nurse. She took several breaths through pursed lips. She closed her eyes for several seconds. "Okay." She looked down again. "You're right, the graft looks okay. It looks like the blood supply is good. I lost what fifty percent?"

"Roughly. You still have some of the tail left, and a portion near the sternum. The muscle flap is from along your side. The reconstruction can be done in phases. You're looking at about eight to twelve months until that can get underway. We'll talk more about that later. In the meantime, we'll continue you in respiratory and physical therapy. With a little luck, you'll be heading home in a few more days."

"Okay." She cleared her throat. "Is there a mirror?"

"In the bathroom," the nurse said.

"I'd like to look."

"Okay. I'll check back in later today." He pulled the gown closed and fastened the shoulder snaps.

"Thank you." As the doctor left, her parents walked in.

Irene hugged Kris. "Good morning, sweetheart. How are you doing?"

"I'm going to need a few minutes. I was going to get dressed."

William turned toward the door. "I'll go get us some coffee. Be back soon."

Kris told the nurse she could go and started to get out of bed. Irene came around to help her. "I'll be your walking chaperone."

"I think I can do it myself." Kris huffed as she shuffled into the bathroom.

Irene pulled the door shut. "I'll be out here. Let me know if you need anything."

Kris stood at the sink staring at herself in the mirror. She had dark circles under eyes, her cheeks were drawn, and her hair was a jumble of tangles and clumps. She bent over to wash her face and gasped with the intensity of the pain. Quickly grabbing onto the sink with one hand she steadied herself until her vision cleared. With a trembling hand, she cleaned up as best she could. Finally, she looked in the mirror again. It was time to look closely. She fumbled with the snaps and ties on the gown until it fell open. She took a deep breath and focused her attention on her wound.

Her breath caught in her throat as she stared at her chest and arm. *Oh dear God. There's practically nothing left.* A trapezoidal area of skin, swollen and soft pink served as a large patch over the area where her left breast should be. All that remained of her left breast was a gentle swell near her sternum. There was no nipple. Kris traced her finger gently over the grafts. *No sensation.* Dragging her finger down her lifeless arm her breath hitched. *Nothing.* Her hand was swollen and still slightly yellow from bruising. A fine line of sutures ran along the edges of the graft. Across her shoulder the skin was puckered and discolored, a mass of scars crisscrossed her upper arm until they reached a smaller skin flap. It was also swollen and softly pink. She tried in vain to clench her fist and bend her elbow. *Lifeless. How did this happen?* Tears ran down her face.

A soft knock on the door startled her. "Kris, are you okay?"

Kris pulled the gown up. "Yes. No. Mom, oh God, oh God."

Irene pushed against the door, took a step into the room and wrapped her daughter in her arms. "Shh, let it out, sweetheart, let it out."

Kris leaned against her mother weeping and trembling. After several minutes she calmed, and whispered, "I'm sorry."

Irene grabbed tissues and wiped Kris' face dry. "Why are you apologizing? Because you cried? Because you finally let go? Because you let yourself be a patient and not a doctor?" Gentle hands cupped her cheeks. "Listen to me. It's okay to be scared. It's normal. Let's get you dressed and go talk. Would you like another gown or some of the pajamas or clothes Shelly brought you?"

"It doesn't matter."

Kris stared at the floor when her mother returned, and stood silent while she wiped Kris' face and neck with a warm washcloth. "Honey, if you want you can dress yourself, but I'd like to see if you don't mind. Let me tell you how it really looks."

"Okay," Kris whispered.

Irene smiled at Kris before she looked at her daughters' chest. "Both the grafts look good. They have a soft pink color to them." She pressed the back of her hand to the grafts. "And they're warm, so it's getting blood. They have you on anticoagulants, so that will help the blood get through. There's still some breast tissue left, here by your sternum and the tail, near your arm. Your shoulder and arm look pretty good, Kris. The scars will fade. Give it time. Give yourself time. How does your arm feel?"

"It doesn't."

"They'll do a few more tests on your arm. Think about it, honey. What else could be causing this? Where would you look if this happened to one of your patients?"

Kris stood silently for several seconds. "At the neck. Even if there wasn't an injury, I'd look there."

"Exactly. Now let's get you into this pajama top. Your father will be back with coffee any minute. And probably with Danish for the staff."

While her mother buttoned the shirt, Kris stood biting her lip. *What am I going to do?*

Chapter Fourteen

SAM TUGGED ON HER shorts. Using the support rails, she pulled herself up, hopped several steps, before she reached for her crutches. Looking in the mirror, she ran her fingers through her thick, black hair pulling it into tufts. She studied her face. *I look like a raccoon. A coon with a yellow chin. Add a little foam and I'd be rabid.* She jutted out her chin and ran a finger over the stiff stitches that protruded. "Looks like a teenager's whiskers."

After brushing her teeth, she leaned against the counter, lifting her arms overhead and turning slightly to look at her ribs. The bruises had yellowed at the edges and were no longer as deeply purple. She could move well without hurting, although a sneeze or a cough would take her breath away. She yanked on a red marine corps t-shirt, and then crutched her way out of the bathroom. She nudged a chair over to the window so she could look outside and was pulling on a stump shrinker when there was a knock on the door.

"Major Davies?"

"Yes?"

The door opened slightly. "You have visitors. Would you like to see them here or down in the lounge?"

"Visitors?"

"Jim and Nancy Kline."

"Here, in here is good." *They came?*

"I'll bring them down."

Sam took a long drink of water to wet her suddenly dry mouth. She recognized their hushed voices as they came down the hall, and her heart pounded in her chest. *What if they're grossed out?* She rubbed her hands across her shorts, drying the dampness. Using her crutches, Sam stood as the door opened slightly.

"Samantha?"

"Come on in." Sam smiled as her foster parents walked in. "Hi, it's good to see you." She started to come toward them but stopped when Nancy hurried over to her and wrapped her arms around her. She gave her a one-armed hug back and watched as Jim set a box and suitcase on the floor.

"Oh, Sam, I'm so sorry you were hurt. Thank God you're back here safe." Jim reached out a hand to her, stopped short, and hugged her.

"Nancy, why don't you let Sam sit down?"

"I think I better." Sam sat in the chair and leaned her crutches against the wall. She forced herself to stick to small talk, anything to avoid the elephant in the room.

Jim cleared his throat. "Lauren wanted to come but was working this weekend. She sent her greetings and was hoping you would call her. She said something about you losing a bet and going out to karaoke with her. I have her new phone number and email addresses for you." Jim pulled a piece of paper out of his wallet and handed it to her.

"I will. She's living closer now?"

"About a half hour away, over on the West side of Chattanooga." He looked at her closely. "How are you doing, Sam?"

"I'm doing okay. Go ahead and look. I still find myself staring at it in disbelief, especially when my toes start itching."

"It itches?" Nancy's hand trembled slightly as she brushed back a lock of her light brown hair behind her ear.

Sam smiled. "The part that's not there does."

"The phantom sensations?" Nancy asked.

"She's been reading everything she can get her hands on about injuries like yours since we found out," Jim said.

"I wanted to be able to help you...In case you needed or wanted our help."

Sam felt her eyes fill. *You're always there for me. Every time something goes wrong. Why? Everyone else left.* She inhaled tightly and turned her head toward the window as she fought to control the tears that threatened to spill over. *You're a Marine for God sake. Don't cry. After several seconds, she looked back.* "Thank you."

Nancy came over, stooped down in front of Sam, and placed her hands on Sam's shoulders. "Oh honey, we love you. We wouldn't let you go through this alone. We've known you since you were four and you've been part of our family since you were eight. What we feel for you didn't end because you moved out. I wish you would have let us come sooner."

Sam muttered, "I didn't want anyone to see me like this."

Jim stared at her. "Like what?"

"Weak—"

"Weak? Why do you think you're weak? That's the most ridiculous thing I've ever heard come out of your mouth."

Sam's eyes opened wide, her mouth opening and closing several times. She looked at Nancy and back to Jim. "I...."

"That's bullshit." Jim stood abruptly, his six-foot frame blocking Sam's view as he approached. His face was flushed right up to the edge of his graying hairline. "Let me tell you something, Samantha. If you honestly think you're weak, you're going to need to talk to a shrink while you're in here—"

"Jim!" Nancy scolded.

"No, let me finish." He turned to Sam "I get that you're scared and that you have pain."

Sam jolted at his unusually harsh words. Her cheeks burned. "You have no idea."

"That doesn't make you weak." He dropped to one knee in front of her and took her hands. His voice softened. "You always were one to confuse not being able to do something physically as a sign of weakness. You would push yourself so hard. But that's not because you were weak. It's because you were so strong."

"I'm not strong now," she murmured.

"Why do you say that?"

"How can I be strong? Look at me. I get tired moving from the bed to the bathroom. Physical therapy is down at the end of the hall. It takes me ten minutes to get there. Last week I couldn't wash my own hair without hurting. Without getting out of breath."

"A few weeks ago you almost died. So what, you need some help. What's wrong with that?"

Sam punched down on her thighs. "I don't like it! I want to do things for myself. I don't want to be dependent on anyone—" *Like when I was a kid.*

"And now you are. So, you see that as weakness. Sam, you're learning how to do things differently. It's not dependency."

"What if I can't do this? What if I can't learn to use a prosthesis? Do you really want to have to take care of me again?"

Nancy interrupted, "Is that what has you worried?"

Jim pulled his chair in front of Sam. "Sam, you can be so damn hardheaded, exactly like Lauren and Justin. Although you're in an unusual situation, that doesn't make you weak. Right now you're beginning to heal, and probably still in shock that this happened. Somewhere inside you is your warrior. All you have to do is rediscover her. These folks here will help you unlock it again. But it doesn't make you weak. Only you can do that to yourself."

Sam looked at him and saw the love in his eyes. A sense of calm she hadn't felt in months came over her. She released a long breath. "I'm sorry I told you all not to come by. I didn't want you to see me this way, broken, and bruised."

Nancy rested her hand on Sam's shoulder. "We understand. You need to understand that we needed to see you. To be with you. Haven't you learned by now, you are one of our kids, Sam? We're not going to leave you."

Sam remembered climbing out of the car with her siblings in front of the church. Her older brother opened the door, while she took the twins' hands and led them up to the heavy doors. She looked back once as her father drove away to park the car. She recalled waiting on the steps outside during the next service for him to return. And the next. She remembered the Klines and another family taking them home, feeding them, and the hushed conversations. The hugs and the tears through the first few weeks. Every time she'd needed them they'd been there for her. "This doesn't repulse you?"

"No," they said simultaneously.

"You've done so much," Sam spoke barely above a once as her father drove away whisper.

Nancy dragged her teeth over her bottom lip and glanced at Jim. "You're not getting rid of us, Sam. No matter how much you push. No matter what you think you look like. You're our daughter, and we love you. This is what parents should do for their kids."

"I'm scared."

Nancy wrapped Sam in her arms and held on when Sam finally let go and cried. After a few minutes, she calmed. The next few hours were spent sharing stories about the family and playing cards. They promised to return later after her next therapy session.

Chapter Fifteen

"HOLY SHIT! WHAT THE hell is that? Where the hell is the rest of your tit? God! I...I can't look at that. Cover it up. I thought you had a little wound."

Kris winced as if struck. Her cheeks grew hot, and her eyes brimmed with tears that threatened to overflow. "Shelly," Kris whispered, "I told you I lost my breast."

"I didn't think you meant the entire thing. How the hell are they going to fix that? And when?"

With her hand trembling Kris lifted the gown to cover herself. The pounding in her head started immediately, and she swallowed hard against the rage bubbling up. She bit her lip hard to keep from crying. Unable to hold her anger in, she snapped out, "For God's sake, Shelly! Keep your voice down. You think this is disgusting?"

Kris ground her teeth together. "The graft has to heal before they can do anything. The muscle underneath is healing too. It's probably going to be about a year."

"What?"

"It is done in stages. I can't explain it to you right now. Do you want to know how my arm is doing?"

"It looks fine except for those scars."

"I still can't move my fingers."

"Still? Why is it taking so long? Are you sure these docs know what they're doing? I mean how often do they treat female chest injuries?"

"They know what they're doing, Shelly." Kris rubbed her thigh, soothing the buzzing of the new skin.

"Why are you rubbing at your leg?"

"It itches. From where they took the graft."

"I don't understand."

"They took the skin from my leg to cover my chest, as the new skin grows back it itches. Have you not been paying attention this week?"

"How many scars do you have?"

"Does it matter?" she said through clenched teeth.

"It does."

Kris sat silently. *What the hell? You're rejecting me? All this time and...* "You need to go, Shelly. I'm tired, and I need to think." She grabbed the buzzer and rang the call bell for the nurse.

The speed of the nurse's appearance caused Kris to blink. "What can I do for you, Commander?"

"I'm tired. Can you show my guest out?"

The nurse looked over at Shelly and back at Kris. "Sure thing. Come on, miss, I'll walk you out."

Kris sat rigid and looked away. Her jaw clenched tight as Shelly left without a word.

***

"Good evening everyone. I'm Tom Reider, and I'm your facilitator today. I had twenty years on active duty, Marine infantry and am here today to let you know it is okay to be mad. It's okay to be scared, and it is okay to feel lost. If you want to talk today about what you're thinking and feeling, great. Feel free to share. If you want to sit and listen, that's fine too."

Sam sat in the room, her leg bouncing rapidly, unable to stop it for more than a few seconds. *Although I could get up and pace, it would only draw attention to me. Besides pacing wouldn't be as satisfying as it used to be. Soon my missing foot will start to itch, and my leg will throb. My leg is probably out there somewhere bouncing, tangled in machinery. Stop it. Get it together. This isn't normal. Am I going crazy? Pay attention, see how the guys talk about it. Maybe they do the same.*

She looked around at the close to forty people in the room. Marines, sailors, men and a few women, with missing limbs, deformed jaws, bandaged heads. Some stared blankly ahead, others talked incessantly. *Good God! The wars in Iraq and Afghanistan have been going on since two thousand two. Some of these old guys have probably seen action in the first Gulf War.*

Sam ran her hand across her clenched and rigid stomach muscle as her eyes filled. She lowered her head and stared at the floor willing the tears not to fall. After several minutes, Sam looked up and noticed a few people now mingled in groups. She had seen them at physical therapy and knew they had been back longer than she had. She was about to get up when she heard a voice next to her.

"Hi, Major. How are you doing?"

Sam looked up to see the facilitator watching her. "I'm fine, sir."

"Uh-uh. It's Tom now. Besides you outrank me, Major. You look like you're feeling a little nauseous."

"I am. It hit me all of a sudden. It must have been something I ate. I should probably go back to my room." She leaned forward to pick up her crutches but stopped when he put a hand on her shoulder.

"It probably was something you ate. Probably a couple hundred MRE's and a couple pounds of Afghanistan sand. How did you lose your leg?" Sam jerked with the directness of the question. He smiled. "I tend to be direct, Major. No time for bullshit in this world. You can choose not to tell me."

"No, its fine. My chopper was shot down. I was pinned in the wreckage. Lost my leg." She lowered her head, cleared her throat. "Lost half my crew."

"That's rough. Do you feel like you did something wrong?"

"What? No. No. I did everything I could to get it down safely. We lost the tail rotor and ended up coming down on the side of a mountain. We rolled a few times."

"You're damn lucky any of you made it out at all. What's your bird?"

"CH53E."

"Super stallion. That's a big ass bird."

Sam smiled slightly. "That it is."

"How's your rehab going?"

"Good. They took a few more inches off a week ago. That set me back."

"You have any questions you haven't asked your medical team?"

"Ah, well, yes." She looked at him and then toward a group of marines with their prosthesis on.

"Ask away."

"I..."

"It's confidential, Major. Unless you tell me something that makes me think you would endanger yourself."

"No. No, nothing like that. I was wondering, is it normal to think of my leg as having its own feelings." He gave a quizzical expression. "Sometimes when my foot is hurting I wonder if it is laying out there in the wreckage and wondering where the hell the rest of me is? And I wonder am I losing my fucking, uh, excuse me, if I'm losing my mind."

He laughed, looked across the room. "Frank! Come over here and talk to the Major."

A huge man, with the build of a linebacker, walked over on two prosthetic legs, one above the knee, one below. His hair was buzz cut so close it looked like he had a five o'clock shadow on his head.

"Major wants to know about her leg missing her."

"Thinking about what your leg is feeling, Major? Yeah, it's normal. It's been six months for me and talking with other vets helps me deal with things, so I still come in. But to answer your question, yes, there are still times it happens. It's a strange thought, although most of us who've lost a limb have it. It's common while you have the phantom pain. I know my legs aren't feeling anything. You know your leg isn't feeling anything. As long as you don't really think that your leg is out there alive, you are sane as anyone else."

They spoke for several more minutes, and several others joined their group. They brought over bottles of juice and plates of fruit slices, and they shared their experiences. A couple hours later, the session ended, and Sam whistled as she headed toward her room. She stopped to chat with the nurses and shared a joke with them, before going to her room. She smiled as she changed into her pajamas, *I'm not going crazy.*

She pulled out a novel and started reading. A half hour later her eyes grew heavy, and her thoughts drifted. The book fell from her hand. *How many people had passed through this same hallway? This same hospital? They're bodies broken. Probably more than a few with shattered minds too. How many years had these Middle Eastern conflicts been going on? Tom had spent virtually his entire career in the middle east. How much blood had been spilled? And for what?*

***

The distinctive thwack, thwack, thwack of the rotor blades echoed in the moonless night sky. Scanning the instrument panel, she ensured everything was operating normally. The crew was subdued in the back. The quiet was justified because they were carrying the remains of several coalition forces. From the few words that were spoken, she knew that her crew was performing their checks and lookouts. Her copilot was looking at map coordinates and gave her updates as needed. Her gaze returned to outside.

Suddenly a bright light rocketed toward them, Sam called out, but the big helo shook with the impact. The sickening sound of metal tearing overpowered the sound of the engines failing and grinding. The smell of fuel and hydraulic fluid saturated the hot, dry air. Working together her crew shouted out instructions as the helo dropped toward the ground. The altimeter spun crazily four thousand, three thousand, two thousand, one thousand, five hundred. The voices of her crew shouting rung in her ears, one hundred. Sam braced for impact and hollered.

Sam jerked up in bed, drenched in sweat and shaking. Reaching up she turned on the light above her. Raising the head of the bed higher, she worked to control her breathing and slow her heart rate. Deep breaths in through the mouth, hold, and exhale through the mouth and nose. Over and over she repeated it until slowly she calmed. She ran her hand through her sweat soaked hair and shivered. She grabbed the water cup on the hospital tray and drank greedily, washing the dust of the desert from her parched throat. After a few minutes, she rang the call bell for the nurse.

"Can I help you, Major?" The nurse asked as she entered the room.

"I need to get up."

"Is something wrong?"

"I need to get up and walk around for a little while."

"Okay, Major. Can you wait for a minute while I get a corpsman to go with you? Do you want new pajamas? Looks like you sweated through those. Are you feeling feverish?"

"No. It was just a dream."

"Do you want to talk about it?"

"No, I want to walk."

Roslyn Bane

Chapter Sixteen

SAM SAT IN SILENCE staring at the wall above the psychologist's head. *Leave me alone. I don't want to talk to you.*

"Major, how are you feeling?"

"Irritable. I'm not in the mood to talk right now."

"Your medical team wanted me to stop by and speak with you. They said you had a rough day, with some setbacks in therapy. And you didn't eat anything at lunch."

"I usually don't eat if I'm irritated. So, don't waste your time telling me I need the food so I can heal faster."

"I won't. You'll eat if you're hungry. Tell me what's bothering you, Sam. I've only known you for a few weeks, and this is unusual."

Sam crutched over to the window and stared outside. "I feel like I'm going to explode. And I don't think you're ready for that. It's going to make a hell of a mess."

"I'm not afraid of that."

"I am!"

"What are you feeling, Sam? Tell me."

Silence held in the air and Sam set her jaw, her muscles tensed before she finally exploded, "This sucks! I hate being an amputee, I want my life back! I want to be able to go to work every day. I don't want to have to retrain and start over in some new career. I have a career! One I'm damn good at.

"I am mad. I am pissed. I look out the window and see people passing by, walking, running, laughing, playing...taking their life for granted, and I am stuck inside wondering if I'll ever walk again. Will I be able to return to my home or will I be stuck in some little handicapped apartment trying to scrape by on disability pay?"

Sam pressed her head against the window frame, pausing for a second before turning back around. "I feel useless because I am stuck in a wheelchair, or on these crutches. I am stuck in this room, and I feel..."

"Feel what?"

"Such hopelessness." Sam didn't cry, she shouted because it was anger, rage that consumed her. She placed her hand on her heart and pressed hard. "God, I hate this." She sat down in a chair, letting her crutches fall to the floor. Her hands balled into fists that she pressed against the side of her head. "Why couldn't I have died with my crew?" Sam grabbed a stress ball off the table and clenched it. Her knuckles turned white, and her fingers throbbed as she squeezed it repeatedly. The cords of her neck stood out, and she bounced her knee in a staccato rhythm "It's not right that I lived."

"Sam, this is all new to you. You'll have days like this where you ask, 'Why me?' You have to push through a little every day. A little more and a little more until the bad days become fewer and the good days increase. You can do this, but it's going to take time."

"The good news is once you get fitted for a prosthetic, and you learn how to walk again, you'll start to feel like you have more control over your life. What you're feeling is common especially in the beginning. And that includes questioning why you survived, and your crew didn't. I have no answer for that other than it wasn't your time. Sam, I have to ask, are you thinking about hurting yourself?"

Sam glanced up at her counselor.

"Major Davies, are you thinking about harming yourself?"

"God no. No, I would never. No, I have no intention of killing myself. That would be throwing my life away. That would hardly be fair to all the ones that didn't come back. I want to visit the families of my men. I need to see how they're doing. And I want to apologize."

"Apologize?"

"I was responsible for getting them back safely. That didn't happen."

"I hear that often. I understand the sentiment. Still, you must realize that you were not responsible for the accident. You were shot down and did your best in a difficult situation. And though you lost some of your crew, half of your crew survived. I want you to remember that too."

They sat quietly for several minutes. "This whole thing is hard to accept. I'm thirty-one years old for God's sake. I was supposed to have a good and productive life."

"Sam, you will have a good and productive life. And acceptance is often confused with the notion of being 'all right' or 'okay' with what has happened. Allow yourself time to feel sorry for yourself, to feel anger, to feel whatever you need to feel. Don't try to suppress your emotions. If you need to, take fifteen minutes, or longer, and allow yourself to feel. There is nothing wrong with what you're feeling. In fact, I would be more than a little worried if you didn't feel this way."

Sam grabbed the crutches and paced around the room. "This is normal? This rage, this anger I have inside? It...it surges up out of nowhere and it...it..."

"What's it do, Sam?"

"It takes control. It takes me over; it barges into everything. It scares me. What if I snap? What if I go berserk?"

"Confusion, rage, and fear are part of the readjustment process for anyone returning from a war zone."

"It is?"

"Yes. You are also recovering from a serious injury. Do you want to talk about this more?"

"No. I need to do something. I'm tired of staying in the room."

"Good. You should head down to the activity room tonight. Get out and socialize a little. You don't have to stay long."

"Maybe. Right now I want to see if I can get something to eat. I'm sort of hungry."

"I'll let them know."

"Thanks. Have a good night."

***

Sam peeked out of her door and looked at the nursing station. Two nurses were looking down at something on the desk while another was entering a room. *Now's your chance. Move fast. Please don't squeak. Great the couch is still near the window. Perfect.* Sam lay down and pushed her crutches under the seat. She looked out the window at the nearby highway. *Lots of traffic still. Not as bad as it will be in a few more hours. Cars are still backed up at the light cycles. Back home the lights would have switched over to flashing by now. More of a friendly reminder to pay attention, not to actually make you stop and wait.*

Sam turned on her side and tucked an arm under her head. She vacantly looked out until movement caught her eye. *Police helicopter. Where's he going in a hurry? Oh, turning back. Searchlights on now. Who you looking for? What did they do? There we go. Police cars too. Time is short buddy, they're gonna get you now.*

The helicopter circled around again. *Am I going to fly again? I wonder how the squadron is doing. They have six more months. Hope they're safe. Don't want to lose anyone else.* She continued to watch the helicopter move back and forth across the sky. Unaware of the movement, her hands twitched as she worked imaginary controls. Her knees flexed slightly as she pressed on the rudder pedals. *I should call Lauren, maybe tomorrow. I wonder if she still runs at night? I want to go out and smell the night air. I bet it smells green and damp. The air in the spring feels different. There's coolness to it, but the pockets of warmth off the ground let you believe that the threat of severe cold is over. Birds will chirp well before the sunrise and rabbits will nibble the fresh green shoots. I bet Nan lost all her daffodils to the rabbits again.* Sam blinked slowly and sighed.

"Major, what are you doing out here?" a female voice called from above her.

The only thing that saved her from flipping off the couch was that she grabbed the back of the seat to keep herself from falling. "I couldn't sleep. I came for a walk." She sat up slowly and reached for the crutches.

"Well, it would be a lot more restful for you if you were in your bed. Come on let's get you back in your room."

Sam grumbled as she stood up. "It was only a few minutes."

"No, Major, I let you stay here for an hour. It's time for you to get back in bed." She smiled. "What? You didn't think I saw you leave your room? Come on, Major, I've been around this block a few times. Now trust me. Get back to bed and rest. Your back will appreciate it in the morning. That couch sucks after a few hours. Besides, you have a big day coming up, it's time to start your fitting process."

Chapter Seventeen

KRIS STARED VACANTLY OUT the window, watching the sluggish morning rush hour traffic. *I can't stay in here. Get moving. Go for a walk. Talk to the staff.* Glad to be free of the cane, she stepped out of her room. She walked the length of the hallway several times, stopping to talk to the staff and other patients. *Where is she? That woman. Sam. I haven't seen her for a few days. I wonder if she left? No. No, it was much too early. She was as tired as I was and still looked a little shell-shocked. I'll have to look when I'm in therapy.* She headed for the big window overlooking the garden. *Perfect. The couch is up close. I couldn't move it. Wonder what's going on outside. Hmm, garden looks nice.*

Kris sat down and sighed. Cars circled the parking lot, the drivers seeking nonexistent parking spaces. She watched as cars made the loop around the third time before they gave up and moved toward the perimeter of the hospital lot. *I should be going home soon. To what though? Shelly can't stand to look at me. I can't work yet. I'll be in therapy for weeks even after I leave here. She's changed. Something else is going on. Who was she talking to on the phone? She's tense, not just scared or nervous. How are Shelly and I going to make this work? If she even wants to try? Do I want to? God, she pisses me off. No, she hurt me. I can't believe what she said. Yes, I can. It is a mess. Scars all over the place. Bruises, swelling. A lifeless arm. Can't work. Can't operate. Medical discharge? Then what? Maybe teach at a medical school. Shelly. One breast. One breast. God, the woman loves breasts. No wonder she's repulsed.*

"Hello again. Mind if I sit?"

Kris flinched in surprise and turned at the sound of the voice. "Hi, Sam."

"You're looking sad today."

"I've been thinking about my future. Wondering what it holds. Here, have a seat." Kris slid over to give Sam room.

"Being here will do that to you. How's the arm doing?" Sam sighed as she sat and placed the crutches on the floor.

"Not too good. We're still trying to figure out what's going on with it."

"That brace looks uncomfortable."

Kris looked down at the brace. "I guess it does look that way. Like some sort of medieval torture device. The problem is, I don't feel a thing. My hand is dead. The brace is designed to keep the tendons from contracting permanently." Kris looked at Sam, noticed the whites of her eyes still held a light pink color and were a fascinating shade of green. Like a stormy sea. *She seems familiar.* "How are you doing?"

"Better. My swelling went down, so they were able to start my fitting process for the leg. I still have a long way to go. I'll be here a few more weeks." Sam pointed out the window. "I want to get outside and sit on that bench. I want to walk to it."

"Sounds like a reasonable goal. If you don't mind me asking, what happ—" Kris stopped speaking when a corpsman appeared.

"Excuse me, ma'ams. Doctor Matthews you have an appointment in just a few minutes."

"Oh. Well, I guess I should get going. I'll see you around, Sam. It was nice speaking with you."

"You too."

***

Kris listened as the elderly woman spoke with her. "There are several bra choices to give the appearance you want. We'll get the bra comfortable, and it won't be noticeable that there is any difference underneath."

Kris waited while the woman took her measurements, smiling in surprise as the woman opened what appeared to be a magician's trunk, and drawer after drawer of bras appeared. They discussed bras and features of the different designs to a level of detail she never would have thought possible. Kris pursed her lips as she considered the selections.

"What's wrong, honey?"

"Don't you have anything that is...well, stylish? No offense, ma'am, but these look like something my grandmother would wear."

"Oh sure. Here look at these." She pulled several catalogs out of her briefcase and pointed out various styles and colors. "I have my van parked outside. I have many different styles and selections."

"You have a van filled with bras and implants?"

"Yes. I service several hospitals and boutiques selling mastectomy supplies, and I make house calls for women who aren't up to getting outside yet."

"That's a good idea."

"I thought so."

Kris thumbed through the catalogs, looking at the different bras. *Ooh, there's red and blue, greens, all the colors.* After several more minutes, she made several selections.

"Vibrant colors. That's good. Don't feel like you can't dress up and be feminine and pretty because of what happened. Have you thought about what you want for swimwear or for exercise?"

"I don't think I will be swimming for a while." Kris frowned at her arm strapped into the brace. "I can get one later. I can use my regular exercise bra."

"Of course, you can. Have you thought about what type of prosthesis you want?"

"I can't have reconstruction for a couple months. Maybe longer."

"I meant in the bra. There are several shapes, round or teardrop, depending on the shape of your other breast. Do you know if you want silicone gel, foam, or fiberfill? And do you want an artificial nipple? The form will have a similar weight and feel like a natural breast. Some breast forms adhere directly to the chest area, while others fit into special bra pockets that help hold the prosthesis in place. It's your choice."

"I hadn't thought about it. Do you have samples that I could look at?"

"Of course." The woman reached into her case and pulled out several different types of breast forms.

Kris started to pace. *I can't believe I am doing this.* Her eyes filled with tears. *Stop, why are you crying all the time. This isn't like you.* "Damn it!" Kris looked around the room and blinked several times.

The saleswoman placed several forms on the bed for Kris to examine. She smiled at Kris and placed a hand softly on her shoulder. "It gets easier. Trust me." She placed a box of tissues closer to Kris. "Do you want me to show these to you or would you like to look at them privately? If you have any questions, you can ask. Remember these are samples. We can have the form made for your measurements, to match your body type."

"I'd like to look over them privately."

"Of course. I have some of these in my van. I'll go get them. It will take me a few minutes, so take your time."

Kris sat and stared at the breast forms. She wiped away the single tear that ran down her cheek. A sound in the hallway drew her attention. *I'd better get to it before the woman gets back.* She picked up the nearest form to examine it. She had set several aside by the time the consultant returned with several styles of bra. After showing Kris how the forms fit inside the bra she left again, giving her privacy. *Oh my God! I didn't know. I sent my patients to see these people, and I had no idea how it worked. Did they feel like I do? I never did this part before.* Kris tried on several combinations and made her decisions. She chose the items she wanted and arranged to have several shipped to her home, and the others she put away. *I don't want to see them now.* After the consultant packed up her supplies and left, Kris sat down in the chair and called her parents. They spoke for several minutes, and Kris wished them safe travels home.

***

Kris stopped in the doorway and watched as Shelly stared out the window. Her heart hitched as she looked at her lover. *She's given me such joy and such pain. What will it be like this time? Can we make it work? Do I want it to? Or is it time to move on?*

Shelly turned suddenly, her eyes opening wide. "Hi, babe. I didn't hear you come in. I'm sorry. I'm sorry for what I said. And for how I acted. I wasn't expecting it…you to look like that. For you to be hurt so bad, it shocked me. I think it finally struck home that I could have lost you. Please forgive me."

Kris watched in silent surprise as Shelly's eyes brimmed with tears. *Whoa. She looks like she's going to cry. She doesn't do that.*

"Kris? Did you hear me? I said I was sorry."

"Yes. Yes, I heard you." Kris entered the room and closed the door behind her. "What you said hurt me. I'm scared. My life has been upended. Here I am expecting your support, and you rejected me. I'm still trying to remember what happened. Do you understand that it's frightening to be missing hours, days out of your life, and have no idea what happened? To have those missing hours effect everything."

"I wasn't rejecting you." Shelly opened her arms. "I didn't mean it. We can get through this. Together. I'll be with you, I promise you. Come here, let me hug you."

Shelly's arms wrapped around Kris, the subtle scent of her perfume mixed with the smell of bourbon on her breath. Kris turned her head when Shelly tried to kiss her, the kiss landing on her cheek. "Were you drinking?"

"I had a drink at lunch. It's not a big deal. I need to head back home today. Apparently, there's a problem with a big contract. If I leave today, I should be able to get it straightened out before you get home in a few days. That's still the plan, right?"

"It is. I can't wait to get back."

Chapter Eighteen

NORTH CAROLINA

KRIS STEPPED BACK AND waited while Shelly unlocked the door and held it open for her. "Come on in, babe. Welcome home."

Kris stepped inside her home, stopped in the entry, and looked around seeing everything at once. *I'm home. Thank God, I'm home again.* She smiled and let out a deep relaxing breath.

"Is there something wrong?" Shelly asked.

She looked at Shelly. "Not at all. It's surreal. Here I am safe, and a few weeks ago I was in the middle of the desert, living in a space the size of a good closet. It's so good to be home. I've missed you." She stepped forward and stroked a hand along Shelly's cheek before leaning in and kissing her, a soft brushing of lips, a gentle caress of lips. Kris sighed and pulled away just far enough that their lips no longer touched. "I couldn't do this in the hospital, but I wanted to." She leaned in again, the kiss started soft and intensified, sliding her hand along the back of Shelly's neck she pulled her closer, stroked her fingers through the wavy hair that reached her collar. She slid her mouth along Shelly's neck, inhaling the subtle scent of her perfume and tasted her lover's skin for the first time in months. "God I've wanted to do that."

"Let's get you settled. You're looking tired. Do you want some water or juice? I'll bring your suitcase inside in a few minutes." Shelly went into the kitchen and Kris wandered around the living room. *It looks the same, and it's clean. No sand or grit. There's green outside.* There were a few new photos on the wall, two of her in Afghanistan, and several of Shelly and her friends, out on a boat and on the golf course. She recognized most of the women in the pictures, but there were a few strangers. In one of the photos one of the women had her arm wrapped around Shelly's waist, another Shelly was behind the same woman her arms draped over her shoulders. *Hmm, who's that?* Kris studied the picture and then looked at Shelly in the kitchen. "Shelly? Who is—" The shriek of children outside startled her. Kris broke out in a sweat and started to pace. *Get the kids inside, bring them in. Hurry. Be calm, be calm. Breathe, breathe. Just breathe, nice and slow in and out. In and out.*

"Kris? Are you okay?"

She looked down to see Shelly's hand on her arm and looked back up to see a bewildered look on her partner's face. "What?"

"I asked if you were all right? You looked a million miles away, and you're sweating."

"Ah, yes. I'm good." She took a deep breath and wiped her hand on her pants. "Can I have that water?" She took the glass from Shelly and drank heavily.

"I'll go get your things. Do you want to change? Get into something more comfortable?"

"I want a long hot shower. It's been a long time since I stood in my own shower."

"Not a bath?"

"I shouldn't soak yet. I'll have to make do with a shower."

"Well, enjoy it. I'll get your suitcase. Your other stuff, from over there, is in the garage. It was dirty and full of sand, so I didn't bring it inside. It's not unpacked."

"That's okay. I won't be needing it for a while."

Shelly looked at her. "Or ever again, I hope."

***

"Help me! My baby, she is so cold. Her arm is hurt. Help me!"

"Doc! Doc we need you over here! This woman is requesting a female doctor. Hurry." Kris ran outside toward the woman and stopped short when a Marine started screaming, and dragged himself along the ground away from a bombed out jeep." Help me! Help me!"

"There's more coming. We need more help! Over here, Commander! Hurry"

Kris took off at a run. The sound of a passing helicopter covering the wailing of babies.

"Ayy—"

Kris lay on the floor with pain shooting through her chest and face, and she tasted blood. The light flicked on.

"Oh my God! Kris, are you okay? What happened?" Shelly knelt beside her on the floor. "Oh Jesus, you're bleeding everywhere. Let me get a towel." She was back a moment later."Here. What the hell happened?"

Kris held the damp cloth to her face, pinching the bridge of her nose to stop the trickle of blood. She licked her lips, probing the gash with her tongue. She used several tissues blotting at her lip and nose until the blood flow stopped. "I...I was dreaming."

"Since when do you sleep walk?"

"It was a weird dream." Kris stood up, wobbled for a moment, and tried to remember the dream "Can you get me some ice? I need to keep the swelling down."

"Sure, I'll be right back."

Kris looked in the mirror. Her face was already swelling. Her chest was throbbing from where she hit the floor. She removed the brace from her left arm and examined it, not seeing any damage. Shaking, she pulled off her blood-stained tank top and looked at her chest. There was no skin damage or bruising—yet. She breathed a sigh of relief. Bending over the sink, she washed her face. She finished drying her face and lowered the towel when she caught Shelly staring at her chest, with a wrinkled nose, and a grimace on her face. She saw Shelly shudder.

"Shelly?"

"Um...sorry. Here's the ice. Are you hurting?"

"It's not as bad as it was. The muscle and rib pain is not too bad. The skin is not as sensitive because the nerves have to regenerate. It's coming along."

"Well, let's get you covered up and back in your brace." She handed Kris a nightshirt before helping her dress, and get into the brace. While Kris sat with ice on her lips and nose, Shelly read to her. After a few minutes, Shelly fell asleep. Kris climbed out of bed, turned off the light, and grabbed some water from the refrigerator. She paused in front of the entryway closet before opening the door. *They're still here.* Kris stepped into her old canvas flats, went outside, and spent the next hour pacing the yard.

.

Chapter Nineteen

BETHESDA, MARYLAND

I'M WALKING, WITH MY own legs. Sam pressed a hand against her racing heart.

"Relax, Major. Not so tense. Little steps. Your brain will figure things out. Try not to shuffle. That's where you got hung up yesterday."

After several more trips through the parallel bars, Sam sat and drank some water. Lieutenant Shorb gave her a few minutes to recover. "Okay, Major, break time is over, let's try this. You're going to do your up and downs, before you walk to the other side of the room." They placed a walker in front of Sam, reminded her how to put weight on the prosthesis and stood by as she tried standing up and lowering herself into a chair several times. After performing it smoothly, she made her way to the far side of the room, the therapist close by patiently matching her step for step.

When Sam reached the other side of the room, she was sweating profusely. "That's hard."

"You're right, it is, the first few times. It'll get easier, I promise."

An hour later Sam was exhausted and sweaty. "Your choice, Major. Do you want to ride, or do you want to use the walker going back to your room?"

"The walker."

"You should be heading back to North Carolina in the next few days."

"That's what I hear. No offense, but I am ready to get out of here."

"None taken. You've done well. You'll continue to use this prosthesis until they get a better idea of what you can do. Your socket may need to be adjusted periodically. Let someone know if you start to get rubbing or hot spots. Soon you'll be fitted for your permanent prosthesis. Don't let that term fool you though. It will change several times throughout your life."

"That's good to know."

They arrived back at her room. "See you later, Major."

"Lieutenant? In case I don't see you again, I appreciate what you've done for me."

"You did the work, Major. Good luck."

***

NORTH CAROLINA

Kris sat on the back porch reading. *God, it's hot. My arm must be sweating. Take the brace off. Do the exercises again. Shelly will be home soon, and she can help you with some of them.* She released each finger from its pulley and unlocked the brace at the elbow. Pulling the brace off, she attempted to move her fingers. *Come on! Something needs to happen here. Damn it.* Kris completed the exercises, wiped the sweat from her hands and picked up her glass. She grimaced as she took a sip of the over warm wine. She pushed it aside and picked up her book, and had started to get involved in the mystery again when a cool drop of water slid between her shoulders blades. "Whoo." She flinched and turned, "Hi, I didn't hear you come in."

Shelly ran a hand over Kris' neck. "You looked pretty involved with the book. Is it good?"

"It is. Thanks for picking it up at the library for me."

"It was easy enough. I picked up several. They're on your desk. You know, Kris, we can afford to buy books."

"But they get read once and I get rid of them. The library is fine."

"Suit yourself. Do you want some cold wine? I was going to get a gin and tonic."

"I'll take one of those. That should stay cold longer."

Shelly smiled. "I don't intend to let the ice melt."

Kris dumped her wine into the grass, and a few minutes later Shelly handed her the drink. "Is it okay that you have that off?"

"Yes. They said I could spend some time out of it. I just finished some of the exercises." Kris sipped her drink and looked at Shelly. It was obvious that something was bothering her. Shelly's brow was furrowed, and her jaw clenched several times. "Shelly? Did you have a rough day?"

"We were swamped. Things are hectic, but everyone is getting along. I have a couple of big presentations coming up. It helps that I'm ahead of schedule."

"When are they?"

"They're both in four weeks. I might have to put in some long days though, as we get closer to crunch time, especially if there are any changes. I was working on the presentations at night before you came home. That's how I was able to get ahead."

"No problem. I know you had your share of nights alone when I worked late." Kris leaned over and kissed her. "I didn't kiss you when you got home."

"You could make it up to me."

Kris lifted a brow. "I could? How would I do that?"

"You could kiss me again."

"I could." Kris stood up and straddled Shelly's lap, encircled an arm around her neck and kissed her softly at first, and gradually increased the intensity. She shifted on Shelly's lap, her hand soft on Shelly's breasts. Shelly broke the kiss. "Don't do that baby. Not unless we're going to go to bed. I can't get all worked up and have nothing happen. I'm having a hard enough time sleeping next to you and not touching you. It's been three weeks since you came home. I've tried to be patient…"

"Now. I want you now." Kris shifted in her lap and started to slowly rock against her. "Now," she muttered as she covered Shelly's mouth with her own. "It's time." Kris stood and took Shelly's hand and led her inside to their bedroom. She shivered as Shelly's hands grasped her hips and slowly drifted across her stomach. She ran her hand down over Shelly's back and gently cupped her ass pulling her close. "Let's go to bed. I want to make love with you. Afterwards, I want to fall asleep with your arms around me and wake up and do it all over again."

Shelly pulled her close, nipping at her lower lip. Before releasing it, she stroked her tongue gently across it. "That sounds like a great idea." They embraced, their kisses soft and tender soon grew urgent as their hands tugged at clothes, and traveled over the newly exposed skin. Shelly pulled Kris' bra cup down freeing her healthy breast to lavish attention on it. Kris moved to take her bra off, and Shelly stopped her. "Leave it there."

"What?"

Shelly murmured, "Just leave it." Shelly took Kris' left hand, lifted it so it rested on her shoulder. Leaning forward she kissed her lips, her chin, her neck, and drifted down to her chest and abdomen. They lay in each other's arms and explored their bodies. With soft caresses and breathless kisses, their bodies moved together and their cries filled the air as they welcomed each other home.

Roslyn Bane

Chapter Twenty

NORTH CAROLINA

"HI, MAJOR. WELCOME BACK to Camp Lejeune. You're attached to the Wounded Warrior Regiment, Battalion East. You'll be assigned to us as you recover. Your quarters will be with us in the medical barracks. Your treatment and rehab will be at the Warrior Hope and Care Center. We have advanced physical training equipment, a lap pool, underwater treadmill, rock climbing wall, and reconditioning, aerobic and training rooms. You'll see family members and kids around the facilities too."

"That's good to know," Sam replied as she looked around the unit.

"We'll help you get settled in your quarters." The man showed her the schedule. "Your first PT session is at fifteen hundred today."

"Thanks." Sam nodded her head and signed her name in the check-in log.

***

Sam was walking to her counseling session, one hand tight on the cane the other holding a folder as a female naval officer approached from the opposite direction. Her left arm was in a brace, and Sam recognized her instantly. The woman's eyes opened in surprise and she smiled.

"Sam, you're looking good. When did you get here?"

"Kris, it's good to see you. I got in a few hours ago."

"Are you coming in here? It's a group session."

"I am." Sam held the door open for Kris. *She's walking faster. You can tell she's feeling better.* They entered, and Sam saw ten chairs arranged in a circle. Most were already filled, so they sat opposite of each other. Almost immediately the session started.

"Hello, everyone, I am Commander Renee Abbott. I am a clinical psychologist and one of the counselors here at the naval hospital. We have several new faces today so let's do quick introductions. Tell us what you want and how you ended up here, and we'll get started."

They slowly went around the room introducing themselves. Sam listened and observed the others. Everyone was in the Marine Corps uniform except the psychologist and Kris.

"I'm Lieutenant Commander Kris Matthews. I was injured in Afghanistan, Helmand province. I don't remember how. My arm was injured. Like most of you, I spend a good portion of my day in therapy. I spend about half my day back at my command. I'm doing some of my normal job functions but certainly not all of them. I am a physician, a surgeon. Unfortunately, my left arm is my dominant arm, so until I have full function I won't be operating. I joined the battalion about three weeks ago, and like most of you I passed through Bethesda on my way here."

Sam noticed a slight accent. *She's from up north. Not far north. Mid-Atlantic maybe. Being in uniform, and not a hospital gown, changes everyone's appearance. Kris looks fit and healthy, despite the brace on her arm and the lingering pallor. Her hand isn't swollen and bruised. Hair's a little long, past the collar. Well, I'm sure she'll get that back in regs. Not like she doesn't have other things to worry about. God, her eyes are bright blue.* Kris' gaze locked on Sam's, she smiled, and Sam felt an unfamiliar tug deep inside. Sam smiled back and realized she was smiling for the first time in months.

Soon it was Sam's turn to introduce herself. "I'm Major Sam Davies. I'm a helicopter pilot." She patted her right leg. "I lost my leg over there. I arrived this morning and I'm wondering if I will get back to my normal duties. My squadron is still over there and will be for a while."

"Okay. Thank you, everyone, for your introductions. At our last session, we were talking about flashbacks. Have any of you been able to identify what your triggers are? Is there anything that you realize you see or hear or maybe even smell that causes you to relive an event?"

After several minutes of silence, someone spoke up. "I had a flashback the other day. I was home and getting ready to start washing the car, and all of a sudden I was back in Afghanistan. I saw the lead vehicle in our convoy hit the IED again, instantly gunfire was everywhere."

"Do you know what triggered it?"

"I think it was my neighbors. It's a couple of guys, and they were joking, calling each other...rude names...talking about the latest Fast and Furious movie, and BAM I was back on the side of the road under attack."

"Why do you think that triggered you?" Renee asked.

"I've been thinking about that. And it seems like the guys in my vehicle were talking about seeing that movie right before the explosion. At least I think that's what they were talking about. It's not that we weren't paying attention. We were. You can't be out on patrol for eight, ten, twelve hours and not talk about something. You talk and pay attention and do your job."

"That's right. Is there any chance you feel guilty about the explosion happening while your crew was discussing the movie? Do you think you could have spotted the IED and stopped the vehicle before it hit?"

"I...I...don't know."

"Think about it. Could you have been able to spot the IED?" Renee probed.

Sam looked around the room, everyone appeared to be holding their breath.

The sergeant gasped out loud. "No! No! We were too far back. We wouldn't have been in position to see it."

"Excellent. Now tell me, Sergeant, if you were not in a position to see the device, and you didn't have a reason to stop the convoy, is there any way you could have prevented the explosion?"

"No." Relief flooded her voice. "No, there wasn't."

"Now that you know the trigger perhaps you can look back at the incident and interpret it differently. We can dig into this more in a one-on-one session. Does anyone have any questions? I want all of you to remember, even when things seemed to have gone wrong, it doesn't mean that it was necessarily preventable by you."

A short while later, the session broke up, and Sam headed for her physical therapy appointment. Several hours later, she showered, ate her meal, and soon afterward fell into bed exhausted.

***

"Kris, do you understand what we're going to try today?" Renee asked her.

"Yes. We're going to try hypnosis to see if it will help me get my memory back."

"Do you think it's important that you get back any memories that may be missing?"

Kris was quiet for a moment before she answered, "Although I don't recall getting injured I don't think there is a large block of time missing either. If you think this will help my recovery, I'll give it a try."

"Do you believe in hypnosis?"

"It's been proven to be beneficial. I've had no experience with it."

"Fair enough. Do you have any questions about it?"

"Yes. How will you know if what I remember is the truth?"

"I do have some information from your colleagues on what happened on the days around the time you were injured. I think it's a good place for us to start. Are you ready?"

"I am."

"Well let's get started. Where would you like to sit?"

"The recliner." Kris sat down, put her feet up, and wiggled around until she was comfortable.

Renee handed her a pair of dark glasses with tiny lights attached to the inside of the lens. "Put these on and close your eyes, lean back and relax."

Kris looked at the glasses carefully, and inspected the wire that attached near the hinge, "What's this do?"

"It's a light display. The lights will flash and help you to relax, some are red, some green."

"No gold watch?"

"Not unless you want one."

Kris slipped the glasses on, took several deep breaths and closed her eyes.

"Kris, can you hear me?"

"Yes."

"I want you to take several deep breaths and slowly count backward from twenty."

"Twenty, nineteen, eighteen, seventeen…" She took a deep breath. "Sixteen…" Kris became silent.

Renee watched as Kris became still, her breathing slow and steady, her face slack, hands limp in her lap. After ensuring that Kris was comfortable and felt safe she started to question her.

"Tell me about your mission in Afghanistan."

"I was at a field hospital. It's a small emergency room of ten beds, two surgery suites, and a pre-op and post-op area. It allows us to give medical care to injured troops as quickly as possible. We can expand to handle more, as the demand arises. As patients come in, we bring them to the emergency area and treat them until they begin to stabilize. Those that can't wait go right to the operating room. Afterwards they're flown out to one of the higher level of care hospitals. If they don't need to be evacuated, we treat them until they're strong enough to get back into the fight. Sometimes, if they needed further care we didn't even wake them up from their anesthesia before they were shipped out."

"So, you were at the front?"

"Close to the front."

"What type of things did you see there?"

"We saw Marines, soldiers who'd been injured. Explosions, IED's, shrapnel, bullets. Vehicle accidents, appendicitis. Burns. We saw everything." Kris spoke clearly.

"Did you only work on coalition forces?"

"No. Anyone who was with NATO. The ANA, ANP. Civilians. We worked on the Taliban fighters too."

"Who are the ANA?"

"Afghan National Army and the Afghan National Police."

"You helped civilians?"

"Yes."

"Children?"

Renee watched as Kris' hand fisted. "At times. They get sick or hurt. The Taliban takes over a village. They shield themselves with civilians. Sometimes the kids step on IED's. If they can make it to us they have a good chance of surviving."

"Did you ever go out to any of the villages?"

"Y...yes. If it was safe. We would do a medical mission. Primarily checkups on the women and children. Sometimes it was the first experience they had with a trained physician or nurse."

"How did you help?"

"We gave them vaccinations, treated minor burns and sprains, dispensed medicine. We did physical exams. If they were interested, we taught them first aid."

"Did the villagers accept you?"

"Not at first. We had to build trust. And there was always the fear that the Taliban would find out the villagers accepted our help and would retaliate."

Renee softened her voice. "Did you get close to any of the villagers?"

"We started to recognize each other."

"But did you become friendly with any of them?" Renee noticed Kris' foot start to bounce and her pulse visibly showed in her neck with each beat. "Kris, did you become friendly with any of the villagers?"

"I got to know a few of them."

"Tell me something about them."

"They're all so poor. So many of these people have very little…a roof over their head, a mattress, a chair, and table if they're lucky."

"Tell me about them. Their personalities. Tell me about someone you were friendly with."

Kris was quiet for a minute. Renee watched as Kris shifted slightly in the chair, her breathing rate picking up, and she cleared her throat. "There was this woman, Waseema, a girl actually. About fifteen, they don't keep track of birthdays like we do. She was a child bride. She'd been married about four years. She had a daughter, Yagana, who was a toddler, with the bluest eyes I've ever seen. Waseema was afraid of us at first, like all the villagers. But when Yagana was ill she brought her to us. The baby had an ear infection and high fever. We gave her some antibiotics. After that, whenever we came to the village Waseema came by. She knew some English and started to learn more. She acted as an unofficial translator for us."

"She trusted you?"

"Yes. She wanted to see what we were doing. She tried to help out. She said she wanted to be a nurse. Several of the nurses and I were teaching her how to read."

"It sounds like you were fond of her."

"It was like she was a younger sister. She was determined to keep her daughter healthy and safe."

"Kris, you mentioned that civilians came into the camp, and at times into the hospital. How did they get there?"

"Our medics would bring them in. But they'd get there any way they could, cart, car, truck, bus."

"Bus?"

"Yes. We would sometimes get buses of injured in at a time."

"When was the last time a bus of injuries came in?"

Kris fisted her hand again, and her feet flexed. "Right before I came home."

"What happened?"

"We received a call from the gate that a bus was coming and was full of injured children. Security, the guards, had to check and make sure that it wasn't rigged to explode. As soon as the bus stopped, we were ready and waiting. It was about twenty children. The Taliban had attacked their school, and as coalition forces closed in, the Taliban tried to blow up the school. It was horrible. Most of the girls had been raped, some had…"

"Had what?"

"Some of the girls had been circumcised. Everything had been cut off, most were bleeding still. With the explosion many lost limbs…had, disfiguring burns. Many were killed instantly. We helped the few who were left."

"It sounds horrible."

"It was. We lost a few." Her breath hitched, and her voice grew tight. "We did amputations on several of them. Their legs or arms were too mangled to save."

"What about their families?"

"Sometimes there was a parent with them. Rarely."

"Doing amputations on children must be particularly disturbing. Did you do many?"

"Yes, too many."

"The day you were hurt did you see any children?"

"I don't remember."

"Think about that for a moment."

Kris grew silent. Her right fingers stroked along her left arm as if she was cradling something. "Yes, two girls. We had done amputations on them a day earlier. But it wasn't enough. We had to take them back in and take off more."

"That sounds hard. How did it go?"

"They…" Kris' voice broke. "One died. The infection was too much. These aren't strong children. They're already malnourished. Some have nothing left to fight with."

"What happened after that? If a child dies, what does the unit do?"

"Same thing as with anyone. They're cleaned. We have a team that cleans the Afghanis according to their customs."

"Did you ever hold the children?"

"Yes, to comfort them."

"How would you do that if you don't speak the language?"

"The same as we do here. A gentle touch, soft words, soothing tone. I used to like to stroke their hair, rub their heads." Her right hand continued to move rhythmically.

"You're doing well. Kris, I want you to think back. Did anything else happen the day after the bus carrying the school children came in?"

Kris was silent for several seconds before she whimpered, "No."

"Kris? What happened? Did a young woman approach you?"

"No."

"Tell me about what happened with the woman, Kris."

"No, no." Kris squirmed and rubbed at her throat.

"What did you do, Dr. Matthews? What did the woman hand you?" Renee watched as Kris' breathing increased and she pushed back against the chair, trying to force herself away. Her knuckles were white, her neck muscles straining. "The day after the bus came in. What else happened? A woman approached you. She gave you something, Kris."

"Blankets. It was a blanket, rolled in a ball."

"Are you sure? Tell me, Kris. You'll feel better. Who was the woman? What was in the blanket?"

Kris was rocking back and forth in the chair, her right hand tight across her left elbow. She cried out, "It was Waseema." She took several strangled breaths. "Inside the blankets was Yagana. She was dead. Her legs had been crushed." Kris rolled onto her side in the chair and wrapped her arms around herself. "She was gone. It was too late. Babies shouldn't die. No...babies shouldn't die."

"Kris, I want you to take a few deep breaths and try to relax. You're safe here in North Carolina. You've done well. I am going to have you wake up now. You'll remember what we spoke about. Now you'll be able to get the help you need to deal with these memories. I want you to count to five and open your eyes. When you reach five, you'll be wide awake, with full memory and recall of what we talked about."

Kris' eyes opened, she took off the glasses and looked about the room. She took several quick breaths and leaned over and cried. "Oh my God! Those kids, those kids. Those poor beautiful children! Babies raising younger babies."

Renee offered encouragement to Kris as she fought to gain control of her emotions. As Kris calmed, Renee spoke. "I know that was painful and that you're feeling pretty fragile right now. I promise you, we can help you with these memories. You'll learn to deal with them."

"Why am I so weak? I'm an emotional wreck. I'm a surgeon for God sake. I deal with illness and injury all the time. I was trained to do this, to take care of people. You learn how to deal with death."

"You're not weak. Your training and your years of practice did prepare you how to be a surgeon. Your response to what happened over both your tours and especially with what we talked about today is a normal response to an abnormal situation. You dealt with the bus incident and Yagana, the only way you could at the time by forcing it down and forgetting it. Today we used hypnosis to help you recall it. The goal here is to try to get you to let it out in a controlled manner and in such a way that you learn to deal with what happened."

"It makes me feel shaky, lost." Kris rubbed her left arm.

"That's understandable, Kris. Finding someone to talk to will help you heal your wounds...maybe another combat medical veteran. The more you go over it, the more confidence you'll feel."

"I don't see how talking to someone helps. It only tears open the wound."

"Kris, while you were in your residency did you ever lose a patient."

"Yes."

"Did you talk about it with anyone?"

"Yes. My classmates, and my roommate."

"And how did you feel afterward?"

Kris was quiet for several seconds. "It helped."

"That's what we're aiming for. Or write down your memories, and how they make you feel."

"I'll think about it."

"Good. I'll see you next week. Call if you want to talk before then."

"Yes, ma'am."

Roslyn Bane

Chapter Twenty-one

KRIS SAT AT THE table sipping coffee, her plate pushed aside. "Did you see this story? A community near the airfield is petitioning to have a noise ordinance put in place, so the aircraft don't make so much noise. Why did city zoning allow homes to be built so close to the airfield? Aircraft are noisy, that's no surprise. They need a buffer zone for noise and for potential accidents." When Shelly failed to answer, Kris lowered the paper and watched Shelly text furiously.

She's doing a lot of texting and always has her phone with her now. It used to be she would have to try to find the darn thing. Now it's almost an appendage. Folding the newspaper closed, she took another sip and watched Shelly. She was grinning while she responded to a text, and immediately the phone buzzed back, and Shelly snickered.

"What's so funny?"

Shelly looked up, surprise evident on her face. "Oh, one of my pals was telling me about her date last night. Sounds like it was the date from hell. They had absolutely nothing in common. It took her two hours to end the evening."

"That's too bad."

"Yeah, I guess so. But it is funny." Shelly stood up, filled her coffee, looked at Kris' cup and topped it off. Leaning down she nuzzled her neck. "What are you going to do today?"

"Mm. I thought we could go for a hike."

"I already have plans," Shelly said quickly.

"You do?"

"I usually meet for a round of golf with some friends. Remember I wrote to you about it. I've missed a couple weeks since you got back."

"Oh, okay."

"Is there something wrong?" Shelly furrowed her brows.

"No. You need to have time with your friends. Go, have a good time." Kris smiled at her.

"Thanks, babe." Shelly gave her a quick peck on the cheek and grabbed a bottle of water from the refrigerator. "You'll get the dishes right? I'll see you later."

"Okay. Bye."

Kris watched the door close and scowled slightly. After a minute she stood, loaded the few dishes into the dishwasher, and went outside. She walked around the yard several times wondering what to do. Wondering why she couldn't think of what she wanted to do. While she was in Afghanistan, she could think of plenty of things she couldn't wait to do when she was back home. Now it didn't seem important.

Kris walked out to the garage, and to the far corner. Carefully she worked on lifting a large tarp. Eventually managing to lift it completely, she stood admiring her motorcycles. One bright red, the other metallic blue. She ran her hand lovingly over the red bike and stroked the leather seat. She looked it over carefully, checking wires and cables. With a little effort, she opened the gas tank and peaked inside. She closed the tank, carefully folded the tarp and stored it. She squeezed the brake lever and gently kicked the tire on the blue and chrome bike she had bought from her brother. She hadn't wanted to modify her bike, so she bought his for when Shelly wanted to go for a ride.

"Soon. I'll be riding again soon." She stroked the red bike again and walked inside. She found the phone number of her favorite bike shop and called for them to come by and pick up the bikes to have them serviced.

She logged into the computer, did a quick search and found a nature trail through a local park. She rummaged through her closet until she found her old leather knapsack that she used on the bike and adjusted the straps so it would be easy to get on and off single handed. She grabbed a peach, a granola bar, and a bottle of water placing them in the pack along with her wallet. She waved to one of her neighbors who was out mowing the grass. He turned off the mower and came over.

"Hey Kris, how are you doing?"

"Hi, Rick. I'm doing well, trying to get adjusted to being back."

"I bet. How's the arm doing? That brace looks wicked."

Kris looked momentarily at the brace. "Not much has changed. I am scheduled for more testing and still go to therapy. They're keeping it moving and have given me plenty of exercises to do for it."

"That's good. Have you gotten into any type of routine yet, or are you winging it?"

"Ah, I'm still winging it. They have me doing administrative work at the hospital. Otherwise, I'm taking things one day at a time."

"I did too when I first got back. It drove Janice nuts after a few weeks. I needed to do something, you know, like have a daily mission. Once I got a routine, it helped."

"It did?" Kris asked with doubt evident on her face.

"Definitely. I'd wander around looking for something to do otherwise. It took a while to settle back down, sleep through the night. I would come outside and pace at night for hours at a time. I've seen you outside doing the same. I was surprised at first. I didn't think docs walked the perimeter like a sentry. It'll get better. I got back into my hobbies and picked up some new ones through the Wounded Warrior Regiment. I guess you're looking forward to getting back on the bike."

Kris looked at him, "Funny you should mention that. I was just looking at them. I called a shop to come pick them up and get both ready. I had them serviced for storage before I left. I can't wait to ride."

"You're thinking positive now."

"Yes. I'll be riding again. I know it."

"I hope so. Let me know if you want to ride sometime. I got one while you were gone. Janice is enrolled in a rider safety course now too."

"Good for her. She'll love it."

"I hope so."

Kris turned toward the sound of a truck coming down the street. "Looks like they're here for the bikes. I'll talk to you later."

"Sure thing. Hey, Kris?" She turned back around. "If you ever want to talk, you know, about over there, I'll listen. It helps you know."

"Thanks, Rick. Tell Janice I said hello."

Half an hour later she watched the truck loaded with her bikes disappear. She looked up at the bright blue sky and made a decision. *I'm going hiking like I wanted to do, with or without Shelly.* She climbed in her car, reached across to close the door and pulled away from the curb.

***

Early in the evening Kris and Shelly sat outside in a chaise lounge finishing a bottle of wine as Shelly relayed the details about her golf match that day. *How much longer can she talk about this golf match? Is she going to ask me what I did today?*

Unable to listen to Shelly talk any more about golf she straddled Shelly and started to nuzzle her neck and fondle her breasts. Sitting across her legs, she traced a finger down from her neck to the waistband of her shorts and slipped her hand inside to feel her wetness. "Should we go inside?"

They stumbled into the bedroom, Kris grunted as she was pushed back against the wall, her mouth captured instantly in a hard kiss. She returned it with equal vigor and fumbled one-handed with the buttons on Shelly's shirt. Leaning her neck to the side, she gave Shelly access to her neck and enjoyed the sensations of lips and tongue drifting along her skin. Her heart thudded in her chest, and her clit awakened as teeth closed on her collarbone for several seconds before a soft wet tongue soothed. Kris tugged Shelly's shirt free from her waistband and slid her hand up over her chest pushing the blouse free from one shoulder. Shelly pulled back slightly and shrugged out of her blouse, unhooked her bra, and quickly removed Kris' brace.

Kris wrapped her arm around Shelly's neck and nudged her backward toward the bed. Strong arms wrapped around her waist, and she was turned and wrestled across the room to the bed, where they fell, panting and mumbling as they finished undressing each other. Shelly straddled over Kris' waist and tugged her shirt upward, stopping before exposing her chest. Kris moaned in pleasure as Shelly kissed and caressed, before drifting lower. She reached between them and unsnapped her jeans and lifted her hips as Shelly tugged them off and tossed them aside.

She moved her legs apart as Shelly nudged them, and shivered as soft fingers slid up her legs toward her core. Fingers ran through her hair before stroking along her labia, slowly teasing her open before fluttering along her inner folds. Kris moaned and lifted her hips trying to direct Shelly's touch. "Please Shelly." Her hand grasped at Shelly's head, guiding her down. "Your mouth, please."

Shelly stopped, knelt straight up, "Did you forget you don't tell me what to do?"

Kris watched in stunned disbelief as Shelly hopped out of bed and moved away. "Shelly, come back..." Shelly turned to face her, a mischievous grin on her face, as handcuffs dangled from her fingers. A surge of anticipation ignited deep inside her. "Ooh please."

Shelly stepped quickly to the bed and jerked Kris' arms overhead securing the cuff around one wrist, behind a wrought iron spindle and locking it onto her other wrist. Grasping Kris' chin, she lowered her mouth, plundering and demanding. Deft fingers released buttons and Kris felt her skin ignite under Shelly's mouth as each inch of skin was exposed and consumed. Shelly pushed her bra up exposing her chest and focused her attention on her right breast. Kris writhed with pleasure as her nipple was teased and tortured with teeth and tongue, before Shelly roughly sucked it into her mouth. Fingernails dragged along the swell of her breast, and ignited her further. "God. Shelly that's so good."

Kris moaned as Shelly released her nipple with a noisy plop, and her eyes flew open when she heard Shelly hiss. She watched as Shelly cringed as she looked at what was left of her breast. Suddenly, fingers dug into her tender flesh, and she cried out in pain. "Not so hard—" Shelly captured her mouth again and bit hard on her lip. Kris jolted and tried to pull away. She yelped when Shelly squeezed her damaged flesh viciously. Kris pushed with her feet to move away. "Stop. It's too rough."

Shelly murmured an apology into her neck and lifted Kris' hips. Kris gasped as her clit was stroked and flicked and fingers thrust into her.

"You like that baby? God you're so fucking wet."

"You do that to me," Kris groaned.

"That's right. I do this to you. I can turn you into a hot panting, begging mess."

Kris shuddered as Shelly whispered the harsh words in her ears, and shouted out when her clit was pinched, before being released and flicked vigorously. Fingers thrust into her again, probing and she moaned with pleasure. Her hips thrust to meet the rhythm of the strokes and warmth spread up her body.

"That's right baby, ride my hand. Show me how much you want me to fuck you. Tell me how much you need to come."

"Yes. Yes. I need to come." She cried out when Shelly withdrew her hand, her hips gyrating seeking friction to drive her over the edge. "Please, Shelly help me."

"What do you want? Tell me."

"I want you to take me. Make me come."

"Do you want me to fuck you?"

"Yes!" she panted and writhed against Shelly's leg.

Shelly thrust her fingers back inside Kris' wet sex and fingered her vigorously. The pressure on her clit had Kris erupting violently, and she clenched around Shelly's fingers. Gasping for breath, she looked down in surprise as Shelly jerked her higher and slapped down on her inner thigh twice before lowering her mouth to her and demanding with her aggressive tongue several more earth-shattering orgasms. Finally, she could take no more. Her clit ached with pain and she cried out. "Please,

Shelly no more. I can't take any more."

"Good now it's my turn."

"Let me go. I want to touch you."

Shelly moved up, positioned herself over Kris' shoulders. "No. I want your mouth." She pulled Kris' head up slightly and growled, "That's right, baby. Make me come. Show me how much you missed me."

It didn't take long before Kris heard Shelly shout out in release. She froze however when the name Shelly called out didn't sound like hers.

Shelly fumbled for the handcuffs, finding the key, and released her arms. She lowered Kris' arms and rolled onto her side. Drawing Kris close, she nibbled along the back of her shoulder. "I'm so glad you're home. I missed you, baby." As Shelly's breathing slowed and she fell asleep Kris lay quietly next to her and wondered if she had heard wrong. After a long time she drifted into a restless sleep.

Chapter Twenty-two

"SAM YOU SEEM A bit agitated today. Do you want to tell me what's wrong?" Renee asked.

"Not really."

"Well, why don't you try anyhow? We have the next thirty minutes together, and it will get mighty boring if we have nothing to talk about. How is physical therapy going?"

"It's fine."

"I don't think I've ever had anyone say that before. Usually there's some comment about the therapists being sadists."

Sam almost smiled. "Well, sometimes I wonder…"

"Wonder what?"

"Nothing. It's not important," Sam muttered.

"Sure it is. If you're thinking about it, it's important."

"I wonder if…if I'll ever be in a relationship again?" Sam felt the heat rise on her cheeks.

"You will, Sam. Life isn't over. You'll find someone, and the right person will love you. The loss of your leg won't keep them away."

***

Kris awakened slowly, and opened her eyes. Despite the glow of the moonlight through the windows, much of the room remained in shadows. The window was wide open, and the sounds of owls and the scent of pine drifted in on the breeze. Surprisingly she was unafraid. She sensed she was being watched and rolled over slowly. A woman stood in the doorway, her face hidden in shadows. She slowly walked toward Kris and smiled, her white teeth flashing in the darkened room. Kris started to speak but stopped as the shadowy figure approached.

"Don't say anything. Let me look at you. Please take the sheet down."

Kris slowly lowered the sheet, and watched those white teeth flash again. The woman sat on the other side of the bed and leaned over. She kissed Kris softly, and whispered in her ear, "You're beautiful." Her lips were soft as they pressed to Kris and her hands stroked skillfully against her breasts, firm and full. Heat raced through Kris, her stomach quivered, and moisture gathered between her legs. Kris arched into the mouth that teased her breasts, as first one, then the other nipple was caught between sharp edged teeth and light pressure was applied. She writhed and opened her legs as fingers brushed lower seeking entry. They were quickly rocking together, their rhythm matching. Kris arched back as the tension built to peak.

She heard someone moaning and sat up suddenly. Momentarily disoriented she looked around and heard the shower running, and Shelly's off key singing in the shower. With a deep sigh she lay back down, and tried to will the deep ache in her sex away. "Where did that come from?"

Chapter Twenty-three

KRIS WAS STANDING AT the sink struggling to wash a few dishes when Shelly came in. "Hi." She came up behind Kris, wrapped her arm around her waist and nuzzled her neck before quickly nipping her hard on the neck.

"Ow! God Shelly, you can't mark me like that! It'll show when I'm in uniform." She rubbed at her neck, and smelled the whiskey on Shelly's breath. *She's been drinking again, be careful.*

"Relax, it wasn't that hard. Besides your hair is long enough to cover it."

"That's not the point."

"Fine. I'm sorry. God, you are so emotional lately."

"I am not…" Kris turned off the water and wiped her hand on a towel. "Forget it. I already put the leftovers in the fridge."

"You used to wait for me to get home."

"You used to call if you were going to be late. It's after eight, so I ate."

"I didn't realize it was so late. Sorry. What did you eat?" Shelly rummaged through the fridge, and pulled out a beer. She twisted off the cap, and drank greedily.

"Baked ziti and some salad. It's in the blue container."

Shelly pulled the bowl out, dumped some onto a plate, and put it in the microwave. She drank from the bottle again and wiped her mouth with her hand. "So how was your day?"

"It was good. I had a counseling session today. I think it'll help with the nightmares. And I went to the orthopedic clinic. The latest tests were negative. They can't find what's keeping it from moving. It doesn't hurt. It's like nothing is there. At least in therapy they are able to move it all the way. It's so frustrating that they can't find the problem. And I was able to see patients in the clinic today, so I was busy."

The microwave dinged, and Shelly pulled the plate out, set it on the table and grabbed another beer from the refrigerator. "That's good. Are you tired?" She started to eat.

"No." Kris lifted the beer. "Do you mind?"

"Go ahead. Is that something you picked up over there?"

"What?"

"Drinking beer?"

"No, Shelly. It's against regulations. Drinking in a war zone is not recommended. I wanted a taste." *I don't want you drinking more. You already smell like whiskey.* "That's not too bad. What is it?"

"It's called Smoky Mountain Porter. It has a nice flavor."

"It does. How did your day go?"

"Eeh. The client didn't like some of the ads, so I spent the day redesigning. It ran late and when he finally approved the designs a couple of us went out to celebrate."

"That's nice. Build some camaraderie."

"I don't know about that, but it sure was nice to have a drink or two." She finished her dinner and pushed the plate away. "I'm going to take a walk. I'll be back in twenty minutes." She kissed Kris on the cheek and walked to the door. "Can you clean up that mess?" Before Kris could answer Shelly left.

Kris stared at the closed door, and then back to the plate on the table. With a sigh she washed the plate, and dumped out the rest of the beer. She went into her office, logged into the computer, and started to do the journaling exercise the psychologist had asked her to try. *We're in trouble. This isn't working anymore. We're avoiding each other. We don't talk anymore, there's no companionship. It's not only my injuries either, although that's a big part of it. She wants my breast fixed and can't stand to look at me. Why doesn't she understand that it's not forever? I'll get reconstruction as soon as I'm cleared for it. The more time that passes, the more irritated she gets. We text more than we talk. She's working a lot, but something else is going on. I feel it.* She glanced at the clock. Ten-thirty. *So much for twenty minutes.*

Kris saved the document and as an afterthought password protected it. She shut down the computer, turned on the outside light and locked the door. She took a long hot shower and enjoyed every moment of the warmth and the quiet. She finished up, reached out to grab her towel and dried off in the shower. She stepped out of the shower and jumped slightly when she saw Shelly leaning against the counter, naked.

"I want you."

"Shell—" Kris was cut off as her mouth was crushed in a hot, aggressive kiss that tasted of whiskey and beer. Rough hands grabbed her ass and pulled her close, so they stood pelvis to pelvis. Shelly ground against her, and broke the kiss long enough to growl, "Now. Right now." She bit down hard on Kris' lip as Kris tried to back away. Shelly advanced, pushed her against the wall and took her mouth again. Her wrists were tightly squeezed before being wrenched over her head, and her knees pushed far apart by Shelly's leg. Shelly braceleted her wrists with one hand and lowered the other, thrusting it between Kris' legs. She cupped her. "You're not wet. Don't worry I know how to get you there."

"Shelly, I don't want to."

"You never want to anymore. You need to remember how much fun it is."

"Not like this, no." She tried to pull her arms free to no avail. She gasped when Shelly pinched her sex hard and bit down on her shoulder. Shelly pulled back slightly and ripped the towel off of her, immediately stepped between her legs, and pushed herself against Kris. Kris started to struggle, she pushed forward and tried to pull her arms free. Her hands were jerked higher while her damaged breast was squeezed violently.

"Shelly stop. It's too rough."

Shelly let go of her arms but immediately grabbed her jaw, holding it tightly. "I know what you like. I know how to make you purr. I know how much you like to be dominated." Her mouth was crushed again by a bruising kiss, strong hands grabbed her hips and jerked her forward and ground her against her thigh. Hard, rough fingers forced their way between them and stroked roughly. Shelly hissed in her ear, "That's right baby, I know what you need. I can feel you getting wet. You like it rough, such a submissive little bitch."

The harsh words startled Kris and she jerked back, but Shelly continued her quick assault forcing her hand between Kris' legs rubbing her vigorously. Fingers thrust suddenly inside her and she cried out in pain. Kris pushed her and had almost succeeded in pushing her away when Shelly suddenly pulled her forward with one arm, and then slammed her back against the wall. Her head bounced off the wall leaving her dazed. She was jerked forward again and violently shoved back, her head cracking loudly against the wall. Her vision started to fade, and her legs grew weak. Shelly yanked her by her left arm and pulled her to the bed.

Shelly pushed Kris onto her back and covered her body. Shelly kept the pace frantic and rough as she slid down and quickly without delicacy, used her mouth. Kris cried out, "Shelly, stop. Don't do this. Please, no." Despite her protests, Kris felt her body tighten, and shuddered in response as her body betrayed her.

Shelly moved up quickly and knelt above her. She pinned Kris' hands down and jerked her head up to meet her sex. "Hurt me and you'll be sorry bitch." Her hair was yanked hard as Shelly ground down against her. With tears in her eyes, Kris used her mouth to bring Shelly to orgasm.

Shelly pushed back away from her, and smiled wickedly at her. Shelly flipped her over, and bit her viciously on the back. Kris screamed and she sprang from the bed. Shelly threw a shirt at her. "Cover yourself up. I can't stand to look at that mess. It looks like some science experience. Like Frankenstein. Frankentit. That's what it is."

Kris recoiled, the final words stinging, and making everything worse. She stumbled into the bathroom, gasping for breath. Showering again, she stood in the shower dazed, letting the water fall on her throbbing head. Sinking to the floor, she cried and tried to figure out what the hell had happened. She stayed in the shower until the water grew cold. She stood slowly, her body aching and still trembling. Toweling off quickly she pulled on a nightshirt, and cautiously opened the door. Shelly was asleep, snoring lightly. Kris slipped into the guest room, turning the lock on the door as she closed it. She lay in bed, quietly shaking and wondered what she had done to make Shelly so mad. After several minutes she got up, pulled on a pair of shorts and quietly slipped outside.

She paced back and forth, tears periodically streaming down her face. *Good God, did that really happen? Did Shelly assault her? No. It couldn't be assault. You can't come if you're assaulted. Can you? I should have fought back more.* She rubbed the back of her head which was tender and bruised. *I need to think.*

***

Kris lay on the examination table, the crinkly white paper barely protecting her from the coolness of the surface. She stared at the ceiling, waiting patiently for the exam to be over. Fortunately, the doctor's hands were warm and gentle on her breast. "How's the sensitivity?"

"It varies. The scars are numb where the skin is puckered. The red is fading. Most of the graft has sensation, and the area that was undamaged feels okay most of the time. Sometimes it is really sensitive and it still occasionally swells."

"I'm done." The doctor pulled the cape closed and helped Kris to sit up. "How often do you notice swelling?"

"It seems like every four weeks or so."

"Is it at the same time as your cycle?"

Kris looked at her and flushed slightly. "Hmm, yes, it is. How could I not realize that?"

"Because you've been under a lot of stress. Because you're healing. Maybe because you're scared. That's a lot of distraction. The good news is that the breast tissue that was undamaged is working like it should by responding to changes in your hormone levels. But you have to be more careful."

"Careful?"

"Your breasts are bruised, both of them, especially the tissue that remains on the left."

Kris looked down but did not open the cape. "I didn't realize."

"Several small bruises, worse on the left. You need to be careful, the skin graft is still maturing and the muscles underneath. That's the tissue that is going to be stressed the most when we start the reconstruction process. Tell your partner to be gentle."

"I...ah...yes, I will." Kris blushed furiously.

"Don't be embarrassed. The fact that you're having sexual relations again is a good sign that you're healing mentally. Intimacy is not always easy after a deployment. Add in the PTSD and the injuries, and well, not all the reunions are happy. At least for a while. With some couples, the physical intimacy takes months, years in some cases."

"I didn't realize it could take that long."

"For some couples, it can. Other than that you're doing okay? You look tired. Are you sleeping well?"

Kris was silent for several moments, remembering the assault the night before. How she paced the yard for hours before finally coming back inside to sleep in the guest room at three. She looked away before answering. "Yes, I had a breakthrough with Dr. Abbott the other day. She used hypnosis to help me. It's only been a few days, but I remembered some of what happened around the time of my injury."

"Good. I'll see you in about six weeks. If you have any problems, let me know right away."

"Yes ma'am." After the physician left the room, Kris jumped up and jerked the cape off. *Damn it!* A series of irregular circles were on each breast, worse on the left especially along the damaged outside area on the skin graft. Irregular circles consistent with fingers. *The only thing missing were the actual fingerprints.* Kris dressed quickly and left, pausing momentarily to pick up the appointment card for her next visit.

Chapter Twenty-four

RENEE QUESTIONED KRIS. "TELL me why you're not sleeping."

"I sleep, although it's not very long. I keep having this dream where someone is screaming. The dreams all end the same, but the beginning is different. Last night I dreamed I was in a restaurant and had ordered dinner. As the waiter turned away there was a blood-curdling scream. I ran into the kitchen and saw blood everywhere, but no one was there. A few nights ago I dreamed I was at my parents' house and heard a scream. In the dream, I run through their house trying to find out what's going on but only see bloody footprints, barefoot prints on the floor. Night after night, I have this strange screaming nightmare."

"Are you screaming?"

"No, it's not me. It's terrifying. Someone needs help, and I can't find them."

"That must be unnerving."

"It is."

"How long have you been having dreams like this?"

"A few weeks now. It started after I was in Bethesda for a few days. But it's getting worse. Sometimes it's happening twice a night. It's such a realistic dream, and I'm starting to be afraid to sleep. There is always a horrifying scream."

"Any idea what or who is screaming?"

Kris was silent. "No idea." She looked away from the psychologist and focused her gaze on the window. "The scream sounds familiar, but I've had this dream so many times, of course, it would be familiar."

"That sounds reasonable."

"I wish it would stop."

"Well, I can give you a prescription to help you sleep, but I am hesitant to do so."

Kris shook her head, "I don't want any pills."

"Good. Let's see if we can't figure out what this scream is about. How long were you in Afghanistan?"

"Seven months. This was my second tour. My first tour was for a year."

"Any nightmares after that tour?"

"Sure, I had some bad dreams but nothing like this."

"Why do you think you're having them this time?"

"I'm not sure. I think it must be cumulative. Seeing all those Marines and women get hurt. I think it must be getting to me."

"Did you see a lot of Marines?"

"Mostly because that's who we're assigned to."

"But you see all service branches and allies. How many women have you seen?"

"There's been a few."

"How many would you say?"

"I couldn't begin to guess. Some I would have treated directly. There would have been others I didn't treat but saw in the hospital."

"You must have some idea," Renee probed.

"I really don't." Kris pinched the bridge of her nose.

"Are you sure?"

"It's not something you keep track of."

Renee pressed her with more questions. "How many male patients would you say?"

"Hundreds. More."

"And females?"

"I don't know. Why do you keep asking that? I said I don't know how many." Kris stood up and walked away.

"I ask because you said, 'Seeing all those Marines and women get hurt.' So, I'll ask again, how many women do you think you've seen? Guess. Amuse me."

"Maybe one hundred." Kris returned to her chair.

"Do the women being hurt bother you?"

"They don't bother me. My job is to help people. That's why I became a doctor. Some of them stick with you longer than others."

"Who is Major Davies?"

Kris tensed, "I don't know."

"You don't know?"

"No. I don't." Kris brushed at her pants. Crossed and re-crossed her legs.

"Are you sure?"

"Yes...No...I can't remember the names of everyone I may have treated," Kris said with irritation.

"Did you treat her?"

Kris grit her teeth. "No."

"Are you sure? You said you couldn't remember the names of everyone. Maybe you did and don't remember."

"I'd remember her. She has short black hair and green eyes, a hint of gray at the edge."

"Tell me more."

"She's a helicopter pilot, marine squadron."

"So you know her?"

"No. I said I don't. You're confusing me." Kris rubbed at her temple.

"Commander, without looking at me, what color eyes do I have?"

"Um…ah…blue."

"No, they're brown. But that's a good guess, going with the blonde hair. How do you know what color eyes Major Davies has?"

Kris sprang up and paced, pushed at her hair, before pulling her left arm across her chest and holding it there squeezing it tightly with her right arm. "Why are you worried about her eye color? How would I know what color her eyes are? I'm sure you could find it in her medical record."

"It doesn't matter to me what color her eyes are. I find it interesting that you would know that her eyes are green if you don't know her. Green is not a common color. Why do you suppose you know the color of her eyes?"

Kris was sweating. She sat down, stood up immediately, and paced some more. "It was a guess. A lucky guess."

"No, it wasn't."

"It was." Kris tried to stop the trembling building through her body.

"Kris, tell me the truth. How did you meet Major Davies?"

"I don't know," Kris whispered.

"Yes, you do. Tell me."

Kris stared at the psychologist, "I tell you I don't know!" Her voice was frantic, almost pleading. *What are you looking for? Why are you stuck on if I know this woman? I feel sick. I'm going to be sick.*

"You do. Tell me the truth."

Kris paced around the room. She shuddered as memories came back in bits and pieces. She recalled running to the wrecked helicopter and crawling inside. The smells of fuel and blood and dirt. She remembered seeing the copilot was dead. She recalled taking the scalpel and making the cut. Kris stopped pacing. She felt dizzy. She heard the major scream. *Oh dear God. She felt everything.* Kris shouted, "I cut off her leg," and burst into tears. "I cut off her leg, and she screamed, and screamed, and screamed." Kris collapsed into a chair and wept.

A few minutes later Kris became aware Renee was sitting next to her, her arm draped across her shoulders. A box of tissues had been moved closer. Kris slowly brought herself under control. Eventually, she reached for the tissues. She wiped at her eyes, and blew her nose. After amassing a large pile of tissues, she stood and deposited them in the trash can. "May I have some water?"

"Yes." Renee retrieved a bottle of water from the small refrigerator and passed it to her. Kris was unable to hold the bottle and open it. She placed the bottle between her knees and tried to unscrew it to no avail. After several unsuccessful attempts, she put it back on the table and walked away.

"Would you like me to open that for you?"

"I would appreciate that."

"Why didn't you ask for help?"

"Because it's ridiculous that I can't even open a water bottle."

"You have an injury. Why would you think needing help is ridiculous? Don't you expect your patients to use their resources?" She handed the opened bottle to Kris. "Sit down and let's talk."

Kris stared at her, nodded slowly, and walked to the window, staring out while she drank greedily. She returned to her seat, set the bottle on the table and rubbed at the back of her neck. "I'm ready."

"Tell me more about what happened with Major Davies."

"She was trapped in the wreckage. To get her out I had to cut the leg off."

"The leg?"

"Major Davies' leg. Her right one." Kris took several large swallows of water. She related the story she'd tried so hard to forget.

"Why cut her leg off?"

"Her leg was pinned, badly mangled. I couldn't see it, but I could reach my hand down into it. I could feel exposed bone, jagged edges, torn muscle. There were insurgents attacking again. There was no way to get her free. So I did what had to be done to get her free."

"And you saved her life."

Kris was silent. She picked up her water, drank, and studied the label.

"Don't you think you helped her?"

"I got her free."

"If you hadn't gotten her free she would have been killed by the enemy or succumbed to her injuries, correct?"

"Yes."

"Why the rush to get her out?"

"I had no choice. We started taking fire. The medevac chopper was waiting. And she was unstable. She was running out of time. So we gave her another shot of morphine and a dose of Versed."

"Versed?" Renee challenged her, wanting Kris to remember the details.

"To make her forget. I couldn't put her to sleep, we didn't have the time or space. We gave her the medicine, and removed the leg."

"And she did well with it?"

"I don't know if she survived her other injuries. There was blood from under her helmet. I remember there were broken ribs, several of them probably. She may have had internal injuries. I didn't have time to access that. I don't know how she's doing."

"That's not what I meant. During the procedure, did Major Davies do all right?"

Kris looked down, studied her hands, and sweat rose on her back. Her chest tightened, her breathing quickened and grew coarse. She gasped for air and tugged at her collar. She craned her neck around, throwing her head back trying to take a deep breath. Her heart raced, and pounded hard enough in her chest she thought it would explode.

"Doctor Matthews, how did the major respond?" Kris jumped up and was half way across the room before Renee added, "Commander, what happened? Tell me what happened."

Kris shouted "She screamed! On and on and on."

"How long did she scream?"

Kris shouted, "The whole time!"

"Are you sure? I would think that most people would have passed out."

"No, she kept..." Kris bit down on her lip, stared off into the distance trying to remember. After several seconds she corrected herself. "No. She had passed out."

"So, she didn't scream the entire time?"

"She couldn't have."

"The scream you hear at night, does it sound like her?"

Kris looked at the psychologist and with tears in her eyes, whispered, "Yes." She sat down, bowed her head and shook.

"I know this is difficult for you. You've done well. I have one more question for you before we're done. If you can't answer it now, I want you to think about it until we meet in two days."

Kris sighed. "Okay."

"What hand did you hold the saw in?"

Kris looked down at her lifeless left hand, saw it holding the saw, the smear of blood across her fingers, the spray of marrow and bone chips coating the glove. She heard the major scream. She stuttered, "M...my left."

***

Kris slung her bag over her shoulder, placed the key in the lock, jiggled it until the lock sprung and pushed the front door open. Sighing, she swung it closed, leaned against it momentarily before turning the deadbolt. She shuffled the few steps to the closet placing her bag inside and hung up her hat. Glancing around the kitchen, she saw several dishes on the counter and tabletop, a pot on the stove. *Damn you.* "Thanks for leaving me a mess, Shelly." She filled a glass with water, sipping from it as she walked to the bedroom, and saw that the bed was unmade, sheets rumpled.

She shook her head in disgust and walked to the bathroom. She turned on the shower, and undressed while the water warmed. She checked it before stepping in. The water felt great coursing over her body, and the muscle tightness she had throughout the afternoon slowly faded.

It was the Major screaming. It haunts me. She couldn't have stayed conscious. She shouldn't remember, thank God. Now that I have that answered maybe I'll sleep tonight. But what about Shelly? Was that really an assault? I mean she's been rough before, but this was different. Like she was angry. Like she wanted to hurt me. But was it an assault? I came. I need to think about this. Maybe counseling. I need to end this. How the hell will she react to that? Why is she like this now? She lathered slowly, and shampooed and conditioned her hair. It took a while one-handed, but the warm water made it more enjoyable. When the water started to chill, she turned it off, toweled off and slipped into a pair of cotton shorts and a tank top.

Crossing into the kitchen, she looked at the mess. "Damn it, Shelly. Why did you leave this mess for me? Can you not do anything to help out? I'm not your maid." She opened the fridge, pulled out a salad, and ate it quickly while standing at the counter. She placed a lime slice in a glass of water and sipped. Scowling she cleaned up the plates and glasses from the table and counter, loading them into the dishwasher.

Something else was wrong, she just didn't know what. She topped off her water glass, before crossing to the bedroom. Disgusted, she went to the guest room, locked the door and collapsed onto the bed. Within seconds she was sound asleep. She awoke in the morning and was still alone. *Where had Shelly been all night? And do I even really care?*

Chapter Twenty-five

KRIS LEFT THE PHYSICAL therapy clinic, her arm trembling with fatigue. She was glad to be free of the brace and sling. She felt an ache all the way up to her shoulder. She hurried down the hall to the group therapy session, pausing for a moment to collect her thoughts before she entered the room.

She glanced around the room recognizing everyone, and was pleased to see Sam but stopped short when she noticed the hard look on the major's face. Kris bypassed the seat next to her and took a seat directly opposite instead.

A young lieutenant walked to the front of the room. "I'm Lieutenant Jennifer Brown, a clinical psychologist. Commander Abbott couldn't be here this afternoon, so I'll be filling in." As the session started, Sam remained unusually stiff in her seat. Kris watched as the major stole repeated surreptitious glances at the clock. Her leg would occasionally start to bounce and she would grab it with her hand and squeeze until the bouncing stopped. Over and over the cycle repeated. Kris and Sam startled and looked up when the counselor called Sam.

"Major, you've been quiet this afternoon. Is there anything you would like to talk about?"

"No. It's been a rough week. I have a lot on my mind."

"That's what we're here for. If you want to talk about it."

Kris looked around the room, her eyes drawn again to Sam sitting across from her. She had a sense of déjà vu but couldn't quite grasp the thought before it floated away. Sam was staring at her, and that caused a strange, unfamiliar feeling in her gut. She had to consciously avoid rubbing the ache in her stomach.

"No, I don't," Sam said firmly.

"Fair enough," Lieutenant Brown said.

"Is your leg hurting?" Kris asked. "You're bouncing it a lot. Are you uncomfortable?"

"No. I'm ready to go. I am tired of being in this place. I want to get out on my own again. But the docs don't think I'm ready yet. My strength and balance aren't good enough. I need to get better and find a place to live. I want to have something lined up so I can be ready to move in as soon as possible."

Lieutenant Brown asked, "And that's important to you? To get back on your own?'"

Kris almost chuckled at the look of incredulity that crossed Sam's face as she stared at the young woman.

"Of course, it's important. It would make me feel nor—" Sam bit down on her lip and grimaced.

"Finish your thought, Sam. Were you going to say normal?"

Sam was quiet before barely nodding her head. "Yes. It would help me to feel normal."

"You are normal. Everyone in this room is normal."

Kris watched as Sam glanced around the room and looked at everyone's faces. "I'm sorry. I don't feel that way inside. Not to myself." She tapped herself on the chest. "I left part of myself over there. I don't mean just my leg. But something inside is...gone. And I don't know what it is."

"It's hope." A young woman, perhaps in her early twenties, her face heavily scarred and stubby hair emerging from the wounded side of her head, spoke. "Your hope for a future is gone. A future where you were in control. Or at least you thought you were. You knew what you were going to do each day. You had a plan for what your future would hold not only in a year but probably in ten years, twenty. And now that's gone. Right now, you can't even walk out of this building without checking in with someone. And you have to get a ride instead of taking your own car. What do you drive, Major?" The woman grinned a lopsided smile that almost looked maniacal, but her eyes sparkled. "I bet it's a Mustang. All speed and muscle."

Sam looked surprised. "It is. But how?"

"How did I know? It was a guess. But if you have a 'stang it's black. You don't need flashy red or look-at-me yellow. You are in charge. The world was at your fingertips. Now you wonder if you'll drive it again."

"That's enough," the counselor interrupted.

"No. I want to answer that." Sam looked at Lieutenant Brown before she looked back at the young woman. "You're right. That car is my freedom. I can go where I want to. My chopper made it all possible. But the odds are against me getting in the air again. Oh, I'll try. I am trying. I'm doing everything in my power to get up there again. But the car is me. Just me."

Kris interjected, "Because you're strong in it. Powerful." Sam nodded. "You still are strong. We all are. We're finding a new strength. A new courage. We need more time to discover this new part of ourselves and see how strong we can be."

Their eyes locked across the room. Kris stared into the deep green eyes and felt her heart start to race. Sweat formed on the back of her neck as a feeling of dread overcame her. She broke eye contact and looked down at her feet, and repeatedly clenched her fists. She sat quietly trying to fight back what felt like a panic attack as the voices of the others carried on around her.

The session was over and Kris hurried from the room. Her one thought was to get home quickly and shake this feeling off. She was nearly outside when she heard her name called. She stopped and turned, watching as the major limped toward her. "Are you okay? You looked like...well, it looked like you were going to get sick. Are you okay to drive?"

"I'm fine. I needed to get outside. Like you said."

"Let's go outside. What made you sick?" Sam opened the door for her and followed her outside. Sam placed her hand on Kris' back and guided her over to a shaded bench. They sat, and Sam reached out and took Kris' left hand. "Your hand is shaking. When did you get the brace off?"

"A few days ago. It's weak." She poked at the muscles which had gone soft and shrunk. "I have a long way to go."

"But you're getting there. That's was a big step...getting out of the brace."

"Yes. In a lot of ways. Why were you nervous today?"

"I have a lot of stuff bottled up. I think if I let it out in there...well, they probably would lock me up in the psych unit." Sam stared at her. "You're a doc. I probably shouldn't have told you that."

"You have to talk to someone, Sam."

"I know. But there are some kids in there. They can't see their leaders falling apart."

"You are not falling apart. And we're all in this together. Did you ever think by not showing any weakness, some of those young women will compare themselves to you and feel even weaker? They might think that they don't have the necessary strength and courage?"

Sam looked at her. "No. I didn't. I'm not sure I agree with that either. It's not in my nature to admit fear...or weakness."

"School of hard knocks?"

Sam clenched her jaw. "Yeah. You could say that." She took a deep breath. "Does it look like you'll get back to being a doctor soon? I mean, I know you're a doc. I meant operating. Do they think you'll make a full recovery?"

"I know I will."

"You sound confident. Good. That's half the battle."

"Are you winning that battle, Sam?"

"Touché. Apparently not as well as I should." Sam grew quiet for several seconds. "When you were hurt, did anyone else get hurt?"

Kris hesitated, "I don't recall all the details. I don't believe so. From what was explained to me it doesn't sound like it."

"I lost some of my crew." Sam stared off into the distance. "They were good men. I wonder why they were killed and I was allowed to survive."

"That's survivor's guilt. We've talked about it in the group sessions."

"I know. Although, sometimes, at night they haunt me. And I wonder why did I get a second chance? Will I be able to make anything out my life now that I'm not whole? I've talked about it with Renee, but there it is. I feel guilty they're gone. I can't quit, but sometimes I want to. I wish..."

"You wish what?"

"Sometimes I wish I was gone." Kris jerked, and Sam held out her hands, "Don't get alarmed. That's happening less and less. At night, sometimes I am afraid, that I'll not be able to get through this. I wonder if you docs realize how scary that is?"

"I think I have a good idea."

Sam looked at Kris' arm, her gaze drifting up to meet Kris' eyes. "I guess you do. Although you have a good idea what your future holds. Most of us in that room don't know that."

"You'll get a better idea as time moves along. Trust me on this. Give yourself more time. Losing your leg is life changing. Right now you see what you've lost. Not what you've gained."

"What I've gained? You're right. I don't see where I've gained anything."

"It will come. Trust me."

"What have you gained?"

"It's hard to describe. I feel it though. And our injuries have given us the chance to meet. I wouldn't have met you otherwise. I'll take all the good I can gather to help get me through the bad days."

"I'll keep that in mind. Tell me something. One of the first things I want to do when I get out of here is to go see my crew members' families. Do you think that's okay? I don't want to stir up any pain. Still, I need to know that they're doing okay."

"I understand, and that's noble of you."

"It's not noble. I need to know their families are okay."

"And if they're not?"

"I'll do what I can to make it better."

"Like I said, that's noble."

Sam's phone buzzed, and she removed it from her pocket. "Sorry. I have a meeting with my career liaison. I have to go."

"Sure thing." As Sam stood up to leave, Kris reached out and took her hand. "It'll get better. It might be awhile before it gets easier, but it will get better."

"Thanks. See you around."

Kris watched as Sam walked away. The woman was holding something inside. A deep anger perhaps? Sitting quietly she reviewed their conversation. Sam was stable. She didn't fear that she would hurt herself intentionally. There was rage there, barely under the surface. She hoped Sam found a way to let it out. Her own phone buzzed. With a smile on her face she answered the phone. "Hi, Mom. Yes, I'm doing well. You heard right. My arm is moving. It's weak, but it's moving. It's a long story." She stood and walked to her car.

***

Kris and Shelly sat at the dinner table. "The therapy on my arm is helping. It's weak, but it is moving again. I'm getting more shoulder motion back. The hand strength is coming along. I have a tremor in it, fortunately, it's lessening. So I feel good."

Shelly did not respond to her comment. Kris poked at the chicken on her plate, pushing it from side to side, occasionally taking a bite. Despite its seasonings, it tasted bland, and the rice was no better. Finally, she pushed the plate aside and brought her salad closer. She ate that quickly.

"You need to eat something other than salad," Shelly grumbled.

"I'm not that hungry. I'll take it for lunch tomorrow."

"You had an appointment today didn't you?" Shelly drained her wine glass and refilled it.

"I have appointments a couple times a week...physical therapy, counseling. I had one for my arm today."

"I'm not talking about those. The appointment for your boob." Shelly gestured with her fork. "That mental stuff will get better. You have to relax. I want to know when they're going to fix your tit."

Kris stared at her in disbelief. "You only want to know about my breast? You don't want to hear about my arm?"

"Not really. It's moving," Shelly said with disdain.

"It's moving? Do you realize if I can't get my strength back, or get better hand control, I can't be a surgeon? I'd have to leave the military."

Shelly drained her wine glass. "That wouldn't be a bad thing."

"What do you think I would do if I can't operate? In or out of the military, if I can't hold the scalpel, if I can't control it or the other equipment, I can't work."

"Well just be a family doctor, like your father."

"It doesn't work that way, Shelly. Don't you—"

"Listen, you'll get your arm strength back, and those crazy sessions you go to will get you to stop being so twitchy."

"Crazy sessions? Twitchy?" She shouted, "God, who are you?"

"I'm the same person I've always been."

"No, you're not. Christ, Shelly, you assaulted me. You grabbed me. Pushed me against the wall hard enough to hurt my head. I told you no, but you kept going. You hurt me."

"Assault? Bullshit. You came like you always do. You like it rough. Oh yeah, every so often I have to get all soft and gentle for you. But I know what you like. You sure didn't put up much of a fight." Shelly grinned and drained her wine glass. "You're the one who came back cuckoo." Shelly twirled her finger around her temple.

Kris pushed back from the table, scraped her food into the trash and thrust her dishes into the dishwasher. "I'm not crazy. You have no idea what it's like over there. What it does to someone."

"Oh, I think I have an excellent idea. I see you and others like you. Jumping when a car backfires, or there's a loud bang. You'd think you were all babies getting startled by loud noises, not big brave warriors," she snickered.

Kris opened and closed her mouth several times, although nothing came out. She stood speechless, for several seconds before she walked out. Several minutes later she returned, grabbed her keys and wallet and stormed out, leaving without speaking to Shelly. She drove aimlessly for an hour and was somewhat surprised to find herself at the beach.

She kicked off her shoes and walked down to the water, dipping her feet in. The water was warm, comfortable. She watched as the wave wash flowed back and forth over her feet, creating little divots in the sand as she sank in. A seagull landed nearby and eyed her carefully, watching to see if a morsel would be offered. They stared blankly at each other until the bird gave up and moved further down the beach to where a child played as his parents sat nearby. Kris moved back up away from the water and sat in the sand, looking out at the sea. *Which one of us has changed the most? What did I ever see in her? I can't even remember. I've changed. I don't have the patience for small talk anymore. And people whining about some perceived slight makes me want to shake them. How much longer am I willing to try? Will Shelly go to counseling? Do I want this to work?*

She makes me uneasy now. I never know what's going to set her off. She's drinking a lot. Too much. Every night, three to four drinks, usually whiskey, often with beer or wine in the same evening. Drinks with lunch on weekends, sometimes at breakfast with a bloody Mary or a screwdriver. Shelly always drank more than me, but never to the excess that she is now. Is work getting to her? Do I need to give her more support? Maybe the apple didn't fall far from the tree?

***

Two hours later she returned home and sat in the driveway for several minutes contemplating what to say to Shelly. *We both need more time to adjust to being together again. We've been together for five. But I've been gone for two. My nightmares take a toll on Shelly also. She must be sleep deprived too. But over the last week, I've only had one nightmare. Perhaps they're over.* With a sigh, she climbed out of the car. *Please be asleep, I can't stand the thought of you touching me again.*

Kris entered the house quietly, gave a silent sigh that the dinner mess was cleaned up and Shelly was not awake. Or at least she wasn't in the living room watching TV. She peered in the darkened bedroom, saw that she was sleeping. Kris grabbed a nightshirt and went to shower. She lingered under the warm spray, enjoying the water pulsing from the shower head against her shoulders and neck. When the water started to chill, she turned it off, reached her hand out, and grabbed her towel. She was startled as Shelly stood leaning against the counter.

"You finally came home. Where did you go?"

"Down to the beach. I needed to think. You pissed me off, Shelly."

"I know. I'm sorry. Let me make it up to you." Shelly reached out and moved Kris' hands away from the half knot holding the towel closed over her.

Kris grabbed her hand. "I'm tired, Shelly."

"I said I was sorry. Let's make up." She pulled the towel away in a rough jerk.

"Shelly, I don't want to...aggh." She backed away, held her hands over her aching breast as tears sprung to her eyes. She cupped her breasts trying to soothe the pain from where Shelly had grabbed her and twisted. Her voice tight with pain she choked back the tears. "Why did you do that? Can't you see I'm already bruised?"

"Oh please, stop with drama. You've always liked me to be rough with your tits."

"No, not like this."

"I don't see bruises any different than before. You've always liked rough sex. Stop pretending you don't," Shelly snapped as she advanced.

Kris stuck her hand out. "No. I'm not giving in to you tonight. I am going to bed, and you're not touching me. Leave me the hell alone." She pushed Shelly and stepped by her grabbing the nightshirt and pulling it over her head as she walked out of the bathroom.

Shelly followed her into the bedroom, pulled clothes from the closet and dressed quickly, "I'm not putting up with this shit from you. I'm going out." She stomped out of the room, several seconds later the front door slammed. Kris walked to the front door locked it, turned off the lights and climbed into bed.

When she awakened in the morning, Shelly still wasn't home. Kris dressed quickly and left for work early. She wanted to be gone before Shelly returned from wherever she had spent the night this time.

Chapter Twenty-six

SAM FINISHED DRESSING AND left the locker room. Walking down the hall, she noticed Kris stretching in the glass fronted studio. She stopped and looked through the glass window. She waved when Kris looked up. Kris gestured for her to come into the studio and Sam smiled and nodded agreement.

Sam watched as Kris continued to stretch while she entered the room. *Whoa, she is seriously flexible.* "I thought that it was you. I haven't seen you in a while, it looks like your arm is doing better."

Kris smiled. "It is. Now there's a chance I'll get back to performing surgery again."

Sam couldn't help but notice the way Kris' eyes sparkled and how she smiled when she mentioned getting back into the operating room. *I hope I get a second chance too.* "That's great. Any idea when?"

Kris sat down on the floor to stretch her legs, and leaned forward to grab her toes. "No idea. I need to get my fingers moving better and get my strength up. Enough about me. How have you been? How's therapy?"

"Therapy sucks." Sam grinned as she said it. "They're doing their best to kick my ass. I'm on the stationary bike for thirty minutes at a time. That's good, and I'm allowed to work out on my own. I'm almost starting to feel like myself again."

"You're doing well."

Kris stood and reached her arms overhead, as she did her shorts slid up revealing a rectangular scar on her thigh. Sam tried not to stare at the scar, but its symmetry drew her eyes like a magnet. She looked up to see Kris watching her. "I'm sorry. I shouldn't have stared. God knows I know how that feels."

"It's alright. It's from a skin graft. It doesn't hurt. It gets a little buzzy occasionally."

"That's good...that it doesn't hurt." They both looked over when several people started to enter the room and lay out yoga mats. "Well, it looks like I should get going. It was good to see you."

"You too." Kris watched as Sam started to walk away. She glanced at her watch. It was coming up on six o'clock. "Hey, Sam? Would you like to get some dinner? If you can wait until I clean up?"

"Ah sure. That would be good. I'm tired of eating in the unit." *This could be fun.*

"I'll just be about fifteen minutes. You can decide where you would like to eat."

"I'll wait out in the lobby."

***

The pizzeria was small and rundown. Kris hesitated before climbing out of the car. Sam laughed at her hesitation. "Don't let the outside fool you, the food is great. Trust me. You'll love it."

"Let's go."

Sam opened the door for Kris, and they squeezed into a vacant high top. Within minutes they had ordered, and their drinks arrived. "So, Doc, what do you do for fun?"

"I like hiking and camping. Back country, not just going to some campground with trailers parked twenty feet from each other. You look surprised."

Sam nodded her head and smiled. "I am. I can't picture you carrying a pack and sleeping in a tent. Where have you been?"

"The Sierra Nevadas. I was with some friends in the John Muir wilderness. We hiked, camped, and fished. We spent some time rock climbing and rappelling too. I'm not sure that I'll be dangling from the end of a rope off the edge of a mountain again. I discovered that I do have a fear of heights after all."

Sam laughed. "That's not the best time to make that discovery. The Sierra Nevadas? That's serious backcountry."

"It is. You know, Sam, not all doctors spend their free time on the golf course or tennis courts."

"I just thought that you medical types were protective of your hands. So, what type of fishing do you do?"

"I prefer fly fishing. It's great out west. Here in the east it's hard to find secluded places, and the rivers are so narrow here, it makes it more difficult. It was a treat to spend that time out west, in the solitude."

"When were you out there?"

"About two years ago. I went between tours to Afghanistan."

"You went over twice?"

"Yes."

"Why? I thought they rotated you folks."

"They do. I volunteered to go back over. There were some folks who didn't want to go. It made me mad. Some of these guys sign up and are all macho. You know, like, I'm a military doctor, blah, blah, blah, but when the shit hits the fan they want to back out. Most aren't like that, but even one is more than enough. I volunteered to go back over. I thought I could make a difference, especially since I had been through it before."

You're not like I thought. Sam smiled. "You're not afraid to get down and dirty. I like that. I figured you for a Zumba dancing vegan."

It took Kris a good fifteen seconds to stop laughing. "Really? Well, what do you like to do for fun?"

Sam waited to answer while the waitress put the pepperoni and mushroom pizza in front of them. "Do either of you gals need a refill?"

"Yes, please," They answered simultaneously.

When the waitress walked away, Kris spoke, "You were getting ready to tell me what you like to do."

Sam spoke while she slid slices of pizza onto the plates. "Well, I like to ski, downhill and water. I had a boat, but I sold it before heading over to the desert. There was no sense in continuing payments, insurance, and storage on it when it was just going to sit around."

"That's smart."

"I like camping and hiking too. I went up to Denali twice. I was hoping to through hike on the Appalachian Trail, but that was going to be after retirement." Sam shrugged. "That's crossed off the list now."

"That's not necessarily true. The technology in some of the prosthesis is amazing. Just look at what the athletes in the Paralympics do. They're skiing, kayaking, running. It may not happen this year or even next year. As your strength returns and you get used to the prosthesis, I think you'll be amazed at what you'll be able to do."

"I hope so." Sam touched her pizza with her finger before lifting the slice. "I can't believe you've never had pizza here before."

"Well, I know the places closer to my house. This is closer to the airfield correct?"

"Yes. We're about five miles from the gate." Sam took a bite. "I actually dreamed of this pizza a couple times when I was in the desert." Kris laughed. "Wait 'til you try it. Besides let's face it, the chow hall leaves a lot to be desired."

"So, did you dream about a beer to wash it down with?"

"Not that I recall. The sweet tea here is fantastic."

"A true southern girl."

"Born and raised. Chattanooga."

"I thought I detected just a hint of magnolia in your voice. So, southern girl, why aren't you drinking sweet tea?"

"I figure since I'm not quite as active I should cut out the extra calories."

Kris reached out and touched Sam's arm. "I think you're safe from getting heavy. You may not feel like you're doing a lot, but trust me, your body is burning through those calories while you heal. And I know therapy is working you hard."

"That's for sure." Sam took another bite. "I really love this sauce. Tangy. It has some zip to it. It's not sweet, like the chain pizza places."

Kris took a bite and chewed. "Oh, that is good. You're right. It's bold." She took another bite. "I understand why you would dream of this pizza. It's a big step up from MRE's."

"Indeed." They both thanked the waitress when she returned with their drinks. Sam grinned broadly. "I did get some good news today."

"What's that?"

"I should get my permanent prosthesis in a few weeks, and I've been medically cleared so I can move out of the medical barracks." Sam's body lightened as she shared her news and she felt calmer than she had in several weeks. "I already signed a lease, and the landlord agreed for me to make some cosmetic changes to the house. I have to hire a handyman to install some things I need, handrails and a shower seat." Sam shrugged a shoulder. "I told the landlord I would do it, but he wants them professionally installed. At first, I thought he was being condescending, thinking because I was an amputee that I didn't have the skills. But it's more of a liability factor." She grinned. "I'll be able to move in about five weeks."

Kris patted Sam's hand. "That's great. Congratulations. I know you were looking forward to it."

A subtle warmth spread through her arm with Kris' touch and lingered after Kris removed her hand. "I am." She paused to wipe her mouth. "I found a place in town to convert my car to hand controls, so I can drive again. I've been checking online, trying to get an idea of what was involved with the conversion process and how much it costs. The price was reasonable, in line with what other areas charge. I'll have to go back to the motor vehicle department, and I can say I am looking forward to that day. I don't even care if it's crowded and I have to wait."

"When will it be done?"

Sam grinned. "I'm third on his list, so about two weeks. Hopefully, I'll be cleared by medical to give it a try."

"Let me know. I'll help you get your car to the shop. That way you won't have to pay the pick up or a towing fee."

"Thanks. That would be great. I'm starting to feel like things will work out."

"They will. Just keep at it." They each had another slice while they talked about other places they'd traveled to. Eventually, the waitress came by and boxed up the remaining slices of pizza.

"Any place else you want to go?"

"You'll get your stamina back, it just takes a while." A few minutes later Kris dropped Sam off near the medical barracks.

Sam watched as Kris drove off. *It was nice to have someone to talk to. Who would've thought we'd have so much in common?*

* * *

Sam sat at the table sipping her second beer, around her the mating ritual was under way. Young butches eyeing the femmes, circling the dance floor, watching and waiting. Lights flashed, stale cigarette smoke filled the room and the air conditioner failed to keep up with the heat rising from the hot bodies gyrating to the music. A local band with a screeching lead singer, and a guitarist who couldn't keep on the beat entertained, or at least amused.

Sam was eyeing a luscious blonde when her view was blocked. She looked up and into intense blue eyes. The owner of those eyes stopped her breath. Her sundress revealed firm, toned arms and smooth skin. Her medium brown shoulder length hair swung free and framed her face. As she smiled, her glossy lips parted to reveal perfect teeth and a broad smile that reached her eyes.

"Hello, would you mind if I shared your table? It's so crowded."

"Not at all." Sam gestured to the chair across from her. The woman sat down and placed her wine on the table. She glanced around the room and back to Sam.

"This crowd gets younger and younger all the time."

Sam was intrigued by her bright blue eyes. "It seems like it. I don't think I was ever that young though."

When a hip-hop song came on the woman sighed. "How can they dance to this? What's wrong with a song that encourages you to dance as a couple with your hands on each other?"

Sam leaned forward. "Like what?"

"I know this is a lot earlier than my time, but what's wrong with some classic like 'Hold Me, Thrill Me?'"

"Johnny Mathis or Mel Carter?" Sam smiled.

The woman broke into a broad smile. "Mel Carter." She took a long sip of her wine, and Sam motioned to the waitress for a refill of both their drinks.

When a slow song came on, Sam held out her hand. "Care to dance?"

"I'd love to."

The DJ kept the music slow for the next few songs. Sam was amazed and how well they moved together. When the DJ picked up the tempo, and the dance floor once again became crowded they stayed on the floor and continued to dance. It wasn't long before their close body contact had them both aroused. The woman held out her hand. "Sam, come with me."

Sam hurried while she was pulled along, they pushed through a door that Sam had not previously noticed and were in a back hallway. The woman turned and jerked Sam toward her, wrapping her hands around Sam's head and pulling her forward in a hard, passionate kiss.

A quick punch of desire jolted Sam. Instantly aroused she pushed the woman back against the wall, and slid her hands down over her full breasts. Sam nipped the woman's bottom lip then soothed it with gentle flicks of tongue.

Moans filled her ears and emboldened her more. No longer thinking rationally and not afraid of being discovered Sam brushed her hands along her collarbone, found the sundress straps and pushed them down. She tugged the top of the dress lower freeing breasts. Sam paused momentarily to appreciate the most beautiful pair of breasts she had ever seen, before she lowered her mouth to them. Strong hands pushed against her head, driving her into that wonderful cleavage further. Sam shifted and ran a hand down across a firm, slender thigh, and then lifted it over her arm.

Sliding her hand along smooth skin, Sam groaned with pleasure when she realized there were no panties covering the firm butt. She slid her hand further and discovered the woman was soaked, her sex hot and slick. Running her hand across her vulva, Sam slowly teased her folds apart before penetrating her, sliding two fingers in. Her thumb teased around the woman's clit and groans filled the air. The scent of their *arousal grew thick. Their kiss grew more frantic as Sam stroked into the woman. Nails racked down Sam's back, biting into the skin. The woman arched and screamed, as voices came from over Sam's shoulders.* Sam froze momentarily, and after a few seconds of confusion reached out and slapped at the radio alarm silencing the DJ's morning banter. "God dammit!" Sam sat up in bed, rubbed her hands over her face and groaned in frustration. Two more seconds and she would have orgasmed in her sleep. *Where the hell did that dream come from? And why did the woman seem vaguely familiar?*

Chapter Twenty-seven

"HOW IS YOUR ARM doing?" Renee asked.

Kris looked at it and smiled. "It's moving well and getting stronger." She wiggled her fingers, clenched her fist and finally rolled her wrist around. "It seems odd that my brain could shut off my arm like that. It was a conversion reaction."

Renee sat back. "In part. In conversion reactions, there is no physical injury only the mental one from a traumatic event. You do have a physical injury, and that will improve with therapy and time. You were hurt emotionally when you lost a child that was special to you. Shortly after that, you had to do a necessary procedure on a patient that on some level violated your oath of 'to do no harm,' because you couldn't properly anesthetize her. Even though you had done amputations before, this one was different. This time, the patient was awake. I expect you'll continue to progress with your therapy now. I wouldn't be surprised if you're not back operating within the next few weeks."

"That's good. I'm left handed. And a one-armed surgeon isn't good for a lot."

"There's more to you than your surgical skills."

"I know. Surgery is what I'm paid to do, and that's what I need to get back to."

"I understand. Kris, you're aware that they will reintroduce you to the operating room slowly. You'll have to assist on some cases. They'll watch to see how you do."

"Yes, I've thought of that. I understand that it's for the safety of the patients. I was able to arrange some time in the procedure lab at one of the medical schools up in Raleigh. I think it will help me get back up to speed and see what my limitations are."

"Good. If you want to talk about it as it gets closer, or at any time, let me know."

Kris hesitated for a moment. "Would it be possible to find out where the major is and how she's doing?"

"What do you mean?"

"I'd like to know if she's doing all right. I don't know anything about her or where she's from. She had many injuries, and her face was swollen and bloody. I remember that the whites of her eyes had hemorrhaged. I think I said last week her hair was black but it may have been brown. There was a little peeking out from her helmet. I keep remembering a little more each day, and it's not as upsetting. I don't remember getting hurt. It had to happen around that same time, correct?"

"I think that's a reasonable assumption. I think as time passes you'll remember additional details. Some will be important, others not so much. Write them down in your journal, if you wish. If anything surprises you or leaves you unsettled call me and we can discuss it."

"All right," Kris replied, feeling good about the session so far.

"How is your relationship with your...ah, partner?"

"Why do you ask?" Kris was instantly cautious.

"Re-integration comes with family difficulties frequently. You've done two tours over there. You've seen things and are injured. That takes an emotional toll on the family too."

What is she getting at?

"What are you thinking about?" Renee asked.

"I...I wonder what you know about me? I wonder what's in my medical file. I've never looked."

"Relax Kris. It doesn't say anything about your sexual orientation in your medical file. I saw you at the Pink Flamingo a couple of years ago. I knew you looked familiar, it took me some time to place you."

Kris studied her. "I didn't realize..."

"What, that I'm gay? Well, it's not like I go around with a sign on my forehead that says lesbian on it. Neither do you."

"But I usually—"

"Oh yes, the gaydar. Well, it's probably off right now while you heal. You've been through a lot and are still healing. I'm sure it will turn back on eventually."

"I'm not so sure." Kris was silent for several seconds, before she blurted out, "It bothers me...my breast. I don't feel...feminine. Don't get me wrong I'm much more concerned with my arm, getting it strong again. And with getting rid of these flashbacks as much as possible. But my breast...does it make sense if I say it feels more personal?"

"It certainly does. It's a more intimate injury. Your breast is covered most of the time. You see it when you bathe, dress or when you're being intimate."

"Shelly, my partner, dislikes it. I do too."

"How does she demonstrate that?"

"She generally won't...uh...touch it. Or if she does, well, it's not so enjoyable for me."

"She's rough with it?"

"Yes." Kris shifted in her seat.

"And have you told her she's hurting you?"

"Yes. But she forgets. She gets caught up in the moment."

"Is she rough..." Renee cleared her throat. "Is she as rough on the other side?"

"It doesn't seem like it." Kris thought for a few seconds. "No, she definitely isn't."

"Have you asked her to stop or to be more careful?"

"Yes."

"Is there any other way she shows her dislike for your injury?"

Kris was silent and looked away. Focusing out the window, she tried desperately to keep control of her emotions. Her throat tightened and her eyes filled. She brushed her fingers under her eyes catching the tears as they started to fall.

"Kris?"

Kris shuddered, and bent forward covering her chest. "She...she called me Frankentit." She cried quietly, fighting to keep some control of her emotions. It took several minutes, but she regained some control. Using tissues from the ever-present tissue box, she dried her face and cleared her throat several times. "I guess when you think about it, it is funny."

"Do you think it's funny? Do you like her saying that?"

"No. Not at all." She sniffed.

"Is there any other way she shows dislike for your appearance?"

"We don't shower together anymore. Lately, she's even wanted me to stay covered when we're...intimate. Recently we stopped sleeping together."

"How does that make you feel?"

"Hurt. But now talking about it, seeing it all put together like this, it makes me mad. She keeps asking about the reconstruction. I've told her several times that it'd be several months before it can start, maybe even a year."

"And how does she react?"

"She wants me to get a second opinion. She thinks the military is drawing it out."

"Do you?"

"No. Not at all. I understand the healing stages and dangers."

"Kris, I have to ask you, are you thinking about the reconstruction for yourself or for your partner?"

"Both."

"How has Shelly reacted to your arm injury?"

"She gets a little frustrated. I do too. It takes longer to do everything. But now that my movement is coming back and I'm able to do some things with it, things will get better," Kris said hopefully.

"Has she hurt your arm?"

"She has pulled it several times, when the brace was off."

"Kris, I have to ask you this. Are you in a safe relationship? Do you feel safe in your home?"

Kris hesitated. *Do I? If Shelly comes home drunk again will I be safe? She needs help. It's the alcohol. Or work. Or something.* Aware of the long silence Kris answered, "Well, yes. Of course, I do."

"If things get worse, or Shelly refuses to change, do you have a safe place to go?"

"This is ridiculous," Kris huffed.

"Answer the question, Commander."

"Yes, I feel safe in my home. Yes, I have some place I could go if I felt I was in danger," Kris said, the discipline back in her voice.

"Good." Renee reached over and took a business card from the table. She scribbled on the back. "Here is my card. My cell number is on the back. If you need to talk or get away for a little while call me. Any time. I mean it. Call me if you need help."

"Yes, ma'am."

Kris drove home taking the long route, replaying the conversation from the afternoon. *Renee was right. Her relationship was bordering on abusive. No. It had become abusive. When had that started? More importantly, why was she tolerating it?*

Chapter Twenty-eight

KRIS KNOCKED ON THE door frame and stuck her head in. "Aunt Kat?"

Dr. Katherine Matthews looked up. "Kris, it's so good to see you." She came around her desk and hugged Kris. "Let me look at you. Oh, you've lost weight. How's your arm? When your father called and said you'd been hurt, I was scared. Finally you got to Bethesda and your parents were able to visit. We finally got details. Thank God, you're getting better."

Kris saw sympathy cross her aunt's face. "I'm doing as well as can be expected. I've actually picked up a few pounds. I had lost some weight over there. Therapy is going well." She lifted her arm overhead. "It's weak, but I have great movement, and my finger dexterity is coming back." She wiggled her fingers.

"I'm glad you trusted me enough to tell me about your counseling sessions. I think what we have planned out is going to be beneficial. I would love to sit down and have dinner with you, but I know that you want to get to the lab right away. In your situation, I would too. Let's go. I'll need to stay with you because of security reasons."

"I understand."

They walked to a locker room and changed quickly into scrubs. They walked the short distance to the lab and hesitated at the door. "You wanted to start with an adult?"

"Yes."

"I have one picked out. Several procedures have already been done on this specimen. The abdomen has been untouched so you can do the procedures you want to."

"Thank you."

They slipped on surgical garb and walked to the table.

"My pleasure, Kris. When the medical school admin heard that a military surgeon had been injured and was trying to get back into the operating room, they backed the idea of giving you lab time. The hospital board approved it too. Are you ready?"

"Yes."

Katherine pulled the drape back on the cadaver. Kris took a moment to look at the deceased, and then picked up the scalpel.

***

The next morning Kris stood silent, trying to control the shake in her hand as she stared down at the child cadaver. Sweat poured down her back. *I can do this. Breathe. Take a minute. Get a hold of yourself. Come on. Focus. Think about what you need to do. Deep breath, in and out.*

"Kris? Come on, step back. It's all right."

Kris looked up and saw the compassion in her aunt's eyes. "No. I can do this." She took a deep breath, held out her hand. "Scalpel."

Two hours later Kris sat in her aunt's office sipping on juice. "Overall I think that went well. I had a little problem with the child at first."

"You recovered well. You stayed calm and thought about what needed to be done. So far you've done eight procedures. Is there anything else you want to do?"

Kris nibbled at a sandwich. "Can we do rounds?"

"I was able to get you visiting physician privileges so we can. Let's finish lunch and go see my patients. I don't think anything will be as exciting as what you've had over the last year."

"It's all important, Aunt Kat."

"That's true."

***

Two hours later Kris stood outside the children's wing and wiped sweat from her brow. *Dear God, children can smell fear. The longer I was in there, the worse it was. I have to get better with kids.* Kris looked up when her aunt emerged from the children's rooms. "It's okay, Kris. You did well. I know you don't think so, but you did. Especially with Bobby. He's a pistol, always challenging the staff and generally causing havoc. What do you say we call it a day, go soak in the hot tub, and you can get me up to speed on what else is going on? Afterward, we'll go someplace nice for dinner tonight."

"That sounds good. Aunt Kat? Thanks again for getting this

arranged for me. I know you had to call in some favors."

"My pleasure. It's a joy to see you work."

***

Kris pulled into the driveway, and looked at the car parked in front of the house. It looked vaguely familiar, but she couldn't place it. Perhaps one of the neighbors had a new car. She went down to the mailbox and retrieved the mail. Glancing through it, she realized it was nothing but junk mail. She went into the house, pausing momentarily to put her bag in the closet. She was halfway to the kitchen, when she stopped suddenly, turned and listened. Her pulse quickened, a cold knot formed in her stomach and she turned to walk down the hall. She stopped outside the door listening, recognized the sound, and quietly opened the door. The mail fluttered to the floor as she watched, their hurried grappling, their frantic violent kiss, their smell was thick in the air.

"What the hell are you doing?" Kris shouted.

They flew apart like thieves in the night. "Oh, shit!" The woman grabbed clothes from the floor and ran into the bathroom. Shelly pulled the sheet up covering herself.

"It's not—"

"Do not even tell me it is not what I think! I know exactly what I saw! Get dressed and get that woman out of my house." She struggled to control her voice, to not shriek in anger. She swallowed hard. "Now." She stomped out of the room, stood at the kitchen entryway, and waited. The woman emerged and looked cautiously at Kris before she ducked her head and ran out of the house.

Shelly emerged a few seconds later and Kris saw the anger in her eyes. But this time she wouldn't cower in the face of Shelly's temper. "How could you do this to me?" Kris shouted.

"To you? Please. You've been gone more than you were here the last three years. You left me."

"I deployed! I was working. I didn't have a choice."

Shelly snapped, "Sure you did! You didn't have to go back."

"I needed to go back. Christ, Shelly don't you understand the concept of the military?"

"I do. And it's volunteer service. You could have gotten out."

"No, I couldn't. Not yet. And I didn't want to. They needed me over there."

"There are other doctors," Shelly hollered.

"That's not the point."

"That's exactly the point! You chose to go over. Did you even try to get your orders changed?"

"That's not how things work. You know that."

"Well, I know you sure as hell don't put a priority on this relationship so why should I? For all I know you could have been fucking some hot nurse over there," Shelly shouted.

"What? God damn it, Shelly, it's not some freaking beach party. It's a war zone."

"You mean to tell me no one is getting laid over there? No one is getting personal? Getting friendly?"

"That's against—"

"Policy. Oh, I know that. But let's be realistic. People find ways to hook up."

"I didn't. I don't cheat," Kris screamed.

"Well, what was I supposed to do? Wait until Uncle Sam decided to send you home again? And you came back damaged! Pacing the floor at night, crying out in the middle of your sleep like some psycho. Christ, you sweat half the night. If I wanted sweat like that I'd sleep with a man."

"What?"

"You heard me. That's only the half of it. Look at you. You've lost weight, you don't even look decent anymore, and that's with your clothes on. Take those off, and well, you're hideous. Why would I want to look at that? So, I wanted to be with someone who looks good...who is sexy...who is normal."

"Get out!" Kris thrust her arm out and pointed to the front door.

"What?"

"Get the hell out of my home," Kris screamed.

"I live here."

"Your name is not on the mortgage, or on the bills. Get out." Kris stormed into the bedroom, grabbed a suitcase from the closet and started stuffing Shelly's clothes into it. Shelly watched from the doorway as Kris slammed the bag shut, and flinched when she threw it at her. "Get the fuck out. Go to your sexy perfect girlfriend. I'll get your stuff packed. You can pick it up tomorrow. It'll be in the driveway."

"Don't you think you're being ridiculous? It's not like you've wanted to have sex."

"Get out. Get out!" Kris picked up a bottle of perfume and threw it at Shelly. It busted against the wall spraying her with perfume, the smell instantly saturating the air. "Get out and don't come back."

With her suitcase in her hand, Shelly hurried to the door. "Freaking psycho." Shelly ducked out the door as a book slammed into the wall inches away from her head.

.

Chapter Twenty-nine

KRIS STEPPED OUT OF the shower, wrapped her towel around herself, and rapidly moved to her locker. She spun the combination, opened the lock, and pulled her clothes out. Toweling off she put her bra on quickly and pulled her shirt over her head. She finished dressing at a more leisurely pace. She stepped over to the counter and applied some makeup before returning to the locker and gathering her gear. As she was walking out of the locker room, she saw a familiar face. "Hey, Sam, how are you doing?"

Surprise crossed Sam's face. "Hey Kris. I'm okay. How are you?"

"I'm well. How's therapy going?"

"Good. I'm able to do stairs now, and they have me getting up and down from the floor with and without the prosthesis."

"Oh, that's good." Kris pointed to a flyer hanging on the wall. "Are you doing any of the events next weekend?"

"I don't feel up to it."

Kris looked closely at Sam, saw the tiredness in her eyes, and the sadness. "It could be fun."

"I'm not ready."

"Well, maybe not for some things. Surely you could shoot a basketball? I can't imagine a marine not being ready to do a little competition. You don't have to play full court ball."

"I didn't know that." Sam looked at Kris, studying her.

"You should sign up. Get out and socialize a little." She reached a hand out, touched Sam on the forearm and felt an unusual warmth pass under her hand. "It's a good program, Sam."

"I know. I..." Sam was mortified to feel herself choking up, as a wave of sadness washed over her.

"You what?"

"Ah...nothing. I have to go, I wanted to get a workout in, and they close early on Fridays."

Kris touched her arm again, the same warmth tingled through her hand. "Talk to me. I can see that something is bothering you."

"I'm fine."

"I'm worried about you now." Kris searched Sam's face for some sign of her emotions.

"Kris, I want to go work out."

"Okay. Go ahead. I'll give you an hour. But, I'm coming back, and I hope you'll join me for a coffee before I head home."

"I was going to be here longer. How about if I meet you down at the Coffee Bean around six?"

"I'll see you soon. Have a good workout." Kris smiled broadly and felt her own mood lighten as she agreed to the plan.

***

Kris walked into the coffee shop and looked around. It took a few moments before she saw Sam sitting at a corner table. She noticed the crutches propped against the wall and hurried over. "What happened? Did you get hurt during your workout?"

"I got a blister on my stump. I can't put the thing back on until it heals. I'm going to be crutching around for a few days."

"Oh, that's bad."

"They said to expect it and warned me not to ignore little skin problems. So, I'll be hobbled for a few days. What would you like?" Sam motioned for the waitress to come over.

The young redhead arrived and smiled. "What would you like, hon?"

"I'll have a dark roast, one cream," Kris said.

The waitress turned to Sam and gave her a long, appreciative look. "How about you, Sam? Do you need a refill?"

"Sure, thanks."

Kris couldn't help notice the long appreciative look the waitress gave Sam before she walked away. Kris turned her attention back to Sam. "Are you a regular here?"

"I was before I went over to Afghanistan. Not so much now." Sam finished her coffee. "So where are you from?"

"I grew up in western Maryland. Both my parents are physicians."

"So, medicine is a family business?"

"You would think so, although they didn't push me into it. Despite the fact I tried to avoid it for a long time, there was nothing else that interested me as much."

"Where did you go to school?"

"The University of Maryland for undergrad and USUHS for medical school."

"USUHS?" Sam looked confused.

"Sorry, Uniformed Services University for Health Sciences. It's medical school for those who plan to work in military medicine. Uncle Sam foots the bill. We sign on the dotted line going in for an eight-year commitment when we're done with school."

"So, you were commissioned before you finished?"

"Yes."

"You could have worked anywhere. Why the military?" They barely acknowledged the waitress as she returned and put the coffee in front of them.

"Probably the same reason as you. Deep down, a love of country. And I wanted to help those who put everything at risk to protect us. Why did you join the Marines?"

"I wanted to fly. I had a choice to select Navy or Marines. I chose the Marines."

"The few, the proud."

Sam smiled. "Absolutely."

"You said you selected. Were you at the Naval Academy?" She looked at Sam, noticed the fierce pride in her leaf-green eyes. A vague sensation of familiarity fluttered through and disappeared instantly.

"I was."

"That's quite the accomplishment. Your parents must have been so proud." Kris saw her eyes flicker, and the slightest momentary change of expression.

"They didn't know. I like to think they would have been."

"I'm sorry, I—'"

"It's okay. I really don't know my family. I have an older brother and a younger sister and brother, although I don't know where they are. We were placed in foster homes when I was eight. For a while the youngest two were together, eventually even they were split up. I know they were adopted. I lost track of my brother when I was twelve. He was four years older and just disappeared."

"What happened to your parents?"

"My mother was injured in a car accident and has a traumatic brain injury. She is incapable of taking care of herself. She's been in a home since. She has the mental capacity of a young child. My father couldn't handle the stress of that and four kids. He dropped us off at a church for Sunday school and never came back."

She reached out and touched Sam's hand, surprised by the softness of her skin. "I don't know what to say. I'm sorry."

"There's not much that can be said." Sam picked up her coffee, blew on it before sipping it carefully. "She's been a ward of the state for a long time. I visit a few times a year. She doesn't know who I am. I send money for clothing and extras. I go when I can to visit my mom, but it's...well, it's hard to describe. I'm older now than she was when she was injured. Although she's in her fifties, she acts like she's five. The last time I was there, before deployment, she asked if I was her mom. I told her I was an old friend."

"Oh God! That must have been hard."

Sam shrugged and sipped her coffee.

"Wait." Kris reached out and touched Sam's hand again, felt the unusual warmth, "When you were in the hospital, in Bethesda, did anyone, any family come to visit?"

"My foster parents visited. I had friends that stopped by. I didn't like having visitors. I spoke on the phone with my sister...foster sister." Sam turned her hand up and held Kris' momentarily. "It's okay Kris, it is what it is. You can't imagine it because you grew up in a secure, loving family. I did too. I was in the foster system until I graduated from high school. Families from our church took us in, but no one could take the four of us. I was frightened for a long time. The Klines made me part of their family, and they treated me like one of their own kids. I was fortunate that they kept me. I was lucky again when I was accepted into the Academy. The Academy and the Marines are my family. It's a hell of a good family." She picked up her empty coffee cup. "Do you want a refill?"

"No, I shouldn't. I'll be up all night."

"Can I buy you dinner?"

"Oh Sam, I'd like to, but I need to get home. I have some records I need to review." She saw the disappointment on Sam's face. "Can I take you up on that some other time?"

"Sure." Sam smiled.

Kris picked up her bag and touched Sam's hand for an instant. "I'll see you later." She walked to the door and looked back and saw Sam reaching for her crutches. She hurried back to her. "Sam, how are you getting home?"

"I have someone coming in a few minutes to pick me up."

"Oh, okay. I'll see you later." Kris looked in the window as she left and saw Sam talking to someone on the phone. She was almost to her car when two teenagers walked by carrying a huge bag of Chinese food. The smell of eggrolls and kung pao chicken wafted along behind them. She changed directions and walked to the restaurant. She ordered, and sat down on the cheap plastic bench seat to wait for her food. Fifteen minutes later she left with her bag of food and rain drops began to fall. By the time she reached her car it was a steady rain. She drove down the street carefully as people rushed by. She was waiting for an older lady to clear the crosswalk when she noticed a figure on crutches hurrying down the street, toward the bus. The bus pulled away and the person stopped and slumped in despair. "Oh shit, it's Sam." She drove over to the curb, shifted to park, and climbed out. "Sam! Sam! You come over here right now! What are you doing?" Kris hurried over to her, reached for her arm, but Sam backed away.

"I was trying to catch the bus."

"I can take you home."

"I'll catch a ride."

"I am not going to leave you out here in the rain waiting for a bus when I can get you home faster than the next bus will come by. Don't be foolish Sam, take the ride."

Thunder rumbled in the distance, and they stared at each other with the rain pouring down. "Okay. I appreciate it." Kris reached out to guide her to the car, and Sam recoiled. "I can get there myself."

"I'm sorry. Of course, you can." Kris watched as Sam got to the car, placed her crutches across the backseat and swung the rear door closed. She used the roof for support and hopped twice before getting into the passenger seat. Sam pulled the door shut and Kris went around and climbed in. She looked at Sam sitting in the seat, stiff as a board, jaw set, eyes straight ahead. Water streamed down her cheeks from her soaked head. "There are some napkins in the glove compartment if you want to dry off a little."

"Thank you." Sam opened the compartment and pulled out several napkins. She passed a few to Kris and used several on her own face and hands. Kris quickly wiped her face and hands, pushing the used tissue into the center console. She turned on the heat and pulled away from the curb. They drove for several minutes in silence. The smell of the food permeated the air. Sam's stomach rumbled and she pressed her hand to it. When they passed the turn that would have taken them back to base Sam spoke up. "Where are we going?"

"To my place. We're both soaked, and I have that delicious Chinese food that we've been smelling. I have some dry clothes you can change into. And don't even try to say no. Stubborn damn Marine. You can't afford to catch pneumonia. You're still not at full strength."

"Okay."

"Don't even try to argue with me...I'm the doctor here."

"I said okay," Sam grumbled.

Kris gave her a quick sidelong look. "You did. Well, then...good." They drove for several more miles before turning into an older established neighborhood of ranch-style homes. The houses were well spaced with large yards and mature trees. Large stately oaks, magnolia, red cedar, and wax myrtle adorned the lawns. Well-maintained gardens and shrubs surrounded many houses. Flowers that she couldn't identify burst with colors from gardens lined with pine straw.

Kris pulled into a driveway wide enough for two cars, and jumped out. By the time she got to the other side of the car, Sam was getting out. Kris retrieved the crutches from the back seat and handed them to her. She reached back in and grabbed her purse and the Chinese food. "Watch the walk it gets slippery when it's wet." She unlocked the door and held the screen door open for Sam to enter. "Come on in."

Kris flipped on lights as they entered. "Home sweet home. Let me put this in the kitchen, and I'll get you some clothes to change into and show you around."

"Okay, thanks." Sam shivered.

"Did you want a shower to warm up?"

"No, that won't be necessary."

"Okay here's the bathroom." Kris pulled a bath sheet from the linen closet. "You can use this to dry off. There's a hair dryer under the sink if you want to dry your hair. I'll be back in a moment with some clothes. We're close to the same size."

Kris hurried to her room, rustled through her drawers, selecting a few items and returned to the hall bathroom. "Here you go. I'll go set the table. Take your time." Kris set the clothes on the counter and shut the door behind her.

Chapter Thirty

SAM DISROBED QUICKLY AND checked to see if the bandages around her leg were wet. She assured herself it was dry. She rubbed with the big fluffy towel vigorously at her arms and back to warm up. She picked up the sweatpants to put them on and was pleased to see that they were solid black. She smiled when she saw a familiar red t-shirt with gold letters, USMC. She slipped it over her head. A pair of thick white socks were next. She pulled one on, reached to put one on the other, and shook her head in disgust. She placed the remaining sock back on the counter. She towel dried her hair, finger combed it, and with a quick glance in the mirror she stared at her own eyes. *God, I look like shit. I must be down ten pounds. My cheeks are hollow. I need some sunshine. I look like a vampire.*

Shaking her head, she turned away from her reflection and turned on the tap to wash her hands and saw that several safety pins had been placed on the counter. She stared at them for a moment, common sense and safety warring with pride. After a minute of internal debate, Sam sighed and leaned against the counter. Reaching for the pins, she tacked the pants leg up so she couldn't trip over it, picked the wet clothes off the floor, and folded them neatly. She stacked them on the vanity and avoided looking at her reflection again. She followed the scent of the food back to the kitchen.

***

"What would you like to drink? I have tea, juice…wine if you want it," Kris asked.

"Any chance of beer?" Sam asked.

"I might have some."

Kris rooted through the fridge before finally digging one out from the back and looked at the label, "It's an India pale ale, is that okay?"

"That would be great."

"Do you need a glass?"

"No. This is fine." Sam leaned a crutch against the counter and took the beer from Kris. "Why don't you go change?"

"Okay. I'll be a minute. Let me put this over on the table for you." Kris placed the beer and her glass of wine on the table. "I'll be right back." She hurried down the hall, stripped off her clothes, and quickly dressed in a pair of jeans and a squadron t-shirt. Coming back to the living room she found Sam looking at the pictures on the wall.

"That's my family, a couple years ago. Before I went to Afghanistan the first time. We were at the beach vacationing together."

"Looks like everyone was having a good time."

"For the most part, although there was underlying tension...fear because of the deployment."

"Probably so."

They moved back to the kitchen table, and Sam sat down at one of the place settings. Kris pulled the eggrolls and sauces from the oven and placed them in front of Sam. She returned quickly with the rest of the food. "It's kung pao chicken, wonton soup, and some pot stickers." She caught Sam's stare "What?"

"That's a lot of food for one person."

"Well, I wasn't going to eat it all tonight." She laughed. "Come on let's eat."

As they ate dinner, Sam asked her about the house. "This is a nice place. It's peaceful here. It has a solid feel to it. In a lot of newer homes, you don't get that feel."

"That's true. This was built-in the seventies when houses were still built with lots of wood. It's a good neighborhood, close to the hospital and the base. I had some walls knocked out, to open up the floor space a little, and eliminated one of the bedrooms so now it has three larger rooms. The bathroom is roomy, and there's a patio out back. I'd thought of selling it a few times, especially with the deployments but I wanted to know I had a place to return to right away."

"You weren't worried about the house being empty while you were gone?"

Kris hesitated. "I, ah..."

"Sorry I didn't mean to pry."

"You weren't. My, ah, ex-roommate moved to a condo at the beach." Kris shrugged.

"Pretty view in the morning."

"Probably so, although she'll never see it. She always slept in." Kris noticed the empty bottle, gestured to it. "Would you like another beer?"

"Sure."

Kris cleared the plates from the table and looked for another beer. She called out, "I don't have any more beer." She looked back in time to see Sam yawn and shiver. "How about if a make a pot of tea? We can crack open the fortune cookies and see what good fortunes are coming our way." She rubbed her arms lightly. "Hmm, I've caught a chill, I'm going to get a sweatshirt, do you want one? The rain must be cooling things off."

"That would be good."

Kris came back with two sweatshirts, one was pink, the other gray. She extended the pink sweatshirt toward her guest. Sam's hand froze in midair. She looked up and saw Kris watching her with an amused look on her face. After a few seconds, Kris burst out laughing, and handed her the gray sweatshirt. "Your face was priceless. You looked at that sweatshirt like it had teeth." She pulled the pink one over her head and flipped her hair out from under the collar. "I can't picture you in pink."

"I probably haven't worn it since I was four."

"Would you like your tea here or in the living room?"

"Here's fine." Sam pulled the sweatshirt on. "This feels good."

Kris served the tea, and they cracked open the fortune cookies. "Hmm, this one says, 'Be on the lookout for coming events. They cast their shadows.' That sounds ominous." She pushed the plate of cookies to Sam. "Go ahead. Pick."

Sam looked at the plate of cookies, amused by the little ritual. Her hand hovered until she finally chose one. "Meeting adversity well is the source of your strength." She put the cookie down, fingering the slip of paper.

Noticing her silence, Kris interrupted the quiet. "Pick one for me."

Sam picked up one of the two remaining cookies and handed it to her. She sat back and sipped her tea while Kris cracked it open. "There will be a happy romance for you shortly." Kris laughed. "Oh please. Who has time for one of those? Your turn, last one." She drank her tea while Sam stared at the cookie on the plate and continued to finger the tiny slip of paper in her hand.

Finally, Sam picked up the last cookie, cracked it, slipped a piece of the cookie into her mouth and chewed slowly, not looking at the fortune.

"Come on," Kris urged.

"Patience, grasshopper." Sam looked down at the words, and

stared at them. "Find a peaceful place where you can make plans for the future." She put the tiny slips of paper down and picked up her tea, "The day before I left for the academy I had Chinese food with a friend of mine. I still have that one."

"It must have been special."

"It said, 'You are about to embark on a great adventure.' Strangely it gave me reassurance."

"That's almost eerie, the coincidence of it." Kris shook her head.

Sam smiled. "You're not superstitious, are you?"

"Not at all. I avoid walking under ladders because something could fall on me."

"An apple a day keeps the doctor away," Sam teased.

"Well, that one is true, especially if you throw hard enough and have a good aim."

Sam stared at her wide-eyed before she burst into laughter. "Now that's funny."

They finished the tea, and when Kris cleared the pot from the table, she saw Sam stifle a yawn. "Oh, it's getting late. I should get you back to base. Or you could stay here if you like. There's plenty of room."

"No, I need to get back. I have medication to take...for the pain in my foot. Well, it's not really in my foot."

"For the phantom pain? Is it bad?"

"It's getting better. The medicine helps, and my dose is coming down."

"That's good. Well, I guess I should get you back."

"My clothes?"

"I'll get them washed. I can't imagine laundry service in the medical barracks is ideal. I can do them unless you need them right away."

"It isn't fast that's for sure. I don't need them right away. Thanks."

"It's no problem. I'll be throwing mine in too. I'll bring them by tomorrow. I can drop them off if you're not there."

"Okay."

They drove back to the base, and as they approached the barracks, Kris noticed a lot of activity outside it, considering the hour. "Is it always so busy? So late?"

"Not always. There's usually a few people up at night. Nightmares, insomnia, the adjustment back can be hard."

"Yes, it can." Kris reached out, touching Sam's hand. "I'm glad I ran into you. I'll bring your clothes tomorrow."

"Thanks. Thanks for dinner too. Good night." Sam looked carefully at Kris and smiled slowly.

"Good night."

After Kris returned home, she quickly cleared the table of the tea cups. She wiped down the table and noticed that Sam's fortunes were gone. She smiled, feeling like she discovered a secret. She sat down at her desk and pulled out the files she needed to review, and in the back of her mind, she wondered why Sam seemed vaguely familiar.

***

Sam undressed, tossed the clothes in the hamper, and removed the ace bandages from her leg and examined it. She removed the smaller bandage from over the blister. Using a large hand mirror, she looked at the back of her leg and the bottom looking at the blister and for any additional hotspots or skin damage. Finding no others, she moved to the shower, pulled down the seat, and sat before placing the crutches outside. Reaching up she grabbed the handheld shower head, aimed it away from herself and turned on the water. She waited for it to warm, holding back a shiver as the airborne mist dropped the temperature slightly. As the water turned warm, she directed the spray onto herself and hung it back on the hook.

That was a fun evening. I'm glad she convinced me to go for coffee. That's the best night I've had in over a year. Kris seemed like she enjoyed herself. She didn't mention her boyfriend at all, not even to bitch about him. He hasn't been gone long. There were markings from the furniture being moved. Grease stain on the driveway too, from another car. Should I tell her I'm gay? She might not be open to having a gay friend, even though we get along well. God, I hope she's not like that. I could use a pal.

Sam rinsed, dried off, and crutched over to the sink. She continued her night-time ritual of applying a special moisturizing cream to her stump. She slathered lotion over the rest of her body, wiping her hands on a towel before picking up the crutches again. Clicking off the bathroom light, she moved to the bed, reached into the drawer of the nightstand and pulled out a compression sleeve. She held it for several seconds, looking at it and with a deep sigh, rolled it onto her stump. She flipped off the light and lay back, enjoying the coolness of the sheets against her skin.

Gradually she drifted off to sleep, and as she did, she remembered Kris' hands. *Long and narrow, the skin looked soft and unblemished.*

Long tapered fingers with short, perfectly shaped nails. Unpolished, but obviously manicured. Her knuckles were small, her fingers straight. The skin was warm and smooth. Her touch was reassuring. Kris had grasped the steering wheel firmly and shifted gears flawlessly as she drove. Her hands were steady as she poured tea, not a single misplaced drop. Her hands looked competent, no, they were elegant.

Chapter Thirty-one

SAM SAT AT A shaded table and turned the empty water bottle over and over in her hands. Around her other participants ate, laughed, and joked about the competition. Several large tents had been set up and volunteers stood manning the buffet lines serving food to the participants. Assistance was given to help carry food to tables and refill beverages. Sam felt she had spoken with nearly everyone in attendance. She launched the empty water bottle into the nearest trash can before standing and moving steadily on crutches to the mess tent to get something else to drink. Leaning against the table, she filled a cup with water and drank it. She bent to the fill the cup again when someone came up beside her.

"Want me to carry that for you?"

"That's all right." Sam turned toward the voice. "Hey, Kris, I was wondering if you were here today."

"I've been around. I did one of the runs and some swimming. Do you want to sit down? I'll carry that over if you would like." Kris held out her hand to take the cup.

"Sure thanks." Kris filled two cups with water, and they moved to a picnic table. "So how did you do today?"

Kris took a sip of water, and wiped her mouth. "I did a five-K, I'm not particularly fast. I don't particularly like to run. I run enough to pass my fitness test with a respectable time. With the swimming, I'll have to wait and see. It was fun to have some competition again. My arm is recovering well, and the swimming is good for it. I swam in high school and college, so there's muscle memory. You're still on crutches, is the blister healing?"

"It is. It just wasn't fast enough for me to compete without the sticks though."

"How did things go?"

"Pretty good. I did the basketball shoot. I did well enough that they won't pick me last in gym class. I didn't want to do this. They're right though, you have to get out and do things. And it's easier when you're with your peers, colleagues."

"It is." Kris took a sip of her water and stole several quick glances at Sam. *Why do I feel like I know this woman? Green eyes the color of a stormy sea, and short black hair. About five-ten, her cheeks were hollowed with dark smudges under her eyes. Possibly from loss of sleep. Certainly, she was going through a lot. Losing a limb was hard for anyone, but a woman surrounded by men with the same injuries was still a woman.* "Sam, would you like to head off base for a little while? Maybe for some ribs or a burger? I could use a good burger and a glass of—"

"Hey, Davies! How are you doing?" They turned to look at the big Marine who lumbered over to the table.

"I'm doing fine." Sam shook the Marine's hand. "It's good to see you. How are you? This is Doctor Kris Matthews. Doc. this is Major Doug Peterson."

Kris could barely respond politely as the words reverberated. A wave of nausea swept through her.

"Hello. It's nice to meet you," Doug said, shaking her hand. He turned his attention back to Sam. "I got the new leg a couple weeks back. It's so much smoother than the first one. I'm telling you, it makes everything seem normal, well almost normal again."

As they spoke, a helicopter approached. Unconsciously Kris' hand traveled to her chest when her heart started to hammer. The helicopter passed overhead, and Kris felt the world start to spin. She was vaguely aware of a petite woman about five three that approached. As Kris struggled to breathe, she heard Doug speak. "That's my wife. I have to go. Hey, Sam, next year, you and me, the Marine Corps Marathon. Don't worry if you can't finish it, I'll carry you over the line." He walked off laughing.

"That'll be the day he beats me in a race. God forbid that would happen, someone would have to shoot me," Sam said with laughter ringing in her voice.

Kris struggled to breathe normally. *Just shoot me.* She stared at her empty hands and saw the blood on them. *It's her, oh dear God.* Her mouth was suddenly dry, her stomach flipped, and she started to shake.

"Are you all right? You look sort of pale."

"I'm…a…fine." She wiped sweaty palms on her shorts and swallowed hard against the butterflies that were swarming in her stomach. "Ah, would you mind a rain check on that burger? I'm pretty tired and should get going."

"Sure. I'm tired too. Are you okay? Are you feeling well? You're sweating. I'll get some help." Sam started to get up, but Kris stopped her with a hand to her waist.

"I need to go. Do you need a ride back to base?" *Please say no.*

"No. They have shuttles for us. I'll catch one in a few minutes."

"Okay. Take care." Kris left the field and started walking to the parking lot. Once she got out of sight, she took off at a full run.

Oh, God. It's her. How could I have not recognized her? What am I going to do? Does Renee know the major is right here? Of course, she does. By the time Kris reached her car, she was in a full panic. She fumbled with the key fob to unlock the doors. Finally getting it open she slipped behind the wheel, started it, and blasted the air conditioner. With her head thrown back against the headrest, she tried to make sense of the last several months.

How could I not have recognized her? It's not like there are loads of female marine pilot amputees around. Calm down. Breathe, breathe. Sam hadn't spoken much, and her voice had been strained with pain. Weak and hard to hear. Her face was filthy, streaked with dirt and grime, and blood from her nose and mouth had dried on her swollen face. The female marine she helped in the field was strong, fit, with dark hair, and green eyes. The whites of her eyes were deeply red, stained with blood from hemorrhaging vessels. This Sam was thin, her cheeks hollowed. Like someone in a battle for their life. Someone who had lost weight relatively quickly. Her face was pale and gaunt. They said I was hurt helping someone. I didn't realize it was her. We were running to the chopper with her. She rubbed at her chest. *That's when I was hit. Oh, dear God what am I going to do?* Kris remembered the relaxation exercises they had been taught and started performing them. After several more minutes, she backed out of the parking space and drove home.

Chapter Thirty-two

KRIS PACED AROUND RENEE'S office. "I remembered everything. Major Davies. Samantha. She's here. We've been in the same sessions. We were at Bethesda at the same time. You knew this."

"I did. I thought when you recalled the amputation you also remembered all the details of it. I didn't realize you hadn't made the connection until the last time when you asked if there was a way to find out if she was doing all right."

"And you didn't think it was important enough to tell me?" Kris shook her head and sucked her bottom lip tight against her teeth.

"Kris, you had repressed certain painful memories. Those memories were revealed when you were able to handle them. My revealing that Samantha was your patient would not have helped you. And it wouldn't have helped Sam either."

"She doesn't know that I did that to her?"

"She was severely injured and already in distress. Close to death. You said yourself that she was given Versed to make her forget what was happening. I can't go into the details of Major Davies counseling sessions with you but, I will tell you the drug worked as advertised."

Kris rubbed at the bridge of her nose. "Should I tell her?"

"Do you think it would help her?"

"That's why I'm asking you."

"I'm not sure it would benefit Sam to know. Most injured warriors don't know who performed their surgeries in theater. If you find yourself wanting to tell Sam, you need to consider carefully if it would help or hinder her. I would also appreciate a heads up if you're going to do that. I will need to find out if Sam is interested in finding out who performed her amputation. If she is agreeable, a session with the three of us would be best."

"I'll think about it and let you know."

***

Kris was walking to her office and passing the elevators when Sam stepped out. Her heart leapt in her chest, and a fluttery sensation filled her belly. "Sam, what are you doing here?"

"I was in the building so I thought I'd try to find you. I wanted to see how you were doing. It's been a few weeks. The last time I saw you, it seemed like you didn't feel well. Are you back to work? I mean operating?"

"I'm doing well. I've been operating for two weeks now. A few cases a week. Do you want to go sit down? My office is right down here. I was going to eat some lunch before I start up again."

"I don't want to interrupt your lunch."

"Don't be silly. I have enough for both us. Come tell me what you've been up to."

Kris walked matching her pace to Sam's and trying to unobtrusively notice how she was walking. Other than the slow pace she didn't appear to be having any difficulties. Kris led Sam into a small office. A couple of desks, a bookcase stuffed full of books and medical journals filled the space. A small window faced the parking lot. Medical degrees hung above each desk.

"Let me grab you a chair." Kris pulled the chair away from the other desk and rolled it in front of hers. She held the chair steady as Sam sat down. "Do you want something to drink? Can I get you a coffee? I have some bottled water here."

"Water is fine."

"How about some salad?"

"I'm not going to eat your lunch."

"I have enough for both of us. I don't want to waste it, and I won't want it this evening."

"Sure."

Kris pulled two water bottles out of the small fridge and a large container. "Do you like beef? I have some leftover flank steak I was going to put on the salad." She pulled two plates out from her desk and divided the greens, and placed strips of beef on it. She rooted around in the fridge. "I have ranch dressing and, hmm, more ranch dressing."

Sam grinned. "I'll take the ranch. Do you always pack so much food?"

"Not usually. I was in a rush to leave this morning. I grabbed the whole thing." When her cell phone rang from somewhere in her desk, she did her best to ignore it. *Damn it, Shelly, leave me alone.* "How are you feeling?"

"Good. They made another socket. As the swelling went down the old one started to rub and was causing blisters. Apparently, it can take up to a year to get to your normal size although most changes are in the beginning. They say the changes are continuous, even years later size and fit will fluctuate. That's why the rechecks are so important." The phone rang again. "Do you want to answer that?"

"No. I'll get it later. What comes next?"

"More PT. Keep building the strength and activity level. I'm doing several flights of stairs, and they have me taking some hops. They're letting me do more on my own, so I don't have someone with me one-on-one all the time. Any day they'll decide what type of prosthesis I get next. This one is temporary. They need to see how well you can do with this thing and what you can accomplish before they drop the big bucks for something more high-tech and versatile. I'd like to get back to being active. To run again and go hiking. With any luck in a few weeks, I should be sporting something a little less clunky. I move next week. I'm looking forward to being in my own space again."

"That's great. Jot your address down and I'll come by." Kris pushed a paper and pen towards Sam.

"Are you okay? You seem a bit down."

Kris looked at Sam. "I haven't slept well the last few nights. I've been thinking some things over." *Like if I should tell you? Is Renee right? We're becoming friends. I feel it. Does that change whether you need to know?* "I find it interesting that so many people worry about us going to war and coming back changed. Well of course we do. You can't be in an environment when your life is in danger and not be changed by it. What we see, and what we do changes you. But it doesn't stop there. While we're gone, life goes on for our family and friends. And they change too. They see the changes in us. And we usually see and feel the changes within us. Yet somehow they remain blissfully oblivious to their own changes during that same time period."

"I know I've changed, and not just because of my leg. I just look at things a little different now. So how's surgery going?"

"I have some fatigue on the longer cases, and occasionally my fingers cramp at the end of the day. All things considered, I'm doing well."

As they were finishing eating Kris was paged to the operating room. Sam stood up to leave. "Thanks for lunch, doc."

"My pleasure. It was nice to see you again."

"You too. I need to get going. I have a PT session in the pool this afternoon."

"Have fun." Kris walked Sam to the elevator bank. As Sam stepped onto the lift Kris couldn't help but notice her well-toned butt. *Don't even think it.*

Chapter Thirty-three

SAM STOOD OUTSIDE THE door and directed the movers on where to put the boxes and furniture as they brought it into the house. She marked off the boxes on the inventory sheet as each item was unloaded. Around noon the movers took a lunch break, and with a sigh, she sat down. She munched on an apple and a banana. *I didn't think this would make me achy.*

"Sam?"

"I'm back here, Kris. Follow the path. What are you doing here?" Sam smiled.

"I thought I'd stop by. I hope you don't mind."

"No, it's good to see you."

"Did you eat lunch? I have an Italian sub in the car, and a half-gallon of sweet tea."

"I don't want to eat your lunch again."

"You're going to make me eat a foot-long sub by myself? It's from the pizza shop you like."

"Hmm, you've twisted my arm. Let me find some plates."

"I'll go get it out of the car."

Sam managed to find two plates and mugs, and was rinsing them when Kris returned. They rearranged some boxes before sitting down to eat.

Kris handed her the package. "I hope you like Italian subs. I had it warmed up."

"Oil and Vinegar?"

"Of course." Kris smiled as she poured tea into the mugs. "I'm so happy for you, Sam. I know you were looking forward to getting back on your own. Do you have a date for your car to go to the shop?"

"It's already there. There was a cancellation, so mine was moved up. I had someone drive it over for me. It'll be modified and inspected. I have to apply for a new license too."

"It sounds like everything is working out." Kris took a sip of sweet tea.

"It feels like it. I'll show you around later after I get things unpacked."

"I'd like that." Kris looked around the kitchen. "I like the hardwood floors. The kitchen is nice and bright."

"The wood is real. I had to sign an agreement that I understood how it needed to be cleaned. It's throughout the house, except for the bath areas. There are three bedrooms upstairs. I'll turn one of the extras into an office."

They finished lunch right as the movers began bringing in the next load of boxes. The movers started asking Sam where she wanted bedroom furniture placed, as she was directing them Kris rinsed the plates and mugs and set them to dry on the counter.

Sam stood at the bottom of the stairs watching as her bedroom furniture was taken upstairs. "Penny for your thoughts." Sam jumped at Kris' voice. "Sorry, I didn't mean to startle you. You looked lost in thought."

"I was thinking of some things I needed to do now that I am getting back to normal...or, my new normal."

"Pace yourself. I know you're strong and healthy, but remember you don't have to do everything in one day. If you need help, don't be afraid to ask. I'll help any way I can."

"Thanks. I'll keep that in mind."

"I need to head back. Really, Sam, if you need anything let me know."

"I will. Thanks for lunch."

***

Sam sat on the examination table in shorts and her bra, the gown was opened in the front. She sat and waited quietly while the physician examined her. Sam tried not to stare at the doctor's bright blue eyes. She had never seen such a brilliant blue. She followed the doctor's finger with her eyes. Stuck out her tongue and said, "Aah" when told. Long, slender, perfectly tapered fingers glided along the front of her throat, her heart accelerated. She breathed deeply when her lungs were listened to.

"Good, your lungs are clear. Now let me listen to your heart." The doctor moved the stethoscope across the front of Sam's chest listening. She closed her eyes as she repositioned the instrument every few seconds.

Sam watched as the woman dragged her teeth over a lower lip that looked soft. Sam's heart fluttered, and she smelled the subtle scent of orange wafting from her. Suddenly the doctor opened her eyes and made eye contact with Sam. Without thinking, Sam reached out and placed her hand on the back of her neck and pulled her in for a soft kiss. There was no struggle, the kiss was returned with a gentle pressure and a soft sweep of tongue across the seam of her lips. Sam groaned with pleasure. Firm hands nudged her backward, and Sam moaned again when the doctor lowered her mouth to her suddenly bare breasts and sucked a nipple into her mouth flicking it with her tongue. Her body erupted in sensation.

Sam sat up with a shout and looked around. She was in her new place. She leaned forward and ran her hands through her hair. Now without any doubt, she knew who the woman in her dreams was. And that was a problem because Kris was straight and Sam learned long ago to not get involved with straight girls.

Chapter Thirty-four

SAM SAT ON THE DECK, rocking slowly. Oblivious to her surroundings, and completely focused on the pages of the adventure novel she read, *the loud clack-clack sound common to the cocking of a shotgun pierced the still night. A menacing disembodied voice from the forest followed seconds later. Real careful now, put your guns aside and raise your hands.*

"Hi, Sam."

Sam's heart leaped in her chest. She screamed, and jumped out of the chair, flinging the book away. *Fuck!* Sam smoothed her hand over her jittery stomach as she turned around and recognized Kris. *Damn.* She took a deep breath and rubbed at her racing heart.

Kris burst into nervous laughter. "Oh my God! I didn't mean to scare you. Are you okay?"

Still speechless, Sam nodded her head and walked over to pick up the book that had landed on the lawn. "I didn't hear you come up."

"That's obvious. Are you okay? You didn't get hurt when you jumped did you?"

Sam saw the amused grin on Kris' face that she was unsuccessfully trying to suppress. "Only my ego. What time is it?" Sam looked down at her prosthetic leg. *Damn, this thing did great.*

"Five. The movie starts at seven, so we have plenty of time for dinner. What are you reading? You were really into it."

Sam turned the book around. "It's an adventure story. <u>Journey to You</u> by AJ Adaire. It's a post-apocalyptic story."

"Ooh, I love her books. I haven't read that one."

"It's excellent. The bad guy just told the women to put their hands in the air when you surprised me."

"Oh geez, no wonder you jumped." Kris laughed. "I'm sorry. I've never seen anyone jump so far from a seated position or squeal so loud."

"I didn't squeal. I believe that was a scream." Sam laughed. "You scared the hell out of me."

Kris chuckled. "I am sorry. I'll make a little more noise next time." They walked inside. "Any ideas where you want to eat tonight?"

"There's an Italian place I've wanted to try, Luigi's. They are supposed to have unbelievable meatballs and lasagna." Kris reached for her keys, but Sam stopped her. "I'm driving."

"What?"

Sam grinned. "I'm driving. I got my car back, so I want to drive."

"Congratulations. Let's go."

Sam grabbed her keys and wallet from the kitchen counter, and they headed into the attached garage. Sam pressed the door opener and as the garage door lifted the light flooded onto the convertible. The black surface gleamed, reflecting light back to her. The charcoal gray roof was a subtle offset to the unbroken black.

"Oh, very nice. Slick. It looks powerful. Can we have the roof down?"

"Absolutely. It's a beautiful night for it."

"It smells new."

"It's a few years old. I had it stored while I was deployed. The shop detailed it for me when they converted the controls. Ready?"

"Let's go."

When they cleared the garage, Sam opened the top so they could enjoy the early evening air. Slipping the Mustang into reverse, they backed out of the driveway. Smiling broadly, enjoying the freedom of driving again, Sam drove with controlled precision. The engine roared with power and hugged the curves. The air blew over them as the car moved down the highway.

They eventually pulled into the parking lot of the restaurant. Sam raised the roof while the two teenage valets ran over to provide parking assistance. Before Sam had to decide who to hand the keys to, a woman approached. "Samantha Davies, is that you?"

"Hi. How are you doing, Valerie? When did you start here?"

"I'm part owner. We opened a few months ago. I'm glad I came out to check if the boys were behaving. They would knock each other down trying to get to this car. How have you been?"

"Pretty good. This is Kris Matthews. A friend of mine."

"It's nice to meet you." Valerie and Kris shook hands. "Why don't you two go on in? Tell the Maître d' I said to give you table number nine. I'll park the car for you."

Sam started to hand Valerie the keys and hesitated. "I need to show you something in the car. Look here. Do you see that switch? For you to drive it, you need to flip it to the off position. That will re-engage the gas and brake pedals. If you try to drive it in the on position, you'll have to use the hand controls. That takes some time to get used to."

"What on earth?"

"I lost my leg when I was in Afghanistan." Sam lifted her trouser leg slightly.

"Oh, God. I'm so sorry, Sam. Is everything going all right? Do you need help with anything?"

"I'm good thanks." She looked over at Kris and smiled.

As Valerie slid behind the wheel, she whispered into Sam's ear. "If Kris is your date, you're doing better than good." Sam shifted her gaze to Kris, and let her eyes drift across her body. Sam's pulse quickened, and her mouth went dry. Both women stared at Kris.

Sam whispered back, "We're friends. Besides she's straight."

"Oh, that's too bad. You could try for a toaster oven though." The car rumbled to life, "Now back up, I want to get this baby parked before my boys over there drool on it. I'll see you inside."

As instructed Sam requested table nine. The walls of the restaurant were exposed red brick and cream-colored plaster. Their table was screened with a four-foot-high glass block wall that hid them from other diners. Lush green plants sat atop the block wall, and on the table, a candle flickered. Mediterranean music played in the background adding to the ambiance but not preventing conversation. The waiter appeared and recited the specials. Sam ordered spaghetti with meatballs, and Kris ordered seafood linguini and a glass of Muscadet. When the waiter offered Sam wine she refused, sticking with water since she was driving.

"Are you settled in your house?" Kris sipped her wine.

"I am. It's been going a little slow. I have the downstairs and my bedroom set up, the garage is good. The other rooms are still a wreck with boxes everywhere, but at least I have them pushed to the walls and have a little space to move around. Two of the rooms are a hideous fluorescent green. The landlord has agreed to have them painted. I think I'll do it myself. I can't imagine he won't agree if I do the work, and he can reimburse me for the supplies. It would be cheaper than him contracting a painter. But I'll check with him. How's your arm? Are you operating more?"

Kris flexed her fingers. "It's doing well. I'm operating about five hours a day, and am starting to do some longer cases. I was out for a while, so I deconditioned some and start to get a little achy in the afternoon, but it's improving. I figure another week or two, and I'll be back to a full operating schedule."

"Why did you become a surgeon?"

"I like taking things apart and putting them back together. You look surprised."

Sam chuckled. "I thought you would say you like helping people, or you don't like seeing people in pain."

"Those are true also. But those are the reasons why I became a doctor. I became a surgeon because I get to reassemble things." Kris grinned.

"What was the first thing you dissected?"

"Hmm, seems like it was a giant grasshopper in seventh-grade science. It was gross. I was adamant about not going into medicine. I wanted to do something fun, like be a lifeguard. Of course, the aspirations of a twelve-year-old can be somewhat limiting. What did you want to do at twelve?"

"I wanted to be a detective, a private investigator actually. I wanted to find my dad and siblings." Sam sipped her water.

Kris reached out her hand. "I'm sorry, Sam."

"It's all right. It wasn't long after that I went to a military airshow with the Klines, and everything changed. That's when I knew what I wanted to do. I talked to one of the female pilots for a long time. Everyone was watching the show, and she kept talking with me about flight training and college. She told me about the service academies. As soon as we got home, I started looking at what it took to get into the academies. I started being a better student shortly thereafter."

After the waiter brought their food, they continued small talk and shared stories from their childhood. When Sam went to pay the bill, Kris insisted that they split it. While they were waiting for Valerie to return with the car, several motorcycles rumbled by.

Both women looked up. "Those are some nice bikes."

"They are. All of them are Harleys except that last one. That's an Indian Scout." A smile curled at the corners of Sam's mouth as her eyes followed the bikes until they disappeared. As the sound of the throaty roar of the engines drifted away in the wind, Sam sighed. "I miss my bike."

"You have a bike? What kind?"

"A Victory Gunner."

"Oh. That's a nice bike," Kris exclaimed.

"What do you know about it?"

"It's a V-twin engine, with six speed overdrive."

Sam's mouth fell open for several seconds before she spoke. "So you're a bike fan?"

"You could say that. I have two."

"You're kidding me?"

"No, I'm not. I happen to have two Victory cycles. I liked the Gunner, but I wanted some color, so I went with the Vegas. I also have a Victory Vision for when I was traveling or going two up. I bought my brother's a few years back. He was living in Connecticut and was going to give up riding because the season was so short. He lives in Florida now and rides it when he comes up here. I'm looking forward to getting back out there."

"You're serious?"

"Yes. What? Do you think because I'm a doctor I wouldn't ride?" Kris challenged her.

"Well, I never pictured you on a bike. Zumba dancing vegan, remember? But yeah, being a doctor, you guys take the fun out of everything."

Kris stared at her blankly.

"Oh, that didn't come out right. I meant that…"

Kris laughed. "I know what you meant. I know several doctors that ride. With helmets."

"Of course, so is your bike red? The Vegas came in red."

"It is. The Vision is metallic blue."

"I'd like to see them sometime."

"I got them back from being serviced a few weeks ago. Next time you come over, I'll show you."

They stopped talking as Valerie brought the car to a halt beside them. "Sam, this car is sweet. Give me a call sometime so we can get caught up. Enjoy your night, ladies."

While Sam drove to the theater, they discussed their favorite motorcycle rides in the region. They arrived at the theater, decided to split a popcorn and settled down with their drinks to watch the sci-fi thriller.

Two hours later they were on their way home and passed the time discussing the movie. Sam pulled into the garage. "Do you want to come inside?"

"I need to get going. I have to be up early to round in the hospital tomorrow, and I'm on call the next 24 hours. I'm supposed to be within twenty minutes of the hospital when on call, so I'll be staying home tomorrow and doing some chores. I had fun tonight, Sam. Enjoy the rest of the weekend. Would you like to come over for dinner on Wednesday? Swing by after work."

"Sure, I'd like that. I'll see you then." Kris pulled out of the driveway and waved as she drove away. Sam waited until her lights disappeared before going inside.

Chapter Thirty-five

SUNDAY AFTERNOON SAM WALKED back and forth across the lawn, pushing the mower. Her hair, damp with sweat, clung to her neck. She watched when motorcyclists and bicyclists rode by. *I want to ride again. I should check to see if it's possible. It's the brake foot, not the gears. It would need a hand brake. That seems easy enough.* Sam refocused her attention when the blue and chrome bike pulled into her driveway. The rider lifted their visor and Sam smiled broadly when she realized it was Kris.

Kris called to her over the rumbling of the engine. "Come on. Get your gear. Let's go for a ride."

Sam shut off the mower and hurried over. "You're looking good." The bright blue sky had a few small puffy clouds drifting by. "It's a great day for a ride."

"It is. Go change into some long pants. Will you be able to get a boot on?"

"I haven't tried. It's supposed to fit."

"Well go check. I brought an extra helmet, in case yours isn't unpacked yet. I'll put your mower away. Go on. Time's a wasting."

Sam hurried inside, washed her hands and face, and rummaged in her closet for some jeans. She searched for her boots, and sat on the bed to try them on. *Think about this. You don't usually ride on the back. What do you know about how she rides? Don't be silly. She's not going to be reckless. I'll ask her to stop if she is.* It took a few minutes for Sam to get the boot on her prosthetic foot.

"Sam, are you okay?" Kris called from downstairs.

"I am. I had a little trouble, but I'm good. Do you want some water before we go?"

"I have a couple in the saddle bag. We can stop and get something to eat if you haven't eaten yet."

"That sounds good." Sam locked up her house and closed the garage door. After they donned helmets and climbed on, Kris started the bike. The familiar growl of a bike, vibrating with power beneath Sam caused her heart to pound. As the bike began to move, she hesitated for a moment before placing her hands on Kris' waist. Kris accelerated the bike smoothly, and as the bike picked up speed, Sam had to wrap her arms around Kris. *Oh, her abs are firm. She smells good. What is that? Orange and maybe ginger? Mmm. Stop it. Stop sniffing her. She'll think you're a creep.*

Sam refocused and realized they were on a county highway with light traffic. They flew down the road, the air warm and balmy against her body. It was a tonic to her soul, as it blew away her fears and doubts. She smiled when Kris leaned the bike into the turns, hugging the curves. The scenery whizzed by and the longer they rode, the more Sam relaxed. Her mind emptied of deadlines, and appointments, meetings with counselors, and the guilt of losing her men blew away like feathers in the wind.

Kris slowed the bike and pulled into a small parking lot. "Are you hungry? This place has great subs, and homemade fries."

"Great."

Kris switched off the bike and held it steady while Sam got off. She dismounted and they headed inside. After ordering sandwiches at the counter, they filled their cups with sweet tea and sat at one of the booths. The plastic table top was well worn but spotless. The vinyl-covered bench seats were bumpy and creaked as they sat down. From an old jukebox, Garth Brooks sang about having friends in low places. "That was fun. Thanks for inviting me."

"My pleasure. It was much too nice a day to spend all day doing chores."

"It is beautiful out. How was your day yesterday? Did you have to go in?"

"Yes. I did an emergency appendectomy and rounded on patients. I spent most of the day at home getting chores done."

They paused as the waitress brought over their sandwiches and a basket of hand-cut French fries. Kris swiped a few fries while Sam bit into her shrimp po'boy. "Mmm, that's good." They were silent for a few minutes while they ate.

Sam wiped her mouth on her napkin and cleared her throat. "Kris, I like spending time with you. I feel a connection with you that I haven't felt for a while. I'd like to spend more time with you when our schedules permit."

"That sounds great. We have a lot in common. It would be fun to have someone to pal around with." Kris placed several fries on her plate and sprinkled cider vinegar on them. She took a fry and started to nibble on it.

"I need to tell you something though. I feel it's important for you to know this before we start to spend more time together."

Kris put the fry back on her plate. "This sounds serious."

"It might affect our friendship. I hope not, but if it does, I'd rather know now. I'm a lesbian."

Kris picked up her napkin and wiped her fingers off. "I see. And you're afraid that I wouldn't want to associate with you."

"It's been known to happen. When homosexuals reveal themselves to straight people, they often lose that relationship."

"Well, then I guess it's a good thing I'm not straight." Kris picked up two fries, munched happily and watched the emotions as they showed on Sam's face.

"You're not? I didn't realize. I usually get a feeling." *Like the butterflies I'm feeling now.*

"Ah, yes. The gaydar. If you're anything like me, my gaydar was jammed after my injury."

"But you had a boyfriend. The first time I had dinner at your place you said something about your roommate moving out."

Kris was silent for a few moments trying to remember the conversation "I said she moved out."

"I guess I missed the 'she' part."

"Seems like it. Sam, I have to tell you. I do enjoy spending time with you. I'm not looking for a relationship, or should I say an intimate relationship. Just a friend."

"Me too. Well, here's to friendship." Sam lifted her glass of sweet tea and tapped it to Kris' when she did the same.

"To friendship." Kris sipped her sweet tea. "Tell me something about the Klines. You're close to them, so they must have accepted that you're a lesbian. When did you know?"

"They have. Let's see, when did I know I was gay? Bobbie Martin kissed me in ninth grade when we were arguing about me wanting to be a Marine. He told me I couldn't be one because only men could be Marines. I pointed out to him that there were women marines, he said I couldn't be a pilot. I argued with him, showed him articles on women pilots in the military. Not one to admit defeat he kept arguing and said girls couldn't think about anything but kissing. He reached over and grabbed me, and did his best to jam his tongue into my mouth."

Kris gasped, "Oh God, what did you do?"

"Kneed him in the balls, followed by an uppercut, and finished with a punch to the eye."

Kris looked at her, the surprise evident in her voice. "Really?"

"It all happened very fast."

Kris laughed. "Did you get in trouble?"

"At first for fighting, but Jim said the boy started it by grabbing me. His parents said, 'It was just a kiss,' but Jim stuck to his guns and said, so if he had grabbed my breasts would that be okay? What if it was their daughter? They got the point pretty quick. I believe he got a three-day suspension and the reputation for being beat up by a girl. I had an afternoon of detention, and the Klines took me out to dinner to celebrate standing up for myself. I was surprised by that. I realized they had my back. It was a great feeling. Anyhow, the day it happened when I got home, I was so upset, I got sick. They thought it was because of the fight. I was totally disgusted by the entire ordeal."

"The funny thing was two days later I was at a friend's house after softball tryouts. We were up in Valerie's room working on a history project when she leaned over and kissed me. I thought my head was going to blow off. My heart started pounding. I felt like someone had pulled on my stomach from below. A quick hard tug that released a kaleidoscope of butterflies in my stomach and left me giddy. It was a gentle peck on the lips. She pulled back, and we stared at each other. We leaned in for another kiss. I can remember the feel of her hair tickling the side of my face, the touch of her lips on mine, soft and full, with a taste of berries from her lip balm. We spent the next twenty minutes or so kissing, gradually getting a little more daring.

"When it was time for me to go, I ran the first few blocks, and then ended up walking through the park for an hour remembering everything. That giddy, drunk feeling wouldn't leave. I couldn't sleep that night. Things started to make sense. No matter how much I had tried to be attracted to boys, it didn't work. It didn't feel right. As the other girls were going boy crazy, I was indifferent to them. Boys were just there. Some were fun and nice, but there was no attraction. But that kiss, that first kiss with Valerie, and things finally clicked."

"Wait, is this the same Valerie from Luigi's?"

"One and the same." Sam felt the blush rise to her cheeks. "We quietly dated. Everyone thought we were hanging out together, but we were dating. Her family moved away two years later. I was crushed. It was about that time that Nancy, my foster mom, realized I was gay. She hugged me, told me it would be rough for a while and that in time I would find someone else."

"Oh, that's great."

"They've been very good to me. Sometimes I feel guilty for what they gave up to take care of me. I appreciate it, but I feel guilty."

"So...are you and Valerie still close?"

"Old friends. She and her wife own two restaurants here, and a tavern somewhere in the mountains. They met down here on vacation when I was in the Academy. They've been together since."

They cleaned up their debris on the table and walked outside to the bike. Kris looked up at the sky. "Looks like a storm's brewing, I think we should head right back. If we're lucky, we'll be back before it hits."

"You think so? It took us two hours to get here."

"We're only an hour away. I won't take such a scenic route on the way home if it's all right with you."

"Let's go." They climbed onto the bike, Sam wrapped her arms around Kris' waist, and they headed home. *Kris is gay. How could I have missed that? Of course, she is...she was reading AJ's books.*

Chapter Thirty-six

SAM PARKED THE MUSTANG and climbed out. She pulled on a daypack and glanced around. "I love this area. I first came to Point Lookout when I was in high school. Jim brought my foster sister, Lauren, and me here because we were arguing too much."

"He brought you to the seashore because you were arguing?" Kris strapped on a fanny pack as they headed to the trailhead.

"We camped in a tent on the beach. Had to tote water back and forth. Cooked over a fire. We had sand everywhere. We did most of the work, and he sat back and watched. He had a tent next to us. It was so miserably hot. The flies and mosquitos treated us like a smorgasbord. He didn't intervene when we argued. He let us figure out that we needed to work together to get things done."

"Ah, teamwork."

"At that time, it was more like misery loves company. One night a big storm came up. The wind was buffeting the tent. Lightning flashed, and the thunder was deafening. We could hear the surf raging but had no idea how close it was."

"Sounds terrifying."

"We were camped well above the high tide line, so we were safe from the water. But we clung to each other and reassured each other and got through the storm. The next day we felt like survivors. We had a new found appreciation for each other."

Kris whispered, "That's great. Oh, look over there, about two o'clock, beneath the scrub pine, egrets are feeding." They stopped and admired the white birds and watched as one cocked its head, and like a flash plunged its beak into the marsh water and came up with a small fish. The bird waded away as soon as it spotted them.

They hiked for about an hour stopping frequently to observe the herons, egrets, and black skimmers that were abundant. They found an old sea turtle nest and saw racerunner lizards along the path. They spotted a downed tree and stopped to rest. Kris was stooping to sit down when a snake slithered out from next to the log. "Ayyyyyyeeee."

She sprung away and was down the trail fifteen yards before she stopped and heard Sam laughing. "Relax. It's a black racer snake. They're not poisonous."

"I don't care. It's still a snake. Where did it go?"

Sam pointed to the side of the trail. "That way. It was almost as fast as you were." She gestured at the ground near Kris' feet. "You need to tie your boot."

Kris looked down and startled seeing the laces, coiled around her ankle. Sam saw her flinch and burst into peals of laughter again. Kris shook her head and bent over to lace up.

Oh good lord look at her butt. And her legs. Those are the holy grail of legs. Sam fumbled trying to retrieve a water bottle from her pack. She felt overly warm. She guzzled the water trying to wash the blush from her face before Kris noticed. As Kris approached, she held out the bottle. "Want some?"

"Yes." Kris drank while Sam kicked at the log.

"Okay. Nothing else is in there. Let's sit and have something to eat. I brought some sliced oranges, grapes, and a few granola bars."

"That sounds good. Phew. I'm a little tired. I guess I'm not in as good a condition as I thought. I've been working on getting my arm back into shape and neglected the rest of my body."

"Doesn't look like it."

"Thanks. Sit down with me." Kris patted the log and smiled up at Sam. "How are you feeling?" She took an orange slice from the bag Sam offered and bit into it.

"To tell you the truth I think we should head back. I think the loose surface is fatiguing my thigh muscle. I need to rest for a few minutes." Sam grabbed a handful of grapes and started to eat them. She held one out to Kris, who leaned forward, but stopped and took it with her hand.

"Are you having pain?"

"No, it's muscle fatigue, nothing serious. Listen to the birds, and you can still hear the surf." They sat and enjoyed the solitude as they ate their snack. Soon human voices could be heard approaching from further down the trail. A family of four approached, and they greeted each other as they passed by. They split a granola bar and drank more water before leaving. Kris stood up quickly and repacked their gear. When Sam struggled to get up, she held out a hand and helped her up. Sam came up quicker than expected and they stood mere inches apart. Their eyes met momentarily before they both looked away.

Sam cleared her throat. "Thanks for the hand up. We should get going."

"Sure thing. Lead the way."

***

Kris stepped out of the shower and tugged on some cotton briefs and a tank top. She went to the kitchen, filled a glass with ice water, and checked to make sure her doors were locked. Settling into bed, she picked up her novel. Several minutes later, when it dawned on her that she'd read the same paragraph repeatedly, she put the book aside and turned off the bedside light.

As she relaxed, her mind drifted. *This was a nice day. Sam is so laid back and comfortable to be around. I like that she wasn't afraid to mention that she was starting to get achy. I would have hated for something to happen and have her have a setback. I love her laugh. It's a deep down, come-from-the-belly laugh. I don't even mind that it was at my expense. Damn snake. Made me shriek like a little girl. You need to be more careful. You almost took that grape from her hand with your mouth. Friends don't do that. Use this time to get your head on straight and figure out what you want. I want a friendship. Renee doesn't think Sam needs to know. I understand her concerns. I don't know that I agree though. We're friends. Shouldn't I tell her? Sam has some guilt from losing her men. Will she feel guilty about what happened to me? God, what should I do?* Eventually, Kris rolled onto her side and fell into a restless sleep.

Chapter Thirty-seven

SAM PUSHED OPENED THE door to the control room and peered inside. The glow of numerous computer screens cast an eerie blue light in the dimly lit room. Large box-like structures moved almost soundlessly, as mechanical arms lifted and moved them. Sam wondered what flight profiles were being run by the simulators. It took several seconds for her eyes to adjust to the decreased light. She caught the reflection of blue light off of a highly polished bald head, and she smiled before calling out. "Hey, Paul is that you?"

She watched as he spun around and a broad smile crossed his face. "Well, I'll be. It's my favorite Marine." He reached a hand out to her, and they shook. "You doing okay with everything?" He gestured toward her leg.

"I'm doing well enough, thanks. I was hoping I'd be able to get some time in the flight simulator. See how I do with the unleg." A look of confusion crossed Paul's face. "With the prosthesis. I was hoping to give it a try."

"Are you going to try to get back on flight status?"

"Definitely. That's what I am trained to do."

"Well, let's see what I can do. With several of the squadrons deployed there is usually plenty of sim time available." He flipped open a log book. "Hmm. Looks like tomorrow around ten hundred is open."

Sam frowned slightly. "Do you have anything else. They have me over in headquarters, and I don't think I can get away."

"Ah, they have you pushing paper, Major?" She nodded. "Tell you what, if you can wait a couple of days and can come by around eighteen hundred, I'll get you about two hours. Unofficial."

"I can do that. Why not official time?"

"Major, I don't want to discourage you. But I'll tell you the same thing I've told the others who have tried what you're trying. It's not easy. You won't get the same feedback. Everything's going to feel different. Let's keep it unofficial. You can get a few practice runs, with no one looking over your shoulder and grading your performance."

"Is this going to get you in trouble?"

"It hasn't so far. I don't expect it will now. Uncle Sam pays a lot of money for this contract on simulator time. Someone ought to be using it."

"If you're sure."

"Absolutely. See you on Thursday, eighteen hundred."

Sam reached out and shook his hand. "Thanks, Paul."

***

Kris knocked on the door, balancing the pizza box in one hand and holding a bottle of wine and her bag in the other. She was getting ready to knock again when Sam opened the door.

"Come on in. Let me take that." Sam took the pie from Kris and let her pass. "Sorry, I'm running late. I had to make a stop, and it threw me a little behind. Here, let me open that for you." Sam reached into a drawer and found the corkscrew. As she opened the bottle, she gestured to a cabinet. "Plates are up there. Wine glasses are to your right above the toaster."

Kris stood motionless. Sam's hair was damp, and in disarray, with spikes and clumps. Her tank top clung to her damp skin and her breasts pressed against the tight fabric. Her nipples peaked against the material. Well-muscled arms bunched as she moved. A drop of water fell from her hair and slid down her chest heading for the space between her breasts. Kris felt her core grow warm and swallowed hard. She stuffed her hands in her pockets to keep from reaching out and capturing the droplet. *Tell her now.*

"Are you okay?"

Kris was aware of Sam watching her and felt her cheeks heat. "Um, yes. I need to tell you something."

"Okay. Let's eat though, I'm starved." She filled a wine glass with chardonnay and handed it to Kris along with the bottle. "Go sit down." Sam gathered the plates from the cabinet, added napkins and pulled a beer from the fridge. She sat down. "That smells great."

"It does. It's from that shop we went to. It's Canadian bacon, jalapenos, and pineapple. You said you didn't care what kind."

"That's right. I don't know that I've had this combination before. It should be a sweet and spicy combination."

"It is. How was your day?" Kris held her plate as Sam slid a slice onto it.

"Busy. I don't know how people can do administrative stuff day after day, year after year. I'd run off into the night screaming and pulling my hair out." Kris started to laugh. "What's so funny?"

"Your hair. It's all messed up and looks like you did pull at it."

Sam ran her hand through her hair trying to smooth it out. A single Alfalfa clump remained, and Kris reached over to smooth it down. Her fingers lingered for a second as the silky strands slid under her fingers. She pulled her hand back suddenly. *What are you doing? Don't play with her hair.* "There, that's better. Now you don't look like that kid Alfalfa, from that old television show."

"Gee thanks. That's very reassuring to know I don't look like a seven-year-old boy from the early nineteen thirties." Sam pretended to pout and took a bite of the pie.

"I'm sorry. Please continue, how was your day?"

Sam finished chewing and wiped her mouth. "I went by the flight simulator building. I spoke with one of the contractors about getting some time in the sim to see how it goes. He can fit me in Thursday evening."

"Oh, Sam, that's good."

"It is. It'll allow me to see how well I can do with this thing." Sam patted her leg and then picked up her slice. "This is a good combination. It has the right amount of kick."

They continued to talk about their day as they ate. As they were cleaning up the few dishes, Sam's phone rang. "I need to answer that. Afterward you can tell me what you wanted to talk about that had you looking so serious before."

Kris paged absent-mindedly through the newspaper and decided how she would tell Sam. Ten minutes later Sam emerged, her eyes red and shoulders slumped. Kris hurried over to her, "What's wrong?"

"That was the wife of one of my men. I had called earlier to offer condolences and see if they needed anything. They're really hurting. She was mad. She blamed me, she cried. After that she apologized. But she's right."

"No, she's not. Sam, it wasn't your fault. You were shot down. No one's injuries were your fault. You did the best you could while under attack." *You can't tell her. This is what Renee meant, that it won't help her.* "Come on let's sit down and talk about it."

"I'd rather not. Can you stay for a while? We can watch some television. I have no idea what's on, but I'm sure we can find something. Or how about some cards? Do you play cards?"

"Oh yeah. Deal 'em up, sister. I'm feeling lucky."

Two hours later, Kris smiled and laid her cards down. "Rummy. That should make five hundred."

"God dang it." Sam laid her cards out. She was missing the ten which would have given her a straight. "Well, that was a good game."

"It was." Kris glanced up at the clock. Ten-thirty. "Oh, it's getting late. I should get going."

"You're okay to drive?"

"Yes, I had two glasses of wine, but that was a couple hours ago. I've been drinking water. I'm good." Kris picked up her bag and walked to the door. "I had a good time, thanks."

"Me too." They hugged each other before Kris left. As she walked to her car, she looked back and saw Sam smile and wave.

"Good luck Thursday." Kris pressed a hand to her chest to still the pounding of her heart. *God, she felt good.*

"Thanks. Good night." Sam watched as she drove away.

***

Sam tossed and turned in bed and finally sat up in frustration. She ran her hands through her hair and squeezed her head. "This is going to be hard." *I want her. I want to kiss her. I want to find out where that orange-ginger scent is strongest and nibble there. But she said friendship. That's all she's looking for. And that's all I can handle. Probably. But I want more.*

***

Over the next few weeks they saw each other frequently. They went out to dinner, took walks in the park, exercised at the gym together, and their friendship bloomed. Kris realized she was growing increasingly fond of Sam, who seemed to remain oblivious to her attraction. She remained troubled and indecisive on revealing to Sam their common history. Kris' nightly dreams were vivid, bordering on the erotic. She awakened aroused and frustrated in the morning, which was considerably better than having flashbacks.

After dinner at Sam's one evening, they were sitting outside enjoying the sunset. Sam was sipping a beer and Kris a glass of wine. "I had an interesting group therapy session today."

"What happened?"

Sam tugged at her ear. "There was an Army guy in the group counseling session today. He lost both his legs at the thigh. He wanted his wife to divorce him. They'd been married ten years and have two kids. She wouldn't do it though, no matter how poorly he behaved. He said she called him stubborn and stupid for thinking she should."

"He was."

"He said he did everything he could to push her away."

"She's a smart woman. She loves him."

"But she married him when he was whole."

"He's still the man she loves."

"I get that. They've got a stake in what they had. But for single people, how often do they find that? Someone who wants them despite their missing parts?"

"You mean who would want you?" Kris stood up and walked to the porch rail, glaring at Sam.

"Look at me. I am missing my leg. I have scars. I can't do things."

"It doesn't change who you are. You didn't stop being strong. So what? You have scars. Lots of people have scars. Wouldn't you date someone with scars?"

"Of course, I would. Renee said the right person would accept it. They wouldn't have anything to get over."

"I think you're the one who can't get over it. Stop feeling sorry for yourself, and you'll see someone standing right in front of you, someone who's hoping you'll see how much she's attracted to you."

Kris' words sank in as Sam looked up slowly, her eyes widening in surprise. "What? No, no you aren't."

"I am."

Sam shook her head in disbelief.

"Who said I can't be attracted to you?"

"But I don't—"

"I already know that you don't see me that way. And that's hard. But don't sell yourself short, Sam. There's a lot of things about you to love. You'll find the right person." Kris walked inside.

Sam stood speechless, her thoughts racing as she followed Kris inside. "I didn't realize...that's not what I meant."

"It's okay." Kris picked up her pack. "I've got some errands to do before I get home. I'll see you later."

"Kris wait—"

"Sorry, Sam. I have to go. I put the leftover chili in the fridge."

Sam watched as Kris left, the door closing quietly behind her. Her mind raced as she stared at the door. She finally crossed to it, locked it, and sunk down into the rocking chair. She turned on the television and flipped through the channels for a few minutes before she shut it off and rocked. *Kris was attracted to her? Wanted to be with her? How had she missed it? And more importantly, why would Kris want to be with her?*

Chapter Thirty-eight

KRIS HEADED OVER TO Sam's immediately after leaving the hospital. She knocked on the door several times without an answer. She glanced at her watch, knowing that Sam should be in. She knocked again before trying the door. It opened. "Sam? Are you in here?" She stood in the dark room, letting her eyes adjust. The blinds were drawn tight, and only a sliver of light came in around the edge. "Sam?" She heard movement from across the room.

"I'm here."

It didn't sound like Sam. It was nasally, and she heard her clear her throat several times.

"What are you doing in the dark? Let me turn on a light."

"No! I want it dark."

"What's wrong? What happened?"

"Nothing. Nothing happened. I don't feel well. I left a message for you. I don't feel like going out tonight."

"I got the message. I know I've been avoiding you since I spilled my guts the other night. I didn't mean to hurt you by staying away. I'm sorry. I still want to be your friend. Something is wrong. I can hear it in your voice. Turn on the light. I'm not leaving until I see you."

Sam sighed, and a light came on. Kris walked across the room and saw Sam icing her stump. Several empty beer bottles sat on the floor nearby. Kris sat on the ottoman in front of her. "What's wrong?"

Sam turned her face slightly away from her. "Sam?" She reached out, and with a gentle hand turned Sam's face back toward her, her breath hIssed as she saw Sam's bruised and swollen cheek. "What happened?"

"I fell."

"You fell? Did you put ice on it?"

"Yes."

Sam pulled back, and Kris reached out again. "Let me see."

"I don't need your help! I'm a grown woman," Sam snapped.

Kris jerked back with the admonishment. "I realize that." She looked closely at Sam and saw her eyes were red. "Please tell me what happened. If you don't want to talk as friends, at least tell me as a doctor so I can make sure you're all right."

"I was seen at the clinic. I'm okay."

"Well, at least you let someone look at you," Kris said with a frown.

"Well, you don't always get a choice on who sees you. Now I do."

"What do you mean?" Her gut clenched. *Did Sam know? Had she somehow found out? I should say something, now.*

"After I fell I had to go to the clinic and be evaluated. I wasted an hour to be told I had bruises."

"How did you fall? There should have been someone working with you. What were you doing?"

"I started doing stairs with the new prosthesis. It didn't go well."

"What happened?"

"I couldn't control it. It felt different. I fell. Several times." The frustration was evident in Sam's tone.

Kris started to speak, but stopped, knowing Sam was proud. She was herself. To fail in front of someone would be hard for anyone. To have fallen in therapy in front of people would have been humbling. "Okay, Sam. I understand where you're coming from. Please let me help you now. Can I bring you some ice for your cheek? It will help with the bruising."

"Okay," Sam whispered.

Kris returned a minute later with the ice, and when handing it to Sam she saw bruised knuckles, she started to say something but remained silent. Sam placed the ice against her cheek.

"Do you mind if I get something to drink? I'm thirsty," Kris asked.

"Sure go ahead."

"Do you want anything while I'm up?"

Sam looked at her, furrowing her brows. "Sure I'll take some water."

After placing the water on the table in front of Sam, Kris sat down. "I am going to ask you a question, and I want you to answer truthfully. What did you punch with your hand? And does it hurt?"

"It doesn't hurt. My fingers move fine. Don't worry about it." Sam flexed her fingers and avoided eye contact.

Kris took a deep breath. "Can I ask you one more thing? I hope you don't bite my head off, but I'm not leaving until you answer me. Did you eat dinner? You've had a few beers, and I wouldn't want you to pass out and fall again. You don't seem like you're in the mood for company, and

I don't blame you. I want to make sure you'll be all right before I go. Will you call me if you need something? Or want to talk?"

Sam spoke quickly. "Don't go. I'll make you something to eat. Don't you say no. You'll piss me off." She picked up her crutches and walked over to the kitchen. She looked in the fridge, and scowled. "Hmm, I don't have much for dinner. How about some BLT's?"

"With real bacon?" Kris asked with a hint of a smile starting to curve at the corners of her mouth.

"Of course. And don't give me a doctor lecture that bacon is bad for you."

"I wouldn't dream of doing such a thing. A BLT sounds good. I'll set the table while you cook."

"That sounds fair."

As Kris set the table, she watched as Sam moved around the kitchen, using the crutches, leaning on one while she cooked. She wanted to help and could get it done faster so Sam could rest. It was evident she was exhausted. She understood that Sam was frustrated and needed to do things herself, to regain her confidence, since finally getting out on her own again. Several of the marines that had arrived at the same time she did had left several weeks ago to return to their homes, but they had a family to help them. She couldn't force Sam to take her assistance.

It didn't take long until the sandwiches were ready. As they sat down to eat, Sam spoke in a voice tinged with regret, "I'm sorry for snapping at you before. I know you were trying to help. I get so frustrated. I want to do things the way I did before, and it's not possible. It won't be for a long time. There are some things I probably won't ever do again."

"Name one."

"I like to play basketball. I won't do that again. I enjoy scuba diving."

Kris stared into Sam's sea green eyes. *Tell her now.* "Sam, I need to tell you something." Sam's phone started to ring, as she reached over and grabbed it off the counter, Kris walked away to give her some privacy. She opened the curtains slightly to look out. *Tell her. Explain what happened.*

She heard Sam end the call. "Sorry for the interruption, that was the therapist checking to make sure I was okay. She was upset today."

"I imagine so. You shouldn't have fallen. They should have been there for you."

"They were. I slipped," Sam said with frustration.

"That's no excuse. Part of their job is to anticipate—"

"Hey. I appreciate the concern, but it's okay."

"No, it's not. You could have been seriously hurt."

"Well, I believe their department head took a big chunk out of their asses today, so that will have to be enough. I'm still hungry. Do you want another sandwich?"

"I'll split one with you."

"Okay." Sam returned to the kitchen, and began cooking the bacon. "You know what I miss the most? The time." Sam tapped at her watch.

"The time?"

Sam flipped the bacon over and took a quick glance at Kris. "Yes. It takes so much longer to do everything. Especially when I'm on the crutches. Setting the table, cooking. Everything is slow. Without the crutches, I feel like I have to watch every foot placement."

"You'll get there."

"I hope so. I want to get back to normal. Even as I say that I know I won't but—"

"Stop it. Turn that burner off. Come here." Kris strode out of the kitchen.

Sam shook her head, turned off the burner and followed Kris down the hall, wondering where she was going? She followed Kris into the bathroom. "What?"

"Look at yourself and tell me what you see," Kris demanded.

Sam looked at herself for a split second. "Just me. On crutches...minus my leg."

"No. Look in the mirror and tell me what you see."

Sam looked at her reflection. Her cheeks were pale and drawn, a bruise was forming on her cheekbone. Dark smudges under eyes still pink from her earlier crying jag. She shook her head. "I don't like this."

"Too bad, Major."

Sam hung her head, as a dull ache formed in her stomach. Her voice hitched, "Don't call me that."

"Why? Isn't that who you are?"

Sam clenched her jaw. "No, it's a title, it's a rank. You know that."

"I can't call you Major?"

"No," Sam said vehemently as the ache grew and crept into her chest. Its cold tendrils tightening her throat.

"Isn't that what you are?"

Hard and choppy, the waves of grief came fast. Her stomach

dropped, and her muscles weakened. Sam recalled how proud she'd felt when graduating from the academy and later earning her wings. She remembered how she'd struggled the last week, on the stairs, and rising from a kneeling position. And how today with a room full of her colleagues she fell on the steps while using her new leg. The humiliation shook her to the core. "When I was an able-bodied Marine. But not anymore."

"No! You are a Marine." Kris' strong voice rang out in the small space.

"Not anymore." Sam rubbed at the heavy feeling in her chest.

"Who said that?" Kris' eyes narrowed.

"I'm not. I should be able to stand on my own two feet. Not one real one and one fake one." Sam dropped her eyes.

"Look at me. That's bullshit. You would tell some private who lost his leg he was no longer a Marine because he lost a limb?"

"No!" Sam shook her head, and repeated softly, "No."

"So, it's only you? You had a shitty day, and now because you had a hard time doing something that is extremely hard for all amputees you don't consider yourself worthy of being called a Marine? I call bullshit, Major. It's time to dig down inside and find the courage that you've had your entire life. Now, what do you see in the mirror?"

The cold in Sam's chest started to turn to heat. *What did Kris want?* Her pulse throbbed in her temple, and acid like anger started to rise. *Leave me alone. Stop poking at me. I don't know what the hell you want! Shit! Breathe. Calm the fuck down. Breathe.* Sam huffed out a breath. "Me. With one leg. And a stump."

Kris met her eyes in the mirror, and asked softly, "Is that all you see?"

Sam swallowed hard against her throat closing up and lifted her hands. "I give up. What else is there?"

"Look again."

Sam slumped over the crutches and rubbed a hand over her face. Tears threatened as weakness spread through her muscles. She closed her eyes tightly and shook her head before looking in the mirror at Kris. She frowned and shrugged. "Okay, you're there too."

Kris saw Sam's shrug and the sad look on her face. "Let me tell you what I see. I see an incredibly strong woman. A brave woman, who is going through a life-changing event right now, with no family around to help her. She's a bit stubborn, but that's okay because that's how she'll get through this. She's friendly, outgoing, and probably a hell of an athlete."

"I was."

"You are. You will get your strength and balance back. You'll be able to run. You'll be able to ski."

"You don't know that," Sam shot back quickly.

"You can try. You might not be swooshing down black diamond slopes, but you can try skiing when you're strong enough. You're getting your independence back. You're driving again. I don't know if bikes can be modified, but you can cross that bridge later."

"Look in the mirror. Let me tell you what I see." Kris stepped up behind Sam and placed her hands on her shoulders. Her voice grew softer, "When you look in the mirror, you see that you're missing a leg. You see, you remember what you could do and how you did it. But when I look at you, I see everything. Everything that you are. Everything that you can be. I don't see weakness. I see strength. And courage. I don't see anything missing, Sam."

Their eyes met and held in the mirror. Kris saw Sam's eyes widen in awareness. Her own heart sped up. She let her hands drift from Sam's shoulders and down her back to her waist. Slowly Sam turned, and Kris stepped forward and into her, their mouths met in a soft, delicate kiss. Their lips moved gently against each other, the kiss lingered as Sam leaned back against the counter and pulled Kris close. Warm moist lips slid along Kris' throat. Kris stroked her fingers along the side of Sam's face nudging her back up, so their mouths met again. Soft sensual kisses that explored slowly and without demand.

They pulled apart, and Sam was flushed and had a confused look on her face.

"What's wrong?"

"I hadn't realized. You said you were interested but...I didn't believe you. How long has it been since your...ah...roommate moved out?"

"She wasn't a roommate."

"I realize that."

Kris looked over at Sam in surprise. "How did you know that?"

"Little things that added up. There were markings in the carpet of the rearranged furniture. The way the bedrooms were arranged. Only one was being used as a bedroom. The beer in the fridge. You almost always drink wine if you're having a drink. You weren't sure if you had beer, and you had no idea what brand it was. Most people have some idea of what brand of beer, or wine for that matter, they have."

"You're quite observant." Kris walked to the other side of the room, and turned back to look at Sam. Her arms held tightly across her chest. "My ex, Shelly. We had been together about five years. I had two tours in Afghanistan in that time period."

"Two? That's tough."

"During the second tour, she cheated. I knew something was off, but I couldn't put my finger on it for a few months. She would be kind and loving, and then vicious. She became abusive. I didn't recognize her anymore. Her hours became erratic, and she was moody. At first, I thought it was me. You know, with the adjustment of coming back. With my injury and the flashbacks, I was overwhelmed, and scared. I felt lost. She couldn't handle my injury, and I wasn't tuned into what she was doing. Or what she needed."

"Or what she needed? You were the one who was hurt." Sam was flabbergasted.

"Yes, but I was in a fog. I wasn't able to keep up with her...well...needs." Sam watched the blush rise on her cheeks.

"She blamed it on you? She blamed her cheating on your tour and your injury. That's bullshit. I hope you realize that."

"I do now. I went off base after I found out she cheated and got tested for STDs. I didn't know who or how many partners she had. Fortunately, she was careful. Or lucky. After I found out she was cheating, I threw her out. It's my house. She'd moved in with me. I packed up her stuff, set it outside, and the next day it was gone. I haven't seen her since."

"Let's go sit down." Sam turned toward the door.

They went back out and sat on the couch. Kris sat next to Sam, reached out, and stroked Sam's cheek before leaning in and touching their lips lightly together. Delicious soft kisses that lingered and explored. Kris arched her neck offering it to Sam's silken lips. Her heart hammered as Sam ran her tongue over her pulse point, before returning to her mouth. They both startled when Kris' pager alerted that she was needed at the hospital.

Sam stood at the window on her crutches and watched Kris drive away. *Holy mother of God can she kiss.* Smiling broadly, Sam lay down on the sofa and flipped on the television.

.

Chapter Thirty-nine

KRIS RETURNED TO THE kitchen and finished with the sauce for the chicken piccata. She was transferring it to a serving dish when Sam nuzzled her neck.

"That smells great." She inhaled. "How can I help?"

"You can bring the rice out and the wine. It's chilling in the refrigerator."

"I'll get it." Sam removed the rice from the burner and scooped it into a serving bowl. Tossing the towel aside she walked to the fridge, found the bottle of wine, and uncorked it. Suddenly beeps filled the air as the shrill blast of smoke detectors and smoke filled the room. Sam dropped the bottle of wine on the floor shattering it as she turned and froze.

"Major, we're hit, we're hit!"

"We lost the tail rotor. Hold on, we're going in fast."

Hands on the collective and cyclic she pushed the controls trying to gain control of the helicopter as it started to spin. The lieutenant was calling out on the radio a mayday and helping her with the alarms going off as she fought to slow the spin. Her crew in the back were shouting over the noise of metal tearing and the rumble of the engines. The big helo shuddered as it fell spinning toward the earth and she manipulated the controls to coax every available pound of lift to cushion the impact.

"Sam, what the hell is going on?" Kris pushed Sam aside, reached under the sink and grabbed a fire extinguisher and extinguished the blaze. She opened the kitchen window and back door. Turning to look at Sam she noticed the sweat on her face, her posture rigid, jaw tense and the faraway look in her eyes.

"Sam? Hey, Sam, look at me. Look at me!" Kris wrapped her hands around Sam's face and pulled her close, so they were face-to-face inches apart. "You're okay, look at me. Do you see me?" She gave her a shake and Sam startled, her eyes focusing as she took a sudden gasping inhalation.

Sam sunk to the floor, shaking, and mumbling. Kris pulled a chair over, climbed up and pulled the batteries out of the smoke alarm in the kitchen and then ran down the hallway, returning with a blanket. She wrapped it around Sam's shoulders, sat on the floor next to her, and draped an arm around her shoulders. "It's okay Sam. You're safe."

"I'm sorry. I don't know what happened. All of a sudden, I was in the chopper and the alarms were going off. We were going down." Sam looked up, saw the soot on the stove and splash guard, the broken wine bottle sitting in a puddle on the floor, and the fire extinguisher on the counter. "There was a fire?"

"It was an accident. Everything is all right. Do you feel okay now?"

"A little shaky. Let me get up."

"I'll help you. Careful the floor is wet." She helped Sam to her feet and pulled a chair over. "Sit. I'll get you some water." Kris brought a glass of water to her. She looked closely at the burned fabric on the stove top. It took her several seconds to realize it was a towel. She tossed what was left of it in the trash.

"What was that?" Sam questioned.

"It was a dish towel."

"Oh shit. I tossed it down. It must have hit the hot burner. I'm sorry. Damn, I almost burned your house down." Distress was thick in her voice. She stood up but stopped when Kris held her arm.

"It was an accident."

"I froze. I couldn't do anything."

"Sam, you had a flashback. Have you had any before?"

"Not like this. Not when someone could have been hurt."

"No one was hurt. The house is fine. I'm more concerned with how you are."

She held out her hand. "I'm a little shaky...and thirsty. I think maybe the smoke detector beeping did it. Not the smoke. I don't think I saw the fire. I'm sorry, Kris."

Kris placed her hand on Sam's cheek. "I know you are. You have wine all over your pants. Do you want to go shower? I'll get you something to wear."

"Ah, I need to sit down to shower."

"There's a seat built in."

"Okay," Sam said softly.

"Let me get you a towel. I'll put some pants out. Is your shirt dry or do you need another?"

Sam ran her hands over it. "It's fine."

Kris led her down the hall to the master bath and reached into the closet for a large towel. Sam looked around the bathroom, a whirlpool tub sat in one corner, and a double-headed shower was fronted with etched glass doors.

"Here you go. Take your time." Kris closed the door to the bathroom, set out several pairs of pants on the bed, and went back to the kitchen. She grabbed a mop and cleaned up the mess on the floor. She began to clean the stove top and splash guard. The range hood was scorched heavily. It would take a lot of scrubbing to get it clean.

She opened a few more windows to let the smoke out and lit a few candles. After washing her hands, she placed the chicken back in the oven to warm along with the rice. After opening a bottle of wine, she poured herself a glass and sat down to wait for Sam. She thought about the movie she had planned on them watching for tonight and decided to make a change. She was reasonably confident that if Sam even wanted to stick around after dinner and watch a movie, she was not going to want to watch something blowing up. The look on her face when she realized the towel had caused the fire was a mix of horror and humiliation. She hoped she could reassure Sam, and make her comfortable. Her confidence would have taken a major hit.

***

Sam ran her fingers through her damp hair and looked at herself in the mirror. *Jesus Christ, you almost burned her house down! And freezing like that. Good God, you need to be able to function in an emergency, not stand there scared to death or completely unaware. Any interest she had in you...despite the leg...well, that's gone now. People need someone they can rely on. Get out there, eat dinner, help her clean up and get going as soon as possible.*

Sam sighed, straightened up and went out to see what pants Kris had set out for her. With a half-smile on her face, she looked at the pink sweatpants, pink shorts, yellow capris and the well faded blue jeans. Shaking her head and chuckling she picked up the jeans, sat down, and pulled them on. Standing back up she found that they did fit relatively well. She pulled the belt from her own pants and put it on to snug the jeans up a little bit more.

***

"Hi, Sam. How are you feeling?" Renee asked her.

"A little better than when I called but…I'm not sleeping well. I had a flashback, and ever since I've felt off."

"Why don't you tell me what happened?"

Sam nodded and sat down. "I was at a friend's house, and we were getting ready to eat. I picked up a pot from the stove and tossed a towel aside. Apparently, it landed on a hot burner and started a fire. I…I didn't notice it. I had grabbed a bottle of wine and was opening it, when there was a blast of loud beeps. All of a sudden, I was back in Afghanistan. When my chopper crashed. It was like everything was happening again. I could feel the heat from the desert, smell the dust in the air and the grease of the bird. I felt the vibrations as we flew and the impact of the rounds as they hit us. I was right back there. Right before the helo would have hit the ground my friend hit me."

She saw Renee's eyebrows arch with an unspoken question.

"Well, not a punch, but she pushed me out of the way. The kitchen was filling with smoke, and the dishtowel was burning. The smoke detectors were beeping. We think…I think, it was the beeping that triggered me."

"That sounds reasonable. Did the smoke detector alarm sound like the warning beeps in the helicopter?"

"Close enough. There were more of them. But what bothers me is I wasn't even aware that there was a fire. I could have burned her house down. Hell, if I were alone I might not have realized it at all."

"When did you realize there was a fire?"

"She helped me sit down and was talking to me. I was confused. It took a minute or so before I realized there'd been a fire. She used a fire extinguisher to put it out. I was completely useless."

"And that worries you?"

"Yes! What if it happens again? What if I have another flashback and don't realize it? What if I hurt someone?"

"Including yourself?"

Sam was quiet for a moment. "Yes."

"Have you had any more flashbacks since?"

"I have dreamed about it in a dozen different ways. Not the flashback, but the fire or other accidents where I am in a daze, unable to help. My friends or family are getting hurt. I wake up, and I feel nauseous. I am trembling. I'm afraid to sleep because of what I might see."

"I think your reaction is understandable. Sam, the more you worry about this, the bigger it gets. How many times have you dreamed or flashed back to your crash?"

"Too many to count."

"Do you think you did anything wrong that led up to the crash?" Dr. Abbott asked.

"No. I've replayed it over and over. Everyone was doing everything right. But that doesn't mean it wasn't my fault."

"You lost colleagues, friends you had trained with, worked with. These are normal feelings. Sam, you have identified one of your triggers as the beeping of alarms. I suggest you change your alarm clock if necessary. Perhaps find a different noise for a smoke detector or get a visual smoke detector, which flashes a strobe light, like they use for deaf individuals. You want to minimize your exposure to the trigger until you desensitize to it. This may take a while. But give yourself permission to talk about this and process it. You were right to come here. I want you to try to get better quality sleep. Fatigue and disrupted sleep will leave you more likely to have flashbacks."

"I'll try."

"How is your friend?"

Sam shrugged. "She's fine...I think."

"You think?"

"I was embarrassed. We haven't spoken since. She's called and left messages that everything is okay. She's said she's not mad, but I can't imagine that she wouldn't be."

"Sam, you have to trust your friend. If she says she's okay and isn't mad, then that's what she is. If she's smart enough to realize you were having a flashback, I'm sure she's sympathetic enough to understand."

Sam sat quietly again. "You're right. If anyone would understand she would."

"Good. Is there anything else you're worried about? You're living off base again, is everything going well?"

"Yes. I'm renting a house. I didn't want to buy since I don't know when my medical board will be."

"That's a reasonable plan. Small steps, Sam. You'd hoped to get back to running, have you done that yet?"

"Not yet. This prosthesis feels a lot different than the other one did. I have to get used to it again. It's more advanced and can tolerate a higher workload. I am doing a lot of pedaling on the stationary bike, and I've started to use a rower. I'll get the running blade soon."

"Good. I hope it goes well for you. Think about desensitization therapy for your triggers. If it gets to be a problem we can give it a try."

"Thanks for squeezing me in."

"That's what we're here for, Sam. Be careful."

"I will. Especially in the kitchen."

Chapter Forty

IT WAS LATE AFTERNOON when Sam stopped by Kris' office. She stood in the doorway and watched Kris as she spoke rapidly into the phone. It took her several seconds to realize Kris was dictating and not having a conversation. As Sam watched, a pleasant warming sensation settled low in her core. Kris pivoted slightly back and forth in her chair as she spoke. She ended the dictation, scribbled something down on paper, and pressed some buttons on the phone. Suddenly she looked toward the door and surprise crossed her face, followed by a smile. She held up a finger to silence Sam, spoke into the phone, and disconnected. She stood and walked over to Sam.

"I was beginning to wonder if I'd see you again."

"I'm sorry."

"For what?" Kris stopped and leaned against the door.

"For everything."

"That's not good enough, Sam."

"Ah, okay. Well, I am sorry. It looks like you're busy I'll—"

"I don't want you to leave. Come in here, please close the door." Kris waited as Sam stepped inside and closed the door. "Why are you here?"

"I wanted to say I'm sorry."

"And I'll repeat my question, what are you sorry for?"

"For setting your kitchen on fire."

"That's it?"

"Yes. I mean, I can pay you for the damage."

"That's all?" Kris scowled at her, disappointment shone in her eyes. "You disappoint me."

Heat rose in Sam's cheeks "What do you want from me? I said I was sorry, and I'd pay for the damage."

"It's not the stove. I'm upset that you haven't returned any of my calls, even if it was only to leave a message that you were okay. I was worried about you. I know what happened shook you up, and I didn't want you beating yourself up over it."

"I was embarrassed. I could've burned your house down."

"Maybe if I wasn't there. But I was there. And you didn't burn my kitchen down. I did get a new range hood, but the old one was junk. The fan didn't work well, and the light didn't work half the time."

"Can I pay for it?"

"That's not necessary."

"I want to. I insist." They stood silent for several seconds staring at each other.

"Only half though." Kris nodded.

"How much do I owe you?"

"You don't mess around do you?" Kris sighed. "It was two hundred fifty dollars at the hardware store. So, one twenty-five."

"What about the installation fee?"

"Well, I was hoping you would help me install it. And we could try dinner again. Maybe with candlelight instead of an open fire." Kris grinned, but Sam stood speechless. "Why do you look shocked? Did you think I wouldn't want to see you again?"

"Yes. Why would you?"

"You can't be that dense. I like you. I am attracted to you. I want to be with you." *I can't help but wonder about being with you and wondering if your strong body has stamina. If you're gentle or if you like a nice rowdy romp in bed.* "The fire? Sure, it scared me. But I've been more worried about you. If you're one of those people who can blow off other people and their worries, I need to know now. I'll still want to be your friend as much as you'll allow me. I can cheer from the sidelines as you get your life back together and get your confidence back. And if you get your bike modified, maybe we can ride together. But romantically, Sam, if you can ignore me, not take the time to reply when it's obvious I'm worried about you, then that part of our relationship doesn't need to develop. I've been in a relationship where my feelings, my concerns were minimized. I won't go there again. I'm not high maintenance. I won't be ringing your phone off the hook or texting you nonstop. I expect common courtesy."

Sam gestured with her hands, and gave a little shrug. "I'm sorry. I wasn't thinking about it that way. I've been worried about if something like that happened again. If I was in danger, or someone else, would I even recognize it? Would I be able to take action?"

"And what did you decide?"

"Nothing. But I spoke to the shrink, and she helped me make some sense out of it. She gave me a pep talk and some things to think about."

"That's good. I hope it helps."

"Well I should get going so you can finish up. Do you want me to come by later and help you hang the new hood? I'll bring some Thai food, and we can hang the hood up afterward."

"That sounds good. I should be home in an hour."

"Good." Sam looked at Kris closely, desperately wanted to kiss her goodbye, but instead raked over her body with her eyes, appreciating her curves. She smiled wickedly when she saw Kris blush. "I'll see you soon." Sam strode down the hall whistling.

***

Kris got home and had time to shower. She dressed quickly, pulling on matching panties and bra, light blue capris, and a sleeveless white button blouse. She opened a bottle of white wine and had set the table when Sam arrived. She opened the door and let Sam in. Her hands were full, one holding the carryout, the other a tool box. Kris kissed Sam warmly. "I wanted to do that before but couldn't."

"It was worth the wait."

Kris took the toolbox from Sam and led her into the kitchen. "We should eat first while this is still warm. Do you want wine?"

"Do you have a beer?"

"I do. I picked up some on the way home. They're already cold." Kris pulled one out, "Do you want a glass?"

"No. Another kiss would be nice," Sam said with a blush creeping up her neck.

"I can take care of that." The kiss lingered, and Kris felt a low warmth begin to spread through her abdomen, and she sighed softly.

When the kiss broke, they stared at each other for several seconds. Sam touched Kris' face. "We should eat so we can get that hood hung up. What time do you have to be in tomorrow?"

"By six. I have surgery by seven and want to round before that."

"Okay. Where are your bowls? I picked up some chicken tom kha kai soup and red curry with chicken."

"I'll get the bowls. It smells delicious."

Sam opened the containers, while Kris poured wine and gave Sam her beer. They ate and talked about their day. Sam told Kris about her work at headquarters and that she would soon start working as part of the advance return team for her squadron, preparing for their arrival back home. After they finished eating, Kris loaded the dishes, while Sam looked over the installation instructions.

Sam ensured the power supply was off before she removed the old unit. She reconnected the power supply to the new unit, and she was surprised when Kris was able to hold the range hood in place with minimal assistance as she fastened it to the wall and cabinet. They finished the job quickly. Kris reset the circuit breaker, and Sam turned the unit on, pleased to see that the light and fan both worked as they should.

"That wasn't too hard. Would you like to stay and watch some TV?"

"That sounds good. By the way…" She reached out and squeezed Kris' bicep. "You have some seriously ripped arms there, Doc. You're stronger than you look."

"Oh, you think I look like a weakling?" She pulled Sam toward her, pinned her arms against her sides. She moved to within an inch of her lips. "I am definitely," she leaned forward, flicked her tongue against Sam's lips, "stronger than," she flicked again, "I look." She lowered her mouth to Sam's and kissed her urgently. Kris pulled away when Sam tried to deepen the kiss. "Let's go watch something. Want to watch the L word?"

"You have it? I haven't seen that in years. Yes, definitely."

"Do you want another beer? I'll get it while it starts."

"Sure." Sam searched the rack holding discs, found it quickly, and slid the disc into the player and sat down.

Kris brought Sam a beer and curled up next to her on the couch sipping her wine. Halfway through the show, they were lying down, kissing passionately while the on-screen action got hot and steamy too.

Kris froze when Sam's hand reach under her blouse. Sam withdrew her hand. "Is something wrong? Sam whispered.

"Ah yeah. I think maybe we should cool it." Kris saw the puzzled look on Sam's face. "I…got my cycle. We need to stop now before anything else happens."

"Um. Okay. But there are ways around that."

"Not tonight. I'm sorry if I led you on."

"No, it's okay. You're right. We can slow this down." They watched the rest of the show and snuggled close, but Sam was careful not to push Kris, who suddenly seemed skittish.

A few minutes after the show ended, Sam left. Kris walked her to her car and kissed her good night. A soft lingering kiss, which soothed while promising more. "I'll see you Friday?"

"Definitely." Kris nodded and smiled. She watched as Sam drove away, waiting until the taillights disappeared before going inside. She tidied up the living room and went to bed.

Chapter Forty-one

SAM WAS ALMOST HOME when she realized she'd left her wallet at
Kris'. She wouldn't be able to get on base the next day without it. She
glanced at her watch—eleven forty-five. *Shit.* She pulled to the side of
the road, checked her mirrors and U-turned. She pulled into the
driveway, noticing the lights were off. With a sigh, she stepped out of
the car and walked to the door. She stopped suddenly, listening closely.
The hair on the back of her neck rose up. She stood motionless and held
her breath. There again, it was faint, but she knew she heard it. A
muffled scream, followed by a deeper noise, a groan as she heard
something or someone banging inside. *What the hell was going on?*

She pounded on the door. "Kris, open the door. Come on, open the
door." Another groan, another impact, and a feminine yelp. She heard a
loud crash and then silence. "Oh geez" Sam hammered against the
door, and would have thrown herself against it but knew she couldn't
generate the force. "Hey, what's going on? Open the door! Come on,
Kris!" She bent over and grabbed a rock and was ready to heave it
through a window when she heard shuffling, and finally the locks being
released. Kris stood, soaked in sweat, a huge knot on her forehead,
blood seeping from a cut by her eyebrow and from her nose. She looked
dazed and looked at Sam with confusion on her face. A few seconds
passed before she seemed to recognize her.

She swiped at the blood dripping from her nose. "Sam? What are
you doing here?"

"Jesus, are you all right?" Sam pushed her way inside and ran down
the hall searching the rooms. "Who did this to you?"

"Sam, there's no one here. I heard a scream I got up fast
and...tripped or something. I realized there was banging on the door."

Sam watched as Kris dragged a hand across her face, wiping at the
dripping blood.

"Um, did you want something?" Kris asked.

"For God's sake go sit down. I'll get you a cloth."

Kris followed Sam into the kitchen and sat down. She sniffled and wiped at the blood again, while Sam got her some wet cloths. Kris placed one over her nose, pinching it gently and the other over her brow. She watched as Sam started pulling open kitchen drawers.

"Where are your plastic bags?"

"Third drawer by the stove."

Sam grabbed two and filled them with ice. "Here. Put this on your nose. I'll hold this one on your eye."

Sam sat next to her, pressing the dishcloth and ice to her eyebrow. She hoped it wouldn't need stitches. She looked down at Kris' shirt. It was drenched with sweat and blood. She listened as Kris gagged several times and jumped up moving to the sink. She coughed violently several times and spat blood into the sink. Sam followed her over.

"Come on, Kris, let me see."

The bleeding had stopped. Sam rinsed the washcloths, warming them and gently washed Kris' face, removing the blood smears. She held the cloth in place when her eyebrow started to ooze again. "This one is still oozing. Let's sit back down. Can you hold this? I'll get you a clean shirt."

Kris took the cloth and leaned back. *Were these flashbacks ever going to stop?*

Sam came back and handed Kris a t-shirt.

"Here put this on."

Kris took the shirt and started to remove her stained nightshirt but stopped. "I'll be back." As she walked away Sam saw Kris weave and nearly bounce off the wall. Sam rinsed the cloths again and waited for Kris to return. *What the hell had happened?*

***

Kris removed her nightshirt and set it to soak in water. She washed her face and then looked at herself in the mirror. "Damn it. That needs to be closed." She rummaged through a drawer until she found butterfly bandages and was able to pull the wound closed. *When are these nightmares going to end? Why can't I have normal ones where I just wake up screaming. Why do I have to run through the damn house chasing ghosts.* She sat on the side of the tub for several minutes trying to decide what to tell Sam. No doubt she would have plenty of questions. When she could delay no longer she went out to talk to Sam.

"Kris, what happened?"

"I fell running to the door."

"But I heard you scream."

Kris was silent. She turned her head momentarily before looking back at Sam. "I hollered when I fell. That's what you heard."

"No, I heard you—"

"You're wrong. I know what I did." She pulled a wine glass down from a cabinet, gestured toward Sam with it. "Do you want some wine?"

"No. I want to know what's going on. And you don't need to drink anything now." Sam took the wine glass from her.

"Nothing was going on. I heard you pounding on the door and I ran and tripped. Why were you banging on my door?"

"I heard you scream."

Kris shook her head, looking down at the floor. "I don't think so."

Sam reached out, placed a hand on her chin, lifting her face up. "I know what I heard. What are you hiding?"

"I'm not hiding anything. Why are you upset about it?"

"Oh geez, I don't know. Could it be that you were screaming in the middle of the night and came to the door with blood running down your face?"

"Oh, for God's sake, Sam, I fell and bumped my head." She turned to walk away, but Sam grabbed her arm. They stood staring at each other for several long seconds.

She knew Sam was studying her face. *Does she see the dark circles under my eyes?*

"You're having nightmares."

"Everyone has bad dreams."

"Flashbacks," Sam stated empathetically.

"Don't be ridiculous. I didn't see combat." Kris could feel the nausea rising. *God was it that noticeable? If anyone knew they wouldn't let her operate.* She turned to walk away, but Sam spun her back around.

"Maybe not, but I bet seeing people ripped apart every day affected you."

"I'm a surgeon. I see people every day with injuries. I deal with it. It's what we do."

"No, not of the magnitude you saw over there. You would have to be a cold bitch to not have it affect you."

"Well, I guess I'm a cold bitch. I've been called worse," Kris snapped.

"Kris, listen." Sam took her by the elbow and kept her from walking away. "That's not what I meant, and you know it. All I'm saying is that maybe you should talk about it."

"I'm not having flashbacks," Kris shouted.

"What would you call it?"

"It was a nightmare, Sam. Just a nightmare, and I ran to the door when I heard you pounding on it, and I fell. That's it. End of story."

Sam squinted her eyes and looked around. "I don't think so." Kris opened her mouth to speak but Sam continued, "I'll have to take your word for it. I'm sorry I woke you. I left my wallet here."

"You did?"

They looked around and finally found it down between the sofa cushions. Kris almost smiled. "It must have fallen out when we were kissing."

Sam brushed a lock of hair behind Kris' ear, but kept her hand on her cheek. "I guess so. Are you going to be okay tonight?"

"Yes. I will. You should go. Drive safe."

Kris led Sam to the door, and guided her out. "I'll see you in a few days." She gave Sam a peck on the cheek and smiled. "Good night" and closed the door.

Kris watched through the peephole as Sam stood outside on the steps, her hands shoved deep in her pockets. After a minute passed Sam shook her head, and walked away.

Chapter Forty-two

FRIDAY EVENING ARRIVED AND Sam and Kris went out to dinner. They arrived at the seafood restaurant and the Maître de seated them at a secluded table. The waiter instantly appeared presenting them with the menus and filling their water glasses. Sam ordered a Kabinett Reisling. They looked over the menus until the waiter returned. He poured Sam's wine. She sipped and nodded. "That's very nice." He filled Kris' glass, and topped off Sam's.

"What are your specials tonight?" Kris asked.

"There is blackened grouper, with roasted fingerling potatoes and sautéed spinach. The grilled swordfish with pineapple salsa is very popular tonight. We also have scallops over spinach linguini and gingered carrots."

"I think I will have the swordfish with pineapple salsa," Sam said.

Kris hesitated a moment longer, "I'll go with the scallops with spinach linguini. Could I have a side salad also, with the balsamic vinaigrette."

"Excellent choices." As the waiter stepped away, another server delivered a basket of warm bread to their table.

Kris looked around the restaurant. "I've never eaten here before. I've heard it's very good." Sam reached for the basket of bread, and she removed a slice. She placed a small swipe on butter on it. "Oh, that has cinnamon in it."

"It does. Don't worry. It shouldn't ruin your appetite." Sam sipped her wine. "How was work today? Were you busy?"

"I did a few cases. There were no surprises in the operating room, that's always good news. I have a fourth-year medical student for the next month."

"A student? For what?"

"So they learn their way around the hospital, and get more hands-on experience with the electronic medical records. There is a method to the madness of the hospital. It is intimidating when you first start to experience it as a student."

"Do you ever teach? I mean in a classroom?"

"No. Maybe someday, when I get older. Right now I am thrilled to be back in the OR doing what I am trained to do."

"I bet you are."

The waiter returned with the meals. While they ate they talked about current events, including the latest shark sightings at the beach. They sampled each other's food. Sam offered Kris a taste of swordfish from her fork, and their eyes met and held. Sam watched Kris' mouth as she took a sip of her wine. She licked a drop from the rim of the glass that threatened to run down the side. Sam nearly quivered imagining that tongue on her skin.

"Are you okay? You look flushed."

"I'm fine. It's a little warm in here." Sam took another bite, and then placed her knife and fork on the plate, and used her napkin.

Kris looked up and smiled. She reached over and touched Sam's face. "Missed a spot, here." Her fingers lingered and slid along Sam's jaw before she withdrew them. When the waiter returned and asked if they wanted dessert they declined.

After paying the bill they left. They walked to a nearby art gallery, side by side, hands brushing when no one was near. After standing in line for a few minutes they entered the gallery. The exhibit was crowded but they were able to steal a quick kiss or an enticing stroke across sensitive exposed skin.

After forty-five minutes of looking at the bizarre collection of abstracts, including a particularly horrid self-portrait, Sam whispered to Kris, "Please tell me you want to leave."

Kris whispered back, "Absolutely." They placed their plastic glasses filled with overly sweet wine on a tray and hurried out the door.

When they returned to Sam's, she opened a bottle of wine. Kris selected some blues from the playlist, and its smoky sound started to play softly. Sam handed her a glass of wine and they both sipped while staring at each other. Sam sat their glasses down and pulled Kris close. They danced in each other's arms, slowly circling the room. Kris snuggled into Sam's neck.

"I love the way you smell."

Sam slid her hand up Kris' jaw, tipping her head up and lowered her lips. "I love the way you taste." Soon they both were heated. Sam lifted Kris' hand to her mouth, kissed her knuckles. "Come to bed with me."

Kris stroked a hand along Sam's cheek and smiled. "I thought you would never ask."

They moved into the bedroom where they kissed without urgency, enjoying a slow sensual exploration. Kris wanted to show Sam what she saw in her...her beauty, her strength. She stroked her hands through her short black hair, kissed her on the brow, the cheek, and finally on the mouth. A gentle caress of lips that touched briefly together before she drifted to the corners of her mouth and her tongue flicked out, tracing their outline. Sam pulled her closer, so their lips joined again.

They caressed through clothing. Kris lifted Sam's shirt off and released her bra. Sam unsnapped Kris' pants and lowered them to the floor. She kissed along her abdomen as she straightened, and tugged her own pants down. She ran the tip of her tongue along Kris' neck and started to unbutton her blouse.

Sam reached to remove Kris' shirt. Kris stopped her and removed Sam's hand from her shirt. "Wait. When I was hurt...I lost my breast. There's nothing there but scars. It—" Her breath hitched, and she glanced away before returning to meet Sam's intense green eyes. "It's bad. But I want you. Please let me lead. This time, this first time, please let me lead. Let me take you where you need to go."

"Yes."

Kris left a trail of soft wet kisses along the column of Sam's throat. The smell of her soap, spicy with a hint of vanilla enticed. She guided Sam to the bed and rubbed her shoulders and nibbled her neck.

"Give me a sec." Sam removed her prosthesis. She stared at her leg, now fully exposed, and sighed. Her jaw clenched. "I'm sorry I'm not...I wish..."

"Sam, don't. I'm here because it's you I want to be with. Come here and let me love you."

Sam sighed and turned toward Kris.

Kris nudged Sam onto her back and continued her exploration. She kissed the pulse on Sam's neck, its rhythm accelerating against her lips. Her hands traced along soft skin, ran lightly along collarbone, as her mouth continued its slow discovery. Sam's fingers tangled in her hair and she was pulled back toward Sam's mouth again. The kiss remained unhurried. Kris would not rush this. She wanted Sam breathless and trembling, and she wanted Sam to moan and quiver beneath her. She wanted that sense of power that would come from pleasuring a strong woman. She moved higher and kissed Sam's eyelids, her cheeks, and for a split second the tip of her nose.

Kris ran a finger across Sam's lips, barely touching until Sam smiled and whispered, "That tickles." She lowered her mouth tracing along Sam's lips and finally sought entry with her tongue. Their mouths stayed joined, and Kris feathered her fingers down the sides of Sam's neck and finally down over the tops of her breasts. She slid down, her tongue leaving a damp trail along her skin, while her fingers explored, staying soft and caressing gently. Her mouth drifted down the sides of Sam's breasts, and she heard her soft gasp as she finally took a nipple into her mouth and flicked it softly, before releasing it to lavish attention on the other.

Kris moaned as she explored, relishing the way Sam's heart stuttered under her mouth. She moved back to her throat, exploring the skin, and drifting up under her jaw to suckle gently on an earlobe. She moved lower, stopping briefly at Sam's mouth again before kissing her chin and the hollow at the base of her neck. Her hands swept down over Sam's firm flat abdomen, tracing across the subtle curve of her hips. Sam's stomach quivered under her touch, and when she groaned, the vibration from her throat, soft and delicate against her lips empowered Kris. Sam's eyes were closed, and her breathing ragged as sighs of pleasure filled the night air.

***

Sam was overwhelmed with Kris' tenderness. There was passion but no urgency. Kris left no skin untouched by her caresses or kisses. She murmured to Sam, describing what she was feeling. "I love how soft you are here. This spot is my favorite to kiss…it tastes so sweet." Kris' fingers danced lightly over her skin, awakening Sam and leaving her desperate for another caress, and another. She had never experienced this gentle exploration. She had always led. She had given this attention but never received it in return. This languid pace of discovery was something she'd never known, and it left her shaking with emotion, with desire. Kris made her gasp time and again as she discovered and exposed sensitive places that Sam didn't know she had.

Kris' hands drifted low over her abdomen and across her hips. Sam's stomach quivered, and she gasped as her skin grew hot. She felt her own wetness pooling between her legs and smelled their mutual arousal. Kris placed a line of kisses across her abdomen and flicked her tongue lightly against her navel. Kris' hair tickled as it brushed across her abs as she ran her hands through it. It felt fine and soft. She gripped Kris' shoulders and pressed her fingers into the soft slope of Kris' flesh.

Kris' fingers drifted lower in no particular hurry, igniting her skin and leaving her near breathless in anticipation of where her burning touch would next ignite her skin. Moving toward her thigh, Kris' hand slid down across Sam's mound and played momentarily with her hair before continuing, making the skin tingle and burn hot beneath the light touch. She loved it, she hated it, and she tensed as fingers crossed the crease to where her leg joined her torso. Kris slid lower, nibbling along her thigh and her hands drifted down close to her knee.

Sam flinched. "Don't touch that leg."

Kris whispered something unintelligible against her abdomen, and Sam felt her hand pull away, and slide back up along her side as Kris shifted slightly. She gasped as teeth closed gently on her nipple, and instantly soft tongue laved and soothed the quick flash of pain. She thrust her head back arching her neck, and lifted her breasts toward Kris' mouth. Sam shifted and reached for Kris' head to hold pressure against her breasts. She tried to dig her heels into the mattress and slipped off balance, collapsing back down. "Stop," Sam whispered. Embarrassed that she had collapsed. "Please stop." Her hands against Kris, she pushed her away. "I can't do this. I'm not ready. Please."

Kris moved off of her, a confused look on her face. "What's wrong? I thought you wanted this? Did I hurt you?"

Sam sat up on the bed, reached to grab her shirt off the table from where it had landed. "I'm not ready. I thought I was, but...I can't." She tugged the shirt over her head and pulled the sheets up to cover her legs. "Please, will you go?"

Kris' hand swept across her cheek, cupped her chin, holding her face until she met her eyes. "What's going on in there, Sam? What's happening in your head?"

"I...um...I thought I was ready, but I'm not."

"Let's talk about this."

"I'd rather not," Sam whispered.

"Well, we need to. I'm going downstairs to fix us something to drink. And when you're ready I sure hope you'll come down and talk to me. You need to tell me what happened, because something clicked off in your head so loudly, I could practically hear it. Let me help you, Sam." She leaned over and kissed Sam on the cheek. She pulled Sam's robe from the back of the door and handed it to her. Kris picked her pants up off the floor and pulled them on. As she walked out the door, she looked back over her shoulder. "Don't keep me waiting."

Sam waited and tried to clear her head. Her body was alive and quivering. As she ached for release, her mind had interfered and shut off the moment Kris approached her leg. She looked down at the stump, ran her hands over the skin and was suddenly aware of how soft and sensitive that skin was. She bent over and retrieved the prosthesis from the floor next to the bed. She looked at it, and after a deep sigh she pushed herself into it, stood up, slipped into the robe, and walked to the kitchen.

Kris stood over the sink and looked out the window into the blackness of night. Sam came into the kitchen and she turned and smiled at her. She brought Sam a hot mug of tea. "Don't look so surprised. It's tea, but I did put a splash of bourbon in it. I didn't look to see if you have any honey."

"No, this is fine." Sam sat down and sipped at the tea. The burn from the whiskey had her inhale sharply as it made its way down to her stomach.

"Sam, tell me what happened. You were right there with me. We were together emotionally, physically, and poof. Did I do something wrong?"

"No. Not at all. Everything was right."

Kris reached out and took Sam's hand, interlacing their fingers. "So what happened?" Kris asked gently.

Sam felt her cheeks heat. "I wanted more. I tried to lift up. To push up into you and I couldn't. I slipped. I tried to push with my legs and fell."

"I didn't notice."

Sam looked at her and saw that she spoke the truth. "You didn't notice?"

"I was getting pretty excited, feeling you respond, watching you let yourself go."

"But I slipped."

"I don't know who you've been with in the past, but I don't expect perfection. I don't keep a score sheet."

"I'm sorry."

"You didn't like me touching your leg."

"No, I didn't. I'm...I don't know. I wasn't ready. I hadn't thought about you touching it. It's a big flaw, an imperfection that I'm still learning to deal with. I hope you can understand that."

Sam noticed the quick flash of something in Kris' eyes but before she could say anything Kris smiled. "I'll be patient, but remember imperfections can be hidden and concealed. We all have imperfections.

Some are physical, and some are mental, but most are an unequal blend of both."

"Yeah, but this is pretty obvious. I can't conceal this. I wondered how I would be if I ever got to the point of wanting to be intimate with someone again, you know. If I'd be able to. I don't think I'm ready."

"I understand. More than you realize. I still want you. Let me come back to bed with you. Let me hold you. Let me be with you while you sleep and it'll be enough."

"That sounds nice," Sam said, a slow smile appearing on her face.

Sam turned off the kitchen lights and led Kris to the bedroom. Kris slid her pants off and climbed into bed while Sam removed her prosthesis and placed it gently on the floor. She dimmed the light but did not turn it off all way. "I leave it on low, I wake up confused sometimes."

"I know the feeling."

They lay on their backs not touching each other. Kris reached over and took Sam's hand. "Thanks for letting me stay."

After a minute, Kris rolled onto her side and soon felt Sam roll against her spooning her. Sam shifted, stroked her shoulder and pressed a kiss to it. Kris rolled back over and lifted her mouth to Sam's. Slow and sensual the kiss spun out as their desire slowly rekindled.

Sam slid her hands under Kris' shirt and caressed up her sides. She stroked the smooth skin puckered and roughened near her shoulder, gently released the buttons and pushed Kris' blouse aside. Kris tensed momentarily. "Shh. Let me touch you." Sam pressed her mouth against the long column of Kris' neck, smelling the subtle scent of her soap. Her tongue flicked gently, and she felt Kris shudder and moan.

Sam moved her hands slowly over the silky bra. The smooth globes of her fabric covered breasts, and felt the uneven heaviness of them in her hands. She stroked across a taut nipple and found the closure in the front of the bra. She gently opened it, brushing the bra off as her hands stroked backward. Their mouths pressed together, tongues exploring, moving against each other. Sam stroked against the soft, smooth skin which suddenly roughened under her fingers. She moved her fingers further, finding a firm knot along the side of breast, and a deep depression, she broke the kiss and looked.

A rectangle of thickened skin ran along Kris' chest where her breast should be. Dark pink scars ran along the edge of the patch and towards her collarbone. Scattered, scars trailed along her ribs and her arm. Sam felt her fingers fumble and realized she had stopped moving. Time passed, three-four–five seconds. She looked up and saw Kris was watching her closely, her eyes filled with tears. Sam grabbed her hand when Kris tried to scoot away. Sam tried to speak and heard her voice crack. She cleared her throat, tried again. "Does it hurt?"

"No," Kris whispered blinking rapidly against the tears.

Sam lowered her head, ran her lips along the damaged tissue, and stroked the tip of her tongue along the scar following it up until it ended where arm joined chest. She heard Kris gasp and felt the air rush out of her lungs. She nibbled along collarbone, to the pulse point where she felt the beating with her tongue. She rose up, placed a hand on Kris' chin and cupped it. "You're beautiful. God, so beautiful." Sam lowered her mouth and kissed her, soft and sensual.

"Tell me if it's too much. If you're too sensitive." Her mouth slid slowly down the newly exposed flesh, and she heard Kris gasp softly and arch slightly toward her mouth. Sam ran her fingers over unbelievably soft skin. Down over her torso, along her hips, and down her legs. She touched everywhere finding sensitive spots that had Kris trembling. She was unrushed in her discovery and made her way back to Kris' mouth. They kissed deeply, their hands caressing each other. Sam drifted back to Kris' breast and laved attention on both of them until Kris was panting. Her hand slowly drifted down until she felt the soft hair. Kris moaned. "Yes," as Sam cupped her.

Sam continued to explore although she was now trembling with desire. Her hand slipped through the wet folds, and she slowly entered Kris. She slid down leaving a trail of moist kisses along Kris' abdomen and along the inside of each thigh. Sam moved higher back toward her heated core and Kris' scent filled her, and she softly kissed her. Kris' moan filled the room, and Sam quickened her pace. She used her mouth and hands to bring Kris up and finally over.

Kris lay in Sam's arms, trying to catch her breath. As her breathing slowed, she whispered, "Let me touch you."

"Please."

Kris rolled over and knelt between Sam's legs. Her hands caressed the smooth skin, and she appreciated the strong firm muscles beneath. Skin quivered under her hands, and Sam's breathing increased. Kris lowered her mouth to Sam's abdomen and layered it with kisses. She leaned forward taking a breast in her mouth and placed her thigh firmly against Sam's sex. She playfully tormented each breast as she slowly flexed her leg against Sam. Soon Sam was moving against her leg as Kris slipped a hand between them and slid fingers inside. "That's right, let go. Let go." Kris nuzzled Sam's swollen breasts with increasing intensity as Sam rocked faster beneath her until Sam lifted her head and shouted, her fingers digging into Kris' shoulders.

They lay breathless, draped across each other. Their skin glistening with sweat as their heart rates slowed. After a few minutes, Sam sat up.

Kris rolled over, propping herself up on an elbow. "Where are you going?"

"I need to do something." Sam had turned her back to Kris and was looking around, not looking at her.

"Hmm, okay." Kris stood and reached for her shirt on the floor, a little stab in her heart. Never had she had a lover so quick to leave the bed. *Did Sam not want to see her? Was she really that hideous?* She turned away from Sam, tried to put her bra on, but her arms started to tremble. Unable to fasten the clasps due to her shaking, she quickly pulled her blouse over her head instead. She held back a sob, and picked her jeans off the floor, tugging them on. She shoved her bra into her back pocket the best she could and wiped her hands across her wet cheeks.

She felt Sam take her elbow. "Come here. What's wrong? Why are you getting dressed? Did I do something wrong?"

"No."

"Where are you going?" Sam stood, a hand braced on the footboard. "Why are you crying?"

"I'm not crying." Kris wiped at her cheeks and dried her hands on her pants.

"Why are your eyes leaking?"

"I was hoping this...you...us...we would be different, but I understand." Kris struggled to control her emotions.

"What? It wasn't good?"

"It was fantastic."

Sam started to smile, but stopped as she saw the look of sadness in Kris' eyes. "If it was fantastic, and it was, why do you look so sad? What did you want different?"

"I...I was hoping you would...never mind. I'll get going."

Sam grabbed her arm, pulled her back. "What's going on? I can't chase you, and I'm afraid if I take the time to put that leg on you are going to be out of here before I finish. What's wrong? Why are you in such a hurry to leave?"

"You said, 'You needed to do something.' I know what that means."

"I am completely confused. I said I needed to do something. I didn't ask you to leave my bed. Why would I want you to go? I just made love with the most exciting woman I've ever met."

"But you said—"

"I know what I said. I want to know what you heard."

Kris hesitated. "Shelly, she said...she said I was hideous. Eventually, she complained if I even took my blouse off." Kris tried to keep her voice level, and calm, but her throat was tightening. "She started to hop out of bed as soon as we were finished."

Sam reached out to grab Kris' hand and tugged, bringing Kris onto the bed. Sam opened her arms. "Please, come here to me."

Kris moved close, and Sam hugged her in closer. "I'm not Shelly. I need to take care of my stump. I have to sleep with a compression sock on it. I didn't want to fall asleep or become preoccupied again and forget it."

"Your stump? Oh God, Sam...I feel like an idiot."

"Shelly called you hideous? That bitch." Sam touched Kris' face. "Please don't go. I want you to stay with me."

"I will."

Sam kissed Kris and turned to sit up. "Wow! This is sure some afterglow, don't you think?"

"We'll get back to where we were, but first show me what you have to do to your..."

"Stump. Residual limb, the unleg, whatever you want to call it."

"Can I just call it your leg?"

"Okay. Although I was thinking of changing it to Barney."

"Barney?"

"Yeah. Like that short stubby guy in the Flintstones."

Kris laughed and kissed Sam on the cheek. "Show me what you have to do."

They sat on the edge of the bed. "I have to sleep with a compression sock on. At first, it was a stump shrinker, but now I use these. It forces the swelling out and helps with circulation. For some strange reason, it also helps with the phantom pain."

"How long do you have to wear this?"

"I wear it when I sleep, or when I don't have Betty on."

"Betty? I thought you said Barney."

Sam grinned. "Betty is the prosthesis, Barney's the stump. Hey, it's my leg I can call it what I want to."

"Ah, okay."

Sam put the compression sock on. "I have some silicone liners I can use at night, but they're too hot. If I don't use something at night my leg swells up, and Betty doesn't fit right in the morning."

"Can I see the prosthesis?"

Sam picked up the prosthesis, and pointed to the end that attached to her leg. "This is the socket, it's made from polyurethane. I wear a gel liner against my skin. Next is a prosthetic sock. The socket goes over the top of it. Finally, over the top of it all goes a sealing sleeve. It helps form a vacuum, suction, so it all stays on."

"It sounds complicated. I've never looked at one before."

"Here." Sam handed the prosthesis to her.

Kris took it carefully. "It's lighter than I thought." She turned it over, and around looking at it thoroughly.

"It's about four pounds. Different feet add a little more weight."

"Different feet?"

"Yeah. I can change out the foot depending on what I want to do. When I am ready to try to run I can switch to a blade foot."

She handed the prosthesis back to Sam. "Thank you for showing me. It seems like such a private thing. I mean you can't walk up and ask someone, hey, how's that work? So, thanks."

"Would you like to come to my next fitting? It's in a week. It's a checkup, but you can see and ask questions. I can tell that doctor brain of yours has some questions."

"I'd like to."

Sam placed the prosthesis against the nightstand. She looked at Kris. "That has to be the strangest after sex conversation I have ever had."

"I can't say I've had any even remotely similar."

"You know what? I think we've spent entirely too much time talking, and that you are way over- dressed." She stroked her hands down along Kris' sides and lifted her shirt off. Pushing Kris onto her back, she leaned forward and kissed her; a slow, tantalizing kiss meant to arouse. When they grew breathless, Sam slid lower, released the snap on her jeans and eased them down. Her mouth and fingers gliding down exploring the newly exposed skin.

***

Kris awakened, enjoying the feel of Sam pressed up against her, spooning her, and felt more content than she had in a long time. The night had been wonderful. She was amazed with the gentleness Sam displayed as a lover. Although she'd pictured Sam as a rough lover, her softness, and gentleness had nearly brought her to tears. She was surprised that through that gentleness, through that incredibly slow pace that she was able to come so forcefully, so frequently. Without the roughness, without the pain, without the power play. Maybe she should have looked at that as a danger sign, when she and Shelly had transitioned to only rough, nearly violent sex. She shook her head. *Do not think of Shelly now.*

Sam stirred, snuggled in closer, her breathing slow and regular. Kris couldn't help but smile, the night had been fantastic, and she wouldn't be filled with bruises. Sam stroked her warm hand along her arm, kissed her on the shoulder. "Good morning."

"Good morning." Kris turned over, pulling the sheet up over her chest.

"Don't do that. Don't hide yourself from me."

"But it's ugly," Kris said, looking away.

"That bitch told you that?"

Kris nodded.

"Now I understand why you didn't want to be intimate a few nights ago. She made you see yourself as flawed. As not enough. It takes a certain kind of mean to make someone feel bad about something they can't control. I think we're both dealing with the emotional scars of our injuries." Sam reached out and ran a finger over Kris' collarbone, making her flesh erupt with sensation. As her finger moved lower and slowly teased its way under the sheet, she whispered, "If you want to cover yourself that's fine, but don't do it because you think I want you covered. I don't. I want you comfortable."

Kris looked into Sam's eyes, and seeing the sincerity in them, she rose up onto one elbow and leaned forward to place a kiss on Sam's welcoming lips. After the kiss broke she moved over Sam, straddled her and pressed her mouth to Sam's collarbone. She savored her flesh and moved slowly down over her firm breasts. Her hands played with Sam's breasts while her mouth enflamed. Sam moaned with pleasure, "So good, don't stop." Kris traced a hand along her torso, and across the firm, taut expanse of her stomach, smiling when the flesh quivered under her touch.

Kris laughed. "You're ticklish."

"No."

"Really?" She repeated the stroke, smiling when Sam hissed and tightened her stomach. "I'll have to remember this spot for later." She rose up on all fours, her leg between Sam's and as her hand slid lower. She leaned forward her mouth covering Sam's in a slow, sweet kiss. She teased, she soothed, and her confidence surged as Sam quaked and gasped below her. She slowly brought Sam to peak and kissed her softly as Sam moaned through her release. They lay wrapped in each other's arms for a few minutes, and Kris murmured, "Is it okay if I cook breakfast? If I stay in bed any longer, I can't be responsible for what might happen next. Besides after last night, I could use the energy boost."

"You want to cook?" Sam sounded surprised.

"I do. Any preference?"

"Not oatmeal. I ate that twice this week."

"Bleh. Definitely not oatmeal. You stay here, I'll cook. You want coffee?"

"Sure."

"I'll bring it in." She bent and kissed Sam, appreciating the gentle stroke of hands along her breast and a quick mischievous grin. "I'll be back in a few minutes."

They sat in bed eating omelets and sipping coffee. "Will you tell me what happened?" Sam spoke quietly.

Tell her, tell her now. Renee said to let her know first. No, it's too late. It's not going to get easier. "I went out on a medevac run. They needed a doctor in the field. We had all done them before. Not often, but it happens when someone might need something advanced done en route.

"We were getting back to the chopper when there was an explosion near me. I didn't have body armor on. I had taken it off. I was doing a...procedure...and it was getting in the way. I didn't put it back on. I was running to the chopper when I felt something hit along my side and chest. I ended up with a collapsed lung and several shrapnel pieces in the chest muscles and near the shoulder. It would be a few days before I realized that my breast was hit too."

Sam stroked gently over a shoulder scar. "You're lucky your arm didn't get hit worse. How is that possible?"

"I was lucky. My face and the rest of my arm were spared somehow." *Tell her. All of it.* Kris swallowed hard and looked away. She gulped a large mouthful of coffee.

"It's okay if you don't want to talk about it. Trust me, I understand. I don't like to talk about my injury. I spend far too much time thinking about it. I'd rather find other things to do."

"That sounds good." The knots in Kris' stomach relaxed. "What were you going to do today?"

"I was hoping to make love with you again, but we spent too much time talking instead of touching and moaning." Sam grinned as she ran her finger across Kris' collarbone.

Kris laughed, put her coffee aside, and placed the dishes on the tray. Sliding into bed, she rolled across against Sam.

Sam groaned. "I have an appointment in ninety minutes that I have to get ready for. I'm sorry. Can I have a rain check?"

Kris leaned over to kiss Sam. "That's all right. I have some work I need to catch up on, and I was going to spend a few hours at one of the pediatric clinics in town. I should get going too. It sounds like we both need to get ready. Duty calls. Maybe a few more minutes to be close?" They lingered as long as they dared. Sam donned her prosthesis, slid into a pair of shorts, and pulled on a t-shirt. She followed Kris to her car and stood by as Kris climbed in and fastened her seat belt. Sam leaned in through the window and kissed her. "I'll call you later." She gave her arm a tender touch and backed up as Kris pulled away.

Chapter Forty-three

KRIS WATCHED AND LISTENED as the therapist worked with Sam. Sam was wearing the assist belt and stood straddling the belt on the treadmill. The belt circled slowly as he gave her some final instructions. *Sam looks nervous. I am too. I hadn't ever thought about it. It's not going to feel the same.* Sam's hands were tight on the rails her posture rigid as she stared at the moving belt. Slowly Sam lifted her leg and placed the running blade on the belt. Her leg shifted backward, and Sam lifted it up and repeated. She did this skating motion ten times before fully stepping onto the treadmill.

Kris let out the breath she didn't realize she'd been holding when Sam started walking on the treadmill. After a minute she realized that Sam appeared to be slightly less stressed than she was when they first arrived for the session. The therapist raised the elevation and Sam adjusted beautifully.

"Excellent. Sit down and take a break. In a few minutes, we're going outside."

"Okay."

Sam took the empty seat beside Kris. She drank from the water bottle Kris handed her, and they watched as other Marines worked with their therapists.

"That looked pretty scary."

"I thought I was going to wipe out there for a second."

"You didn't."

"Thank God. I've kept saying I want to get back to running, but that was pretty intimidating."

"I was thinking the same thing."

"He told me I was going outside next. You don't have to stay."

"I really shouldn't. I'm glad I was able to see what the prosthetist does to check your socket and to ask him questions about the fit, but I can't stay for the rest of your therapy."

"That's okay. What time do you have to be in?"

"By sixteen hundred. I have the overnight tonight. I'll see you

Friday night."

"That sounds good. I was going to cookout."

"I'll bring the wine."

They stood for a second looking at each other, and Sam whispered, "You know want I want to do now right?"

"I do. Right back at you. Bye." Kris paused for a few seconds and spoke with the therapist who had worked with her during her own recovery, and left.

Chapter Forty-four

SAM WAS TURNING THE potatoes on the grill when Kris came up behind her. "Is that a charcoal grill?" Kris nibbled on Sam's neck.

Sam turned and kissed her. "It is. Nothing comes close to the flavor you get with charcoal. The potatoes will be another twenty minutes. I have steaks for tonight."

"Fantastic. I'm starved. I'll take mine medium rare. I brought some wine. Would you like a glass?"

Sam pointed to her beer. "Too late. You have to make a toast to the grill god when you fire it up to ensure a great meal."

Kris laughed. "Is that so?"

"It is. But you can have wine. I think we're safe. I've paid homage appropriately."

As Sam placed the lid back on the grill her cropped t-shirt rose up and exposed her hard abs. Kris felt a quick kick of lust. *God, I want to run my lips over those abs.* She wrapped her arms around Sam's waist and stroked her stomach. "I missed you. I made you something."

"You made me something?"

"It's in the trunk. I need help getting it in."

"Let's go."

Kris opened her trunk and lifted out a large planter filled with brightly colored flowers in full bloom.

"These are beautiful. Thank you." Sam reached into the trunk and pulled out a second planter. "These will look good on the deck."

"I noticed you were looking at mine, but I didn't think you would make some."

"You're right, gardening isn't really my thing," Sam said sheepishly.

"That's why this will be good. All you have to do is remember to water them if it doesn't rain. There are tulip and daffodils bulbs in there too. They should come up in the spring. I have something else, but I'll get that myself. I'll be right back."

Sam went inside, opened the wine, and poured Kris a glass. She was stepping back outside when Kris stepped back onto the porch carrying a large potted tomato plant. Several green tomatoes clung to the vines. "I know you like tomatoes. I have too many plants, so I brought this one over. These should start to turn in a few days. I put a bag of ripe ones on the counter when I came in before."

Kris set the pot down. Sam placed her hand on the back of Kris' head and guided their mouths together. The kiss was soft and sweet. She gave Kris her wine. "Thanks." Sam picked up her beer, "Happy weekend." She leaned in and kissed Kris.

"Happy weekend." They tapped glasses and kissed again. Kris' stomach growled. She pressed her hand to her belly. "I'm sorry. I skipped lunch today."

"Well, let me put the steaks on."

They dined outside enjoying the steaks, summer squash, and baked potatoes. They finished dinner, and Kris did the dishes while Sam cleaned up the grill. Sam came inside and kissed Kris on the neck before going into the living room. She searched through her music collection and slid a CD into the player, and then moved to the window. As Kris finished tidying up the kitchen her phone rang. She stepped outside onto the porch to answer it.

A few minutes later Kris entered the room and stopped. Sam stood staring out the window motionless but for her breathing. A faraway look in her eyes, she did not hear Kris approach. Just before Kris reached her, she turned her head suddenly, a look of surprise on her face.

"I didn't mean to startle you. You looked so far away. Almost sad."

"I'm fine. I was thinking. Well, daydreaming."

Kris stood next to her, wrapped an arm around her waist, and looked out the window. "About what?"

Sam sniffed at Kris' neck, and started to nibble along the soft skin. "Hmm? Oh, it doesn't matter."

"Sure, it does. Especially if it makes you seem sad. Most people daydream about fun things, something exciting, different." She turned to face Sam. "I'd like to hear it."

"I was thinking about the beach. I always liked to go there. Listening to the surf, seeing the constant motion of the waves, it helped to clear my head. It makes you feel small and inconsequential."

"Did you ever go when you weren't so philosophical?"

"Sure. Fun and sun. Volleyball, scuba diving. I tried surfing a few times, but I couldn't get the hang of it. Morning runs along the beach. There's nothing like it."

Kris remained quiet; her hand resting on Sam's hip as they looked out the window.

"But when I needed to get away, to figure things out, to center myself, the beach was my solace."

"Let's go."

"What? It's thirty minutes away. It'll be dark soon."

"Then we need to hurry so we can watch the sun go down. Come on." Kris held out her hand, waited, and when Sam took her hand she kissed her on the cheek. "This will be nice."

***

They walked along the water's edge, as the sun lowered, their hands occasionally brushing. "I wish these people weren't here. I want to kiss you," Sam whispered.

"I want that too." They stopped walking and faced each other.

"I want to lay with you in the sand and kiss until we're breathless," Sam said, and tracing a finger along Kris' jaw.

"The sun sets in a few minutes. If you can wait."

"Well, maybe for a few more minutes. My impulse control is not what it used to be. I must have stored it in my unleg."

"I have the same problem. They say it can be attributed to stress. One of the many PTSD symptoms is the lack of impulse control, but for me, it's because of being around you. I don't want to behave when I'm with you."

Kris looked around, and as the sun slipped below the horizon she leaned into Sam, and their mouths met in a slow, warm kiss that enticed. When she was breathless, when her fingers itched to undress Sam, she broke the kiss. She nuzzled against Sam's neck, her fingers toying with her hair. Returning to kiss her again she whispered, "Come with me, Sam. Come with me to the beach for a few days."

"We're at the beach."

"No. Somewhere we can be ourselves. Where if we want to kiss, no one will mind."

"Where would we go?"

"My family has a house down in the Keys. It's secluded. We could fly down, rent a car."

Sam pulled back and studied Kris. "You're serious?"

"I am. I'll put in leave papers. I have the time."

"I do too."

"Let's pick a few days and go. Get away from everything, and be ourselves."

"That sounds enticing."

They kissed again, broke apart as voices carried toward them, and then headed back.

***

Kris unlocked the door and stepped inside, Sam was unusually quiet on the way home. At first, she thought Sam had fallen asleep but soon realized that she was awake and staring out the window. Kris turned on the lights and turned around in time to see Sam limping. Obviously trying to minimize the weight on her unleg.

"Sam, what's wrong?"

"Nothing."

"Don't tell me nothing. I thought we'd moved past this. It looks like you're hurting. Is something wrong with your leg?"

"It's burning. Like it's hot."

"Sit down. Take it off," Kris demanded.

"My clothes or my leg?" Sam sat down on the couch.

"Don't be funny. Take your prosthesis off." Kris had dropped to her knees in front of Sam and was reaching for her leg when Sam grasped her hand and stopped her. Sam paused for a moment and stared at Kris when a sense of déjà vu swept through her. She pushed Kris' hands away as nausea roiled up suddenly.

"Stop. I'll do it."

"You're shaking. Why are you shaking?"

"I don't know. Give me a minute." Sam shuddered. "I haven't felt like this in a while." When the nausea passed, Sam released the seal and removed Betty, and the liner. She looked at her stump and ran her hands over it. "How does the end look, and the back?"

"Lean back a little and let me check. Hmm, there's a blister. It's about the size of a pencil eraser. And another area that's red, but the skin is intact."

"Let me see."

Kris hurried to get a hand-held mirror. "I'll hold it, you look."

Kris watched Sam's face as she looked at the area. "Okay. It's not as big as it feels. I need to clean it."

"Go take a shower. I'll cover them when you're done."

"Okay." Sam looked around and realized her dilemma, "Kris? I don't have my crutches with me. Will you help me to the shower?"

"Of course. Why are you looking at the floor? Look at me." She waited until Sam looked at her. "I'm here for you, Sam."

Kris helped Sam to stand up and slipped her arm around her waist as Sam draped her own across Kris' shoulder. Together they moved one step at a time down the hall.

Sam stripped off her clothes, and Kris helped her into the shower. Sam stopped in surprise. "You had rails installed."

"I want you to be comfortable when you're here." She turned on the water. "It takes about a minute to warm up." Kris leaned forward, kissed her softly on the cheek. "Call me when you're finished."

"I will." Sam lowered herself to the built-in seat and took the hand-held shower head from Kris.

"Save me some hot water."

"You could stay in here with me. We could conserve water."

"That's tempting, but I want to get those bandaged as soon as possible. It'll be better if you're not waterlogged. Do you have your medications with you?"

"There are some nerve pills in the nightstand. I left some here."

"I'll get them."

Kris was waiting with Sam's towel as soon as she turned the water off. She was worried. A wound on the stump could be dangerous. Sam wouldn't be able to wear the prosthesis until the skin completely healed. And they had to figure out what had caused the blisters. When Sam called that she was ready, Kris helped lift her to standing and supported her until she got to the chair she had placed in the bathroom. "Here's some shorts and a t-shirt."

Kris brought the prosthesis to the bathroom and placed rubbing alcohol and some clean clothes on the counter. She kissed Sam on the head, quickly undressed, and stepped in the shower. Following a short shower, Kris dried off.

"I found some sand in there. I don't know how it got in, but it did. That has to be what happened."

"Okay. But make sure you talk to your doctor about it. And your prosthetist."

"I have a recheck tomorrow. I guess that's good timing."

"Are you ready for bed?"

"I need to brush my teeth and take my pill. I could use a hand getting to the bed." A few minutes later they were settled. "Kris, do you mind if we don't..."

"Not at all. It's been a long day. We both need the rest."

"Thanks, babe." Sam put on her compression sleeve and lay back.

They kissed and said good night, Kris turned to her side and smiled as Sam spooned into her, and within minutes they were asleep.

Chapter Forty-five

KRIS KNOCKED ON THE door and got no answer. She walked around the back of the house and didn't see Sam outside. She went back around to the front and placed her hand on the hood of the car. *It's not warm. She can't be running. She's doing well, but running along the side of the road with no backup is a long way off.* She knocked again, and when there was no answer, she used her key and entered.

The house was quiet, and it took her eyes a few seconds to adjust to the dim light. She saw Sam asleep on the sofa, curled on her side, her head on a pillow, a colorful quilt draped over her. *She looks soft, almost innocent. God, she's beautiful.* Kris wanted to lie down with her but knew Sam would wake instantly. She sat in the chair and watched as Sam slept. *You need to tell her that you did the amputation. Leave out you were hurt helping her.*

"Hi there. When did you get here?"

Kris looked up surprised when she heard Sam's voice. "Hi, about twenty minutes ago." Kris moved over to her and knelt on the floor. "Don't get up." She kissed her. "I missed you."

"I missed you too. Come up here."

Kris climbed onto the couch with her. They kissed several times before Kris lay on her side, her arms and legs draped over Sam. "What have you been doing?"

"I'm starting to pick up speed and elevation on the treadmill. I am side shuffling well. I played a little basketball with the guys the other day. Of course, we were all a little timid, but it went well for all of us. How was your conference?"

"It was interesting. They reviewed some new techniques and approaches to abdominal surgery. There are some interesting new products out. I know you don't want to hear about new ways to anastomose bowel loops."

Sam cringed. "No. I'm not sure what that even means, but no."

"I found something we can do this weekend. If you don't already have plans."

"I was planning on spending it with you."

"Good! How about going to a beer tasting?"

"A beer tasting?" Sam couldn't hide the surprise in her voice.

"Yes. It's like a wine tasting but with beer."

"You don't particularly like beer."

"I'll be your driver. It's at an auto museum. Classic cars, antiques, even some vintage motorcycles. You can kick back, relax, and I'll take care of you if you get tipsy."

"Marines don't get tipsy. We might get drunk, but we don't get tipsy."

"I'll be your wingman if you get drunk. I'll take good care of you." She slid her hand up under Sam's shirt. "I'll make sure no one bothers you." She stroked across a bare nipple and felt it pucker. "I'll get you home safe." She rolled her thumb and forefinger causing Sam to moan. "I won't take advantage of you."

"Please do." Sam pulled Kris up, so she sprawled on top of her. "Please do."

***

The three-story museum was packed with a friendly crowd. People were dressed in everything from Bermuda shorts and t-shirts to coat and tie. A good portion of the revelers appeared to have come directly from work. Two bands entertained and twenty microbreweries offered up samples of over seventy different beers. Restaurants had partnered with the breweries to offer small portions of their specialty foods which paired perfectly with the beer served. A cigar station set up outside was busy.

"Where did you hear about this? This is fantastic." Sam sipped from her glass. A tiny line of foam rested on her lip.

"When I got back from my conference I passed the tourism booth at the airport. They had a banner up advertising it." Kris reached out, wiped her finger along Sam's lip, gathering the foam, and licked her finger. "Mmm, that is good." She smiled at Sam. "I might have to try a taste or two."

"You should since we're not driving home."

"When I found out there was a hotel right across the parking lot it was an obvious choice. They opened this week, so most people didn't realize it was there. The manager said they didn't sell out until late this afternoon."

"Well, that was lucky for us. Let's go over to that table. This brewery has a pale ale I think you might like."

Kris tried sips of several beers and found a few that were agreeable. She was careful not to consume too much and soon switched to water. Sam was obviously enjoying herself, and Kris liked watching her let her guard down.

They ran into a group of helicopter pilots from a sister squadron, and Sam had a lively conversation with them. They asked how she was doing and also shared some good-natured ribbing. Kris caught Sam's attention and indicated that she was going to go get some water. The guys spoke with Sam for a few more minutes before they moved on.

Sam started looking for Kris. While she was searching, she was interrupted several times by women determined to flirt with her. Sam politely discouraged them. She was about to give up her search and text Kris when she caught sight of her. Dressed in snug blue jeans and a black sleeveless button shirt, she looked sexy. Her long legs looked even longer, and a small strip of stomach was exposed when she walked. Their eyes locked and Sam saw a flare of passion in them. A quick punch of lust filled Sam. She grew damp, and her breasts tingled. A gnawing sensation deep inside started to grow. She moved toward Kris quickly.

Kris smiled. "There you are. Are you okay? You look flushed."

"Yes. I want to go." Sam spoke quickly and took her hand.

"Already?" Kris glanced at her watch, "It's only been ninety minutes. Don't you feel well? Is your leg hurting?"

"No, it's fine. I'm fine. We need to go."

Alarmed with the urgency in Sam's voice she started moving with her. "Okay. Would you like some water?"

"No, come on." Sam tugged her along.

"Sam, please tell me what's wrong." They hurried out of the building and down the path toward the hotel. "Sam?"

As they approached a small storage building, Sam stopped and spun Kris around pressing her up against the wall. "I need you." She captured Kris' mouth in a smoldering kiss. Her hands raced over Kris' body, seeking skin. Kris' groan enflamed her more. Sam slid her mouth along Kris' neck and settled on the pulse point. Her hands slid under the cotton blouse and stroked across soft skin. "I want you."

Kris gasped. "Sam, good God, you need to slow down." She hissed as teeth closed on her collarbone. "We can't do this here." She tried to push away, but Sam pulled her back and kissed her hungrily. Sam broke the kiss and grabbed Kris' hand, and they hurried the rest of the way to the hotel. Kris fumbled with the key card when the electronic reader didn't accept it. After several attempts, the door buzzed to allow them into the hotel. Sam yanked the door open and pulled Kris behind her. They hurried down the hall to their room, again the key didn't work. With a growl of frustration, Sam pulled it from Kris' hand, shoved it into the reader and pulled it clear. The light flashed to green, Sam pushed the door open and grabbed Kris pulling her through. She tossed the key card onto the floor, spun around and pushed Kris up again the wall.

Hard, urgent hands stroked up Sam's sides, her mouth captured in steaming hot kiss, which stoked her desire. Sam jerked Kris's arms overhead and continued to devour her mouth, the mildly pungent taste of the beer noticeable. Kris responded, her mouth eager. Sam forced her legs apart with a knee, her hot, moist tongue left a trail of fire down her neck. Kris arched and offered the soft skin there to Sam's hungry mouth. Her arms nearly dropped as Sam released them unexpectedly but she quickly raised them when Sam tugged her shirt off before being tossed aside.

Sam reached around and had her bra off in seconds. "God," Kris hissed as mouth and hands closed on her breast. Sam's moans vibrated against her chest and Kris pressed at Sam's head holding her tightly against her chest. Kris let go and hurried to unsnap her pants. Sam's hands tangled with hers as they tugged her clothes to the floor.

"My turn." Kris reached out and pushed Sam's hands aside as she fumbled with the buttons on her blouse. She released three buttons before she grabbed the center and pulled it apart. Sam released her own bra and pulled Kris back to her.

Their breathing was hot and harsh, their mouths frantic, groans filled the air as they groped and stumbled their way to the bed. They tumbled and rolled, mouths fused and hands groping, their hands seeking, finding vulnerable places, and exploiting them. They moved across the bed and back again. The sheets sprang free, pillows were shoved to the floor, Sam slid lower and wasted no time on teasing, she hurried along, and Kris gasped and reached for the sheets to hold on.

Kris was racing upward on sensation and pleasure until she erupted and felt herself flood with her release. As she lay gasping for breath, she became aware of Sam standing and rapidly jerking her own pants down. The jeans got held up trying to clear Sam's leg, she pivoted, sat down and pulled the leg off, letting it fall tangled in her jeans to the floor.

Kris reached up and pulled Sam down onto her. Their mouths met again, and she tasted herself. She rolled quickly, reversing their position and pressed Sam down. Her heart hammered in her chest, and she felt powerful and strong as she pleasured Sam. Sam's groans and gasps emboldened her. She would give Sam this. Hot, and urgent, letting the animal in her out. Kris tugged and tickled, and when Sam tried to flip her with her legs, she pushed them down and wide without thinking about it. Kris slid lower, using her mouth to wrench an explosive orgasm from Sam again.

Giving Sam no rest, Kris moved back up her body tasting the salt on her skin. Kris straddled Sam, reached between them and stroked into her. The sounds of flesh on flesh were rhythmic, and Kris watched as she drove Sam upward again; her face filled with shocked pleasure and her bright green eyes lost focus a moment before she erupted.

Sam's breathing slowed, and she started to tremble with aftershocks. Kris wrapped her in her arms and pulled the blankets off the floor, covering them both. She spooned against her and placed soft kisses and an occasional quick bite on her shoulders. Each nibble triggering another shudder. "Are you okay?"

"Oh my God," Sam moaned, the words garbled. "What the hell was that?" She rolled and propped herself on her elbow. "I guess you're pretty proud of yourself."

"Yes, I am. I love that I could get you, the strongest woman I know, to surrender completely. Yes, it was...empowering. I hope to bring you to that point again. Soon." She pushed up to a seated position, pushed hair back away from Sam's eyes. "What happened in there?" Kris tapped Sam's forehead.

"I saw you. The sexiest woman in there walking toward me. And everyone was watching you. The men, half the women, and I thought, 'God she's here with me.' And you had your eyes on me. Only me. It was hot. I couldn't help myself. I needed to have you." Sam reached out and cradled Kris' cheek. "I was rough. Did I hurt you?"

"No." Kris leaned forward and nudged Sam over onto her back. She straddled her immediately and lowered herself, so they lay breast to breast. "No, you couldn't." She lowered her mouth again.

***

Sam awakened and lay quietly for a moment trying to figure out where she was. Kris lay beside her, breathing slow and deep. Her bladder demanded she get to the bathroom. Sitting up she looked around the room for her prosthesis. In the darkness, she couldn't find it.

She leaned over reaching out to find her jeans, still no luck and she had to hurry. *Damn that beer*. She eased down onto the floor, now frantic to find her prosthesis. After several more seconds, she gave up, and crawled to the bathroom, cursing herself and praying that Kris remained asleep. She made it to the bathroom and relieved herself. She finished washing her hands and exhaled sharply as her body heated. She used her hands on the counter to help her hop to the tub and sat down. Unexpected anger bubbled up, like lava, her hands shook with rage, and she clenched them over and over, her ears pounded and heart raced.

There was a soft knock on the door. "Sam? Are you ill?"

"No. I needed to use the bathroom." *Damn it!* She swiped a towel from the rack and twisted it violently.

"Can I come in?"

"Wait a minute." Sam pushed up and got back to the sink. She splashed cold water on her face and was drying it when Kris knocked again.

"Sam? What's wrong?" Kris opened the door a few inches. "Are you sick?"

"I'm fine, I—" Her voice cracked, and she turned away.

Kris pushed in. "Oh, Sam what's wrong? Are you having pain? You don't have on the compression sleeve. I'll get it. Do you need your medicine?"

"I don't need any pills!" Sam saw Kris wince with the sharp tone of her voice. "I'm sorry. I don't need the medicine. It wouldn't go well with the alcohol."

Kris stepped up next to her and placed her hands on Sam's cheeks. "Tell me what's wrong. What happened?"

"It's nothing." Sam turned away.

"Look at me. I can tell you're mad about something. What is going on?"

Sam twisted the towel and fought the unfamiliar impulse to hit the wall. "I had...I had to go the bathroom." She growled and leaned over the sink. "I couldn't find my leg. I had to hurry. I...I had to crawl. God this sucks. This sucks! I hate being an amputee."

"Oh, Sam. I'm sorry."

"It's... it was humiliating. I kept hoping you wouldn't wake up and see me."

"I didn't see you." Reaching out she placed a hand on Sam's shoulder. "You could have asked me for help."

"I should be able to go to the bathroom by myself."

"You did."

"On my own two feet."

"You can't. You only have one. So you have a choice to make. Always keep Betty close by, ask for help, or do what you did. As far as keeping Betty close by, I know you usually do. But we didn't think about that before. We were preoccupied."

"You don't understand."

"You're right. Emotionally I don't know how you feel. But I like to think that I am compassionate enough to. Will you sit down?" Sam hopped to the edge of the tub, and Kris sat down next to her and leaned against her shoulder. "Can I ask you a question?"

"Sure."

"Do you know what vertigo is?"

"Well, yeah every pilot does. It's where everything seems like it's spinning, and you can't tell up from down."

"Pretty much. If I told you that when I get a head cold I have a tendency to get vertigo and that leaves me unable to walk. And that I end up getting sick to my stomach, would you ignore me? Deny me help if I asked?"

"No, of course not."

"If I had vertigo and didn't want to ask for help and you saw me crawl to the bathroom, would you think less of me, or would you offer to help?"

"I...I'd help you. Whether you wanted me to or not."

Kris knelt down in front of Sam, grasped her hands. "Then don't deny me the opportunity to help you. There are many things I can't help you with. This is something I can."

Sam looked down and saw the compassion and sadness in Kris' eyes. Again, she was surprised when she had the sense of familiarity of Kris kneeling next to her. She was silent for a long moment before shrugging it off. "I'll try to keep that in mind."

"I appreciate that. Now would you like some assistance getting back to bed?"

"Absolutely, I'm freezing. And from the looks of you, you could use some warming up to." Sam gestured to Kris' turgid nipple. "Let's go get warmed up."

Chapter Forty-six

SEPTEMBER FLEW BY WITH Kris on a full operating schedule and clinic duties. Sam continued to progress through therapy and was the liaison for her squadron, which remained overseas, but she worked on readying the squadron spaces and maintenance shop for their return. She spent a portion of each day with the wounded warrior regiment, now working as a peer counselor/advisor for others as they transitioned into the unit. And three or four times a week she managed to squeeze some time into the flight simulator and practice her skills.

Kris was rediscovering herself as she slowly realized she had surrendered much of her autonomy to Shelly through their years together. She deleted the occasional angry email or phone call from Shelly without responding to any of her promises or threats.

Sam spent a lot of her free time researching and talking to pilots across the different services that had lost legs and found out more about the medical evaluation board. She was trying to find a pattern to what the pilots who had been retained for flying had done differently from those who were not retained. Sam exercised relentlessly, pushing herself a little harder each day to help control her increasing anxiety about her future. She spoke to her foster parents weekly keeping them updated on her progress, and she joined several online amputee support groups. She frequently found herself wondering what Kris was doing, and promised herself she would cautiously enjoy the present.

***

Kris and Sam returned from dinner out and were outside enjoying a glass of wine as the sun set. "Kris, would you like to go away for the weekend? Maybe head out toward Asheville? They have a nice arts district and some excellent restaurants and clubs. We could do some hiking too, not too rugged."

"That sounds like fun. Why don't you pick the trail? Do you want me to make arrangements for the trip?"

"No, I'll take care of it. Are you able to leave on Friday?"

"Yes. I should be home by five."

"Great." She leaned over and kissed Kris. "I'll pick you up here."

"It should be fun." Kris placed her hand on Sam's cheek. "Do you want to go inside and watch a movie?"

"No. I want to go inside and go to bed. I missed you last weekend when you were on call."

"I missed you too." Kris took Sam's hand and led her inside.

***

Sam and Kris had been hiking on a looped trail for about two hours when they stopped back at the parking area and refilled their water bottles. After having lunch, they started walking again. They had been hiking for twenty minutes when they heard someone running toward them.

A man ran through the brush. "Help! I need help. My daughter fell. She's bleeding. Please help."

"Show us."

Kris took off running with the man, and Sam followed as quickly as she could. They arrived several minutes later; a pregnant woman was kneeling on the ground peering over a ledge. "Stay still honey Daddy is getting help."

They stopped and peered over the edge of an eight-foot drop. A young girl about five years old lay on the ground crying. There was a small pool of blood around her. Kris moved to the edge. "I have to get down there. Help me down." She got on her hands and knees and grasped an exposed root. She was unable to reach down and was worried about the drop, if she rolled at all she would have a dangerous fall. Sam arrived, and Kris told her what she needed. Sam and the father, lay on the ground and hooked her arms, and lowered her a few feet. They lowered her as far as they could before letting go and Kris dropped the last few feet landing on her feet like a cat.

"Hi, honey. My name is Kris. I'm going to help you, okay?"

"Mommy!"

"It's okay, honey, the lady can help you."

"What's your name?"

"Robin."

"Hi, Robin. Can you lay still? Where do you hurt?"

"Mmmmy arm, mmmmy leg. It's all bloody, and it hurts so bad!"

she stuttered, crying softly.

"Let me look." The arm was deformed at the wrist, bone protruded through the skin. Blood oozed slowly from the wound. Kris looked at the leg. It was obviously broken, and more blood was pooling around it.

Kris called up to Sam. "Give me the pack. Sir, did you call nine-one-one?"

"Oh God, I forgot!" He replied with panic rising in his voice.

"I'll do it." Sam pulled the small knapsack off her back and dropped it to Kris. She pulled her cell phone from her pocket.

"Tell them she has compound fractures of the right wrist and lower leg. The patient is stable at this time." After Kris finished taking the child's pulse, she opened the bag and pulled out a first aid kit. She covered the exposed bone ends, secured the dressings and used a collapsible splint on the arm. She applied direct pressure to the bleeding wound on the child's leg but would have to wait for help to get the leg splinted. She spoke reassuringly to the child and listened while Sam called, and tried to reassure the mother. Kris looked down at her hands, saw the blood on them, and more blood next to the small leg, and heard a bizarre whizzing noise.

"Doc we got kids out here! Holy cow! They have blood everywhere." She ran down the hall, stopping over a small girl, her leg was a mess, bone shattered, small ribbons of muscle and flesh somehow hanging on and supporting the mangled foot. Shrapnel peppered her body. She assessed the patient, shouted orders to the corpsman and moved on to the next patient. "Dear God almighty." She assessed the boys' wounds. His arms were bundled tightly with blood-soaked rags. She felt along them, peered underneath, his fingers were gone off of one hand, the other hand nearly severed at the wrist. More orders and she moved on to the next patient. Another girl, lying still, her eyes wide open watching, as blood pooled on her tunic. Kris looked at her, took a pulse. She was warm but lifeless. She closed the child's eyes and had a fleeting thought of a prayer before she moved on to the next injured child. "Good God what happened?"

"Taliban bombed the school while kids were inside. These are the only ones who made it."

The last child had burns on her arms and face. Kris called out instructions before hurrying off to change. She entered the operating room as the children were brought in for surgery. The sound of sirens filled the air, warning of incoming mortars that created a bizarre whizzing noise the moment before their sickening crack and the earth shook.

"Kris? Kris, do you need some help?"

She looked around, surprised to find herself on rocks, in the middle of lush green woods. The child at her feet sniffled, and Kris looked at her momentarily confused. Nausea roiled up, sweat beaded on her face and trickled down her back. Despite her confusion, training kicked in, and she took the child's pulse and spoke reassuringly to her. "Yes. Is anyone coming yet?"

Voices and muffled footfalls could be heard approaching. Soon an EMT was lowered to the outcropping. The EMTs lifted Kris up with a harness and lowered another EMT with a stretcher. They worked quickly on the narrow ledge, barely fitting in the space. After a few minutes, they were all back on the path. Kris finished her report to one of the EMT's and quickly the crew and the family left.

Kris watched them go and looked down at her bloody hands. Grabbing leaves from a tree she scrubbed her hands vigorously, panting as her heart raced. Sweat stains formed on her shirt. Her hands trembled.

"Kris? What's wrong?"

"I...I need to go...I need to..." She tried to run, but Sam grabbed her arm.

"No. Wait, just stay still. Sit down."

"I can't. I have to..."

Sam wrapped her arms around her. "Stay still. I got you. Everything will be all right. Shh." She kissed Kris' head.

The muscle tremors intensified and after several minutes Kris sunk to the ground. She heard Sam's voice reassuring her. Warm hands stroking along her shoulders. Finally, the tremors stopped and her breathing normalized. Sam offered her a bottle of water, and she gulped it, nearly groaned, and would have sworn that dust and sand was washed from her parched throat.

Sam held Kris' chin in her palm. "Are you okay?"

"Yes. I'm okay."

"What happened?"

"I...must have flashed back. With the kid, and the blood. I'm okay, can we go now? I want to get away from here."

"Sure thing." Sam reached out offering her hand to Kris.

Kris accepted Sam's hand and was pulled to her feet. Soft, strong hands cupped her face, fingers brushed over her cheeks. Sam moved forward until their foreheads touched. "You'll be okay. We'll get through this. We'll head back the way we came."

When they reached the parking lot, Sam opened the door for Kris and helped her inside. Sam slipped in behind the wheel. "It's late enough that we can check into the hotel. How about if we go get cleaned up and rest a little?"

"Thanks, I appreciate it." Kris yawned. "I'm sorry."

"It's all right. We should be there in about twenty minutes or so."

"Good, I could use a shower." Kris leaned her head against the headrest and fell asleep instantly.

***

Sam glanced at Kris while she drove. She was pale, her hands twitched periodically while she slept, and she groaned as if in pain several times. Kris had clearly had a flashback, the blood or the child had triggered it. *Had Kris worked on kids while in Afghanistan? Or was it the blood? But she was a surgeon, surely the blood wouldn't have triggered it. She would see blood whenever she operated.* Sam glanced over again, the afternoon replaying in her mind. She would have to try to get them to bed earlier tonight. In her experience fatigue made the flashbacks more likely to occur.

Pulling into the parking lot, Sam shut off the engine. "Stay here, I'm going to get us checked in." A few minutes later Sam returned and pulled the car around to the assigned parking spot. She moved the bags into the room, before awakening Kris. "Hey, babe wake up, we're here. Wake up." She stroked her hand up Kris' arm.

Kris awakened slowly, opened her eyes and looked around slightly disoriented. "Wow, I fell asleep. Sorry."

"For what? You needed to rest. Let's go inside. I already took the bags in." Sam took Kris' hand as she exited the car. They held hands until they got to the room. Before they entered Sam stopped, and looked at Kris, "I...it's a handicapped room. I didn't want to be on an upper floor."

"That's not a problem. Now open the door. I have to pee."

While Kris was otherwise occupied Sam hung their clothes in the closet, and drew the curtains closed.

Kris emerged from the bathroom. "Did you see how big that bathroom is? That shower must be big enough for two people. We'll have to take advantage of that." She grinned mischievously. "The counter is big enough to lay on. But I'd rather use the bed."

"Oh really? Feeling a little frisky are you?"

"I had a power nap. I'm good to go." Kris wriggled her eyebrows.

"Why don't you find a place you want to try for dinner tonight while I take a shower?"

"Why don't we take a shower together, and decide later about dinner?"

"That sounds like a much better idea."

They disrobed quickly, and Sam sat down on the shower seat. Kris watched as Sam removed the prosthesis and passed it to her. She placed it carefully on the counter before rejoining Sam in the shower. Kris pointed the shower head away from them, turning on the water and letting it warm. Sam reached for the grab bars and started to stand, but Kris nudged her back down.

"Sit. Let me do this." Kris made sure the water was warm enough before directing the spray against Sam's body. She wet her hair, squeezed shampoo into her hand, and slowly shampooed Sam's head, massaging the scalp, easing away tension. Her stomach quivered when she felt light strokes across her abdomen and fingers teasingly moving upward. "Behave." She poured soap gel into her hands stroked her hands across Sam. Working up a rich lather, she palmed Sam's breasts and stroked her thumbs playfully over nipples that puckered. Her soapy hands slid across her strong back and firm abdomen "Lift your leg." She stroked her hands down the hard muscles of her leg, gave a gentle twist on her toes. She reached for Barney, pausing when Sam grabbed her hands. Their eyes held, and Kris waited and watched the emotions play out on Sam's face before she released her hands.

Sam lifted her leg, and Kris gently cradled it with one arm, slicked it with soap and silently marveled at the bulk of the muscle in the leg. She stroked carefully over the end, quietly amazed, with the softness of the skin, and the strange Jello-like feel of the end of the stump. Lowering Sam's leg she leaned forward, and her hand moved up across inner thigh, and she trailed her fingers through the dark patch of hair. Sam's ragged intake of breath had her own heart accelerating. Kris leaned over and cupped Sam's chin before gently tracing along her lips with her own, collecting the water as it fell upon them. Kris straightened and reached for the soap again. "Let me—"Sam leaned forward suddenly and nipped at her ribs. She gasped, and tugged tightly at Sam's head. "Stop, or you'll get soap in your eyes. I wouldn't want to be responsible."

"Hurry and rinse it out. There's something I want to do," Sam demanded.

Kris grabbed the shower hose, nudged Sam's head back, and carefully rinsed the soap from the front of her head. She rubbed her hands lovingly through Sam's thick black hair, before nudging her head forward to rinse the soap from the back of her head. Strong arms quickly came around her and pulled her down until she was straddling Sam. Soft kisses quickly intensified, leaving a trail of scorching hot kisses down her neck and across each collarbone.

How the water didn't turn to steam, she didn't know. She moaned and clutched at Sam's head, as her breasts were nuzzled. Warm, open-mouth kisses that teased her nipple until it tightened. Sam stroked her damaged breast with feather light strokes of fingers and followed with her lips. She showed no preference and paid attention to each breast. Kris was overwhelmed with emotion as Sam accepted her, all of her, without hesitation, or complaint. Warm hands caressed and she shuddered as slow, lingering kisses along the sides and tops of her breasts enflamed her. Kris moaned and sighed with pleasure and tangled her fingers in Sam's hair, pulling her closer. She lowered her mouth to Sam's head kissing it, ran her face along it, feeling its texture, and smelling the fragrance of the shampoo. Her breast was engorged and heavy, and when she could take no more, she eased Sam away and slipped to her knees in front of her.

Kris knelt between Sam's legs, ran her hands up along her smooth, strong arms and across her shoulders. She nuzzled into her neck, lips and tongue playing along the curves of her throat and at the angle of her jaw. Leaning forward, her tongue stroked one earlobe before gently drawing it into her mouth, toying with the gold stud in the lobe. Sam's quick inhalation relayed her pleasure and the thrust of her hips, her growing excitement. Fingers tugged Kris' hair pulling their mouths back together, and warm water coursed over them. Her hands slid over slick flesh exploring Sam's subtle curves and eliciting murmurs of appreciation. Their mouths moved slowly against each other. Their exploration slow, unrushed, without demand or greed. Their discovery nourishing each other, healing, not devouring.

Sam broke the kiss. "Your knees must hurt, let me wash you." She quickly soaped Kris' upper body, lingered at her breasts, caressing each carefully, learning more about the sensitivity of the injured side. Sam reached her hands under Kris' arms and gently helped Kris to her feet. She soaped her torso, letting the bubbles rinse away. Her hand moved between Kris' legs, stroked gently, separating her before moving on. She soaped Kris' shapely legs, and when she could reach no lower, she pressed a kiss to her belly. "You'll have to finish."

Kris quickly finished washing and made sure they were both rinsed. She shut off the shower and handed Sam a towel. She stepped out of the shower drying herself. She was aware of Sam's eyes upon her, and of the fact that she hadn't moved from the seat. Without saying a word, she handed Sam another towel and walked from the bathroom. She returned a moment later with the crutches. She positioned them next to the shower, leaned down. "Don't take too long, I want you. I need you." Her kiss was fierce and quick, and then she turned and walked away.

She sat on the edge of the bed, hoping she was right in assuming that Sam wouldn't want help. That she would want, no need, to come out without assistance, the capable, strong lover. She was debating on getting up when Sam emerged, her eyes bright and focused. Kris smiled, moved up onto the center of the bed, and lay on her side. She patted the bed next to her. "I need you right here. I need to touch you."

They lay side by side on the bed facing each other. Sam reached out and brushed a stray hair back from Kris' forehead. She ran a finger down to the edge of her brow, and along her temple. She stroked across her high cheekbone and down along the side of her nose to her lips. She placed two fingers on Kris' lips and traced them lightly. She rose up slightly before rolling on top, and covered Kris' mouth, their tongues entwined as they started to move.

***

Sam lay awake as Kris slept next to her, an arm and leg draped over her. Her head rested on Sam's shoulder, and her hair tickled her chest. Kris' breathing was deep and slow, and Sam enjoyed the soft puffs of air that blew across her chest. She wanted to shift but didn't want to wake Kris. They hadn't spoken about the flashback earlier in the day, but Sam was worried. It seemed as if the injured child had set off this flashback. She remembered that Kris had said she was spending time at one of the pediatric clinics in town. *Had something happened with a child? It would have to have been a villager.*

Her heart gave a little lurch as she thought of what would have had to have occurred for it to have had such an effect on Kris. She seemed to have a lot of flashbacks or at least bad dreams. Several had caused her to get up and run, but Sam didn't know if she was running to or from something. Regardless, she had bumped into things or fallen several times and received minor injuries. Lately, it seemed to be getting worse.

Kris murmured in her sleep and flinched. Sam stroked her fingers through Kris' soft hair and nuzzled her head. Kris sighed and rolled over. Sam moved in against her, spooning her and quickly fell asleep.

***

Oh God, she's stuck, her leg is stuck between those trees, and she's bleeding. I have to cut it off. Oh God, I have to cut it off. She reached for the saw. She looked at Sam writhing in pain. "I have to Sam. I have to take the other one." She removed the prosthesis from her leg, setting it aside carefully. "I'll be quick." She drove the scalpel in deep, quickly cutting through the tissues, blood spurted. She grabbed for the saw and turned it on. And the screaming started.

"Kris! Kris! Wake up." Sam pushed at Kris trying to get her to move. Kris was kneeling astride her, facing her feet and squeezing her good leg with all her strength. She had already ripped the compression sleeve from her stump. Kris stiffened and muttered. Sam was able to scoot out from under her and turn on the bedside light. "Kris, are you all right?"

She looked around, dazed and confused in the unfamiliar room and the sudden bright light. "My God! Did I hurt you?"

"No. You just scared me."

"I'm sorry. Oh, my God, I am so sorry."

"Hey babe, it was a dream." She didn't like the way Kris looked. She was pale, and her skin damp with sweat. Her eyes appeared overly large, and her pupils were wide. Reaching out she took Kris' wrist and felt her racing pulse. "I'm okay. Look at me, I'm good. Come up here and let me hold you. You can tell me what happened. Or not." She saw Kris shake her head. "Do you want some water?"

"I'll get it. I need to—" Kris bolted from the bed, banging off the door frame as she ran into the bathroom. Sam grabbed the crutches lying next to the bed. By the time she got to the bathroom, Kris was kneeling on the floor in front of the commode, vomiting. Sam retreated to get a washcloth. She wet it with warm water and went back to Kris. Sam wiped the back of her neck and handed her the cloth. Sam placed a towel over her shoulders to keep her warm, knowing the shakes were going to start.

"No." Kris pushed to her feet and went to the sink. Sam watched her carefully. Her hands were shaking, and when she tried to squeeze toothpaste onto her toothbrush, it missed and went on her hand. "Shit."

Sam moved to her, took both from Kris, applied the toothpaste to the brush, and handed it back to her.

"Do you need to take something?"

Kris met her eyes in the mirror and shook her head from side to side. She finished brushing her teeth and took a moment to wash her face. She accepted the towel Sam handed her. "I'm all right. It was a bad dream."

"Not a flashback?"

"No. I dreamed I had to amputate your other leg. We were in the woods though, where we were today with the girl. It was…well, not good."

"Do you want to talk about it?"

"Not really. I would prefer to forget about it." Kris shook her head and walked away.

"That's your second one today."

"No, it was my first. The other was a flashback, this was just a dream."

"Don't you think you're splitting hairs? Besides since when do nightmares make you sick? That's more consistent—"

"Sam, I know what the symptoms are! Now please stop! I don't need a pill, and I don't want to talk about it."

Sam tightened her lips and bit down to keep from saying anything. She couldn't take it personally. Kris was scared, that was obvious. Something with the child set her off today. She would make sure they took it easier tomorrow. "Okay. Let's go back to bed."

Sam sat on the edge of the bed, pulled on a t-shirt, and rolled on a new compression sleeve. She'd find the other in the morning. "Can I hold you?"

"Yes." They arranged the pillows and Kris snuggled in against her. "Did I hurt you?"

"No."

"What did I do to you? I need to know."

"I woke up when you grabbed my unleg." She heard Kris gasp. "You didn't hurt it. You pulled off the sleeve, and started shouting and squeezing my other leg. You didn't hurt me. You surprised me. What I was worried about was that you were going to take off running down the hall naked. I wouldn't be able to catch you, and it would look mighty odd me chasing you down the hall on crutches naked too."

Kris smiled against her shoulder and pressed a kiss to it. "That would be quite the scene. Thank you for helping me. Thank you for being here."

"You're welcome." Sam reached over and turned off the light. They lay together in the quiet of the night, comfortable in the warmth of their bodies and eventually Kris' breathing slowed into a deep, slow rhythm.

Sam was awake for a long time, keeping watch for a demon she couldn't see and couldn't fight. And as the sky started to lighten she fell asleep.

Roslyn Bane

Chapter Forty-seven

KRIS STEPPED OUT OF the shower and grabbed both towels. She handed one to Sam and dried herself before grabbing her robe off the back of the door. She reached in and took the towel from Sam, who pulled her into an embrace, kissing her gently. "Your hands are magical."

Kris nuzzled Sam's neck. "Liked that, didn't you?"

"I think that was pretty obvious. I plan on returning the favor." The ringing phone interrupted her, "Can you get that?"

"Sure." Kris hurried to the phone and after a few seconds brought it into Sam. "It's Nancy. I'll go make some breakfast."

Sam's eyes widened, and she blushed. She hurriedly finished pulling on her clothes before accepting the phone. "Hi, Nan. I'm doing well. Um, Kris. She's a friend." Sam cleared her throat. "Well, my girlfriend actually. I'll do that. I'll ask her. I promise. Love you too. Bye."

Several minutes later Sam joined Kris in the kitchen. While they ate strawberries and bananas topped with yogurt Sam relayed her conversation. "Nancy wanted to know if I'm coming home for Thanksgiving, I haven't been home for two years."

"You should go."

"She invited you too."

"That would be great. My parents will be in Europe visiting some friends. The trip has been planned for months. I told them not to cancel it just because I was home. Visiting your family will be fun. I'd love to meet them."

Sam looked down at the floor momentarily before lifting her eyes to Kris. "I've never brought anyone home before." Sam felt the heat rise on her cheeks. "Are you sure?"

Kris moved to Sam and hugged her. "I can't wait."

***

Kris pulled the car into the driveway and shut it off. She took Sam's hand in hers. "Are you okay? You look nervous. I should be the nervous one."

Sam offered a small smile. "I'm fine. Thanks for driving."

"My pleasure. It was fun with all the curves." Their conversation was interrupted when the door opened, and a couple walked out. They both climbed out of the car. Sam hugged Jim and Nancy before introducing her foster parents to Kris. They enjoyed an early dinner of lasagna, salad, and homemade bread. After the dishes were finished, Sam showed Kris around the rest of the house, and they went for a walk in the surrounding woods.

As darkness descended, Sam and Jim went outside to start a bonfire. While Sam laid kindling in the ring, Jim sipped at his scotch. "I'm glad you could make it back to see us."

"It's good to be here. I've missed you all." She looked up and into his eyes, stood up, and moved close to him. "There were a few minutes…in the desert…when I was afraid that I wouldn't get to see you and Nan again." Sam brushed at the tears that filled her eyes. "All I could think was that I wanted to tell you how much I love you two, and how much I appreciate everything you've done for me."

"Sam."

"Please let me finish. I know I hurt you when I didn't want you to come to Bethesda right away. I'm sorry for that. I needed some time to get my head around what was going on."

"We understand, Sam. We spoke to one of the counselors while we were there. They explained to us that it's common for that to occur. We miss you, Sam, but we understand what your career entails. Are you getting back to flying yet?"

"I'm trying, but it's not going well. The odds are against me too. There are healthy pilots coming up all the time." Sam took several deep breaths. "I'm not doing well in the flight simulator. I can't get the pressure on the pedals right. I'm consistently missing my headings, and that can't happen. Landing on a pitching deck is out of the question."

"Is there anything you can do?"

"Just keep practicing in the simulator until I get a feel for the pedals. I can't actually get in a bird because I'm not on flight status now."

"Catch-22."

Sam sighed. "Yeah." Sam looked up when the door opened and smiled as Kris walked out, followed by Nancy. Her heart thudded in her chest, and she swiped a hand through her hair.

Jim followed her eyes. "Your Kris is very nice. She's a doctor?"

"Yes, we met at Bethesda, when we had some sessions together."

"She was hurt too?"

"Yes. Her arm was injured. I really can't say more."

"Of course not."

Sam walked toward Kris, "What do you have there?"

"Cocoa with." Kris handed Sam a steaming mug of cocoa spiked with spiced rum.

"Yum. Let's sit down and enjoy this. Come on Nan, we've got a chair for you."

***

Several hours later when the fire had died down to glowing embers, Kris yawned. "I'm sorry, we were up early for our flight, and had the delay. It's been a long day."

Nancy stood up. "Come on, I'll take you up. Can you two make sure that fire's out all the way before you come in?"

"Yes, ma'am," Sam replied.

Kris followed Nancy inside and upstairs, when she stopped outside Sam's bedroom Nancy opened the door. "Your bags are in this room. You seemed surprised that we would have you and Sam in the same room."

"I...ah...wasn't sure."

Nancy walked forward and placed her hand on Kris' shoulder. "We don't stand for a lot of pretense in this house. You're sleeping with our daughter, and it's obvious you both have feelings for each other. Sam's never brought anyone home before. She brought you home, and that means something. We want you both comfortable while you're here. There are fresh towels in the hall bath. Sleep well. Wake up when you feel like it tomorrow."

Kris smiled broadly, and bounced slightly on her toes. "Thank you. I'm so happy that you accept Sam and I, as we are. I appreciate that more than you realize. Good night." As Nancy closed the door, Kris did a little happy dance.

***

Sam awakened slowly and smiled. Kris lay half sprawled against her body, their arms and legs entwined. Kris' breath puffed across Sam's chest stimulating her breasts. Kris repositioned and murmured, her hand cupping Sam's breast. *Oh God!* Sam's nipples pebbled and she tried to will away her increasing arousal. Kris muttered again and repositioned her hand now resting on Sam's abs. Sam swallowed hard. "You're killing me." A few minutes later Kris awakened. "Morning." She freed Sam from beneath her leg and reached up to kiss her, a soft, pressing of lips. "It was nice staying in here with you. It was sweet of your folks to do this."

"It was." Sam shifted uncomfortably.

Kris leaned up on her elbows. "What's wrong?"

"I…oh God. It feels so good to have you lying next to me. Before you woke up, your hand was on me, on my boob. And on my stomach."

"Okay. Oh…oh. So, you're ready to go?"

"I need to shower."

"Let me help you out. I'll be slow and gentle. You can't be as energetic or as vocal as usual. Pretend you don't want to wake up children."

"No." Sam shuddered when Kris ran her hand down over her shoulder and across her collarbone, her touch sending heat into her core. "Oh, dear God. Yes. Please."

Kris' kiss was soft and teasing, Sam's abdomen quivered under Kris' soft exploration as her fingers drifted lower. Sam shifted, opening slightly to give Kris access. With a few gentle caresses Sam's breathing quickened, and when her breath grew ragged, Kris kissed her thoroughly capturing her moan.

"Do you feel better now?"

"Mmhmm." Sam's eyes grew heavy.

"Go back to sleep. I'm going to go shower."

***

Fresh from her shower and dressed in black jeans and a paisley print blouse Kris headed for the kitchen. Nancy was closing the oven door after placing the turkey inside. "Good morning, Kris. Would you like some coffee or tea?"

"Hot tea would be great. Something smells good."

"There's a breakfast casserole on the warming tray. Want to give it a try? It's Sam's favorite. She usually puts a healthy dash of pepper sauce on it."

"That sounds good. How can I help?"

"For now, just sit down and enjoy the morning. There'll be plenty to do later."

***

Throughout the day Kris helped in the kitchen and enjoyed chatting with Sam's mom. She didn't think of Nancy as Sam's foster mom, as she saw so much of Sam's sense of humor and mannerisms in Nancy. As Kris watched Sam and her family throughout the day she had no doubt that Sam had grown up in a loving family that cherished her and fully accepted her.

Her foster sister, Lauren, regaled them with stories of celebrities and some of their antics she'd experienced as a talent scout in California before she returned home to work in the country music industry. Her foster brother, Justin, and his wife, Penny, doted on their baby girl, Madeline; and despite the extreme fatigue that came with being new parents, were fun. The football games were on but for the most part ignored, as the family celebrated being together for the first time in several years.

In bed later that night, Kris snuggled into Sam, "You have a wonderful family. This was such a great day, and we both have much to be thankful for. Thank you for inviting me."

"I'm glad you enjoyed it. It was nice to be home again."

Chapter Forty-eight

KRIS OPENED THE SHOWER door and poked her head in. "Sam, dinner will be ready in ten minutes. Do you want wine?"

"Sweet tea. I'll be out in a few minutes." Sam flicked a few drops of water at Kris. "Close the door, you're letting cold air in." Kris closed the bathroom door and went back down the hall. She stopped in surprise when the front door opened and Shelly walked in. Kris' stomach sank, and her heart raced.

"Hey, sweetheart, what are you doing? Are you just going to stand there with your mouth hanging open or come over here and greet me?"

Cold settled into her core. "Wha...what are you doing here?" Kris stuttered.

"I came to visit you. You've been ignoring my calls."

"How did you—?"

"Get in? I still have my key. Obviously. You never asked for it back." Shelly grinned at her.

Kris glanced down the hallway. *How long would Sam be?* "I don't want you here."

Shelly scowled, "Now that's not nice. I came all the way over here with all that traffic to see you, and you won't even talk to me."

"You cheated, you lied. There is nothing for us to say to each other." Kris took a step away from her.

Shelly advanced further inside, glancing into the dining room. "Table set for two? My, my, do you have a date tonight?"

"As a matter of fact, I do. And I want you to leave." Kris gritted her teeth as heat started to rise from deep within.

"Well, I think I'll stay until your friend gets here." She stepped closer.

"What do you want, Shelly?" Kris watched Shelly carefully, noticing the slight hitch in her step and realized she had been drinking. She remembered how argumentative Shelly could become after a few drinks and the more recent descent into rage-induced violence. It suddenly stuck Kris that most of the problems they'd had in their relationship somehow had alcohol tossed into the mix. It wasn't just jealousy. It wasn't only Shelly's infidelity. Those things were part of it, but underlying it was her now obvious abuse of alcohol which shortened her temper. She was certain that Shelly would fly into a rage when she saw Sam. *I've got to get her out.*

"I told you I wanted to see how you're doing." Shelly rearranged some candles on an end table. "I think I was a little hasty moving out before. I should have given you more time to get things fixed."

"Fixed? Get what fixed?"

"Don't be stupid." Shelly pointed to Kris' left breast. "To get your tit fixed. I know we can get things back on track again."

Heat rushed through Kris, racing out and across her flesh. Her body tensed, and her heart pounded. "How dare you come in here, uninvited, and demand that I let you back into my life, but only if I have myself fixed. Why on earth would I want you back? Get out! And give me the key." She thrust her hand out for the key and shrieked in surprise when Shelly grabbed her and jerked her forward.

"I didn't ask to come back into your life. I am back in your life. We were good together. You've forgotten that because your head is all messed up."

Kris backed up and struggled to pull her arm free. "Let me go. Get out."

"I'll go when I'm ready. What are you going to do? Kick me out? That's not going to happen again. Remember I know what you like. I know what makes you tick." She yanked Kris toward her, spun her around, and placed her in a choke hold, with the other hand she reached up and clawed at Kris' chest, squeezing hard. "Shit! You still haven't gotten that fixed?"

Kris gasped from the pain, felt herself going lightheaded. *Not again.* "Let me go." She brought her elbow back hard into Shelly's side, and stomped down on her instep. Shelly loosened her grip momentarily, and Kris jumped away. Kris turned and faced her. "Get out!"

"Make me." Shelly bluffed to the right, and when Kris tried to run by her, she reached out and pulled her hair jerking her closer. She punched Kris in the chest, and drove her hard into the wall, knocking pictures down.

Kris screamed. She landed a weak blow to the side of Shelly's head. "Let me go."

"I will when I'm ready," Shelly hissed.

"No! You will let her go now," Sam growled.

Shelly spun around and stepped back. She looked at Sam, back to Kris, and returned again to Sam. Her gaze swept along Sam's body. "You think you can make me?"

"God, Shelly just leave." Kris groaned, her arms clutched across her chest trying to soothe her damaged breast.

"I don't think so." She turned back to Sam. "Nice shorts. You really know how to dress." Shelly snickered. "Are you really her date?"

"Yes." Sam silently moved closer and now had Shelly within reach. "I believe Kris has told you to leave and to give her the key."

"I don't think I'm the one who is going to leave. So why don't you take yourself and that fake leg and get the hell out of here. Before I hurt you."

"Oh God!" Kris started to step forward, but Sam glared at her and shook her head subtly, effectively stopping her movement.

"Oh, you're warning her away." Shelly laughed. "That's rich." She stared at Sam, glanced over at Kris, and turned back suddenly with her arm swinging. Sam ducked, and when the punch flew by her right shoulder, she pivoted, grabbed Shelly by her arm and used momentum to throw her to the floor.

Kris stood and watched in disbelief as the two women eyed each other. Shelly was somehow back on her feet and charged. Time slowed as Sam ducked and Shelly's momentum carried her forward. Sam stood back up neatly flipping Shelly over and onto her back. This time Sam dropped down onto her, sitting across her chest and squeezing her with strong thighs. Sam took a hard punch to her jaw, and Kris cried out when Sam's head snapped back. Sam let out a groan when Shelly hit her in the chest. The sound of Sam's gasp for breath broke Kris' spell and she grabbed the phone, dialing nine-one-one. Sam wrapped her arms around Shelly and rolled with her to the side. They banged into furniture sending it toppling.

Shelly broke free and sprang to a crouch and started a kick aiming for Sam's midsection. Sam's arm shot out blocking the kick. She grabbed Shelly's leg and jerked it upwards, holding on while Shelly crashed unprotected to the floor. The sickening sounds of body, and head smacking into the floor filled the air. Sam was on her in a second, driving a knee into her stomach and forcing the air out. She landed a quick backhand and two hard punches to Shelly's ribs. Kris saw Sam pull her arm back to swing again screamed out, "Sam stop, stop. It's over. She's done." She placed a hand on Sam's shoulder.

Sam flinched with the touch, turning her head to look for the next threat. She glanced up and saw the fear on Kris' face. She looked down at Shelly and saw the glazed look in her eyes and realized Shelly was no longer capable of fighting. Sam straddled Shelly's chest and pinned her hands to the floor. She squeezed with her knees preventing Shelly from taking a deep breath. Staring at Shelly, she spoke to Kris, "Come get your key."

Sam kept the pressure on Shelly's hands and chest while Kris reached into Shelly's pocket and drew out the key. Her heart pounded, and her muscles remained tense as Kris removed a key from the ring, and she slid the remaining keys back into Shelly's pocket. Shelly suddenly kicked out and almost hit Kris in the head, and Sam drove her knee into Shelly's stomach forcing the air out. Kris scrambled away while Sam shifted her weight so that she kneeled on Shelly's forearms. She put one hand on Shelly's forehead and her other gently across her throat. "Give me one reason to squeeze. Just one more reason."

"Let me up, you stupid bitch," Shelly spat.

Sam pressed her hand to Shelly's throat until her eyes widened and her muscles started to slacken. Removing her hand, Sam leaned forward and whispered in Shelly's ear, "I can hurt you in ways you can't imagine. Come near Kris again, and I will hunt you down and make you pay."

Sam kept her eyes locked on Shelly and called out to Kris, "Did you call the police?"

"I did." Even as she spoke the sound of sirens could be heard. Kris walked to the door and opened it. "She's in here." They entered and quickly assessed the scene. They took control of Shelly as Sam got up. As they handcuffed Shelly she screamed at them, a stream of obscenities spewed from her mouth. "I'll get you both. I'll kill you both."

"You will be pressing charges, ma'am?" The officer looked at both of them.

"Yes," they said simultaneously.

"You bitch. Fuck you. What the hell did I ever see in you? You two deserve each other. You bunch of freaks."

"Hey, that's enough, Miss." The officer jerked Shelly forward and out the door.

Sam and Kris stood in the doorway and watched as they put Shelly in the back of one of the cruisers. Sam's feelings were mixed, embarrassment for Kris, as her neighbors watched the unfolding drama. Although she would never admit it to anyone else, she was pleased that she had been able to defend Kris and kick Shelly's ass. Hitting her had felt good. Damn good. They listened to her continued shouts of profanity and watched as Shelly kicked the back of the patrol car's seat. Sam reached for Kris' hand and held it firmly when it quivered. They ignored the neighbors who had gathered on their porches. As a cruiser pulled away, Kris followed the female police officer inside, and Sam rubbed at her jaw where she had taken a hard punch. She wriggled it side to side and took several deep breaths before following Kris in.

They spent the next twenty minutes with the female officer giving a report and explaining what had happened. After the officer left Sam locked the door and leaned her forehead against it for a moment. She turned and saw Kris walking toward the windows and draw the blinds closed. She noticed Kris' slumped shoulders, and downcast eyes. "Kris, are you okay? How bad did she hurt you?"

"It's just words." Kris' voice was flat and trembled. She straightened the coffee table and replaced the lamp on an end table.

"No, she grabbed you. I heard you scream."

"I'm okay."

"Look at me. Tell me what you're thinking." Kris made eye contact and held it for several seconds before her face flushed, and she looked away, biting her lip.

Sam hurried over to her, when she touched Kris on the arm she felt her flinch. "What are you thinking? You look—"

"Embarrassed? I am." Kris' lips flattened, and a wrinkle appeared between her brows. She unclenched her fist to rub at the furrow. "She came into my home, and I couldn't get her out. I wouldn't have been able to make her leave. She hurt me and I wasn't able to keep her away."

"She surprised you."

"It's more than that."

Sam reached for Kris' hand and held it gently between hers. "Did she hurt you? Before?"

Kris' voice hitched and tears formed, "Sometimes she…she would get a little too rough especially if she'd been drinking." She tugged at the hem of her shirt and looked at the floor. "She was drinking tonight I could smell it. Her favorite is vodka because it doesn't smell as much. But it doesn't matter. If it's alcohol, she'll drink it."

"She hurt you…during sex?" Sam pressed a hand against the sick feeling in her stomach.

Kris shrugged and tucked some hair behind her ear. "A few times. I don't want to talk about this."

Sam ground her teeth together. "Did she…force you?"

"Does it matter?" Kris walked to the window, pushed the curtains back and peeked outside. *Thank God the neighbors had gone back inside.* Kris sighed. She considered not telling Sam, but since she was now caught up in this to, she needed to know the extent of it. She turned around. "Yes. Yes, she did." Kris' face was bright red, and she wouldn't keep eye contact.

"You never said anything about her being violent."

"She wasn't usually violent." Kris moved the hair from behind her ear and immediately tucked it back again. She shifted the candles back into the position she'd had them in before Shelly had moved them. She brushed her hands over the hem of her shirt before making quick eye contact with Sam. "Occasionally she would get pushy. But after I got back this time she was different. She was mean and hurtful. And yes the sex became rough. The intimacy was gone."

Sam held her tight, and wouldn't let her go when Kris tried to back away, "Why didn't you tell me?" Kris shook her head but said nothing. "I'm sorry you went through that." Sam hugged her close and kissed her forehead. "I'm sorry I couldn't get here faster. I had to get my leg on. I tried to hurry."

"It's not your fault. It was a lesson learned the hard way. Can we talk about something else? Please? Let's not let her ruin our evening any more than she already has," Kris pleaded with her voice and eyes.

The pain in Kris' eyes had Sam relenting. They would return to this topic when Kris looked more sure of herself. "Okay. We'll talk tomorrow. I won't push. I want to say one more thing though."

Kris sighed. "Go ahead."

"I'm changing your locks tomorrow. She might have another key."

"I was thinking the same thing."

***

As Kris showered, she couldn't stop thinking of Shelly's intrusion back into her life and how fast Sam had been able to subdue her. The quick, violent blows that had rendered Shelly defenseless had erupted and ended quickly revealing how strong Sam was. Sam's anger had vibrated through the air more dangerous in its intensity than Shelly's had ever been.

Kris had been shocked by the sense of fear she'd felt when she'd seen Shelly, and the feeling had only intensified as Sam and Shelly fought. Sam had subdued Shelly quickly, and Sam's confidence had surged. Kris had seen it. There'd been a subtle change in how she held herself. Her pride had been restored. And deep down that frightened Kris. Despite the fact that Sam had protected her, despite the fact that Sam had calmed quickly after the altercation, she was frightened.

Shelly had become abusive, and she wasn't anywhere near as strong as Sam. If the anger that had ignited in Sam tonight was ever directed toward her, it could be deadly. Kris started to shake as she remembered Shelly throwing her against the wall, and yanking on her injured arm before dragging her into the bedroom. She remembered the violent words and the vicious bite on her shoulder. The rough sex, no it hadn't been sex, it had been rape. Shelly had hurt her, several times. As easily as Sam had been able to hurt Shelly, Sam would easily be able to destroy her.

No, no, no. Sam was kind and caring. Sam had never been aggressive toward her. Calm down, just calm the hell down. You're upset because Shelly was here. She scared you. That's all. Don't get them confused. They're nothing alike.

Kris stepped from the shower and toweled off. With a sigh she looked at her chest, a bruise was forming where Shelly had grabbed her. Kris ran her hands over the damaged flesh and grimaced. She would have it fixed when the muscle and skin grafts were mature enough to handle the procedure. They had said one year, and that was her plan. Sam wasn't repulsed the way Shelly had been, and that was a miracle. Kris felt the tender areas, and after a few seconds turned her attention to her other breast and examined it.

***

Sam watched as Kris ran her finger along the scars across her shoulder and what was left of her breast. She saw Kris grimace and noticed the quick look of sadness that crossed her face. Kris placed her hand on her other breast, gently stroking it. It took Sam a few seconds to realize she was performing a breast exam. Kris turned slightly and saw Sam watching her and quickly pulled up a towel to cover herself.

"I...I was doing a breast exam."

"I know. I didn't mean to interrupt. Why did you frown when you were looking at yourself?" *Damn you, Shelly. You not only hurt her. You made her feel ugly. You made her feel weak.* Sam knew she had to get Kris to remember how strong she was, how far she had come.

Kris pulled on her robe and tied the belt. "Did I?"

"You did." Sam stepped fully into the doorway and put her arms on the frame, completely blocking the opening. Kris looked at her, and their eyes met and held. Kris' pupils had dilated so large the brilliant blue was barely visible, and her face was unusually pale. Sam wondered what else had happened between Kris and Shelly that would leave her so shaken. She needed Kris to tell her, as much as Kris needed to let go of whatever she was bottling up inside.

"Excuse me, I want to get by." Kris' voice cracked, and she flinched when Sam reached out suddenly and cupped her cheek. Kris' confidence had been shattered. She cursed Shelly and considered what she would like to do if she ran into her again. A sniffle from Kris refocused her attention.

"Why are you upset?"

"Sam, please let me pass."

"No. Take your robe off," Sam spoke softly.

"Sam—"

"I mean it. Take it off."

"I don't want to." Kris backed away.

"Don't back away from me….take your robe off." Kris didn't move. "Please."

Kris hesitated, and looked at the floor, before she placed her hands on the knotted belt.

"Look at me," Sam demanded.

As Kris' fingers twitched on the knot, Sam watched her carefully. Her face was blank, but her mouth and hands trembled slightly. Kris blinked rapidly several times and lowered her head. She held back a whimper when Sam tugged her close by the belt.

"Why are you shaking? What are you afraid of?" Sam rubbed at her temple realizing she was not handling this well either. Her stomach clenched when she saw the tears, "Why are you crying?"

"I don't want to do this. Not tonight," Kris whimpered.

"What the hell are you talking about?" Her voice was sharp and loud, and she watched stunned as Kris recoiled.

"Don't hurt me. I'll do it," she whispered, barely audible. Kris dropped the robe to the floor as tears ran down her face and dropped onto her chest.

Sam felt the anger rise up from deep inside, a thick bubbling rage that erupted within her, consuming her. "What do you mean? What are you doing?"

Kris' eyes flew open, and she bit down on her bottom lip. She stepped back, and her hands moved up in front of her, shielding her, as she tucked her chin. "Please. Sam. You told me to take it off. I'm sorry."

Sam put her hands to her own head and pulled her hair violently, trying to control her rage. *Kris was afraid of her. She had been on edge since the police had taken Shelly away. Was Kris afraid that she was going to attack her? Force herself on her?* Sam turned away and paced back across the room. She took several deep breaths, calming herself, tamping the sick feeling down, deep inside. Turning back she held her hands out, palms up, in front of her. "Kris, I'm not going to hurt you." She bent over picked up the robe and extended it to her. "I'd never hurt you. I will never force you to do anything you don't want to do. I'm sorry if you thought I would. I just wanted to show you something. Something that you're not seeing."

Kris stared at the robe and tentatively reached for it. She watched Sam closely before she took the robe and put it on quickly. She tied the belt and took a calming breath. "I'm sorry. Shelly coming here upset me more than I thought." She wiped at her eyes. "I never used to be this weak, this scared."

"You're not weak. Stop believing the lies you're telling yourself. You're stronger than you think. I wanted to show you something, it's important, but it can wait for now. I want to help you, I want to make you feel better. I don't know how to do that without touching you. I don't want sex. I want to hold you. Let me hold you. Please." When Kris nodded and stepped to her, Sam muttered against her hair. "I'm not like Shelly."

Sam hugged Kris as sobs wracked her. After the shudders stopped, Sam wiped Kris' face with a cold cloth and kissed her on the forehead. "I will never hurt you. Let me show you something. Please take off your robe. Let me tell you what I see."

Sam watched as Kris searched her face, and felt her heart leap when Kris tugged the belt open and let the robe slide to the floor again. Sam approached her slowly, and placed her hands gently on her shoulders, and turned Kris to face the mirror. She kissed one shoulder and then the other before she met Kris' eyes in the mirror. She spoke calmly. "I see a woman who is stunning and strong." She brushed her thumb along Kris' high cheekbones, "I see your beautiful eyes, which are so observant. I see soft skin." She stroked her finger across Kris' lips. "I see beautiful, kissable lips."

She stroked her hand over Kris' shoulders. "Strong swimmers shoulders." Sam glided her hands down Kris' arms. "Well-toned, feminine arms, that hold her lover securely, skilled soft hands, that can save a life and thrill her lover." Sam slid her hands back up, stroked along the sides of her breasts, causing her nipple to pebble. She placed her hand in the center of Kris' chest over her heart. "A heart that beats strong and true. Which has seen horrors beyond imagination but still shows great compassion. A heart that was betrayed, but still has the strength and the courage to welcome another lover."

Sam's hands traced along Kris' ribcage and across her abdomen. "Soft, smooth skin over firm taught muscle. Strong and feminine." She rested her hands on Kris' hips, "Lean narrow hips and a tight butt, the envy of many women and men. Strong thighs, capable of carrying great loads, and of holding a lover close, ensconced in ecstasy. You stood with me in front of a mirror and told me about what you saw. About how strong and brave I was. Let me tell you something, Kris. I see the same things in you."

Chapter Forty-nine

"HERE WE ARE." KRIS pulled onto a small gravel road, not much wider than a driveway. The tires crunched over the gravel and shells, and the trees and brush crowded the road. There were a few places where the lane widened marginally so two cars could pass but it would be a tight squeeze. The smell of the ocean on the light warm breeze enticed, and Sam jumped in her seat as two colorful birds flew by in front of the car.

"Were those flamingoes?"

Kris laughed. "Yeah. Some things never change. For as long as I can remember cars get dive bombed here. Every once in a while someone will run off the road trying to avoid them. Usually, they're high enough to avoid getting hit."

"Usually?"

"My brother got knocked off his motorcycle a couple years ago by one. He and the bird were both okay."

"Is this a goat path?"

Kris smiled. "Actually, it's the driveway. There are only three houses down this way. My folks and my uncle each own one. The third is owned by a family up in Maine. The grandparents winter over. We might meet them if they wander by. But the houses are laid out in such a way to be pretty secluded."

Kris slowed and turned again. Sam hadn't even seen the turn-off. They moved about a hundred meters down further and past extremely thick brush before it opened into a wide expanse of well-manicured grass and lush trees. The house rose up two stories, brilliant white with blue shutters and roof. A plantation style porch wrapped completely around the house. Rocking chairs and small wicker tables tempted visitors to sit and relax. Ceiling fans whirred quietly moving the warm air and ruffling the huge ferns hanging from the ceilings.

As they stepped up onto the porch, the door opened, and a woman their age ran outside and hugged Kris fiercely. "Welcome back. Your mother called and said you would be down for Christmas. I have things ready for you."

"Thank you. Alannah, this is Sam."

Alannah reached out her hand and shook Sam's firmly. "It's nice to meet you."

They exchanged introductions and got a quick rundown of Kris' progress and Alannah's kids. After a few minutes, Alannah offered to make them fresh piña coladas while Kris showed Sam around.

"I have the waterfront rooms opened up but if you want I can get them all changed over. Will you need me through the weekend?"

"That won't be necessary. It's only the two of us."

Sam was surprised at the appreciative look the woman gave her and the sly grin that crossed her face when she turned back to look at Kris. "Well, you give the tour, and I'll get those drinks out on the deck for you."

As they walked away, Sam looked back and saw the woman watching them with a broad smile on her face. "How long has Alannah worked for your family?"

"About ten years. She looks after the place for us. My parents occasionally rent it out. Alannah looks after it. She was in an abusive relationship. My mother helped her to leave, and they got her set up down here. Her kids are great."

Sam looked down at her hand when Kris took it in hers. "She didn't seem surprised that we were here alone," Sam murmured.

"She wasn't. Alannah will have no problem with us being here together. Unless something has changed, she's been living with the same woman for about five years. She'll give us plenty of privacy. Let me show you around."

The downstairs was an open floor plan with Mexican tile flooring, brightly painted walls and oak trim. Oversized windows and glass doors allowed unobstructed views outside. Several small alcoves offered tucked away corners of privacy.

A wide stairwell led upstairs and opened into a large hallway. Four bedrooms were beautifully decorated with bright colors, deep seated chairs or loveseats and sturdy looking antique furniture. Queen sized beds were opposite French doors which offered a spectacular view of the gardens. Each bedroom had a private bath. "Kris this is beautiful. I've never seen anything like it."

"Thank you. It is a wonderful place. My grandparents, my mother's parents, bought it cheap sometime in the nineteen sixties and spent a lot of time and money improving it through the years. They left it to my mother. My parents have continued to improve and modernize it. Let me show you where we'll stay."

Kris opened an oversized door that led into a huge room, the walls were white, and ceiling fans with coral blue blades stirred silently creating a gentle breeze. A king sized bed with a wrought iron headboard filled the center of the room. Coral blue subtly accented the room décor. Intricately carved wood armoires sat against the walls. Vases of fresh flowers filled each table. Wide plank wood floors glistened in the sunlight. Two sets of French doors led out onto a porch wide enough for a table and chairs and traveled the length of the building. A magnificent view of the water welcomed them, and a sailboat sat at a dock.

"My God, Kris. How can your parents not spend all their time in this amazing home?" Sam looked out at the ocean.

"They're not ready to retire yet. They come down a few times a year. I was hoping you would stay in this room with me, but perhaps you want your own room?"

Sam turned around, stunned at Kris' suggestion. When the corners of Kris' mouth started to twitch, Sam grinned at her. "No, I intend to sleep with my hostess."

"The other bedroom is similar to this one but done in a deeper shade of blue. It's more masculine but still lovely. The bathroom is through here." Kris opened the door, and Sam peeked in and saw an oversized shower, with multiple shower heads, a large Jacuzzi tub, and marble-topped counter. A separate vanity table sat with an antique chair nearby and held toiletries.

Sam shook her head, "I think this bathroom is bigger than my first apartment."

Kris laughed, "I know it's larger than mine was. Come on let's go get that drink."

Kris led her down a back stairwell, and they opened into a large airy kitchen with state of the art stainless steel appliances and a wide butcher-block island. A large square wooden table with glass inlay sat to one side of the room and was surrounded by eight chairs.

They walked out onto a back deck that faced west, and Kris pulled Sam into her arms. "I've been waiting to do this all day." Her hands stroked the sides of Sam's face, and she pulled her in close for a kiss that started lightly and quickly became hungry.

Sam moaned with the urgency of the kiss and the quick jolt to her stomach. She felt her core warm, and her heart stutter. She returned the kiss with equal fervor. Her hands slid down to Kris' hips, and around to her butt to pull Kris closer.

"Well, now, that's looking like a right steamy kiss. You might need more than one pitcher of these piña coladas to keep from igniting."

Sam jerked back, but Kris held her close. "Thanks, Alannah."

"Are you planning to stay in for dinner tonight or would you like me to get you a reservation somewhere?"

"I thought we would stay in tonight. We can grill something. How's that sound?"

"Great. I don't think I'm up for a late night." Sam pulled away and reached for the drinks on the tray, handing one to Kris, before taking a sip of her own. "Ooh. That's smooth."

Alannah smiled. "I'm glad you like it. Fresh coconut makes the difference. I went to the market earlier. The refrigerator is stocked for a few days. I picked up some mahi-mahi. Would you like me to prepare some vegetables or a salad?"

"No thanks. We'll take care of it."

"I'll be going now. I'll be by around nine-thirty tomorrow morning. You two should be decent by then." Alannah laughed as she walked away.

They spent the rest of the day relaxing and enjoying the pool which somehow Sam had not initially noticed. They walked along the property and Kris pointed out some of the nesting sites on the grounds. She offered to take the sailboat out, but Sam declined. By late afternoon they were in bed and didn't emerge until the sun was low in the sky. Standing hand in hand, naked on the balcony they watched the sun go down. Finally, they showered and went downstairs to cook dinner. After dinner, they settled onto one of the leather couches and watched a movie. They snuggled in each other's arms until soon the movie was forgotten and their clothes were strewn across the floor.

Chapter Fifty

SAM SAT ON A chaise lounge, her drink now melted and her book lying neglected on the ground. She smiled as she watched Kris approach. *She is so beautiful. How did I get so lucky*? Kris stopped ten feet from her.

"Are you rested?"

"Yes, I woke up about twenty minutes a…" She stopped talking as Kris pulled her top off, slid her bathing suit bottom off. *Ooh, sweet Jesus.* She swallowed and looked around. "What are you doing?" she whispered.

"Let me show you." Kris picked a towel off the adjacent table, dropped it on the ground at the foot of the chaise lounge. She crawled up Sam's body and pressed her mouth to hers. Sam's flesh quivered as skilled hands deftly moved under her shirt and found her breasts, tweaking her nipples.

Sam's nipples hardened instantly and her gut clenched when Kris tugged them gently, rolling them until she shuddered. She raised her arms when Kris lifted her shirt, before carelessly tossing it aside. Kris nuzzled her neck, slowly moving toward her mouth. The kiss was gentle, a soft caressing of lips, a teasing sweep of tongue, asking for entry. Sam opened her mouth and let Kris' tongue sweep in and sensually moved against hers. They kissed until they were breathless.

"We should go inside."

"No. Right here. Right now. No one is around."

"Someone might…" She groaned as Kris nipped at her earlobe, and instantly soothed it with a gentle caress of her tongue. Her breasts swelled as hands lovingly stroked and teased. Kris moved lower, captured a taught nipple in her mouth, and teased it mercilessly. Sam moaned, and a dull ache began to grow deep within her.

Sam groaned as fingers stroked along her torso, her abdomen quivering as Kris moved lower. Kris used her tongue, leaving a moist trail on her stomach, as hands tugged at the snap on her shorts. Kris pulled at her shorts. "Lift up, Sam. Trust me." Obediently Sam lifted, hissed softly as her shorts were pulled down and fingers stroked against her thighs leaving a trail of fire. She watched as Kris pushed the shorts aside, and used fingers and mouth to scorch a trail back up her legs and inner thigh. Her breath caught when Kris slipped her hand between her legs, cupping her, sliding against her wet sex.

"Oh God!" Tipping her head back she closed her eyes, enjoyed the loving strokes of talented fingers as they slipped along, caressing her folds. Her eyes opened suddenly when she felt Kris grab her by the hips and pull her down the chair. She sat speechless when Kris pushed her legs wide, carefully lowering her leg to the ground before she dropped to her knees. Warm hands, slid up her legs, teased across wet flesh. Her hips lifted automatically, and she groaned in frustration when hands stilled.

She looked at Kris, their eyes locking and she saw Kris smile wickedly, holding her gaze for several seconds until an unseen finger stroked across her clit. She groaned and saw Kris smile before she lowered her head. She moaned as mouth and hands worked together to bring her pleasure. Slowly and gently guiding her up. "Sweet Jesus," she groaned as she neared peak, growling in frustration when Kris stopped.

Kris whispered, "Watch me. Keep your eyes open. I want to see you when you come."

Sam watched as Kris lowered her mouth, but kept her eyes on hers. She saw the excitement in Kris' eyes as she gave pleasure. Sam moaned, the sensations overwhelming her, but the eroticism of looking in her lover's eyes as she knelt below her, pleasuring her, was shocking. Her legs started to shake, and her walls started to clench tightly around Kris' fingers. With a slight twist of Kris' hand, Sam erupted, a prolonged wave of pleasure rolled through her, and she shook with release, arching against Kris as a deep moan rumbled in her throat. Sam lay looking up at the sky, soaked in sweat, as she spasmed again with aftershocks. She looked down and focused on Kris as she continued to caress her, her eyes bright and her smile huge.

"What did you do? I've never come like that before."

"Something I learned in medical school."

"Oh really? And who taught that class?"

Kris laughed and pulled herself up to straddle Sam. "I paid very close attention in anatomy."

"I'm so glad you did. If you ever need to study again let me know."

Kris began to rock against Sam. "I'll keep that in mind."

***

Kris and Sam spent Christmas morning on the beach and exchanged gifts under a palm tree. Kris loved the triple braided gold necklace and the signed collection of mystery novels from a favorite author. Sam was speechless when she saw the itinerary for an adventure trip for two in the Grand Tetons.

Kris took them out on the sailboat that afternoon, and they dropped anchor in a shallow spot, where no one else was around and sunbathed nude. The radio played, and they drank wine. They made love on the deck and afterward to cool off Kris persuaded Sam to get in the water. Sam removed her prosthesis and back flipped into the water. Initially, she wore a life jacket, but after her confidence had grown, she took it off and left it onboard. Kris helped Sam climb aboard when they were finished in the water.

Back on board, Kris switched to drinking water and read while Sam fished. It didn't take long before Sam caught a large grouper. Sam cleaned the fish and Kris went below to prepare dinner. They ate dinner on the deck, blackened grouper, a pasta and zucchini salad, and finished with a raspberry sorbet that Alannah had put in the small freezer.

They sailed back slowly so they could watch the sun going down and before the sky completely darkened they pulled up to the dock. Kris expertly jumped off the boat onto the dock and secured the boat. Sam climbed out a few moments later. They strolled hand in hand toward the house.

"I had a great time today. Thank you."

"It was fun. I didn't know you liked to fish. I can see about getting you with a guide."

"Will you come?" Sam asked.

"I'd rather not, but if it's something you would like to do that's fine. Alannah and I can catch up."

Sam looked at her. "You wouldn't mind?"

"Not at all. I want you to have fun."

"I am."

***

"I can't believe how quickly this week has gone by. I admit I was a little worried about being down here for a week and not being able to do much in the water."

Kris grinned at Sam. "You mean not being able to do much in the ocean. I remember we did plenty in the pool."

Sam's cheeks heated. "That's true. I've had so much fun this trip. I don't think I would have visited the Dolphin Research Center if I had two feet. It would have been something I skipped. But thank you for taking me, it was interesting. And the video of the dolphin with the prosthetic tail was amazing. If I ever get to Clearwater, I'm going to see her."

"It's been my pleasure. I'm glad you've had a good time. Sorry, you could only go out on a half day fishing trip, instead of an entire day. I hadn't thought about that to arrange something sooner."

"It was fun. I think any longer, and I'd have been too tired. The rocking of the boat made it harder to stay balanced."

"Is your leg sore? Are you sure that you still want to go dancing tonight?"

"I feel good, my unleg doesn't hurt." She reached over their plates, and took Kris' hand. "Besides I can't wait to hold you, move with you, and kiss you, all in public. With no fear of what others will say."

"The only one who has anything to fear is me. I have a feeling that you are going to attract a lot of attention."

Sam laughed out loud. "I don't think so. I'm going to have to be on guard, so someone doesn't steal you away. You look beautiful. So sexy. I bet you get asked to dance the first time I turn my back."

Sam was surprised as Kris' eyes darkened and grew serious. "That's not going to happen."

The waiter came by to check on them and topped off their wine glasses. Kris was silent and stared at her plate while the waiter was at their table.

"Did I say something wrong?"

"I wouldn't cheat on you."

"I wasn't implying you would. Are you okay?"

"It's nothing. I'm sorry," Kris murmured.

"No, something happened, your whole demeanor changed. What did I say?"

Kris drank most of the wine in her glass and began to twirl the stem in her fingers. "It's just Shelly was extremely jealous and would start arguments in bars when she thought others were hitting on me. What you said made me a little uneasy."

"I understand...I think. And if some woman asks you to dance I'll know that she has extremely good taste in women. I can hardly hold that against you."

Sam was aware that Kris was studying her. Sam lifted an eyebrow.

"Come on, Kris, I want to dance with you." Sam motioned for the waiter, and ten minutes later they made the short walk to the club.

Inside multi-colored lights flashed, reflecting off the mirrors and a stainless steel bar. New Year's decorations hung from the ceiling, and tropical flowers in tiny vases were centerpieces on the table tops. Noisemaker and blowouts positioned among the flowers were pulled free and blown by women ready to celebrate the New Year surrounded by family. The music thumped, heavy on the bass as bodies gyrated. Sam took Kris' hand and quickly moved her onto the dance floor. They squeezed into the crowded space and danced. When others moved between them, they quickly moved back together, ignoring the other women around them. They moved together well, their bodies bumped, slid against each other and lingered. Kris grazed her fingers along the sides of Sam's breasts and stroked over her ribs. Her hips were pulled forward, so she slid against Sam, rocking with the beat of the music.

The music slowed, and Sam pulled Kris closer, her hands locked on Kris' hips as Kris' arms encircled her neck. They moved sensually, lost in each other's arms. Sam pressed a kiss to the side of Kris' head and inhaled the citrusy scent she'd grown accustomed to. The music continued, and they moved slowly in time with it. The songs changed, and they stayed on the floor, as the tempo increased they stayed in each other's arms, their bodies moving sensually together as their blood heated. Their mouths met, and they fed hungrily. Sam slid her mouth down along Kris' neck and nipped at her collarbone, Kris arched her neck to the side and felt her sex begin to throb.

Kris pulled Sam's head back up and whispered into her ear, "We have to go, or I'm going to come right here." Without another word, Sam grabbed her hand and pulled her outside.

***

Kris raced the convertible up the driveway and skidded to a stop. Before she could shut off the ignition, Sam pulled her over and kissed her hungrily. Their hands tugged at clothing and Sam leaned over the console, her arm hit the steering wheel, and the horn sounded. They laughed and shoved open the doors, and stumbled as they clung to each other, grappling the short distance to the house. Kris tried to put the key in the lock but was spun around and pinned against the door. Their mouths clashed, and when they were breathless, they staggered inside.

Sam led her to the bedroom but stopped Kris' hands when she

reached to unbutton Sam's shirt. "Undress for me." Sam noticed the surprise in Kris' eyes give way to mischief. A broad smile crossed Kris' face as she backed away several feet. Without hesitation she released each of the tiny buttons along the front of the dress, gradually revealing the white lacy bra underneath. Sam's breath caught, and her stomach tugged as Kris slowly caressed her own skin and stroked her hand up her arm until she reached her shoulder. Sam swallowed hard as Kris brushed the straps off her arms and allowed the dress to drop to her waist.

A white lace bra revealed most of the top of her breast. Sam took a step toward her but stopped and stared as Kris placed her hands on her hips and slowly lowered the dress over her waist and started a subtle rotation of her hips. The dress fell to the floor, and Kris stood before her in matching white lace bra and panties, her tanned skin in sharp contrast. Sam gasped, making Kris smile and her eyes brightened. Her eyes were sharp and clear, the brilliance of the blue intensified by the flush on her cheeks. *She's so confident now. Not self-conscious at all. God, she's sexy.* Heat spread across Sam's skin when Kris moved toward her like a cat on the prowl, and encircled her arms around Sam's shoulders.

Kris nipped Sam's neck. "Come on, Sam, let's get into bed. We can sleep on the plane tomorrow."

Chapter Fifty-one

THREE MONTHS LATER

SAM SAT IN THE examination room and tried to calm herself. Even though she was dressed in shorts and a t-shirt, she felt exposed. Her prosthesis lay on the exam table next to her, and she struggled not to reach down and scratch at her missing foot. She rubbed her damp hands along her thighs and rolled her neck before taking several deep breaths and blowing out slowly. She was about to take another deep breath when there was a knock on the door, and it opened.

"Major Davies?"

"Yes, sir." Sam was pleased that she was seeing Dr. Bayne, the same orthopedic doctor that she had on her last three visits.

"How are you feeling, Major?"

"I feel good. I feel strong, fit. I am moving well on Betty. Ah...the prosthesis."

"Betty?"

Sam felt a blush rise. "I, ah, call it Betty, sometimes. My leg is Barney."

He smiled at her. "You can call it whatever you want. Humor can help to defuse some tense situations."

Sam lay back and watched his face as he examined her leg. He gave nothing away, and she thought she wouldn't want to play poker with him. She moved her leg when he instructed her to. Straightening her knee all the way, and flexing it fully. He grasped her knee and tried to shift it from side to side. He examined her skin carefully feeling for abnormalities. She rolled over when asked to do so.

"Where were you getting the blisters?"

Rising up onto her elbows she twisted around and showed him the spots. He rubbed firmly over that area. "I don't see or feel anything abnormal, so hopefully it's resolved. If it starts up again though I want to see you. Especially if it is in the same areas."

"Is there a problem?" Sam tried to keep her voice calm.

"No everything looks great. Your motion is fantastic, the knee is stable, and you're active. But an area that keeps getting irritated would need to be followed closely."

"I understand."

He leaned back against the counter. "I've read the reports from therapy. You're doing well. They say your thigh diameter is the same on each leg. That's great. Both your legs are strong, and the therapy team is extremely pleased. Have you moved out from the medical barracks?"

"I've been in my own place for several months. I had my car modified, so I am driving."

"How do you feel about that?"

Sam grinned. "Fantastic. I feel like I have my life back."

"Good. That's what I like to hear. You've adjusted well to this." He handed her the prosthesis. "Go ahead and put Betty on. I want to watch how you move around." While she donned Betty, he made a few notes in her chart. "Let's walk down to the therapy room, and you can show me what you can do."

Ten minutes later they were back in the exam room. "Well done, Major. Now for the administrative stuff. Have you decided if you want to stay in or get out and head back home?"

"The Marine Corps is my home. I want to stay in."

"You are familiar with the process? The petition?"

"Yes, it was explained. I have a list of questions. I realize I'd be on limited duty. But I want to continue to serve."

"You might not be clear for flying."

Sam dragged her teeth across her bottom lip and bit down lightly. "I'm aware of that. They are allowing some to fly with a prosthesis."

"Not as many as are petitioning though. I'm not trying to dash your hopes. I want you to have a backup plan. In any case, you need to start preparing for your board. You've met your milestones, and it's time to start the process if you haven't already. You will initially be found unqualified to continue to serve. You must request to stay on active duty. You have the right to demand a formal board. You'll submit a request for Permanent Limited Duty. I will tell you they have allowed some infantry back into theater overseas. Some pilots, not many, have returned to flying. I can't predict what will happen. How many years do you have in?"

"Ten. Fourteen with my time at the Academy."

"Naval Academy?"

"Yes, sir."

"Well good for you. That time won't hurt you. They look at time in service. Your section leader will help you with the process." He stood up to leave.

"Do you need to see me back here?"

"Once a year, unless you have a problem."

"Thank you, sir."

"Good luck, Major."

Chapter Fifty-two

KRIS KNELT IN THE garden putting in seeds when she heard the door open. She glanced over and watched Sam take a seat at the patio table, her hands wrapped around a mug. "Good morning."

"You're up early."

"I was putting some lettuce and carrots in. I'll be finished in a few minutes."

"Take your time."

Kris returned to her chore and ten minutes later picked up the pile of weeds and dropped it into the compost bin. She went to the garage and put away her tools. Going into the kitchen, she washed her hands. "Do you want some breakfast? I can make us some omelets."

"That sounds good. Do you want some help?"

"Relax, I'll do it." As Kris prepared breakfast, she noticed Sam start wandering aimlessly around the yard. She wondered what was bothering her. She'd been restless the last few nights and had gotten up several times to pace. She tried to ask Sam questions but she wouldn't answer other than to apologize for waking her. Sam would come back to bed and lie still for a little while before again getting up to pace. Kris cut and seeded a melon and placed wedges onto plates. She added tomatoes and feta to the omelets, made rye toast and brought the plates out to the table. "Sam, it's ready."

Kris walked back inside and brought out another cup of tea for Sam and ice water for herself. She frowned slightly when Sam bent over looking at the ground. Kris hurried across the lawn. "Sam?"

Sam looked up, a surprised look on her face. "What?"

"Breakfast is ready. What are you looking at?"

"Sorry, I didn't hear you. These ants. They're so busy scurrying back and forth. Do you ever wonder if they get tired?"

Kris studied Sam's face. She looked tired, soft smudges under her eyes, her cheeks were slightly drawn.

"I can't say I have. Do you feel okay?"

"I'm good. Let's eat." Sam took Kris' hand and walked back to the table. "This looks good."

Sam started to sit, but Kris stopped her, pulled her in close and kissed her lightly. The faintest touch of lips. "Good morning."

"Good morning."

They sat down and ate, and Sam remained subdued. "Sam, what's wrong?" Kris reached out and touched her hand.

"Hmm? Nothing. I have some things on my mind."

"Do you want to talk about it?"

"Not really. I have to figure some things out. There isn't anything to discuss. It doesn't involve you."

"Oh. Well, I see."

Kris used her knife to trim the melon from the rind and cut it into small cubes. She stabbed them with her fork repeatedly saying nothing. "Why so glum, Sam?"

"Looks like a great day to go for a ride."

Kris smiled. "Let's go."

"Funny," Sam answered harshly.

"I'm not joking."

"No. I'm not used to riding on the back of someone's bike."

"That's ridiculous. You did a few months ago."

"That was different."

"How?"

"We weren't dating then."

"That makes absolutely no sense whatsoever. You rode on the back when we didn't know each other too well, but now that we're a couple, you won't? If you don't trust me..."

"I trust you. I just don't ride two up unless I drive."

"Oh, I get it. It's that butch attitude. Can't sit behind the little woman. Can't bother her with your worries." Kris felt her frustration growing and lashed out. "So you'd rather stay here and cling to your butch attitude than go for a ride?" She pushed back from the table and grabbed her plate. Before she could walk away, Sam grabbed her by the wrist.

"You make it sound stupid."

Kris tugged her wrist free. "It is." She walked into the kitchen and quickly washed her plate and utensils, and scrubbed the pan. She placed the dishes on the drain board before walking down the hall to take a shower. She needed to cool off before she said something she would regret later.

***

Sam sat and sulked. Through the open window, she heard the shower turn on. She sat alone with her thoughts and realized that twice in a few minutes she had brushed Kris off and obviously hurt her. *Was not telling Kris that her medical board was coming up not trusting her? Or was she not ready to admit to anyone that she was worried?* She became aware of the sounds of motorcycles rumbling somewhere in the neighborhood. After several more seconds, she admitted to herself that Kris was right.

Butch attitude? Damn right. She wasn't sitting behind anyone like a femme. But she had done that very thing before. Besides she didn't think of Kris as a femme. She was just Kris. Intelligent, skilled and a fierce competitor. Although she was usually submissive in the bedroom, she was never passive. Outside of the bedroom, she was a force to be reckoned with. Time to swallow your pride. She gathered her dishes and went inside to wash them. A few minutes later she entered the garage, found what she needed and walked down the hall to the bathroom.

She watched as Kris turned off the shower and snaked her hand out through the door before snagging the towel and pulling it inside the shower. She sat on the counter waiting for Kris to emerge and saw the surprise on her face when she realized Sam was sitting there holding a helmet on her lap.

"I'm sorry Kris. You're right. Part of it was image. Part is habit. It's a great day to ride. Will you take me out for a ride?"

"Oh, Sam, I'll ride you anytime." Kris laughed at Sam's arched brow. "For now, let's start on the bike." A few minutes later dressed in jeans, t-shirts, and boots, they donned helmets and rode off. Sam holding onto Kris' waist as they roared down the road.

They rode along the coast for about an hour before heading inland and driving through the rolling countryside. Sam enjoyed being on the bike more than she thought she would. At the traffic lights, if time permitted, she would snake her hands up under Kris' t-shirt to her breasts. Several times she rubbed lightly across her tummy, enjoying the feel of Kris' abdomen quivering under her touch.

Eventually, Kris pulled into a diner. She rode around to the back of the restaurant and shut off the bike. Sam dismounted and took off her helmet while Kris lowered the kickstand, and swung off. Before she could say anything, Kris fisted her hands in Sam's short hair and pulled their mouths together in a hot, urgent kiss that Sam swore raised the temperature ten degrees. Kris broke the kiss suddenly and walked away laughing. "I'm hungry. Let's get something to eat."

On the way back they stopped to browse in some antique shops and watched a college softball game under the lights. They returned home shortly before midnight and fell into bed exhausted.

They walked out of the house laughing, and before getting on the bikes shared a quick kiss. Starting their bikes, they gave a thumbs up and pulled out of the driveway. They rode the back roads with long dusty straightaways and paved single lanes with wide turns. The weather was perfect, sunny, with a whisper of a breeze, and a few fluffy white clouds drifting by.

They rode along a shaded area of the road, but the longer they were in the shade, the darker it became. The light at the end of the wooded area receded away from them, and the woods grew cold, and damp as it closed in around them. Soon they could only ride single file, and they slowed as the road filled with potholes. A loud bang and a bright flash caused Sam to swerve to the left, and her bike nearly went down. As she coaxed her bike back to upright, she saw that Kris had moved ahead of her.

Sam straightened the bike and felt a quick, violent tug on her leg that took her breath away. She fell to the ground, her bike disappearing and she lay in the dust and gravel and watched as her leg turned black and withered. She lay on the road and shouted for Kris, who couldn't hear her over the roar of the engine and the sudden chaos of buzzers and beeps ringing in her ears and lights flashing before her. She dragged herself along the ground and called to Kris again, panic rising in her.

At last, Kris stopped and turned around to look at her. She smiled sadly at Sam before she pulled her visor down and rode off, a man sitting behind her on the bike. Sam screamed out "Kris don't go!" and jumped up to chase her.

Sam lay on the floor half way across the room, confused and struggling to get her wind back. She flinched as Kris rolled her over.

"Sam! What are you doing?"

She heard the panic in Kris' voice and felt her move away. A moment later the light came on, and she winced against the brightness.

"My God what happened?"

Sam shook her head, unable to talk. She rubbed at her gut and struggled to breathe. She tried to remember what had happened before she awoke on the floor.

Kris knelt in front of her. "Sam, look at me!" Her hand was gentle on Sam's chin. "Relax. You had your wind knocked out. Take a deep breath, blow it out. There you go. A few more. It'll come back. Here sit up, it'll help." She was pulled into a seated position. After several more tries, Sam was able to start breathing normally. "Are you okay?"

Sam nodded and whispered, "Yes."

"What happened?"

"I'm not sure. I must have been dreaming."

"Did you have a flashback?"

"No. It was a weird dream."

"Do you want to talk about it?"

Sam was quiet for a moment trying to remember. "I dreamed I crashed on my bike and lost my leg. But that wasn't it entirely. Different parts of my life were blurred together. The lights and sounds of the chopper as it crashed were in there, and I heard gunfire. It was strange."

She remembered more, but she didn't say anything about seeing Kris ride off after the crash. Or the fact that she saw her father on the back of Kris' bike as they left her behind. That was something she didn't want to think too deeply about.

"Anything else?"

"My leg turned black, and I tried to run. I guess that's when I hit the floor."

"I heard you scream and heard you hit the floor. I thought you called my name. You're not hurt are you?"

"I don't think so."

"Will you let me check? You hit awfully hard."

"Sure. Let me get up."

"Let me help you up." Kris stood up and taking Sam's hands helped to pull her up. She wrapped her arm around Sam's waist and helped her back to the bed. "Did you hit your head?"

"I don't think so." Sam sat down on the bed.

"Does anything hurt? Are you dizzy? Are your ears ringing?"

"No, no, and no."

Sam sat patiently and let Kris examine her. Kris checked her back, ribs and abdomen. She looked carefully at Sam's stump until she was satisfied Sam was uninjured. "Everything looks good."

"Thanks."

"Why aren't you looking at me?"

"I am."

"No, you aren't. Are you embarrassed that you fell?" Sam was silent. "Damn it, Sam. It's nothing to be embarrassed about. You had a nightmare and fell. How is that different than when I have taken off running in the middle of the night and banged off walls, knocked over furniture?"

"I guess it's not."

"Look at me. You guess it's not?"

"It isn't any different," Sam muttered.

"I am glad you realize that. Now answer this truthfully, did riding on my bike scare you?"

Sam shook her head. "No. It was fun. It was good to be out again. But I look forward to getting my own bike back."

"That I can understand. Are we good here?"

"Almost. I'm sorry about earlier today. I didn't want to tell you that my medical board is coming up, and I'm worried. I'm not getting better in the simulator. I can't get the feel of the rudder pedals with my leg. I thought I'd recognize how much pressure I was applying by how it felt in my knee. But it's not there. I think I might be done as a pilot."

Kris leaned forward and wrapped her arms around Sam. "I'm so sorry. Is there anything else you can try? Are there any adjustments they can make to Betty? Would a different foot piece help?"

Sam smiled. "No. We've tried several things, and it didn't improve the results."

"What are your options?"

"Kris, I'm a pilot. There isn't much else out there for me."

"Don't be ridiculous. You have a degree in aerospace engineering from the Naval Academy. That's nothing to scoff at."

"I know. I guess I still have to figure out what I want to do. I might be able to get a position with one of the aeronautical firms." *I'd have to move away.* Sam brushed her hand across Kris' temple, tucking a lock of hair behind her ear. "Anyhow, thanks for checking me out and making sure everything is okay."

"Sweetheart, I've been checking you out for a long time." She leaned forward and kissed Sam softly. "Let's go back to bed."

"That sounds good."

Chapter Fifty-three

SAM LAY IN BED trying to get comfortable. She wondered how Kris was doing and if her night was busy. She'd never thought about it before that someone had to staff the hospitals at night. She knew it was done, she just hadn't thought about it.

Kris said she would be home in the morning between seven and eight. Sam would make sure to have some breakfast for her when she got home. Nothing heavy because Kris was going to have to sleep and she would sleep better if she wasn't full. *Maybe some herbal tea to help her relax, not caffeine.*

I feel better now, more complete then I ever have before. How is that even possible? I'm still learning how to do things again. I have therapy twice a week, and they continue to kick my ass, but I feel whole. I'm not going to fly again, I know it. I hope I can stay in. But doing what? Please God, not admin. Maybe an instructor position. Why haven't I started giving serious thought to this? Why am I content to lie in bed and wait for morning, so I can cook Kris breakfast? Have I changed that much? Sam rolled over and pulled Kris' pillow close. *Her subtle scent lingered, and with a smile on her face, Sam drifted to sleep.*

***

Sam awakened, and lay quietly, her thoughts immediately drifting to Kris. With a quick gut clench, she realized that she loved Kris. This giddy feeling that kept her on edge and feeling like she was upside down was love. *This want for Kris. This desire, it wasn't only lust. It was beyond that. It was bright and new and terrifying.* Suddenly nervous she got up, dressed quickly, and went for a run. Thirty minutes later, significantly calmer and more in control she returned, looked at the clock and realized she had time for a quick shower.

Sam finished in the shower and was reaching to turn off the water when the curtain opened, and Kris poked her head in. "Morning sexy. Is there room for me in there?"

"Sure." Sam shifted on the bench, repositioning to give Kris some room. "I didn't hear you come in."

"That's because you were singing."

"No, I wasn't."

"Yes, you were. I kissed a girl." Kris lifted the hand-held shower head and directed it over her body before returning it to spray on Sam.

"I don't think so." Embarrassed she pushed the bottle of shampoo into Kris' hands and enjoyed the view in front of her. Kris squirted some shampoo in her hands and started to wash her hair. Sam leaned forward, running her mouth across a firm, smooth abdomen. She heard Kris' gasp and felt her stomach quiver, Kris stopped moving her arms for a second before her hands fluttered down to Sam's head.

"Oh, that feels so good, but give me a chance to rinse."

Sam pulled back as the shampoo bubbles ran down Kris' lean body and were rinsed away. "Was I really singing?"

"Yes. It wasn't bad either. So, is that what's on the agenda today?"

"Is what on the agenda?"

"Kissing a girl?" Before she could answer Kris sunk to her knees in front of her and captured her mouth in a soft, sensual kiss that lasted until they were breathless. Sam pulled back, and held Kris' face gently in her hands, "I love you." She saw the emotion blaze into Kris' eyes, and she trembled when she heard in return "I love you too."

Chapter Fifty-four

SAM AND KRIS SAT in the parking lot across from the courthouse. Sam took Kris' hand and held it gently. "Are you ready?"

"I am. Are you sure you don't mind?" Kris searched Sam's face for any sign of disapproval.

"Babe, this is your decision. We've discussed it, but it's ultimately your choice. If I had known what she did to you, what she put you through, I wouldn't have stopped." Sam looked at Kris, smiled, and reached out tucking some wayward hair behind Kris' ear before stroking her face. "I love you. Do what you think is right."

Kris nodded. "Thank you."

They walked across the street to the courthouse, entered and found the courtroom. Sam took a seat in the gallery and Kris huddled with the prosecuting attorney. Shelly sat at the table looking down as her lawyer spoke quietly to her. The bailiff called the court to order, and they stood as the judge entered.

The judge started the proceedings and called for the prosecution to start. The prosecuting attorney stood. "Your honor we would like to offer a plea bargain. If the defendant, Ms. Shelly Delabrois pleads guilty to harassment and agrees to complete an inpatient alcohol treatment program, as well as agrees to have no further contact with Dr. Kristine Matthews, we will drop the assault and battery charge."

Shelly's lawyer conferred with her talking rapidly, and he stood. "Your honor, we agree to those conditions."

Shelly stood and announced to the court that she pled guilty to harassment. The judge sentenced her in accordance with the plea agreement and dismissed them. As Kris and Sam walked out of the courtroom Shelly's lawyer approached them. "Dr. Matthews, my client would like to speak with you for a moment. You too, Ms. Davies."

With a nod, they agreed and Shelly approached. "Kris, I apologize for everything, the cheating, the lying, but most of all for hurting you. I don't know exactly when I changed. I realize that none of it was your fault. It was all on me and my weakness for alcohol. I am an alcoholic. Thank you for giving me a chance to get my life together. It's more than I deserve." She looked at Sam. "Take care of her." Shelly turned and walked away.

Chapter Fifty-five

ONE MONTH LATER

THE OFFICERS CLUB WAS packed with everyone in attendance dressed for the formal affair. Military personnel were in formal dress uniforms and civilians were in black tie or dresses. A large contingent of public relations staff were present, carefully guiding and kowtowing to the congresswoman and her entourage. The upper leadership of the base and the naval hospital were in abundance. Sam and Kris mingled with the crowd, moving in and out of conversations but were careful not to spend too much time together. Eventually, a group formed which was almost entirely comprised of the members of the Wounded Warrior battalion. As they caught up with each other, the congresswoman approached along with the commanding officer of the hospital.

The commanding officer took responsibility for making introductions to Congresswoman West. "This is Dr. Matthews. She's one of our general surgeons. She has a few combat tours under her belt and is one of our more combat experienced docs. We're happy to have her back and in the operating room again. She gave us quite a scare."

Ms. West lifted her brow in surprise. "Oh really?"

"Our brave doc went out into the field to help free a Marine who was trapped in the wreckage of a helicopter crash. It turned out to be a Major from one of our local squadrons. While the doc was out there, she ended up taking a hit in the shoulder. What was it? A rocket-propelled grenade exploded close by peppered her with shrapnel. It took multiple surgeries to put our doc back together and lots of rehab. It took a while, but she finally got her arm back to full function."

Congresswoman West shifted her gaze to Kris. "I didn't realize medical personnel went out like that. Other than the medics."

"They do when it is possible. If we can save someone en route by having a doc in the air, we'll do it."

"That's remarkable. So, did the Marine make it too? Was the rescue successful?"

Kris swallowed hard, trying to hide the disbelief that her commanding officer had revealed her private medical history. Kris stammered, "Yes." She took a breath and smoothed her voice. "I understand she's doing well."

Kris heard a quick intake of breath and turned to see Sam standing next to her. She saw Sam's expression go from surprise to anger. Her eyes were narrowed, and she ground her teeth, setting her jaw. Her skin flushed starting at her neck and moving up to cover her face.

"She? That's fantastic. What a story. Female Navy doc gets injured saving female Marine. That would be a great special interest story on female vets."

Kris' stomach clenched, and she struggled to take a deep breath. She turned to the congresswoman. "No. Please don't do that. I was doing what any medical staff would do. We're there to help the troops. That's what we're trained to do."

The congresswoman turned to Sam. "Tell me something," She looked at Sam's uniform, saw the rank insignia, "Major, wouldn't you love to hear more of the doctor's story."

Sam looked at the congresswoman. "As a matter of fact I *would* like to hear the *entire* story. With none of the important details left out. Like exactly how and where her injury occurred." Sam turned and glared at Kris.

Kris heard the anger in Sam's voice but before she could respond the congresswoman said, "Of course the details are important. I'd love to hear more of the story."

"I'm sorry, ma'am, but it deals with my personal life, and that's not up for public consumption," Kris said, but her eyes stayed on Sam, noting her rigid posture and the firm set of her jaw. *Oh Dear God. Not now. Not here.*

Sam's eyes were glinting with anger. "I'm sure what you share with other people about your injury is carefully guarded. A select few would need to know the details. If you would excuse me, I need to go. Good night, Ma'am, good night Captain." Sam turned on her heel and walked away.

Kris excused herself from the group as quickly and unobtrusively as possible, and she scanned the crowd looking for Sam. She hurried out to the lobby in time to see Sam leave through the front door. She rushed outside to Sam and placed her hand on her wrist. "Sam, we need to talk."

Sam glared at the hand on her wrist and then looked up. "Really?

You think talking is important? What about the truth? Was that important, Kris?" She pulled her arm away. "Leave me alone. I'm going home." A few people close by turned when they heard Sam's voice.

"I'll drive you home," Kris whispered, trying to defuse the situation.

"Forget it. They've already called a cab for me."

"Don't be ridiculous."

Sam hissed, "Ridiculous? Since when is the truth ridiculous?" Kris reached for her, and she backed away. "Leave me alone. Just leave me alone." She walked away and raised her arm to hail one of the cabs that were pulling into the long driveway.

Kris followed her, caught up with her. "I'll come by later."

"Don't bother." Sam climbed into the cab and pulled the door shut.

Kris stood on the sidewalk and watched the cab pull away. *SHIT!*

***

Sam stood at the end of the pier listening to the waves roll past on their way to the beach. The sky began to lighten, and she sat down, legs dangling over the edge, her chest pressed hard into the lower rail. Every breath hurt. She wiped at the tears that started without warning, and her breath hitched. As the sun peaked over the horizon, a small, animal-like sound emerged from deep within her. *How could I have been so stupid? How could I believe that she would want me? It was all just sympathy, pity for what happened, guilt that she did it to me. God! I am so fucking stupid.*

Rays from the sun blinded her. She stood abruptly, wiped the sand from her dress blue trousers, picked up her shoes, dress jacket and hat. She wiped her hands on her pristine white t-shirt and walked to the shore. Minutes after calling for a cab she climbed into the back seat. Giving the cabbie the address she leaned her head back and closed her eyes.

"Ma'am, we're here."

Sam's eyes opened, and she looked at the meter. She handed him a wad of cash. "Keep the change."

"Thanks. Are you okay, Ma'am? Do you need help getting inside?"

Sam shook her head and cleared her throat. "No. Thank you."

Sam dropped her jacket the minute she got inside. She walked to the bathroom, turned on the shower and stripped. She sat down and removed the prosthesis, eyeing it closely, and squeezing it in her hands until they hurt.

She sat it aside and transferred into the shower. *I've never felt this pain, this emptiness before. No, that's wrong. I did when my father didn't come back. Week after week as he stayed away and Brian, Jamie and Jenny were taken away. First my mom, then dad, and my siblings. One by one they all left.*

Sam sat in the shower with the water beating down on her and washed absentmindedly. As the water sluiced down, her gut clenched and Sam watched vacantly as the suds spiraled down the drain. A choked sob escaped from her, and she leaned forward hugging herself and cried until the water turned cold and she shivered uncontrollably.

She shut off the water, dried quickly and hopped into the bedroom. Exhausted she climbed into bed and curled onto her side. She smelled Kris' fragrance on a pillow and tossed it aside. Staring at the wall, she placed a hand over the twisting in her gut and fell into a deep sleep.

***

Kris and Sam stood facing each other over the table. "You lied to me!" Sam slammed her hand down onto the table.

"Sam, let me explain," Kris pleaded.

"No. Every day since we met you've lied to me. You knew who I was. You knew what happened. Well, I don't need you. I don't need you checking up on your patient." Sam kicked a chair out of the way.

"No! That's not the way it is."

"Bullshit! I don't need you assuaging your guilt over what happened to me. And I certainly don't need you in my bed for a sympathy fuck. Isn't that an ethics violation?" Sam shouted.

"What? I'm not checking on a patient. Sam, I didn't realize, not at first, who you were. I don't feel guilt over what happened to you. Your leg was ruined no matter what. What was I supposed to do, leave you to die? Or should I have pulled the trigger on your weapon, like you asked, and ended your life?" Kris picked up a paperweight and shifted it from hand to hand while she paced. She slammed it down. "Sympathy fuck? How dare you!" She stalked over to the window, spun around "How dare you imply that I would do such a thing. How could you reduce what we've shared to...to a sympathy fuck? If anyone's been lying it's you. Most of the time you shut off your emotions. You're so busy worrying about your image as the tough Marine."

"What we've shared is a lie. I'm just a patient. How many other—"

Kris pointed a finger at her, "Don't you say it. Don't you even imply it. I have never gotten involved with a patient. Never."

"Well, from where I'm standing it sure looks like you did. What was this, some prolonged medical checkup to make sure I was doing all right? Then, when you're sure I'm doing okay you walk out? Well, let me tell you something, Doctor. I'm fine. I don't need you checking on me, making sure I eat right and am taking care of myself. I've adjusted very well. So, piss off."

"Sam, let me explain."

"Explain? Explain what? How you couldn't be honest with me? How you thought I was so weak that you couldn't be honest about your part in this. That you did it!"

"Dammit, Sam! I've done the right thing my entire career! You think I didn't worry about this? I know it was right on the edge of what some would consider inappropriate. But I didn't recognize you in the beginning. And by the time I did, we were already friends. I didn't plan to become your lover. What was I supposed to do? How was I going to tell you that I did this to you! I know it was the only way to save you. But how do I say, 'I took your leg,' when I've seen how much you've suffered? How hard you've worked to overcome everything?"

"Sam, look at me. I know how guilty you felt about losing your men. I see how you've struggled with that. Knowing how I was hurt wouldn't have helped you."

Sam placed a hand on her chest trying to quiet the pounding of her heart. Her head throbbed. She stared at Kris but remained quiet.

"Sam, I am sorry."

"I don't want to hear your lies." Sam stalked to the door, pulled it open. "Get out! I don't want to talk to you. Don't come near me again. If you call me, if you so much as look at me, I'll report you for an ethics violation. What you did was wrong. You don't mess with people like this. I'll never forgive you."

"Sam, please."

Sam stepped aside and gestured to the door. "Get out! I never want to see you again!"

With tears running down her face Kris walked to the door. She paused and reached out a hand toward Sam. "Sam, please—"

Sam slapped her hand away. "Get out!"

Kris jerked back with the contact, lowered her head and hurried out the door. She paused for just a moment and looked back. Sam slammed the door behind her and set the lock.

Roslyn Bane

Chapter Fifty-six

DR. JAMES PLACED KRIS' chart on the exam table. "The skin graft has healed well. Your suture lines are fading and have matured nicely. The scars are fading and no longer tender. You have full motion and strength in your arm, and the chest muscles all work well. Do you get any shortness of breath when walking or exercising?"

"Nothing that's unexpected."

"Are you sleeping well?"

"I've had a few rough nights. I have a lot on my mind. I need some time to figure things out. When can we proceed with the reconstruction?"

"Whenever you're ready. If you recall I said that this would be done in several phases. Your graft and muscles appear to have healed well, so the next step is to insert a tissue expander. This goes under the chest muscle. The expander has a port that is built into the front of the expander through which additional saline can be added. Over the next few months, we add saline to it. This gradually stretches the skin and the muscle to help form a pocket that will later support the permanent implant. Are you thinking of enhancement or reconstruction?"

"No. I don't want to be larger, just symmetrical."

"Okay. Although it won't be absolutely identical. Most women do have one breast slightly larger than the other."

"I understand."

"Of course, you do. You've performed reconstruction before."

"A few times in residency. None recently," Kris said without emotion.

"Things have probably changed since you did the procedure. You'll need about four surgeries. "

Kris sat quietly for several seconds lost in thought.

"What are you thinking about?"

"I never thought about the next step. With my patients, I did my part. I removed their breasts when there was cancer. I made sure they healed, and that they went to oncology and eventually to plastics for reconstruction. But I didn't check, not really, to see if they were healing emotionally. They had to be scared. They had to be overwhelmed. I thought I understood what they felt. I didn't. I didn't have a clue."

"Kris, when we find ourselves in the same situations as our patients, we grow."

Kris sat silently and nodded her head.

"Do you have any questions?"

"If I start this here can I complete it elsewhere? I may be getting orders soon."

"That would be unusual. It's not unheard of. Although if you're going back overseas—"

"No. It would be here in the States."

"That shouldn't be a problem. Well, take some time to think about what you want to do."

"I want it done. I want to get this started as soon as possible."

"Okay. Get some sleep Kris, you look exhausted. You'll need to have someone available to help you the first few days after surgery."

"I'll get that arranged."

***

Sam eyed the landing zone and lowered the collective allowing the helo to descend. She pulled back slightly on the cyclic keeping the nose up, the engines rumbled, and the light flickered as the rotor blades spun. They were coming in fast for a grab and go, picking up the wounded and their corpsman and lifting off again as soon as possible. "Do you see our pick up?"

"Roger that, Major, they're off the nose about 500 meters, down behind those rocks. If you can bring us around a little to the right, they can run for the door. We're ready back here. Mitchell is on the gun. Roberts is on the door."

"Thanks, Chief. Lieutenant stay sharp this should be fast, watch for overhead traffic."

There was a gentle thud as the wheels touched down, and the helo settled fully onto its landing gear. Sam's hands remained in position on the flight controls, ready to take off soon as she got the word from her team in the back of the bird. Two teams of two raced toward the chopper carrying stretchers, their weapons slung over the shoulders. Five seconds later another team raced out. This stretcher was carried by three. She watched in shock as the litter dipped and one of the smaller soldiers fell. They slowed momentarily to adjust their grip on the stretcher but kept moving. The figure on the ground sprung up and took a quick glance around before making eye contact with Sam. It was a woman, determination was on her face, as she started to run toward the chopper.

Sam gasped, "Fuck it's Kri—" Sam screamed as she saw the explosion. She cried out when Kris was propelled up into the air, cartwheeling with the force of the blast. Even while she was airborne, Sam could see her legs were gone. Terror filled Sam as she watched Kris slam onto the ground. Her body bounced once and lay still. Sam screamed, pulling at her harness to get free. She took one step and slammed onto the ground.

Sam found herself on the floor in the dark. Her heart was racing, her breathing was harsh, and after several seconds she realized there were tears on her face. She brushed them away and rolled over, untangling the sheets wrapped around her thighs. She pulled herself to a sitting position and sat back leaning against the bed. Quietly she sat in the dark, and let the shakes course through her body. Her hip and elbows hurt. Her unleg was throbbing, and after a few seconds, she realized she tasted blood.

Sam crawled to the bathroom where she pulled herself to a standing position at the counter. Turning on the light, she looked at herself. Her skin was a ghastly pasty white, her pupils dilated with fear, and her hair was damp with sweat. As she splashed water on her face, her hands trembled. She swallowed a pain pill before turning her attention to her throbbing stump. Pulling out the hand mirror she examined her leg and, once satisfied there was no further injury, she turned off the light and crawled back to bed.

Sam lay quietly in the dark and tried not to think about the dream. She waited for daylight to come and hoped she would slip quietly into sleep. She momentarily considered talking to the psychologist about the dream, but realized she would have to admit to having a relationship with Kris and that she wasn't willing to do. She slid down under the covers, punched at her pillow several times, and drifted into a restless sleep.

Roslyn Bane

Chapter Fifty-seven

KRIS WAS NAUSEOUS AND exhausted, she had tossed and turned all night. Looking at herself in the mirror, her ghostly reflection was barely recognizable. Dark circles under her eyes stained her flesh. Her cheeks were gaunt and hollowed. She rubbed her hands across her aching stomach. Her eyes were wide with…fear? *Would Sam report her? Would her behavior be deemed unethical? Was it? Was someone you treated half a world away one time still your patient?* She had thought about this question a thousand times through many nights. She didn't like the answer. When she had first seen Sam, in rehab, she hadn't recognized her. But she had been drawn to the strong silent woman who was fighting quietly and fiercely around the more vocal men.

Kris jumped when someone pounded on her door. She pulled on sweatpants and a sweatshirt, and before she reached the door, a knock sounded again, and a gruff voice called out. "LCDR Matthews, open the door now!" Kris moved toward the door, took a deep breath and with a trembling hand reached out to open it, her career was over.

Kris stood in shock and blinked several times before she recognized the person standing before her. Her brother laughed out loud. "Geez, sis, you look like you were facing your executioner. How the hell are you?" He grabbed her, enclosing her in a bear hug and spun her around. She wrapped her arms around him and burst into tears. He held her tight and lowered her to the ground. "Easy, sis, I know it's been awhile, but I've been where it's safe." He patted her back. "Are you okay? If I'd have known you missed me this much I would have visited sooner."

She let go and wiped the tears from her face. "God, I missed you, Tommy. Come on in." She looked up and down the street before she closed the door, and led him into the kitchen. "Do you want some coffee?"

"That would be great." He looked at the bottle of bourbon on the counter, gestured to it. "Rough night?"

"Yes." Her eyes followed his to the bottle. "Don't worry, I only had two. What brings you to town?" She measured coffee into the machine, poured in the water, and turned it on.

"I had a legal conference in Raleigh this week and thought I'd come over this way to visit before heading down to Hilton Head. A couple of the guys are heading down for some golf. I wanted to take my old bike if you don't mind, and leave my car here."

She pulled mugs from the cabinet. "Sure, go ahead. Since when do you golf?"

"I don't. I'm staying on the beach to check out the pretty girls, while the guys chase some silly white ball around. While they're bitching about their golf game, I'll be surrounded by scantily clad girls."

"That's the brother I know."

"And I know my sister. What's wrong?"

"I screwed up, Tommy. I seriously screwed up."

"Come on, sis, you never screw up. You're Miss Reliable. Commander Cool."

"I'm not joking. I might…" Her eyed filled with tears, overflowed. "I messed up. I might lose my commission. I could even lose my license."

"Yeah right." He stared at her. "Christ, you're serious. What the hell happened?"

Kris grabbed a paper towel, blotted at her eyes. "I …I got involved with a patient."

"No, you didn't." Kris remained quiet. "Shit. Krissy what were you thinking? What happened?"

With shaking hands, she poured coffee into two mugs and handed him one.

They sat down at the table. "I don't know where to start."

"How about at the beginning, when you met this patient."

"I met Sam twice."

"Sam? Did you switch sides? When did you start dating men?"

"Samantha. She's a Marine Major. Helicopter pilot. Or was. I guess she still is for now. Be quiet and let me tell you." She took her time and told him the story. It felt good to tell him the story again because it helped her feel closer to Sam. She finished and wiped her eyes.

"And you didn't tell her?"

"No." She heard his quick intake of breath.

Tommy leaned back when she'd finished. "I see. So, other than when you were over there you haven't been her doctor? You haven't been involved in her care?"

"Not unless she asked me to."

"What does that mean?"

"That she asked me questions a couple times about things. I offered my opinion. Only if she asked. I tried to get her to ask her medical team. I felt uncomfortable—"

"If you felt uncomfortable, why didn't you tell her that you had done it, the amputation?"

"I was advised not to. But deep down, I didn't agree. The psychologist didn't know that Sam and I were friends. I should have, and I don't know why I didn't."

"You don't know?"

"Dammit, Tommy! I screwed up. I should have. I knew it then, I thought about it several times. I just couldn't."

"Why not?"

"I...I was afraid...I didn't want to lose her as a friend. We became lovers, and well it was too late."

He took her hand, gave it a squeeze. "That wasn't smart. She's feeling deceived."

"Yes." Tears streamed down her face.

He shifted and pulled her next to him, holding her while she cried. She calmed, and he spoke in a quiet, soothing voice. "I think if I were her, I would be pretty mad. She probably feels like you had all the power in the relationship."

"But I didn't."

"Yeah, you did. You knew the truth. And you failed to share it with her. You didn't give her the option of backing away. I can't imagine anyone would be pleased with that power imbalance. Especially a Marine. I'm betting the female ones are as gung-ho as the males are."

She wiped at her eyes and pinched the bridge of her nose. "You're right."

"Um, who made the first move? Sexually?"

"It was mutual. Pretty spontaneous."

"So lesbians have quickies too?"

"Yes. But it wasn't like that. We...God, this is embarrassing. We were going out. Eventually, we made it to bed."

"Eventually?"

"Yes. We both had some issues...about how we looked."

He pulled his lips tight across his teeth and looked down into his coffee. "Yeah, I guess so."

"But it was mutual."

"I...I don't think this is considered fraternization."

"It's not. We're the same rank. Different chains of command."

"And since don't ask, don't tell is gone, that's not a problem."

Kris stood up and looked at the window. "That's gone. We can serve. Not everyone is accepting." She turned around and looked at him. "I've always been discreet."

"But that still leaves the question of whether it violated doctor-patient relationships. I have to tell you, sis, that's a good question. I think you're going to be okay. You treated her once under an emergency situation, and you haven't been involved in her medical care since. I'm not saying that to relax you. I think you'll be okay. I know you've never done anything like this before."

"Oh, hell no."

He stood and refilled his coffee. "You're worried she might report that? A breech of doctor-patient relationships."

"Yes."

"You already know that some people would look at it that way. "

"I do. I'm not proud of it."

"I know." He came over and hugged her. "You'll get through this. Right now, you're primarily scared. But under it all, I know you're hurting. It was more than physical, wasn't it?"

She nodded her head. "Yes."

"What happened with Shelly?"

"She cheated on me when I was over there. It continued when I got back. She started…" Kris stopped, cleared her throat. "She started drinking more than usual. She got mean when she drank, and she got violent a few times."

"She hit you?" Tommy asked, anger thick in his voice.

"Pushed, shoved. Bullied. This was happening while I was in counseling. I eventually kicked her out. Not long after that, I realized who Sam was."

"Did you get involved with Sam because you felt sorry for her?"

"No! I was, am, genuinely attracted to her. God, I love her!"

"Does she love you?"

Kris sighed and shook her head. "She did. I don't think so now."

"Give her some time." He sipped his coffee, took her hand, and looked at it. "How's your arm doing?"

Kris wiped her face dry and looked at her hand. "It's good as new. There's no problem with it. Do you want some breakfast?"

"Yes. I'm starving." He walked to the fridge and started rooting around. "Good, you have eggs. And bacon. Really? Bacon? I thought that was against the doctor code."

She snatched the bacon from his hand. "Keep it up, and I won't fix you any."

"Sure, you will." Tommy took the frying pan from her hand and set it on the stove. "You know, Krissy, I don't think your Marine is going to say anything. She's pissed. Maybe she threatened just to have something to say, or to make you hurt. Ultimately, if she loves you, no matter how mad she is, she won't destroy you. She'll also be worried about looking weak. I'm not a Marine, and that's what I would be worried about. That and appearing foolish."

"I didn't mean…"

"I know, sis. If she really knows you, she'll realize that too…it might take a while. She'll come around."

"I don't think so. It's already been a month."

***

Sam leaned on the counter looking out the kitchen window. Her jaw ached, and she realized she was clenching her teeth. She slapped at the lever for the water, turning it on to fill a glass. She drank it quickly, refilled it, and turned the tap off.

Glaring out the window, she saw the planters, now in full spring bloom. The tulips and top-heavy daffodils swayed on their fragile stems. She shook her head and stared at the flowers, biting down again until her jaw throbbed. She guzzled the water and slammed the glass down in the sink. The crack of the glass was instantaneous with the sharp jab into her hand. "Damn it." She looked at the blood running from her palm, wiggled her fingers, and grabbed a towel. She wrapped the towel around her hand and pressed it firmly against the wound. Sam stormed outside and ripped the flowers out of the pots before knocking them over.

Stomping back into the house she pulled off the towel, turned on the water, rinsed her hand and looked at the lacerations. "That was fucking stupid." She wrapped the towel around her hand again before snatching a plastic sandwich bag from a drawer. She turned sharply to cross to the refrigerator and slipped in the blood on the floor, landing on her side with a thud. Momentarily stunned by the impact, she lay on the floor motionless and groaning. After a minute, she made an assessment of what was hurting. Her right hip and elbow were hurting, but nothing was severe. She slowly stood up, limped the last few steps to the refrigerator and pulled out the entire ice bin.

Moving carefully back to the counter she reached for a few more plastic bags and filled them with ice. Gathering another towel, and the ice, she limped into the living room before lying down on the couch with ice on the painful areas. After several minutes of staring at the ceiling, she started to look around the room. A picture of Kris and herself, from Key West, sat on the end table, their eyes soft on each other. Sam remembered Alannah taking the picture just as they had separated from a kiss. There was a trio of candles, arranged on another table, bought by Kris, set next to a bright blue vase, now filled with dead flowers.

The novel Kris had been reading sat neglected, a bright pink slip of paper serving as a bookmark. Her gut clenched and she squeezed her eyes tight against the tears that formed. After several more minutes, she stood, picked the vase up and returned to the kitchen. She sniffed the trace of fragrance in the wilted flowers, before dropping them in the trash.

Carefully removing the broken glass from the sink, she dropped it in the trash, before rinsing the vase. She went into the bathroom and cleaned and bandaged her palm. Looking in the mirror, she checked her hip and elbow for bruising and poked them to see how tender they were. She looked at her reflection noting the dark smudges under her eyes, unkempt hair, and blood on her shirt. She remembered Kris standing behind her, insisting that she look at herself in the mirror and describing what she saw, right before they'd kissed for the first time. "Damn you, Kris. Why would you do this to me?"

Limping slightly Sam went back to the kitchen and grabbed a beer from the fridge before going outside to sit on the patio. She sat brooding with her beer until her gaze settled on the planters, the flowers already wilting from the heat of the sun. An unfamiliar feeling washed over her, and it took several seconds for her to realize it was shame.

Sam moved quickly to the garage and returned with a bag of dirt and a shovel and carefully replanted the flowers into the containers. She watered them thoroughly and moved them out of direct sunlight hoping they would survive her temper tantrum. She brushed the dirt from her hands and put the supplies away. Returning to the house, she dumped the rest of her beer down the drain and placed the picture of her and Kris into a drawer in the living room. The novel was tossed into the trash. It landed in the bin back cover up and she realized it was from the library. Her gaze fixated on the book for several seconds. With a sigh, she retrieved it and brushed off the crushed flower petals, before picking up her keys and wallet to return the book.

***

An hour later Sam watched the waves slam against the beach as a storm approached. She sipped a beer and thought the waves matched the fury within her. The waitress placed another beer in front of her and picked up the empty plate. "I didn't order another beer."

"Beer is compliments of the blonde off to your left. She said her name is Gena."

"Thanks." Sam looked over her shoulder and smiled recognizing the woman, who was now gliding toward her, hips swaying enticingly. Sam stood up to greet her.

"Sam, I didn't know you were back. I was hoping to hear from you when you came home."

"Hey there." Gena leaned in to kiss her and Sam turned slightly and kissed her on the cheek. "I wasn't in any shape to see anyone for a long time. Sit down. Would you like something to drink?"

"A frozen daiquiri would be good."

"Sure thing." Sam motioned to the waitress and quickly ordered. "How have you been?"

"I've been busy. The business has grown a lot over the past year. I actually had to hire another assistant to help with the clients." Gena shifted in her chair.

"That's great. Everyone needs accountants." Sam didn't react to the stroke of a foot along her leg.

"So it seems. How long have you been back?"

"I've been back in the States a year, but down here, about nine months."

"I'm crushed you never called." Gena laughed her blue eyes sparkling with merriment.

Her eyes are blue but not as brilliant as Kris'.

"I thought you might be getting home in the next few months. Seriously are you okay? It looks like you've lost weight. Are you feeling all right?"

"Yeah, I'm good. I got back early."

"How did you get lucky enough for that to happen?" She sipped at the frozen daiquiri that the waitress had delivered.

"I got injured, lost my leg."

"Stop. You did not." Gena slapped Sam on the arm. "That's a

horrible thing to say."

"I'm not kidding," Sam said flatly.

"Sam?" Gena started to bend over to look but stopped herself.

"Go ahead look." Sam pulled up her pants leg.

"Oh my God! Oh, Sam, I am so sorry. I didn't know. I…"

"It's okay. I've gotten used to it." She reached out and wiped the tear that was sliding down Gena's cheek. "Don't cry."

"I'm sorry. Can I ask how it happened?"

"I was shot down, lost part of my crew. My leg got crushed." Sam spoke quickly, her voice flat. She paused to force down the despair she felt creeping up and cleared her throat. Her eyes focused on the white-capped surface of the water. She exhaled slowly. "Three of us made it." She looked up in surprise when she realized Gena was holding her hand. She watched as Gena turned her palm up to place a kiss there.

Gena sat up and searched Sam's face. "That must have been horrible. Are you okay with…everything?"

"As well as can be expected." Sam looked at a spot on the horizon.

"Would you like to get some dinner? Or I could cook something for us back at my place. We could talk, get reacquainted."

Sam sat thoughtful and quiet. "That sounds nice. But I'm going to have to pass. I…listen, Gena, I appreciate the offer, but I met someone."

"Oh, well, that's too bad for me." Gena looked around. "Is she meeting you here? I'd like to meet the woman who settled you down."

"Um, no. We had a fight."

"So you're down here cooling off. It must have been a doozie if you came all the way down here. I've never seen anything faze you."

"You could say so."

"I'm sure she'll call soon to apologize. I hope everything works out for you." Gena stood and walked around the table before bending over to kiss Sam on the cheek, "Give me a call if you find yourself available. She's a lucky woman, Sam."

Chapter Fifty-eight

SAM LAY MOTIONLESS IN bed, staring at the ceiling. While the sweat dried on her body, she tried to slow her breathing. *Two in the morning. Again*. She thought about the dream that had woke her. She wished she knew whether the dream was a flashback or if hearing Kris try to explain what happened had planted the memory in her head.

Giving up on sleep she walked to the living room, turned on the TV, and flipped through the channels looking for something interesting. She stopped as she came across M*A*S*H and watched for several minutes before it broke to a commercial. She went to the kitchen, rooted through the fridge, pulled out a beer, and leftover Chinese food. She dumped it on a plate and placed it in the microwave to warm. By the time the food was ready, the show had resumed, and Sam sat at the snack bar eating while she watched the episode. As the show unfolded, it revealed how the medical team was inundated with wounded and the staff showed their stress. The episode ended and another began.

The surgeon Hawkeye suffered an eye injury from an explosion, and it was questionable whether he would see again. His career as a surgeon would be over. *Like Kris. Her career could have ended. Because she came out to help me. I've never thought about that. That doesn't say much for me.* Sam lay down on the couch watching, her beer forgotten on the counter along with the remnants of her late night food binge.

Thirty minutes later she sat at the computer searching for the surgical company Kris had been assigned to. The public information on the command website spoke about the mission of the medical team and how they had served in Afghanistan. She read about the numbers of casualties the small hospital handled and looked at some of the photos of the facilities and staff. She found a picture of Kris holding a small girl. Kris was smiling broadly. The toddler's face was animated with laughter, while an Afghan woman stood nearby, a trace of a smile on her face.

"This was before children scared you. What happened?"

Sam sat staring at the picture before continuing to read. She was surprised to learn that the facility had come under mortar fire frequently and had been infiltrated by insurgents several times. The medical staff itself had suffered casualties but had performed admirably. Sam realized that during the time that she was in Afghanistan the medical command had lost more of its members than her squadron had.

She pushed back from the computer, and stared out her window into the darkness and thought to herself that Kris had lost friends, team members too. Maybe more than she had. That she probably had to try to save the lives of her own friends. Kris had most definitely seen more of the ravages of war than she had. As Sam stared out the window, she tried to remember her initial care after her injury. Most of it was a blur, even her time in Germany. She could distinctly remember several doctors and nurses, but she was only one patient. How many had they dealt with daily? She realized for the first time that she wondered how the medical team put up with the urgency and stress every day.

***

Sam sat at the picnic table and picked at the sandwich she'd packed for lunch. She watched as families stopped to eat at the roadside picnic area. Kids were running about, screaming, exercising their pent-up energy after their car ride to wherever.

Sipping her water, she watched as two boys, clearly twins, about ten years old slowly approached her bike. They stood looking at it as they spoke in whispers so that she couldn't hear what they were saying. They moved closer to touch it, she stood up and called to them, "Please don't touch that!"

Walking over to them she asked them again not touch it, and they stood still and waited for her to come over. "Do you like it?"

"It's awesome," they said simultaneously. "What kind is it?"

"It's a Victory motorcycle."

"Why does it have a Marine Corps sticker on it?"

"Because I'm a Marine."

"Na-ah."

"I sure am."

"What do you do?"

"I fly helicopters. Well, I used to." She watched as the mother approached.

"We love motorcycles. They're the best, but mom says we can't have one. Not even dirt bikes."

"Well, it's important to listen to what your mom and dad have to say."

"Dad ran away."

"Daniel, Jacob that's enough." Their mother's voice rang out sharp, but she smiled at Sam. "Sorry they're bothering you."

"They're not. They're just admiring the bike."

"Look, Mom, it has a Marine Corps sticker on it. She says she's a Marine."

"And flies helicopters too! I want to be a Marine when I grow up. But mom says it's dangerous. Did you go to the war?"

"I did."

"Boys leave her alone so she can have her lunch."

"Mom says lots of soldiers got hurt over there."

"They do."

"Did you?"

"Yes, I did."

"Boys come on." She smiled awkwardly at Sam.

"It's okay, ma'am." Sam turned back to the twins. "I was hurt in a helicopter crash. Now I have an artificial leg."

"No way. Cool." The boys spoke together. "Can we see?"

"Boys stop!"

Sam smiled at the woman. "I don't mind. It's best if kids get comfortable seeing people that are...different. To see what we can do."

"Do you have a peg leg? It doesn't look like it."

Sam laughed. "It's not a peg leg like pirates have. It's more like a robot leg."

"Cool!"

"If your mom says it is okay I can show you the bottom of it."

"Ah sure." The woman shifted side to side.

Sam pulled the leg of her jeans up, and the boys saw the prosthesis. After a few seconds, she tugged her pants leg back down.

"That's so cool," the boys shouted. "Is there a foot in your boot?"

"Yes, so I can walk."

"Some people have blades instead so they can run," the one boy stated matter-of-factly.

"That's right. I can change the foot to a blade and go running."

"Wow. How did you get to be a Marine?"

"I went to the Naval Academy and studied hard."

"What does your mom think?"

Sam was quiet for a few seconds before answering. "She was sort of happy and sort of sad." She stood up, glanced at her watch. "I need to get going. It was fun talking to you boys. You know if you want to be Marines one of the first things you have to do is follow directions. Your mom is in charge so you should follow her orders."

The woman smiled at Sam and shooed the boys back over to their picnic table. As she walked away, she turned back to Sam. "Thanks for your service."

Sam smiled and nodded, and had to fight to hold back tears. Sam walked back to her table and finished her sandwich in one large bite and chugged her remaining water. She placed her trash in the bin before she mounted her bike and tightened her helmet's chin strap. She started the bike, gave a wave to the boys and roared away.

Two hours later, Sam sat on her porch and thought about the day. Hearing the boys say their father had run away bothered her. She wondered if the boys would have a good life. She hoped they would and thought they had a good chance because their mom was with them and she seemed to have her stuff together.

Sam sat and brooded about her fractured family. She wondered where her siblings ended up. The closest thing she had to a family was the Klines. No, not the closest, they were her family. And the Corps was. And Kris. But Kris was gone. Sam worried about the high probability that she would be medically discharged from the Corps.

With a sick feeling in her stomach, she moved into her small office, turned on the computer and started to put together a resume. It was time to plan for the future. An hour later she pushed back from the desk in near panic after giving up on trying to put her military experience into something useful for the civilian workforce. She sent a quick text message before changing into running gear, switching to a running blade, and setting off for a run. Thirty minutes later, a grin spread on her face when her phone flashed the text response. Next weekend she was going Chattanooga.

.

Chapter Fifty-nine

SAM PARKED OFF TO the side of the driveway, got out of the car, and reached in the trunk for her suitcase. Before she had the trunk closed, the front screen door flew open with a loud crash and Lauren ran to her, nearly knocking her over. Sam somehow managed to keep her balance.

"God, Sammy, you're home."

"It's good to see you too."

"Where's Kris?"

Sam felt her smile fade. "It's over."

"What? No way. You two were totally wrapped up in each other. Perfect for each other."

"Nothing's perfect."

Sam stood and watched as Lauren, her sister in every way but blood, looked her over closely. Sam fidgeted while Lauren stared into her eyes. Before she could say anything the door opened again and Lauren stepped back to make room for her mother and father to welcome Sam home.

"Welcome home Sam." Nancy and Jim hugged her. "How was your trip?" Jim took her suitcase and led them into the house. The smell of brownies was heavy in the air and the underlying scent of lemon. Sam noticed some changes to the house since her last visit.

"You got new furniture."

"Sure did. And there's a new TV in the back room." Nancy rolled her eyes.

"Dad finally joined this century and got a flat screen," Lauren teased.

"Hey, the other one worked just fine," Jim defended himself.

The friendly banter continued, and soon they were sitting outside enjoying frozen margaritas and nachos. The afternoon drifted by as they caught up with each other. They ate dinner outside, surrounded by tiki torches that cast their flickering light around the patio and warded off mosquitos. A few neighbors stopped by to visit and welcome Sam home. Hours later, Jim and Nancy said good night, and Lauren went inside and made another batch of margaritas. She brought the pitcher and fresh glasses outside and salted the rim before filling them. Handing one to Sam she spoke quietly, "What happened with Kris?"

"I'm not talking about it."

"Fine. How are you doing?"

"I'm getting back to normal." Sam drank from the frosty glass and licked the salt from her lips. "Ooh, that's good."

"This is a no bullshit zone, Sam. It's just the two of us."

"I'm doing good. I like my house. I'm back in the squadron. I had my medical board and am waiting for the results. In a few days or maybe a few weeks I'll find out if I get to stay in." She took a large swallow of margarita. "I had the bike modified so I can ride—"

"What? Don't you think that's a little dangerous? You already lost one leg."

"In a helicopter. I'm not giving up the bike."

"But Sam—"

"No. Drop it. It's one of the things that kept me sane. It gave me something to look forward to. Something for me to aim for once I was back on my own. And it's helped me get through the last few weeks."

"What's so hard about the last few weeks?" Lauren sipped her drink and licked the salt from her lips.

Damn, I walked right into that one. Sam looked at the condensation forming on the glass, stroked her finger through it, and took a large swallow of her drink. She shook her head as it throbbed against the sudden rush of cold.

"What happened with Kris? Mom and Dad won't ask, but we can see you're hurting."

Sam drew her lips tightly closed. "You always saw too much."

"What happened?"

Sam shook her head and rubbed at the aching spot in her chest. "I don't want to talk about this."

"She really hurt you. You finally let someone get close enough to you, to let you feel something meaningful—"

"You don't know what you're talking about," Sam grumbled and tried to push up from the table but the drinks through the day had caught up with her. She stumbled slightly and sat back down. Glancing over she saw Lauren's dimples crease. "You think this is funny?"

"I'm not making fun of you, Sam. I'm worried. Tell me about what happened? You two seemed so happy at Thanksgiving." She topped off Sam's glass and sipped at her own.

Sam remained quiet, stared at the ground, almost burning a hole in the concrete patio. She could wait out Lauren's curiosity.

"Sam, you can sit there the rest of the night trying to ignore me. You've been away long enough to forget that I am more stubborn than you. I can wait all night."

Sam gave her an icy glare and sighed. "She lied to me."

"About what? What was so big that you would break up with her?"

"She was the doc who did my amputation."

Lauren's quick intake of breath, revealed her surprise. Sam paused and pinched hard on the bridge of her nose, trying to stop the tears that threatened. "She came out to the crash site where I was trapped and cut off... cut off my leg to get me free. On the way to the medevac chopper, she was hit. Her arm, and ah...ahm...her left breast were almost completely destroyed. She had a collapsed lung and almost didn't make it. They did muscle and skin grafts to close her wounds. There's a lot of scarring." Sam swallowed hard as she realized Kris could have been killed because she had chosen to come to help her and her men.

"Wow. That's...I can't imagine." Lauren shook her head slowly.

"She said she had hypnosis to help her remember some events...said she didn't realize it until after we were friends that she'd done my amputation." Sam wondered what had been so hard about her amputation that Kris had been injured mentally from helping her.

"Dear God, she got hurt helping you." They sat quietly each reflecting on what Sam said. Sam finished her margarita and poured more of the half melted concoction into her glass, sat back, and sighed. The glass spread the rings of condensation across the table as Sam moved it around aimlessly. Bile rose thick in her throat as her chest tightened. She recalled the swelling and deep bruising on Kris' arm the first time she'd seen her. The pain etched on her face as she'd walked down the hospital hallway.

"I don't know what to say. This is unbelievable." Lauren held her hand over her mouth and rubbed her lips.

"She should have told me."

"Told you what? How she got hurt? Or that she did your amputation?"

"Both," Sam replied angrily.

"I disagree. I understand that you're hurt. But telling you how she got injured had the potential to undermine you. To cause you to feel guilty. She probably didn't want to put that burden on you."

"That's what she said. But she should have told me she did the procedure."

"Why? It wouldn't have changed anything. Did she have amnesia about this?"

Sam thought it would have changed things. She wouldn't have gotten involved with Kris, and she wouldn't be feeling this pain and guilt. How could she ever look at Kris, and not see the scars that were a result of her actions? How could she not acknowledge that Kris' five-year relationship had failed as a result of her injuries?

"She had no memory of it. It was one of several incidents that she needed help recalling. She said it took the psychologist visits to remember what had happened."

"Were you already doing things together when she remembered?"

"Sort of, but we weren't dating."

"But you were friends. She was probably worried about you breaking off the friendship. Sounds like you were both pretty fragile and needed the friendship."

"But…"

"No, Sam. No buts. I think I would have done the same. No good would have come of her revealing how she got hurt."

"She should have told me."

"Fine, let's say she did tell you. Would you have let the relationship develop more?"

"No."

Lauren rubbed her lips and studied her sister. "And if you hadn't it sounds like you would have missed the support she gave you and the good times you shared when you most needed them. You might not want to admit it, but she helped you heal. And I don't mean your leg. I mean your heart."

Sam's chest tightened, and her stomach swam with a vague sickness. "What do you mean?"

"Oh, come on. I've never known you to date someone over three months. And I'm using the word date very loosely."

"I date."

"Yes, but this time you actually got attached to someone. You finally let your guard down and risked something. From the little you've shared in the past, you always kept things light, no promises, no strings attached. Kris made you feel worthy of love. And you've been afraid of getting involved with someone, loving someone, and having them leave. Like your father did."

"This has nothing to do with my father." *But it does. You said exactly that to Kris. 'What was this, some prolonged medical checkup to make sure I was doing all right? Then, when you're sure I'm doing okay you walk out?'* Sam's stomach sank with the realization that perhaps it may have something to do with her father.

"You push people away before they can get close. That way it doesn't hurt if they leave. You push them away so they can't leave you first."

"She betrayed me. She lied to me." Anger dripped from her words.

"She did it to protect you. You're letting that be your excuse to walk away because you're afraid of getting hurt." Lauren placed her hand on Sam's forearm and gave a gentle squeeze. "When someone can bring strong emotions such as love to the surface, they also have the potential to hurt you severely. Love is a vulnerability. She was able to hurt you because you love her and felt loved by her. Even if you were probably too damn stubborn to admit it to her."

Sam opened her mouth to speak and snapped it closed. *I did tell her. Then everything fell apart.* She guzzled from her glass and refilled it.

"What happened after you found out?"

"We argued."

"Did she explain what happened?"

"She confirmed it. She tried to justify it. Just like you. I told her we were through. I didn't want to see her again."

Lauren slammed her hand on the table. "Put yourself in her shoes. You said she didn't recognize you at first. How would you have felt if she had just walked away and said nothing? Or told you she did your amputation and just left? Tell me something, didn't you ever recognize her? Did you ever get a feeling that she was familiar?"

Sam was quiet, as she remembered the occasional flashes of déjà vu.

"Oh, Sam. You can be your own worst enemy. Think about it. You're looking at what happened later and ignoring the fact that everything was happening while she was injured too. That she was going through some heavy shit also. You felt fear. Don't you think maybe she was afraid too?"

Sam rubbed at the back of her neck, as her mind raced. She mumbled weakly, "I can't trust her."

"You're a fool." Lauren's voice was throatier than normal, and she shook her head in frustration. The words were like a kick to Sam's gut.

"Fine. I'm a fool," she snapped.

Lauren shook her head and growled. "You're so damn stubborn! Did you call her? Did you ask her why she didn't reveal everything? I've seen you when you're angry. You're scary."

Sam flinched and went cold as she thought about the abuse Kris had gone through after she got home. What she had done when Kris was trying to explain. How Kris had reached for her hand and she had slapped it away. Kris had flinched and backpedaled. She'd hurried out the door, head down, shoulders stooped. *Oh, God. I frightened her. She left when she thought I would hurt her.*

"Tell me something, did you get up in her face and shout like you used to? Or did the Marines train that out of you?"

Heat rose on Sam's face, and she felt weak. She covered her eyes before dragging her hand across her mouth and chin. She was silent as shame, confusion, and anger swirled inside her. She took a sip of the drink and felt the burn of alcohol in her stomach. Sam looked away.

"I've known you a long time. You're pretty damn stubborn, and you put up this big defensive wall, but inside you have this fragile spot. We all have one. Tell me something. Are you hurting more because she didn't tell you everything, or because she's out of your life?"

"Because she's gone." Sam swiped at her eyes, stood and staggered slightly. Scowling she looked at the melted drink and dumped it onto the grass. "I fucked up. I can't think any more I'm going to bed."

"Let me help you up. And don't try to push me away. You fall over drunk, and I'll leave your sorry ass out here with the skeeters and the hounds."

Sam swayed on her feet but accepted the shoulder to lean on as she stumbled inside. It took several minutes, but they staggered up the stairs together. "I don't know how to forgive her...how to love her." She staggered toward the bed and pulled her shirt off before collapsing onto it. Lauren pulled off her shoes, and placed a blanket over her and closed the door softly behind as she left the room.

Chapter Sixty

TWO WEEKS LATER

SAM RAPPED ON THE door frame of her commanding officer's door. "You wanted to see me, sir?"

"Yes, Major. Come on in. Close the door."

Sam did as he ordered, walked to the Colonel's desk, and stood at attention. "At ease, Major." Sam relaxed slightly. "I have some good news for you, Sam. You have been accepted for retention. I don't have official orders yet but I understand that you are slated for the Naval Research Lab up in Washington, DC. You'll be in the aeronautical research division. You can put that aerospace engineering degree from the Academy to good use."

"Thank you, sir."

"I'm sorry we weren't able to retain you in the squadron."

"I understand, sir."

"When you get up there, keep in mind that the Academy is close by. Build some relationships there, Major. If you play your cards right in a couple of years, you could end up as Academy staff and finish out on retirement."

"I'll keep that in mind, Colonel."

"I'll update you when we receive your orders."

"Thank you, sir."

"That's all."

Sam returned to attention and left his office. A sense of relief washed over her. She was staying on active duty. Sam felt like jumping and shouting out but controlled herself as she walked down the hall.

"Hey, Sam, you look happy this afternoon. Did you get good news?" one of the pilots asked her.

"Hey, Monster. I did. I've been retained."

"That's great." He reached out and gave her a slug on the arm. "Congratulations. You going out to celebrate? I have a night flight tonight, but let's get a beer tomorrow, okay?"

"Sure thing."

"I gotta go."

"Have a good flight," she called after him.

Sam drove home and went for a run to burn off some extra energy. She wanted to celebrate, to tell someone. Restless, she paced around the yard, and fingered her phone. *Should I call? Perhaps it's time. I screwed things up. Don't call, just go. Face-to-face would be best. I've changed. Not just my body, that was easy. I'm letting myself feel. Some of it sucks. Lauren was right. I've never let myself love because it would make me vulnerable. My father scarred me. Am I going to let his actions rule my life?*

Sam pulled up in front of Kris' house in time to see a lean, red haired woman enter. She sat stunned. Kris had found someone else? A spike of anger rose in her stomach, and before she realized it Sam was walking up the sidewalk. She rang the bell not knowing what she was going to say.

The door opened, and the redhead appeared. "Can I help you?"

"Is Kris here?" The anger in her voice had the woman flinching. Sam made an effort to calm herself. "I'd like to speak to with her."

"Kris? You must have the wrong address no one named Kris lives here."

"Kristine Matthews."

"No, I'm sorry." She started to close the door and stopped. "Wait. You mean the Navy doctor? She moved out. My husband and I bought the house. We were just going to rent, but at the last minute she decided to sell. The timing worked great for us."

Sam stood quietly, her thoughts racing, as she tried to comprehend everything. "Do you know where she went?"

"Sorry, I don't."

"Well, I'm sorry to bother you." Sam started to turn away but stopped. "How long have you lived here?"

"We've been here a month."

"Okay. Sorry to bother you." Sam walked away. The hope she had been feeling was replaced with a deep ache.

***

Sam walked into the clinic and looked at the signs on the doors to find Kris' office. She retraced her steps and stood outside the door that now read Lieutenant Commander Murphy.

"Can I help you, Major?"

"I'm looking for Doc Matthews."

"Sorry. I don't recognize that name. Perhaps a different floor?"

"No, it's this one."

"No one here by that name. But I'm new. Let me check." He turned. "Hey Smitty, we got a Doctor Matthews around here? Major wants to see her."

The corpsman walked around the corner. "Hi, Major. It's been awhile since I've seen you down here. You're looking good, ma'am." He blushed. "Well, I uh. I mean you look healthy, fit."

Sam grinned. "Thanks. I know what you meant. I feel good. Is Doc Matthews here?"

"Sorry, Major, she shipped out about six weeks ago. Up to Bethesda. Anything we can do for you?"

Sam improvised. "No. I just wanted to thank her for helping me out with my medical evaluation board."

"You're staying in?"

"I am."

"Congrats, Major. I know she would have been happy to hear that."

Chapter Sixty-one

BETHESDA, MARYLAND

SAM STOOD LOOKING AT the information board trying to find Kris' office. After several minutes of studying the board, she heard someone approach.

"Can I help you, Major?"

"I was trying to find Doctor Matthews, a general surgeon."

The petty officer led her over to a desk, typed on the keyboard. "Let's see, we have five Matthews here that are officers."

"Lieutenant Commander Kristine Matthews."

"Third-floor clinic. Their clinic hours have probably ended for the day. If you missed your appointment, you'd have to reschedule. I can call and see if she's still there."

"Thank you." Sam turned and looked around as he spoke on the phone and saw a tall woman with light brown hair leave. Her heart thudded in her chest. "I see her, thanks." Sam hurried outside and stood in the parking lot trying to find Kris again. She wandered around just hoping to catch another glimpse of who she knew was Kris. She was about to give up when she recognized her car pulling onto the perimeter road. *Yes, it's her. I'll be back tomorrow.*

Over the next several days Sam continued to look for a place to live and tried to adjust to the insane traffic around Washington DC. By afternoon she was back outside the main entrance of the medical compound watching and waiting for Kris. It took several days, but she was eventually able to follow Kris all the way to her home.

She watched as Kris arrived home in the evenings, closing the garage door as soon as she entered. A few minutes later she would emerge and go for a run. *She's thinner. Too thin. Is she sick?* Sam's heart filled with dread, and she rubbed her hand across it. One night Sam arrived late and had to park closer than she ever dared and was in time to see Kris return from her run. Curious she stayed to see what she would do.

Sam watched from her car parked one house away as Kris emerged and sat on a chair on her porch. Several times Kris looked directly at her car as if searching it. Other than that, she sat nearly motionless until the sky grew dark. Before it became too dark to see, she watched as Kris lowered her head into her hands and appeared to cry. Kris finally went inside, and Sam drove away, her hands clenched tight on the steering wheel and a dull ache in her gut. *Just go talk to her. What are you waiting for?*

***

Sam watched from her car as Kris slowed down and appeared to look directly at her before pulling into her driveway, and immediately into the garage, triggering the door to start to close before she was completely in.

Sam waited for one minute. *Go talk to her. This is getting creepy, you sitting out here at night. Someone is going to call the police.* Sam climbed out, locked her car and hurried up the sidewalk. She was about to step on the front porch when the door flew open.

"What do you want?" Kris growled.

Taken aback by the anger in the words Sam did not step onto the porch. "I wanted to talk to you, to see—"

"To see what? To see if I'm dating a patient? To see if I'm seducing them? Is that why you've been parked out here the last few nights? God, Sam, I can't take it anymore! This waiting. Go report me and put me out of misery. So, I can start to salvage something in my life."

Sam rubbed her earlobe. "What are you talking about?"

"I need you to go! Get it over with!" Kris gripped her fists tight trying to keep from doing something rash. "Tell me, when I should expect the call from the CO that I'm being brought up on an ethics charge? Are you here so you can do it in person?"

Before Sam could answer they heard another voice. "Hi, Kris, how are you tonight?" Together they turned to look at the couple who stood in her driveway. "Is everything okay?"

Sam felt their eyes burning into her flesh as they watched her carefully, "Everything is fine." Sam smoothed her clothes and stuck her hands in her pockets.

Kris spoke, raising her voice loudly. "This lady was looking for someone, and she's at the wrong house. She was just leaving."

Sam knew her face registered shock. She looked at Kris in disbelief and turned to look at the couple who had now moved further up the driveway. "I'm sorry to bother you. I'll check my directions." Sam turned and walked down the drive silently past the couple. As she drove away she looked over to see them standing together on the porch watching her drive away.

Sam drove in silence, weaving her way through the traffic as her mind raced. *Kris looked like hell. She was thin, too thin, and it wasn't just from the running. Something was wrong. She was angry, and she looked exhausted.* Sam turned onto the base and passed through the gate. She went to her room at the officers' quarters, changed into workout clothes, and grabbed her gear bag. She loaded in her running blade, gloves, her ID card, and a water bottle. A short while later she was at the gym.

Sam sat on the treadmill momentarily to change her shoe for a running blade. Setting the bag carefully aside she stepped onto the treadmill and ran. At first, she was annoyed by the stares of the people around her. They were all military, so they'd seen others with injuries. Sam continued pushing herself and worried about Kris. She became oblivious to the looks of others around her. *What did she mean? Let me salvage my life?* Sam continued to run and thought about how Kris had responded. It didn't make sense. She could understand Kris being mad at her for showing up unannounced, but what was she talking about with an ethics charge?

As her time on the treadmill expired, Sam stepped off, changed the foot piece back and spoke briefly to the attendant. A few minutes later she was punching on a heavy punching bag until her arms ached. Changing gloves, she started on the speed bag, the rhythm of her blows strangely mesmerizing. Tomorrow was Friday. She was going back. And this time they were talking.

***

Kris sat on the couch for a long time shaking. Tomorrow, the woman she loved would probably tell her commanding officer of their ill-advised relationship. Tomorrow she would find out what the next few years held. She picked up the article she'd been reading. *Three years. It would take three years for her to reapply for her medical license. And then she would have to try and find a job. God how had she screwed up her life so bad? I wish I could go back and tell her. Four simple words 'I amputated your leg.' It would have avoided a lot of heartache for both of them.*

Kris dropped the article on the table, along with the others. The case reports and disciplinary actions she'd been able to find from the different states that dealt with violation of trust between patients and physicians, and questionable relationships. She opened the fridge, pulled out a yogurt and returned to the couch. She sat in silence as she ate and watched the clock hands turn, listening to the ticking grow louder as her fate inched its way closer.

Awakening with a jump when the alarm started to buzz, Kris reached out silencing the alarm on her phone and glanced at the wall clock. Five-thirty. She didn't remember falling asleep or pulling a blanket up. She sat up and pushed the blanket and pillow to the end of the couch. Moving quickly she stepped into the bathroom and showered. Twenty minutes later she looked at herself in the mirror. Her uniform was crisp and sharp. She applied a light layer of makeup to conceal the dark circles under her eyes. She grabbed a yogurt from the fridge, devoured it and dropped the spoon in the sink. She grabbed her bag and hat and walked to the door leading to the garage. Kris looked back over her shoulder once. *What the hell will today bring?*

***

Kris stood at the scrub sink washing her hands. She was exhausted, six surgeries, rounds, and an emergency appendectomy. She was aware of the sounds of the surgical staff around her, moving carts to and from the surgical suites. The faint smell of smoke from the electrocautery probe drifted out of the rooms, as the circulating nurses did their jobs. She closed her eyes and rested her hands on the sink edge. She tried to absorb the sounds around her. To pull them within herself so in the years ahead she could recall the memories and know that she had done something right.

"Hey, Doc, are you okay?"

She opened her eyes and looked at the operating room nurse standing next to her. *She's watching me. She knows something.* "I'm tired." Kris gave a half-smile. "It's been a long day. I fell asleep on the couch last night, so I'm a bit sore. Naps on the couch are fine but an entire night's sleep…not so much."

"I was worried about you today. You were quiet. Well, that's all we have. Hope you have a good weekend. You're not on call, are you?

You've picked up a few extra ones."

"Not this weekend."

"Okay, see you Monday."

Kris went to the locker room, showered, and changed back into her uniform. With her heart thudding, she went back to her office space to finish paperwork and wait for the ax to fall. She heard footsteps approach and looked up to see a corpsman standing in the doorway.

"Staying late, Commander?"

"I'm finishing up some paperwork. Is Captain Brusels here?"

"No, ma'am. He left about an hour ago. He was in a hurry to leave. They're taking the new sailboat out on the bay this weekend."

"That's right. I'll only be here a few more minutes."

"Yes, ma'am. Have a good weekend."

"You too." Kris sighed deeply and felt the knot in her stomach grow a little smaller. *Not today.*

***

Sam parked on a facing side street and watched as the garage door closed. She got out of the car and was nearly to the house before she remembered the flowers. She hurried back to the car, grabbed the flowers, and had just reached the porch as the door opened. She heard Kris gasp in surprise and quickly move into a defensive position.

"Sorry, I didn't mean to scare you."

Kris stood still, not moving, barely breathing, several seconds passed as she stood motionless. "What do you want?"

Kris' voice was higher than normal, and she hadn't moved except to blink. Sam reached out with her hand to touch Kris on the arm. "It's me. Are you all right? I didn't mean to startle you. I needed to see you, now. Can we talk? Inside?"

Kris shouted, "I said I was sorry! I did what you said. I left you alone, I didn't contact you. Believe me, Sam, if I could turn back the clock and change everything I would. Please, I beg you, do not do this to me!"

Sam could see that Kris was nearing hysteria, her voice unusually high pitched, her hands, no, her entire body shaking. "I went to the hospital...shit!" She jumped forward to catch Kris but was only able to keep her head from smashing onto the porch as she collapsed dead weight. The flowers forgotten where they fell.

"Hey, hey, Kris, wake up." Sam tapped her repetitively on the cheek trying to get Kris to wake up. Her own heart was racing, her mind scrambling. She looked over Kris' body looking for any injuries from her fall. She breathed a sigh of relief as Kris started to awaken. "Hey Kris, you're all right. I'm right here. Let me take you inside." Sam propped open the screen door and lifted Kris. *God, she's lost weight. Is she sick?* Entering the house she was surprised to see boxes stacked in the corner, and books scattered around the room, on the floor, on end tables. A lamp stood minus its shade, the bare bulb exposed and burning bright. A pillow and blanket were tossed on the couch, a water bottle and an empty yogurt cup on the floor next to it. She lay Kris down on the sofa.

"I'll be back. Stay there." Sam hurried over and closed the doors, and went into the kitchen. It was immaculate and smelled of bleach. Its surface shone with brilliance. Boxes were stacked against the walls and under the table. Sam opened a cabinet and found two glasses, only two. She turned to the refrigerator, opening the freezer to get some ice, and stood and stared. It was nearly empty except for some open bags of frozen vegetables and a measuring cup. A one cup size. Sam felt her anger start to build. She shoved ice into the glasses and slammed the freezer shut. She jerked opened the door on the fridge and looked at its contents. Yogurt, loads of it, and the makings for salad, some of which looked to be past its prime. A half-gallon of milk which looked new. Sam pushed the door closed, filled the glasses from the tap and walked into the living room. Kris lay on the couch her arm draped across her head covering her eyes. Her breathing was ragged. "Here's some water. Drink it. What the hell is going on here?" Sam demanded.

Kris didn't answer. She didn't move. Sam walked into the small dining room and saw more boxes stacked on the floor, dishes and books stacked on the table, covered with packing paper, the doors on the dining room hutch open with items shoved haphazardly inside. Sam moved a few items and closed the doors. She walked down the hallway, more unopened boxes were stacked in two rooms. The computer was set up in another room, the desk and a card table cluttered with books and papers, a wall of boxes encircling it, like a fortress.

Sam turned to the last room, the master bedroom. The bed was in its frame, clothes stacked on it, boxes surrounding it. The closet doors were open, the uniforms precisely arranged, and spotless. A kit bag lay open, the camouflage uniforms neatly folded. A crumpled paper on the floor caught her attention, she opened it and read through it, her brow furrowing as she read it. She held it tight in her hand and slammed the closet shut.

The dresser drawers were opened revealing their meager contents. Shorts, t-shirts, socks, all exercise clothes, except for a pair of jeans and a sweatshirt. She took a moment to look in the bathroom…immaculate, again the bleach smell, a few cosmetics carefully arranged on the counter, a towel hanging on the rack, a sports bra hanging on a hook in the shower. Her rage grew. She stomped down the hall and into the living room. Kris was sitting up, her head in her hands, and the empty water glass on the table. Sam crossed the room in two giant strides grabbing Kris and jerking her to her feet, "What the hell is going on here?" She shook her, felt minimal resistance "What is this mess?"

"It's my home. Get out."

There was no anger in her words only resignation, and that scared Sam more than what she was seeing. She tightened her grip to shake Kris again and remembered the paper in her hand. She let go of Kris and watched as she dropped back down onto the couch. "What is this about?" She read from the letter. "'Although we do appreciate your request to return to Afghanistan at this time, your current orders will remain in effect. In the future, if the need arises, you may request to join the fleet hospital.' What the hell are you doing? Volunteering to go back over there? Wasn't twice enough?"

Kris stood up, pushed Sam back away from her. "Why does it matter to you? Look around. What do you see? What do I have? Why should I unpack?" Kris lowered her voice, thick with despair. "I've been waiting for this day, dreading it. I was hoping to be overseas when it happened at least…"

"What are you talking about? God damn it, you are not making any sense! Tell me what's wrong. How can I help you?"

"Help me?" Kris' laugh was cold and bitter. She flopped back down on the couch, "Is that what you're doing…following me? Making sure I bring no one home so you can investigate to see if I'm fucking them? Well, look around. Obviously, I'm not hiding anyone. Go ahead and report me and get it over with."

Sam stood motionless as emotions warred within her. She was angry at what she was seeing, scared by what Kris was saying, and through it all a sinking feeling of despair that somehow she was responsible for what was happening. Whatever 'it' was. She considered the words Kris had just spoken, and she gasped. She took several deep breaths, centering herself before she knelt on the floor in front of Kris, "Are you telling me that you are afraid that I was going to report our relationship? Answer me. Please."

"Yes. It was an ethics violation."

"No, it wasn't. It was a mutual relationship. I was every bit as responsible as you. I had no intention of reporting it."

"You didn't know. I should have stayed away. I shouldn't have gotten involved with you."

"Don't say that. I love you. You helped me heal, and I don't mean my stupid leg. I don't understand everything that happened. But I know you lost your memory. You didn't know who I was at first. That's why you were going to counseling. In one of the early group counseling sessions we were in, you said you couldn't remember the details of your injury. A lot of us couldn't."

"But friends trust each other. I violated that trust when I decided not to reveal who I was. And once we became more intimate, I thought it was too late to tell you. But it wasn't. At any step along the way, I should have had the courage to tell you. That was the right thing to do." The loathing in her voice hung heavy in the air.

"I wasn't your patient. You helped me. You saved my life half way around the world. The next time we saw each other we were both patients...I bet I know when you realized it was me. It was during the games. You got pale and looked sick. You ran away."

"I did. You said, 'just take my gun and shoot me.' You said that in the helo, too. I was already starting to get my memory back but that was when everything finally clicked. But I couldn't stay away. I came back because you caught my eye as soon as I'd healed enough to think about something else. I just wanted a friendship. It wasn't till later that my feelings changed. I should have stepped away," Kris said.

"No! You're not listening. I'm glad you didn't. I love you."

Kris searched Sam's face, "So you're not going to file a complaint? An ethics charge against me?"

"No. Dear God, no. I would never." She stopped talking when Kris burst into tears. "Kris?" She leaned forward and wrapped Kris in her arms and held on while she sobbed in her arms. Her own tears mixed with Kris' as they cried together.

Chapter Sixty-two

KRIS COULDN'T BREATHE. *IT was over. Sam would not report her. She would remain a physician.* Relief flooded through her and the stress exited in a torrent of emotion and tears. She had no idea how long she cried. She was aware of Sam holding her, silent and strong. She wiped a hand across her face, let go of Sam and reached for a napkin laying on the table. Wiping her face again, she blew her nose. She took two deep breaths and in a voice that trembled, "Thank you, Sam."

"Look at me," Sam spoke softly as she gently cupped Kris' chin and lifted it, forcing her to look at her. Kris was surprised to see Sam's face streaked with tears, her eyes sad. "I never meant to cause you harm. Not at all. I am sorry I caused you so much...pain. So much distress. I wasn't any better than Shelly. She hurt you physically. I did it emotionally. Please...forgive me."

Sam's heart thudded hard in her chest, and her pulse fluttered in her neck. Kris placed her hand over Sam's where it still rested on her chin. "I do. I should never have deceived you. I will go to my grave sorry for that deception. I took away your choice. I am sorry for that. It was reprehensible. I'm so sorry."

"Don't say that. I'm not sorry for it. I was lost and you saved me. If you'd told me I might have ended the relationship. If that would have happened, I wouldn't have gotten as strong. I wouldn't have kept fighting. I wouldn't have fallen in love. You accepted me for who I was before I could accept myself."

Sam stood up and pulled Kris to her feet. "If I help you, will you unpack?"

"I will. Are you hungry? I've got..."

"Yogurt. I looked. Why don't you order something, and while we wait we can find your dishes and fill some of those cabinets?"

"Okay. How about some Italian? Not pizza."

"And a salad, that stuff in the fridge looks a little old."

"Hmm?" Kris walked to the fridge, peered inside, and pulled out the bag of lettuce, glanced at it and tossed it in the trash. "I'll get an antipasto too."

Sam was starting to tear open a box, "Excellent. Now, where do you want your plates?"

They had the kitchen organized before the food arrived. Kris set the table while Sam paid the delivery man. They sat down to eat, and Sam watched in awe as Kris devoured the salad and bread before starting on her chicken parmigiana. She'd never seen Kris eat so heartedly. And it answered her unspoken question. The weight loss was due to fear that Sam would destroy her career. She would make sure Kris ate while she was around, and they were getting groceries before she left to go back to North Carolina.

"You're staring at me," Kris said between bites.

"You've lost weight."

"A little."

"No, it's more than that...It looks like you've lost ten pounds, maybe more."

"Well, I've been running more. I run daily now. My long run is twelve miles. And I work out more. It's the exercise."

"Maybe. Are you training for something?"

"I was thinking of doing the Marine Corps Marathon in the fall. I won't be ready for a full marathon, but I'm going to try."

"Why? I thought you didn't particularly like running."

"It helps with...never mind...it's good for me."

Sam reached forward and wrapped her hand easily around her wrist. "It helps with what?"

"Stress. It helps with the stress."

"This new position is tough?"

"It'll get better now. It's a matter of adjusting to the new command. Bethesda is a different beast. The volume is higher, and the pace is fast. I see so many that remind me of the fear I felt as I came through here."

"So much stress that you're training for a marathon to tame it?"

"It helps. But I've been looking over my shoulder waiting for the ax to fall. It was the only way I could relieve the stress."

"You could have called." There was silence for several moments. It spanned the months in between and all the hurt and pain. It teased at the edges, and if it wasn't finished now, there would be nothing else left to say. "I need you to know that I never thought you'd get involved with patients. Your ethics wouldn't let you."

"Oh, Sam, that hit so hard because I had questioned myself since the moment I realized who you were."

"Tell me everything. What happened to us? Everything you remember now. I want to know about your flashbacks. About why kids, little kids, but not babies haunt you. Please."

Sam listened while Kris relayed everything she could about the day of their injuries. Deeply affected, she held Kris as they cried over Yagana's death. More tears came as Sam realized what Kris had to do to save her.

As they finished eating Sam looked around the kitchen at the collapsed boxes, stacked to go outside. "Why haven't you unpacked?"

"It seemed like wasted effort. I've been waiting to get called into the CO's office and kicked out."

"Kris, I am so sorry for what I said. For accusing you of...of using me to assuage your guilt. For being unethical. I was hurt. I lashed out. I was mad, and I was scared."

"Scared?"

"Yes. That you were with me, only because you somehow felt responsible. It scared me because I had fallen in love with you, and it hurt to think that the feelings weren't mutual."

"They were though."

"I know that now. It took me some time to recognize it. Once I stopped feeling sorry for myself. I didn't understand it, but I was waiting. I was waiting for you to realize that you didn't have to be with me and to walk away. Like my father did."

"I wouldn't have," Kris said with conviction.

"You left without saying goodbye."

"I started to call and come by so many times. But I understood your anger. I hoped that you would calm down, forgive me, and call me, but I wouldn't...couldn't, contact you. To risk hurting you more. To risk you carrying through on your threat. How did you find me?"

"I went to your house to tell you I was being retained."

"Oh, that's good news. I wondered if you'd heard."

"I won't fly. I have new orders to the naval research lab. In the aeronautics division."

"That's in..."

"It's a half hour away." Their eyes met and held.

A smile spread across Kris' face. "That's so convenient."

They stood up simultaneously and moved toward each other. Kris leaned forward as Sam's hand pressed against the back of her neck, guiding her forward until their lips met. Soft and gentle, she savored the feel of her lover's mouth again on hers. Their mouths slid over each other's lips caressing and soothing. Her fingers stroked over Sam's face as if trying to recall every curve and every angle. Kris broke the kiss and gazed at Sam. She saw the gentleness in Sam's eyes. The concern and the softness she was so skilled at hiding. And she knew she would do everything she could to prove to Sam that she would never have to doubt her intentions again.

They kissed, and it quickly grew frantic. Hands clutched in her hair and tugged. Sam's strong hands grasped her ass and squeezed, pulling Kris closer until they pressed breast to breast through their clothes. Kris moved her hands down grasped Sam's shirt ends and pulled it up and over her head.

Sam's hands tugged at Kris' belt, opened the snap on her jeans, and quickly lowered the zipper. She yanked them down taking her panties along. Kris stepped free of them and started to unbutton her shirt. Sam kicked the pants aside and pulled Kris close again.

Sam backed her against the table. The rattle of silverware distracted her momentarily, and she hastily pushed the remains of dinner to the end of the table. She kissed along the side of Kris' neck. Soft strokes of tongue and quick bites. Her hands finished with the buttons and swept the blouse open. Kris shrugged her shoulders and sent it falling to the table. Their mouths met again in another urgent kiss, mouths demanding more as little moans and gasps escaped with each caress. Sam reached behind and released Kris' bra. She pulled it free and lowered her mouth to take her breast in her mouth. She stopped and stared, slowly she reached out and traced a finger over the scar, now just a fine pink line over a surprisingly full but nipple-less breast. She lifted her eyes slowly to Kris.

"It's not done."

"Can I?"

"Most definitely yes." She used her hands to press Sam's mouth down to her breast. Arching into her mouth as lips nuzzled along the side.

Sam explored each breast, cupped them together and buried her face in between, relishing the scent of her skin. Kris' fingers tugged at her hair, dug into her shoulders, and she pushed forward up into her mouth offering Sam more of her breasts. Sam reached around and grasped her ass, lifting slightly to put Kris on the edge of the table. She wedged her body between Kris' legs and bent her back over the table, their mouths again locked until she had to climb on top of her or break the kiss. She straightened, nudging Kris' knees apart with her hands, and hooked her foot around a chair pulling it close. She sat down while pulling Kris back to the edge of the table. Her fingers stroked along the inside of her thighs, and she nibbled and licked along the smooth skin, gradually making her way to the center. Kris gasped and spread her legs wider.

Sam ran her hands higher, her thumbs stroking upwards until they pressed along the outside edge of her sex. She stroked firmly along the side of her outer lips, and pressed them together, gently rolling them. Kris moaned, and her hips started to lift and match the rhythm of Sam's hands. Sam reversed the pattern she was tracing before lowering her mouth for a soft, slow stroke of tongue along her seam. Kris gasped with pleasure and lifted her hips more. Sam moved her thumbs down to tease the edge of her opening and lowered her mouth again.

Kris gasped and writhed slowly moving across the table. "Where are you going?" Sam asked as she pulled Kris back toward her as her wriggling on top of the discarded shirt was moving her across the table top. Sam slowly entered her with one finger then added another. Her fingers working in tandem with her mouth, as Kris started to rock her pelvis in time with her strokes.

"God, you're making me crazy," Kris groaned. "More."

Sam laughed against her but refused to hurry. Kris squeezed with her thighs, reaching for more friction and Sam nudged them apart and pressed down on her abdomen, forcing her back down onto the table. Sam stood slightly, leaned over Kris and nipped her on the hip bone. She moved her hand, changing her angle and added a third finger. Her thumb traced circles around her clit, and Kris' breath grew frantic. She arched up again to meet Sam, who again bit her on the hip and pushed her down, her mouth now rejoining in her intimate attack on her sex. Kris arched high and tensed, her motion frozen, until with a last gasp, she shouted, "Sam," as she came.

Sam paused momentarily, before she started stroking again. She soon had Kris writhing and gasping again. "Again baby. I want more. Give me everything." She tormented her, alternating between playful teasing caresses and more forceful strokes. Keeping Kris off balance she gradually built her toward peak, but retreating as she came close to release. Finally, Kris was pleading, begging for release, she stood quickly pulling Kris with her. She kissed her possessively, their mouths eager and frantic, she bit down on Kris' lower lip and spun her around, pressing her down over the table. She stepped between her legs, one hand wrapped around her front skillfully teasing her clit while the other found its way inside her and thrust. Sam thrust her hips forward and ground her clit against the smooth, taut globes of Kris' butt. Their moans and gasps filled the room, and with a shout, Kris erupted again. She collapsed under Sam's weight. But Sam was too close. She leaned over, nipped Kris on the shoulder, and pulled her up. She turned her, kissed her brutally and placed her hand on her shoulder guiding her to the floor.

***

Kris knew what Sam wanted and wasted no time positioning herself in front of Sam and between her legs. She knelt and pulled Sam to her and used her mouth aggressively to meet her need. Sam thrust her head back, rocked her pelvis forward and grabbed Kris by the head forcing more contact. With a shout of release, she trembled and released her passion, anointing Kris with her fluid.

Sam collapsed down into the chair and pulled Kris into her lap. They leaned against each other, their breathing ragged. Hearts hammering against their chests, and slick with sweat, they sat enjoying each other's warmth. She felt Kris nuzzle her neck and say something. "I didn't hear you?"

"I said I guess I should make the bed. I don't know how much more rocking this old table can take."

"I'll help."

Hand in hand they walked down the hall to the bedroom.

Chapter Sixty-three

"WAS THERE ANYTHING YOU wanted to do today?" Kris ran her hand across Sam's abdomen.

"I want to stay in bed with you all day. But since I head back tomorrow there is one thing I need to do. I need to go to Arlington. Two of my crew are there."

Kris sat up and looked at her, "Well let's get ready. I'll drive. You can shower here, and we'll stop by ...where are you staying?"

"I'm at Bolling, south side of DC."

"That's along the way. You can put on your uniform. I'll help you pack your gear, and you can check out. I want you here with me for as long as possible."

"You want to come with me?"

"I would be honored." Kris smiled.

"Do you want to shower first?"

"It doesn't matter. Wait. I don't have a chair in there for you."

"Shower with me. But just...you know, a shower."

"Yes, Sam. I am capable of controlling myself for a couple of hours." Kris smiled back at Sam.

Kris helped to support Sam as she soaped up and rinsed. Kris helped Sam from the shower and back into the room. She rooted through a box and handed Sam a pair of jeans and a t-shirt. "Here these will fit." Kris slipped back into the closet and put on her service dress blue uniform. She checked her image in the mirror. The dark circles remained under eyes, but her cheeks had some color.

Sam donned her prosthesis, dressed, and stood up. "When we get back I'll help you unpack in here."

"That won't be necessary. I'll think I'll have the motivation now to do it. Knowing I won't have to move again."

Sam looked over, started to apologize again, but Kris cut her off. "Stop. Don't say it. We've both made our apologies and learned our lessons. I want to move on, Sam. I want to see where this thing goes with us. Now let's get moving." She grabbed a handful of change off her dresser, and they left.

The drive to Arlington was quick with the light traffic. Kris parked, and they walked into the visitor's center. Sam spoke briefly to the attendant, and after several minutes returned.

"It's a bit of a walk."

As Sam started to walk away, Kris reached out and took her hand turning her back around to face her. "Sam, take your time. You don't have to rush. You don't have to explain."

They walked the path for more than ten minutes quietly, as trams drove visitors around the graveyard to President Kennedy's grave and up to the Tomb of the Unknown Soldier. Finally, they came to the proper section. They walked side-by-side looking for the gravesite. Sam stopped suddenly and walked toward a headstone. She looked down on it and stood silent for a long time.

Remembering her crew chief who she had served with for over six years, their paths paralleling several times in their careers. She had met his wife and children at a squadron function several years ago. His son had told her most emphatically that her name couldn't be Sam. It was okay that she could fly, but her name wasn't right. His wife, Joan, had been mortified, but Sam laughed and told the youngster if he promised to keep it a secret she would tell him her real name. Only after the boy took a solemn oath of secrecy, she revealed her name to be Samantha. His eyes widened in surprise. "That's a girl's name," and he scampered off.

Sam remembered some of their more harrowing missions in Afghanistan, and finally, she remembered what she could about their final mission. She apologized and lowered herself to her knees, a hand resting on his headstone, she said a prayer as the tears fell from her face. She felt Kris step up behind her and rest a hand lightly on her shoulder. After another minute Sam stood up and fumbled in her pocket. She withdrew her hand and looked at Kris, who silently took her hand and pressed a quarter into it.

Sam stepped stiffly over to the headstone, and placed the quarter on it, symbolizing that she was there when he died. She took a step back, and Kris walked forward, placing a dime on the headstone. Sam watched silently while Kris said a prayer and backed away. They stood silently side-by-side and rendered a salute, turned crisply and walked away. They walked in silence back to the path. They stopped, and Kris stood in front of Sam waiting while she composed herself and blocked her from people who had stopped to look.

"When you're ready. Let me know," she whispered, her hand gentle on Sam's sleeve.

Sam lifted her head slightly, extending her neck and took several deep breaths. She brushed her fingers over her damp cheeks before pulling the slip of paper from her pocket. She glanced at it. "It should be down here further on the left." She reached out and touched Kris' hand briefly before walking toward her next goodbye.

Kris waited patiently at the foot of the grave while Sam again paid her respects. Several people stood a few rows over, quietly visiting another grave. There were a scattering of coins on the markers, mostly pennies. Nickels and dimes rested on a few of the more recent headstones. Kris saw a few quarters on the markers of fresh graves.

A shuddering gasp brought her attention back to Sam. She turned back in time to see her sink to her knees. Sam leaned forward onto her hands and took several deep breaths before straightening herself. Again, she placed a hand on the tombstone and muttered silently. She rose up, her face marred with tears and, accepted the quarter that Kris had stepped up to give her and placed it on the marble. Sam backed up to the foot of the grave and Kris moved forward, and again placed a dime on the headstone. They stood still momentarily before rendering a salute and moved away silently.

As they walked along the path, Sam was lost in her thoughts, and Kris watched her carefully. She knew that Sam still harbored thoughts that she was responsible for their deaths. She hoped the counseling sessions had helped to alleviate it. They walked for several minutes until they found a bench and sat down.

Sam looked down and brushed the soil off of her knees. "That was something I had to do. Thank you for coming with me."

"Sam, you don't need to thank me." Kris' eyes filled as she looked into Sam's tearful eyes.

They sat looking over the rolling hills, acres covered with headstones evenly spaced, row after row. Sam spoke quietly, "It brings it home, seeing this. Knowing that all these people died wearing the uniform. They ought to make every politician spend a day here. Make everyone who says they hate the military spend an afternoon with a grieving family, so they see the pain these families go through. See the additional grief their words of hate cause. Do you know from here you can see the Pentagon and vice versa? You know what you can't see? The White House or the Capitol building. How ironic is that? The people who so willingly call on the sacrifice of others can't even see the outcome of their actions." Sam stood up and offered Kris her hand, helping her up. "Let's go. I'm done here."

As they walked down the steps, several people stopped them and thanked them for their service. Several older men wearing the Legion hats and old campaign ribbons from World War Two spoke with them offering support.

***

"What have you worn the last six weeks other than your uniforms?" Sam questioned as she hung another armful of clothes into the closet.

"I have a few pairs of shorts and pants out. I've been exercising a lot so mainly shorts and tanks. I haven't really gone anywhere, just to the grocery store a few times."

Sam stared at her. "What have you been eating?"

"Sam, please let's not get into dietary choices."

"Fine. But we're going grocery shopping, and I'm grilling you a steak. A big one. Do you do still have your grill?"

"It's in the back yard. I need to get propane. We don't need to go shopping. Let's go out to dinner."

"No. I leave tomorrow, and I want to know that you won't be here existing on a yogurt and mixed veggie diet." Sam used an open pair of scissors to cut through the packing tape on the bottom of the box she had unloaded and let it fall flat. "Hand me that box and finish that one you have. I'll take them out to the curb on our way out."

"Sam."

"Don't argue with me. I'm getting hungry, and you don't want to make me mad."

"I never noticed you getting hangry before."

Sam stopped unloading the box and stared at Kris "Hangry? What's that?"

"Hungry and angry."

Sam chuckled. "Yes, I guess I do." She wadded some packing paper and threw it at her. "Yes, I get hangry, so let's move."

The steak was grilled to perfection, while the salad, a variety of mixed greens, tomatoes bursting with flavor, and colorful carrots, radishes and peppers, was tasty. Sam had insisted that Kris eat at least a few bites of her baked potato. Kris agreed and promised to finish the rest of the giant spud the next night, topped with chili and cheese.

They sat next to each other on the patio, finishing the bottle of cabernet as the sun started to set. Kris reached out, took Sam's hand, brought it to her mouth, and kissed each knuckle. "Where did you get these scratches?"

"At the gym the other night. I went a little crazy on the punching bags. I needed to let off some steam."

"Is that a good workout?" Kris' disbelief evident in her voice.

"Well, I ran too. But yes, it's good. Arms up, hands up for your whole workout. The rhythm, once you get going, is...strangely soothing."

"I'll have to try it sometime." Kris kissed Sam's knuckles again, turned her hand over and kissed her palm. Her tongue teased along Sam's wrist. "There's another rhythm I find soothing. Do you know..." she bit down lightly on Sam's wrist, "what it is?" She leaned forward, nipped at Sam's lower lip before covering her mouth, and stroking her hand up the side of her breast.

"Hmm. I believe I do."

Roslyn Bane

Chapter Sixty-four

THEY STOOD IN THE living room, arms wrapped around each other. Their mouths drew apart, and Kris hugged tighter. "I packed you a sandwich and some fruit. There's a bottle of juice in there, too. And your coffee should be done soon."

"Kris, it takes a few hours."

"It's over six, and that's if traffic is moving. Call me when you get there."

"I will."

"When do you think you'll come up for good?"

"I haven't signed a lease, so I'll be back up soon. It should be within the month. After that, the move will be quick."

"I want you to move in with me."

"What?" Sam pulled back, her eyes opened wide.

"You heard me. Move in with me. I love you. There's more than enough room."

Sam moved toward her. "Are you sure you want to do this?"

"Absolutely."

"Yes." They hugged, kissing softly, a tender kiss goodbye. "I need to get going."

"I know. Drive safe."

"Eat. I'll be upset if you haven't put some weight back on." Sam pinched gently at Kris' waist.

"I will. Let me get your lunch" Kris walked into the kitchen and filled the travel mug. She picked up the small cooler she'd packed and followed Sam to the car. As Sam loaded her gear into the trunk, she arranged the cooler on the passenger seat where Sam could reach it and placed the coffee in the console. Kris looked up and saw Sam standing in the garage. She walked over to her, "Is something wrong?"

"I need to..." She pulled Kris inside and kissed Kris thoroughly until they both were breathless. "Listen to me. Please. After my father left, I felt worthless, unwanted. The Klines always made me feel welcome, but deep down there was fear, that one day they would realize the same thing my father did and they would send me away. I've avoided serious relationships. But something happened with you. I've felt things I never have before. Despite myself, I wanted more, and I was afraid that you'd eventually leave when you realized my shortcomings." She lifted Kris' hand to her mouth, nuzzled her knuckles. "I love you."

Kris' face broke into a broad smile. "Sam, love is about accepting people as they are, with their strengths and weaknesses. I want you. I love you." She leaned forward and kissed Sam, a feathery light kiss that promised more. "I'll see you in a few weeks."

Kris stood in the driveway and watched until Sam disappeared from view. She went inside and started to arrange the office. She only had a few weeks to get ready for Sam's return.

***

Kris ran outside when she heard the car pull into the driveway. She nearly jumped into Sam's arms, and they kissed fervently in the driveway. They broke the kiss when a car drove by on the street and beeped its horn.

Laughing, they each grabbed a suitcase out of the car and went inside. "The moving company will be here tomorrow to deliver your furniture. I cleared two of the rooms, and we can figure out how to arrange everything."

"Later. Right now, I want to kiss you." Sam pulled Kris into her arms.

The embraced ended and Sam held Kris' hands. "It's taken me a long time, and I've come a long way, but I feel like I'm finally home."

Kris moved back into Sam's arms. "You are. Welcome home, Sam."

THE END

About Roslyn Bane

Roslyn Bane started writing while recuperating from an injury that kept her indoors during a long cold winter. Her debut novel, Time For Terri was a finalist for best F/F Romance at Love Romances Café.

A US Navy veteran she served as an Aerospace Physiologist and earned her flight wings. After leaving active duty she served several years in the reserves before resigning her commission. She continues to work in medicine.

She spends her free time in the outdoors enjoying photography, skiing, shooting, and enjoying the fresh air on her motorcycle. The inspiration for her stories comes from daily life, her love of the outdoors, and people watching. She now lives near York, Pennsylvania with her family and two lovable labs.

She is a member of the Romance Writers of America, Central Pennsylvania Romance Writers, Golden Crown Literary Society, RomVets, and Rainbow Romance Writers.

Contact Roslyn at

rojodek@outlook.com

Facebook: Roslyn Bane

Twitter: @RosBane

Note to Readers:

Thank you for reading a book from Desert Palm Press. We have made every effort to edit this book. However, typos do slip in. If you find an error in the text, please email lee@desertpalmpress.com so the issue can be corrected.

We appreciate you as a reader and want to ensure you enjoy the reading process. We would like you to consider posting a review on your preferred media sites such as Amazon, Smashwords, Bella Books, Goodreads, Tumblr, Twitter, Facebook, and/or your blog or website.

For more information on upcoming releases, author interviews, contest, giveaways and more, please sign up for our newsletter and visit us as at Desert Palm Press: www.desertpalmpress.com and "Like" us on Facebook: Desert Palm Press.

Bright Blessings

www.ingramcontent.com/pod-product-compliance
Lightning Source LLC
Chambersburg PA
CBHW071512260626
47170CB00002B/354